Le Roi Du Sang

Written by Tiana Laveen

Edited by Natalie Owens

Cover by Travis Pennington

This is not your ordinary vampire tale...

Le Roi De Sang

"They say the good die young.

My soulless body has walked the Earth for over four centuries. I've always been a king amongst the living dead, born into royalty and earned – not given. My head is heavy with a gold crown made of blood jewels from the drained essence of vessels all the way from Paris, to Zimbabwe to New York fucking City. Therefore, what they say, whomever 'they' is, that the good die young, is only partially true. Care to guess which part that is?"

– Count Alexandre Marseille

COPYRIGHT

Don't Bite My Hard Work.

Copyright © 2019 by Tiana Laveen
Print Edition
All rights reserved.

ROI & REINE DU SANG

LE ROI DU SANG

BLURB

Alexandre Marseille was born during the Hundred Years' War in France, a member of the royal House of Valois. His parents, both ruthless underworld monarchs, instilled endurance in their children above all else. Yet, while most of his family perished over time, he remained a survivor. For a 400-year-old vampire, staying in power has its share of challenges. Alexandre has now established his empire in New York City, living an opulent life and running a successful law firm. But his ultimate goal is one alone: to find his soulmate, his bestowed Blood Queen. Once he sets eyes on Venus Anderson, Professor of Art History, he will stop at nothing to get her, and the relentless, sensual pursuit begins.

Venus Margaret Anderson remembers vividly what it was like to be human. To smell the yellow Jessamine flowers and feel the warm sun on her flesh in the South Carolina heat. But being human sometimes meant she wasn't treated humanely at all … for Venus once lived as a slave, on a plantation owned by a cruel master. Until the day she made her escape to freedom, changing her destiny forever…

The two twisted soulmates are bitten from the same bloody cloth, but it will take all the demons of Hell and all the prayers in Heaven to convince Venus that Alexandre is not *always* the ruthless monster he appears to be. Separate, they are forces to be reckoned with; together, they are an explosive power couple destined to leave an indelible, blood-stained mark upon the world. But, with all good things, there are those who wait in the shadows, working their black magic to drain and destroy this love at the onset, casket officially closed…

Will Venus step into her destiny and become the Reine Du Sang she was born twice to be? Will Alexandre Marseille prove to her he is capable of love, and that he can provide the sacrifice, training, and protection she so desperately deserves? Turn the pages of this bloody, hell-bound book to find out!

WARNING

This is not your typical paranormal romance...

There will be blood. Lots of it.

The violence is off the charts.

The profanity is abundant and profuse.

The sexual encounters are frequent, extremely graphic, and at times hedonistic.

Some of the topics explored may trigger you: debauchery, racial discussions/slurs, explicit murders, sexual deviancy, homicide, vengeance, African slavery in the United States of America, brutality and more.

This is a dark romance in EVERY. SENSE. OF. THE. WORD.

Please do not read this book if you are bothered by the aforementioned.

A warning is to be heeded – not ignored and then complained about as if never given. If you skip or ignore this cautionary notice, the author is not responsible for that.

Thank You.

DEDICATION

This book is dedicated to the extraordinary, non-cookie cutter authors who are struggling to remain true to their vision in a world that prefers paper dolls over rock solid authenticity. You are a jagged pill that doesn't go down easily… you scrape the throat as you are consumed, but you deliver the greatest remedy. Many of us just wish to write our books in peace, but at times, that seems impossible due to outside pressure, negativity online and elsewhere, and unrealistic expectations. I want to encourage my fellow authors who are bizarre, gifted, capable and different from the norm to embrace their imaginations and step out on faith. Believe in yourself even when it appears no one else does. Do not allow yourself to be strangled by the invisible withering grapevines that attempt to wrap themselves around your neck and extinguish your light from within. Not everyone is going to love your work – but if YOU don't love your work by being someone you are not due to the pressure to appease others who don't know or love you, then you are killing your creativity, your vision, the reason why you became an author in the first place … one stab wound at a time.

You fit in no one's box.

So don't let anyone put your creativity in a coffin.

Embrace your metal spikes, torn, blood-soaked leather, and pointy glass edges.

Sometimes, true beauty is found in the bumpy imperfections, the flagrant flaws, the muddy puddles covered in wilted, black rose petals.

Fall into the silver waters face down.

Invite the masses to

drown in your oddity…

It's a perfect day for a swim.

TABLE OF CONTENTS

LETTER TO THE READER

To my Laveen Queens and Kings, welcome.

I want to interrupt this letter and alert my old and new readers about a decision that I have recently made: <u>I know that 'goddamn' is the proper way to say and spell this particular curse word.</u> I have done so in the past but always cringed. It's just a personal choice and situation that doesn't sit well with me. Therefore, going forward, I wish to write, 'gotdamn.' I am not religious, but I am quite spiritual, and it has always bothered me to write it the proper/correct way so if you will allow me to deliberately spell this word wrong, I would greatly appreciate it.

Thank you.

...Moving along.

Let me tell you a bit about me...

I have written over 45 books, the majority of which are full length novels. I've written

everything from sweet romances to a best-selling
12 book Zodiac series, to tales about paranormal
psychics with sex addictions, to aliens living in
Maryland and murdering drug dealers. I write
whatever strikes me, whatever stories are begging
to be released from inside me, petitioning me to
be shown to the world.

Now, we've arrived here, at the abode of the
Le Roi Du Sang.

Let the games begin.

I have been asked to write a vampire story
several times, but was never moved to do so.

…Until NOW.

I never force anything on myself. I'm either
inclined to write a story or I am not. This idea
came to me and I fell in love with it. It was
then that the story began to write itself,
webbing the details inside my mind and flooding
onto the pages.

All I needed to do was sit down and write it.

Before I continue, I want to take a commercial
break right here. This may seem silly to some,
but trust me, it's necessary in my opinion. Let's
briefly discuss what a vampire is. The official
definition, according to the Merriam-Webster
dictionary:

vampire noun

vam·pire | \\vam-ˌpī(-ə)r  \

Definition of *vampire*

1 : the reanimated body of a dead person believed to come from the grave at night and suck the blood of persons asleep

2 **a** : one who lives by preying on others

  b : a woman who exploits and ruins her lover

3 : VAMPIRE BAT

Okay… so now that we've covered the basics, I want to inform you that vampires, historically, are not sparkly, pretty creatures. They are monsters. Though I appreciate and enjoy, for example, the "Twilight" books, the characters in that series are not remotely close to the original definition of these beings. Vampires don't give a single fuck - by nature. They suck and feed without an iota of care for the host. They kill, enjoy murder, mayhem, and are highly sexual beings. There is no such thing as sharing, consent, etc. When they see something or someone they want, they take it. PERIOD.

The difference between them and zombies is that:

1) They are not rotting. They are never in a state of decomposition, and should they have an injury, they tend to self-heal quickly.

2) They do not crave brains or other human organs - they have bloodthirst. Period.

3) They can learn, speak, read, sing, dance and make conscious choices. They are not slow in movement, either - in fact, they move faster than

the speed of light, depending on what type of vampire they are (turned, pure/true blood, etc.)

4) They can be charming and alluring - they are con artists basically, and innately manipulative. Zombies are not charming or alluring due to their inability to speak in a clear manner if at all. They appear incapable, in most depictions, of learning new information.

5) Zombies are what they are - what you see is what you get. Vampires (many, but not all) are shapeshifters. They can turn into various animals: Bats are the most notable in books and movies, but also foxes, and some in literature have the ability to turn into wolves, snakes, and ravens.

6) Not all vampires written about historically or in Hollywood versions can be killed by garlic cloves, crosses, a stake to the heart, holy water, silver bullets, fires, Christian prayers, sunlight, etc. Some are not fazed by ANY of those 'vampire weapons.' The effective method to kill them truly depends on the type of vampire in question and their individual powers. For some, only beheading works.

7) Vampires are diverse! Zombies, a bit less so … but one thing about vampires is that they are naturally violent. I repeat, they are naturally violent. One more time for the folks in the back: They are naturally violent. They will present themselves at times as gorgeous beings -

but beneath that lies the truth… the monster that they in fact are. Vampires were sometimes human before they were turned. Sometimes they were born a vampire - those are often called Royals, Pure Bloods/True Bloods.

Pure bloods are often depicted in a more stellar light than their 'turned' counterpart. Some people are 'put off' by vampires acting as their true nature in novels and movies because Hollywood and mainstream media have offered us a false narrative about these beings, including those cases looked into by the Catholic Church.

Now, I am not going to give a long ass vampire history lesson right here. You didn't purchase this book for that purpose - but please Google it, look it up when you have time. It's very interesting indeed!

Some professionals and clerics believe vampires to be real while others say that they are not. Some say they are mere demons (which I disagree with. They are a totally different entity and there is definitely more concrete proof that demons are real … but I digress…). But, regardless of anyone's beliefs, the TRUE ORIGINAL definition of a vampire must be considered when reading tales about these beings - yes, even in the case of romance novels.

There is nothing wrong with writers, directors, etc. using creative license in their art and work, but as a reader, it would only be fair that you be told at least a little bit about the true nature of these immortals before we delve any further. Okay, now that that is out of the way, let's continue with our regularly scheduled program…

This hero makes a shadow look like a ray of light.

I am not a stranger to dark tales. I have written many and my consistent readers are aware of this. I refuse to limit myself, so when the mood strikes for me to write something in particular, that is what I do. Writing for me is not only enjoyable, it is therapeutic and a need. Just like air, food, and shelter, which I have to have, I must do this, too.

These characters fulfilled my desire to tell this tale. They came to life and I just sat back and enjoyed the ride.

For those of you that have been reading my work for years -

THANK YOU.

You are much appreciated.

This is a modern day tale with some historical ties. I wouldn't call it a historical romance because less than 10% of the book delves into incidents occurring in a past time period. Only what historical background and reference is necessary is explored in order to allow the reader to understand how these beings came to be. It's important, as they say, to know one's history in order to appreciate the present and prepare for the future. Not everyone's past is peachy keen - and that is immediately realized when the reader is first introduced to Venus, a strong and determined young woman living in the South, during times of slavery in the United States. She was born a slave and is physically strong. She's also brave and believes that if life can't get better, then the only solution is death. She wishes to be free by any means necessary.

Death within itself doesn't frighten Venus; it's the idea of never even trying to stand up for herself, to discover whether freedom is fantasy or fact, that terrifies her.

On the fateful night of her fleeing the plantation that she'd been bound to for years, she discovers far more than she ever bargained for…

Alexandre Marseille, sometimes called Lord, Count, or King Alexandre Marseille, makes others in his bloodline look weak and ill equipped. He trained at an early age for battle, for his family protected the throne and the old way of life for Pure Bloods. He is notorious for his quick temper, superlative physical strength and power, lightning speed, and a penchant for violence straight out of a gory 1980s horror film. He is pretentious, conceited, intimidating, clever, promiscuous and has a unique psychic ability that allow him to tap into the fears and desires of humans - then use them like puppets to get what he wishes.

He has no conscience, has no idea what regret or guilt are, nor does he have any curiosity to find out. For Alexandre Marseille, life is about securing his position, furthering his reign of terror, and continuing the bloodline…

But it will take a special woman to convince him to reconsider his ways…

Sex is to him like sleeping or eating; it means nothing and is just part of everyday life. He fucks frequently, almost as much as he feeds, and female vampires and human women are mere toys, something to look at and play with until he grows bored. When we meet him, his desire for a bride and to settle down are now at the fore-front, and he begins to question whether the wizard assigned to him as a child was correct that he would find her in the United States, as predicted…

Once he meets Venus, however, there is no doubt in his mind and he refuses to ever let her get away.

He begins to feel things… strange things, and his craving for her grows into a full blown obsession. He's never had to romance a woman or vampire; they would easily fall under his spell. But now, he must pull out all the stops, espe-cially when he realizes that Venus is even more than meets the eye.

Their love for one another is explosive, poignant, volatile and all consuming.

Alexandre Marseille now has something new to fight for…

Love.

Can a wickedly cunning, seductive, and habitually cruel vampire that has been in existence for multiple centuries learn to use his natural skills to set free entrapped beings, rather than keep them in bondage using fear tactics? Sometimes, slavery is also a state of mind, and occasionally, freedom is an illusion…

Now, without further ado,
I present, 'Le Roi Du Sang' - (The King of Blood)

Tiana Laveen

PROLOGUE

The Little Cabin in the Woods

South Carolina, December 18, 1837

C OLD, CLAMMY HANDS covered in deep, oozing gashes and stinging cuts throbbed with ache and pulsed with insoluble pain. Covering her watering eyes to shield them from outstretched wild, sharp branches that knifed their way into her dry flesh, she was now partially blind while her blood felt as if it were freezing up right in mid-flow through her veins. Each step she took felt like she was being pulled and prodded, smacked and attacked… one big, walking open wound moving amongst the prickly brush and creatures of the night.

Her fingers, neck, every exposed part of her flesh was bloodied and smeared with dirt from hours of running, hiding, falling, and getting back up all over again. She could feel the itch from the caked-on filth and the malodorous underarms induced by fear. Trickles of sweat drizzled from her pores like water from tipped floral vases. Venus' body jerked and propelled forward from pure cool terror and heated adrenaline.

Her thick, black, wooly hair had been pinned high and away from her face as usual, but from all the running and dodging, it was now in her way. The pins had fallen out miles ago. Coiled, dry tresses bounced in her eyes with each rapid step, tampering with her visibility in the middle of the night. She continued on, working past her brutal exhaustion and all the odds against her, giving herself mental pep-talks each step of the way.

"No!" She hissed as cool air cut across her hip. She paused for a spell and peered at her body. The darkness allowed little visibility, but moonlight shone through the trees every now and again, and she realized she was now half naked, the once thick dress ripped apart, practically reduced to ribbons by the unforgiving wilderness, as if it had fingers, knives, and teeth trying to cut her up and eat her alive.

Venus was certain she'd never forget this date, the 18th of December. She kept on running through the vast forest full of overgrown, twisted trees that almost seemed to come to life. The creepy noises bouncing around, echoing about, sounding much like men, ghosts, and indistinguishable mammals that made the hairs on her neck stand to attention.

I'm gonna catch pneumonia if I don't find this place soon…

Her feet were covered in thick wool socks and black ankle boots, protecting her feet at least, but the rest of her was in pure torment. Her eyes now burned from falling debris. Howling and snarling wild beasts hidden in the brush made her heart beat against her chest like an angry, fist full of white rage. She was no stranger to that, either...

The Panic financial crisis had made the White folks meaner than ever, as if that were even possible. Venus barely knew the touch of cool circular metal in the palm of her hand, let alone paper bills, to afford to know the difference. She sighed for a spell, looked in all directions, and resigned herself to the fact that if she didn't rest for a few minutes, she'd burn out quick, topple over in fatigue, and be as good as caught.

Just a moment or two... then I'll be back on my feet.

She found a large tree and slumped against its rough bark, the sweat draining down her face making her jolt from the chill of the cutting air licking her skin like the rough tongue of a feline. Her thoughts raced...

This ain't right. Did I get lost? I don't think so. Where will I go if I can't find this place? I can't think like that. Gotta stay focused. They say there's a cabin in the woods I can hide in... they say it's safe... they ain't have no reason to make it up, to lie. I gotta keep goin'. I can't go back there. If that's livin', I'd rather be dyin'.

And then, she remembered what had made the monsters within the White man all the more atrocious... Yes, that's right, she'd been thinking about The Panic...

The Panic had made a mess of the White folks' money and though she didn't know the ins and outs of it, she knew enough. Something about President Jackson and the charter of the Second Bank... unemployment and the like. She'd heard them talking, and she recognized a few words here and there, though she was far from fluent. She could barely read, just a wee little bit. Nevertheless, worries like this made people speak their minds, hoping that their tongues would put an end to the worries. The White people had gotten strange. Money woes caused the wealthiest of men to look rattled, to take their aggressions out on the innocent. Fear and panic looked the same, regardless of whether those eyes were bright sky blue or midnight black. Didn't matter if the flesh around them was pale and freckled or smooth and dark mahogany. The Panic caused a madness… a frothing of the brain. It's like the White folks had rabies, but you couldn't see it until they was up on you. The beatings got worse; the abuse had taken a different spin, climbed up to a whole different level…

He gonna kill me… He gonna shoot me dead.

She got up sooner than she'd planned and made her escape, running as fast as her bloodied legs would carry her. She was hungry and thirsty, fighting time. Nobody fought time and won…

I gotta live… I gotta live!

That thought whirled in her head as she heard the faint bark of dogs in the distance, hot on her trail. The same dogs no doubt that watched her and the rest of 'em working the rice and sugar fields. The same dogs that begged for scraps when she helped in the kitchen, while sometimes debating on whether to toss a few drops of arsenic in Master Miller's morning oats. The same dogs that used her little slanted house made of clay and other cheap materials as shelter when it rained. Master didn't want their stinking behinds smellin' up his big, nice house after they'd been caught in a downpour.

Those dogs, the same ones who'd rub up against her leg and beg for a scratch along the head, had now been sent to sink their razor-sharp teeth into her calves, vying to tear her apart like meat from a bone. The thought of their pursuit gave her an extra boost of strength.

She ran and ran, now almost convinced her heart was going to give out before she'd even drawn close to the little cabin the others would whisper about.

Venus, what you gone and done?! But I had to go. I ain't have no choice! Please God protect me!

She zigzagged through the maze of saplings, her eyes wide as the full, white moon that shone its light like a beam. She came to a small clearing, bare of the towering things. Now, everything was crystal clear. The moon lit the way much better, but at the same time, this was sure to make her more visible, too. She tucked her fears away and kept moving, chasing shadows and glints of light. Her tawny limbs were slathered in the oily, dark solvent, just like Joseph had told her to do. Right before she'd made her exit, she'd covered herself from head to toe in the stuff. It would help to mask her scent, he'd said… confuse the hounds. But nothing could stop the crackling of the dried grass and slender broken branches beneath her feet. She believed she was breathing loud, too; even her sweat seemed to scream as it clung to whatever clothing she had left on her.

I ain't have no choice! I couldn't just keep takin' it!

Ahead, there was nothing but blackness. The moon was hiding behind another cluster of high trees; it had closed its mouth and swallowed the glow. Stretching her arms out to feel her way around, she made sure to not deviate from the path. Getting lost wasn't an option. If anyone got a hold of her, she could meet her end.

She'd already tried to run away two years previously and was whipped nearly to death. Her back still bore a thick welt. She'd heard the stories... this second offense would result in much worse. If she was lucky, when caught, she'd be sliced on her face and burned, perhaps branded with an 'R' for runaway for all to know. If she were unlucky, he'd put a bullet in her head...

But the bullet in the head seemed a far better option than one more night on the Miller Plantation in St. James Goose Creek parish...

Just that morning, Master Miller had come to her again, his fists balled up tight. He'd told her to go back out to the rice field. She'd passed out and was allowed to go back indoors for a spell and drink some water. When ten minutes or so passed, she ignored the call to return. He arrived there and demanded she go out. He was three hands short. Paul had died the week before; the man had to have been in his 50s. Betty had given birth that morning to a stillborn and lost a lot of blood, so they let her be, and William's whereabouts were unknown. She surmised he'd been sold since he was accused of causing trouble. She'd caused trouble too, but he wouldn't shake her loose. When she'd tried to explain that she was ill, Master Miller had smacked her so hard, she'd lost consciousness. When she'd come to, her dress was hiked up around her hips and he was nowhere in sight. It hadn't been the first time he'd done such a thing, but she'd meant it to be the last.

She gritted her teeth as anger surged through her once again. The memories took hold, warming her cold body – the remembrance of the dull ache between her legs, the taste and smell of stale tobacco against her lips where'd he kissed her while she was swimming in the black fog of unconsciousness. She hated his scent; his body had a strange sweet stench, like that of a damn pig running all about in the sun. She hated his voice; it was high pitched like a fowl's. He was short and stout, strong and bullheaded. Sometimes she'd size him up and think about attacking him… a fantasy that had been on repeat in her mind for years, but she'd never acted on it. For a moment, before she'd run off that afternoon, she'd contemplated getting the gun William had been trusted with to go hunting, right before he disappeared, and taking matters into her own hands.

It was always in the third cabin near the big house. Bastards were trusting enough to hand them guns to kill their dinner, make 'em chop wood with the axes, but made sure they'd beat the hide off 'em for trying to read and write. She envisioned herself swinging that axe and landing it right in the center of his skull, splitting his fat face clean down the middle… Or shooting that gun, aiming it right between his light brown, beady eyes…

She hated everything about him… his twisted, thin pink lips… the odd shape of his ears… the wispy strands of dark blond hair, visible only when he wasn't donning his wide-brimmed black hat. She hated his long-faced wife, their spoiled, disrespectful children, the land, the alligator-infested rice fields, the smell of death and disease all around her…

She hated the man who had killed her mama right in front of her when she'd been just a young child, and she hated his whole family for it, too. That had been a different master… a man Mama had put roots on. Hatred kept Venus alive. It ran through her veins like the velvety rich history her grandmother had told her of their family… They were from Nigeria and Gambia. She held on tight to that identity, for if she survived, she'd be responsible for telling her children the truth about them, too. Time had no beginning and no end.

She realized that the moon had shifted positions.

The sun gonna come up soon… If they ain't close behind, they camped out and they'll be after me again. This time, their cavalry will be doubled.

Every muscle in her body was on fire, as if soaked in kerosene and lit with a tossed flame. Just as she was about to slump down onto the cold ground and contemplate how to dig her own grave with her bare hands, she spotted a cabin in the near distance.

Jesus! My Lord!

She raced forward, her wobbly legs and knees almost giving out. Soon, she'd reached the creaky steps. The porch was uneven, weathered, and the windows were covered with dark linens. She swallowed, tasting the saltiness of her split lower lip as she ran her tongue across it. Arm up, she said a silent prayer and rapped on the door. There was no sound, no light, no signs of life in that cabin.

Oh yes, I need to do the special knock…

She rapped again, and this time she did three knocks… paused… two knocks… paused… then two more. She waited. The door swung open revealing darkness like she'd never seen. The smell of sweet perfume drifted around her as she stood there, confused. No one was there, but it felt like there was.

"Hello? I… uh…"

"I know why you're here," came a deep, female voice that sent chills up her spine. From the darkness emerged one of the tallest women she'd ever laid eyes on. The lady's skin was so white, it made white look dark… Her eyes were a piercing, icy blue, and her pitch black, shiny hair was pulled tight and pinned up with a sparkling dark red pendant that looked as if it cost more money than one could even imagine. Dressed in a long emerald gown, the woman smiled down at her, studying her from head to toe. She clasped her hands together. "Come in here before they see you."

Venus looked over her shoulder. For a split second, she wondered if what was behind her was worse than what was before her…

Her body tingled with chills; her mind whirled with forbidding thoughts. Making a fast decision, she stepped over the threshold. As soon as she did, the cabin seemed to come to life, becoming instantly aglow with candles, a roaring fire, warmth, and a wooden table laden with large bowls, silver platters full of food, big, glass pitchers of water, and a dark red, pretty drink she couldn't identify.

"Have a seat." The woman pointed to a chair at the end of the table.

Venus made her way over and plopped down. Her spine seemed to give out as her muscles turned to mush and every fiber of her body twisted and flinched, screaming out in agony. Her stomach rumbled at the sight of the feast, though she tried to keep her eye on the woman, too.

"My name is Geneviève." She glided slowly towards the fire, her face split in a smile that was troubling and comforting all at the same time. Picking up an iron poker, she began to work the fire. The flames came to life, almost yelling from her touch. "I first want you to eat and drink, get warm. Then you can bathe. I have clothes for you; they should fit. After that, you will need to get some sleep."

"Hello, Geneviève. I… I can't thank you enough. Thank you for lettin' me in. I'm not even sure I'm alive right now. Feels like I'm dreamin'… feels like I'm half dead."

"Oh no, my dear. You're *very* much alive…I can hear your strong heartbeat, your rich blood flowing… poor thing." The woman kept her back straight as the glow of the fire surrounded her like some blazing halo.

Venus tilted her head to the side and tried to concentrate on what was being said, the odd feeling in the place… but as soon as trepidation crept across her mind like marching ants along a twig, peace transfixed it, wiped the worries away.

"My name is Venus. Venus Anderson," she offered.

The woman nodded and drew closer until finally, she was standing before her. Venus stared up into her icy blue eyes, and a strange sensation overwhelmed her, putting her in a peaceful state, as though someone was singing a lullaby to her. The towering woman gently outstretched her pale, cold hand and tilted her chin upward, then turned her face from side to side, as if doing some sort of inspection. When she was done, she walked to the other end of the table and took her seat. Grabbing one of the glass pitchers filled with something dark red, she poured it into a beautiful goblet and took a sip.

"Venus, eat until you are full. Drink until your thirst is quenched. This time tomorrow, I will be gone and you will be in a wagon headed to a place called New York. Are you familiar with the name of that state?"

Venus nodded. Grabbing a warm, buttery roll from the basket, she jammed it into her mouth. She swallowed hard, and before long, she'd consumed a big bowl of delicious chicken stew, a plate of peppers and corn, and collard greens, washing it all down with two large glasses of water.

The woman offered more and more food. Gooey sweets, hot drinks, and plenty of liquor. Venus passed on the alcohol, but accepted a cup of hot tea with honey and lemon, which made the tickle in her throat go away... the first sign of a cold.

Geneviève barely spoke for quite some time, but her actions showed how much she cared. She placed a thick red blanket along her shoulders, took her hand, and made her settle directly in front of the fire.

"There you go, Venus... lie there and finish your tea. When you feel like yourself again, I will show you to your bath and you can dress in fresh, dry, clean clothing."

Venus looked at the woman whose skin was so light, it appeared to have a blue glow to it, like that of the full moon. She simply couldn't get over it. Her companion was so strange looking, yet mesmerizing, too. She was beautiful in her own way.

"Thank you, Ma'am. I can't thank you enough. If you don't mind me askin', how'd you get into this line of work? Seems you've been doin' it for a long time."

Geneviève's eyes glowed as she hesitated for a spell. She clasped her hands together.

"Venus, I believe man, *all* man, is created equal. Not one of you is greater or lesser than the other. I've been doing this for a long time, indeed. How I got into it is unimportant, but let's just say, I have my reasons."

Venus nodded and took another sip from her cup. She turned towards the fire and stared into it, the flames drawing her in as they jumped and danced like the ancestors Grand-mama had told her about...

When she turned back around, the table was cleared, as if nothing had been on it at all. In fact, the entire cabin looked different... and yet, the same. Another chill ran down Venus' spine, despite her being so close to the fire. In the distance, she heard water pouring, as if someone was dumping a big bowl of it into something. She could no longer see Geneviève, but she sensed the woman's presence. After a few moments, she finished her tea and got to her feet. When she turned around to set the empty cup on the table, she screamed and dropped it... and it shattered at her feet.

"I scared you… my apologies, Venus," the woman stated as she stood so close to her, she could see every nuance of her face. The fire highlighted the details of skin that looked inhuman… oddly, perfectly smooth, like a porcelain doll kept in the master's house for all his little girls to fawn over.

"I—I'm sorry…" Venus immediately dropped to her knees and began to pick up the shattered pieces of pottery, slicing her finger open in the process. "Oh, no." She immediately brought it to her lips and sucked the droplets of blood from her fingertip.

An eerie exhale emitted from Geneviève, and when she looked back up at the woman, her lips were parted, her eyes wide, and her chest was heaving up and down as if she were having some sort of attack. The woman suddenly turned away.

"Leave the broken cup, dear. I will get it. Please…" She pointed ahead. "Come here and take your bath."

Venus looked at the closed cabin front door, then back towards the pitch black where Geneviève had disappeared. For a fleeting second, she wondered if she should head straight for the door and take her chances on the hounds, the horsemen, and the master. Against Geneviève's request, she finished cleaning up after herself and set the pieces onto the now barren table. One of the pieces was dotted with her blood… She stared at it for a long time.

"Venus… come." The woman's tone was a bit sterner now.

On a swallow, she turned and headed into the darkness but soon, she was bathed in light. In a small corner of the room sat a bathtub filled with water. It smelled like rich perfume and oils, powders and everything pretty.

Green floral leaves floated along the liquid surface and several white candles were aglow around the room. Venus discarded her bloodied, soiled clothing and shoes and stood quivering, holding herself. She couldn't ignore the way Geneviève looked her up and down, her gaze lingering on her hips and buttocks. It was the same way Master had glared at her… made her feel dirty and surge with unspent violent thoughts.

"Why are you lookin' at me like that?" The words came out before she could control herself and reel them back in. It was too late anyway; she wanted answers and wasn't against running out of there completely naked if need be. Worse had happened in her lifetime… much worse.

"Because you're beautiful." The woman smiled graciously then dipped her hand into the water. "The temperature is perfect. You should get in before it cools." Venus locked eyes with her and once again, felt a sense of calm wash over her. She drew closer to the bathtub, placed a leg inside, and then the other. She lowered her body until she was neck deep in the water.

She grasped the sides of the tub and leaned back, falling into a cloud of relaxation like she'd never experienced in her life. It was the first time ever that she felt like she didn't have a care in the world… No one wanting anything from her, demanding more than her comfort and smile. Geneviève kneeled down beside her onto a soft rug. She settled on her knees and grasped a thick cloth with her long fingers. Using a white block of soap, she started to wash her neck, shoulders, and arms. Venus was transfixed – unable to move away, even if she wanted to. Before long, her hair was wet and heavy, and Geneviève worked her long, clear nails against her scalp, massaging all of her troubles away. She felt good from her head to her toes… the sores, bruises, and bloody wounds hurt no more. Geneviève hummed a song she'd never heard before. It was soothing, familiar yet foreign.

Moments later, she got out of the tub, dripping wet. The woman wrapped a lush towel around her body and thoroughly wiped her down.

"Put this on." One at a time, Geneviève handed her clothing items. A shift, stockings, garter. She then handed her a stay made of what appeared to be whalebone. Venus had never had such fancy clothing before but had seen them in the big house many times as she took them out to launder and dry in the sun. She then slid on a dark blue mantua. "I have a pair of shoes for you by the bed I've prepared. You won't need them until tomorrow." Venus followed the woman to the other side of the cabin. Once again, they entered darkness. Once Geneviève opened a door, light shone from the small room which featured another fireplace, a small, comfortable looking bed with layers of sheets and quilts, and a table on which sat a cup of water, a book, and a quill pen.

"Ma'am, this seems to be the only bed in the house. I don't feel right taking it. I can just—"

"Nonsense. This is where you sleep tonight. You must

stop thinking like a slave, Venus. You must learn to take what you need, what you deserve!" The woman's tone seemed suddenly angry, then, just like that, a pleasant smile creased her face again and a softer tone prevailed. "You've had a trying time." Geneviève approached the fire and prodded a poker in it, then turned back towards her. "Lie down."

Venus lay down in the bed, shifted under the covers, and got comfortable. Before another word could be spoken, the woman sat next to her, gathered her hair in both hands and began to pull and jerk, straining her neck. Venus soon realized she was braiding her hair...

Seconds later, Geneviève handed her a mirror and stood back. "Do you like it?" She grinned as she played with a shiny black and red necklace that danced against her collarbone.

"Yes. You braid like my grandmama... Who taught you to braid like this? It's beautiful." Venus ran her fingertips along her hair, turning from side to side. Seven braids ran from her forehead to her back, flowing down like black ribbons.

How'd she do that so fast? How'd she clean the table so fast? How'd she move so fast after handin' me the mirror?

"I learned a long, long time ago... from a Negro woman."

Venus nodded, still admiring the handiwork. Not one strand was out of place. Her tight, coily locks were smooth, shiny, and done to perfection... something that had taken Grandmama hours to do... Geneviève approached her, took the mirror from her grasp and set it on the table face down.

"Sleep..."

She ran her fingers along her eyelids and just like that,

16

Venus felt a wave of warmth and slumber approach. A part of her deep within fought it, but another part wanted this rest in the worst way. Her eyelids felt heavy, and she could hear the door close. A strange noise made her stir, but she couldn't manage to open her eyes; she could only lie there and rest until she fell into blackness, a timeless place…

Hours must've passed, but Venus wasn't certain how much or how little. She swallowed hard, her throat dry as her eyes fluttered and she awoke. She grabbed the glass of water beside her and took big gulps until it was all gone. Then… she heard it.

Dogs barking. Close.

She leapt out of the bed and swung the bedroom door open. There Geneviève stood, in the darkened short hallway, her hair flowing, her eyes almost stark white.

"They've found us!" the woman shrieked. "There's been a change of plans, Venus. Go back to bed and close this door."

"But—"

"GO!" Her voice boomed so loud and low, that a window cracked.

Venus raced away and closed the door, then dropped to her knees by the bed. Angry tears filled her eyes. For a brief moment in time, she'd been happy, almost free. Now it was all ruined… Venus heard noises, like heavy furniture moving, being tossed about. Suddenly the bedroom door crashed open and Geneviève was floating in record speed towards her. Venus' heart pounded hard within her, and she experienced fear like she'd never known.

"Get up from there. Lie down on the bed." Venus quickly got to her feet and did as instructed. Geneviève propped the pillow beneath her head and pulled a chair close, taking a seat. "I have no time to explain any of this to you. Do you still wish to be free?"

"Yes!"

"There is a price."

"I ain't got no money!"

"No, not that type of price, Venus. It's a blessed curse, a cursed blessing... stated both ways. It's a gift that will give pleasure and pain for many lifetimes to come but one thing is certain, you will finally be in control of your own destiny. I can give you freedom, right now. This was not supposed to happen this way!" The woman looked enraged as turned her attention briefly to the open bedroom door. "But something went wrong, so now, I have no choice! I ask again, do you want me to give you the gift?"

"I don't understand!"

"Yes or no?!"

"YES!"

Geneviève gripped her chin with one hand, and with the other she cradled her crown. She jerked her head to the side.

"Whatever you do, Love, be still, and *don't* look at me!"

Venus shrieked when a pain like she'd never known radiated in the flesh of her neck. Her throat burned as if had been lit on fire, and her entire body shook and jerked about as if struck by lightning. She nearly bit her tongue, but soon felt the hand against her chin jerk her mouth open, and fingers slid inside. She ground her teeth into the woman's digits, drawing blood against the white knuckles that invaded her orifice. The sound of pounding at the front door echoed in the room… loud and cruel. Geneviève stood to her feet and Venus turned and looked at her…

She tried to scream but had no voice. She tried to run, but her legs wouldn't budge. The woman's eyes were now pitch black, and her hair blew about as if a breeze was blowing through an open window—but there was none and all the windows were closed. Blood dripped down the woman's chin, coating her lips. Geneviève picked her up in her arms, kicked the bed over with the greatest of ease, and opened a hatch in the floor.

"Sleep. I will return in three days."

Still without a voice, Venus screamed inwardly as she was tossed violently down a dark black hole that smelled of old water and stale, rotten wood. She hit rocks and debris, clutching her bleeding neck before she was surrounded by darkness as the hatch was slammed closed and locked. She heard something heavy sliding again… perhaps the bed… and the muffled sounds of heavy walking and yelling could soon be heard. She looked up, feeling weak. She heard voices right above her.

"Where is she?! She had to have come here!" some man yelled.

"The dogs tracked her to this place, but there's no one here!" The scampering of dog feet hit the wooden boards, along with growls and whining.

"What's wrong with the hounds?!"

The beasts snarled, then whimpered.

"Musta known she was here, that's all. We've checked everywhere. Ain't nobody here. Come on."

"Wait a second!" someone else yelled. "Does not look like anyone has been here, but I can smell fire… The fireplaces are not lit, however." Another voice bellowed. "Something isn't right."

"I can smell food but don't see anything."

"We don't have time for this. Nobody is here! She and whoever helped 'er musta taken off. Damn niggers! I say we kill 'er soon as we catch her! Come on, let's go before she gets too far!"

She heard a bunch of running until the place was finally quiet once again. After a while, she felt safe, as if the men had finally left for good. A foreboding feeling came over her, though. She felt alone…vulnerable. The woman who'd taken her in, treated her so well, then bitten her so roughly had vanished, too. She could simply feel it…

Gift? A blessed curse… a cursed blessing? Back in three days? I hope she ain't leave me here! Maybe I should pretend I'm dead? Why do I wanna get help from someone who did this to me?!

But she felt no fear thinking about the woman. She couldn't explain it, but somehow, someway, she knew the attack hadn't been born of malice…

Venus tried to call out once again.

"Geneviève!" She strained, coughing up blood, feeling weak as she tried in vain to make her voice carry. She ran trembling fingers along her neck for the wound pulsed and throbbed, the pain unbearable. She tried again to scream out, but there was no answer. Venus stayed there, looking up at the ceiling of the cave-like dwelling she was in and then, the urge to sleep came over her with no warning. It was almost as if she'd been knocked out from behind by an invisible force that blanketed her with a deep, slow slide into torpor, for she couldn't keep her head up or her eyes open for even a second longer...

...Three and a half days later

HER EYES FLUTTERED, sensitive to the sudden light...

Venus brought her forearm over her lids, blocking the abrupt illumination that almost hurt upon sight. She could hear flapping... a sound like a bird's wings moving...

After a few moments, she lowered her arm and looked up to see a large, shiny-feathered black raven flying from left to right. Her entire body was cold, and she could barely remember anything that had transpired.

I ran away... that's right. Am I alive? I AM alive...

The cabin... am I still in here?

Had it all been a dream? She stared at the raven that went back and forth, back and forth until finally, she couldn't see it anymore. A loud thud brought her quickly out of her confused state. She reached for her neck; the wound was dry and crusted over. She began to speak, then stopped herself.

Master might be back!

She moved out of the light in the hole, pressing her back against the rough, dank walls. The fear of the horrid man's possible return sent her into an instant panic.

I'll fight! They'll have tuh kill me just like they said they would!

"It's okay…" said a familiar voice.

Long black hair fell down into the opening of the hole. The bluish white, smooth flesh could be seen and long fingers, covered in jewels, wrapped around the rough edges of the circular opening.

Geneviève smiled, her lips now painted a bright red. The woman extended her arm. "Grab my hand."

Venus did so and she helped her out with little to no effort. Before she could say a word, ask a question, the woman zoned in on the bite she'd inflicted upon her. Geneviève ran her finger along the wound, then nodded.

"It's irregular… not my best work. But it's doing fine."

"What's goin' on? Why'd you bite me?! Where'd you go?!"

"Venus, you have many questions. That's to be expected. I will answer some. First, though, let's address your wellbeing. Are you hungry?"

"Yes."

Geneviève took her hand and led her out to the table, which was covered with platters of food again. Gigantic icing covered cakes, buttery rolls, green beans, strips of fried bacon, and apples covered in cinnamon… The sight of it made her feel a mixture of deep hunger and revulsion. Suddenly, she gagged, feeling a knot in her throat. The sting of vomit climbing up her gullet stung her esophagus and before she knew it, she was shivering and standing in a puddle of her own vomit. She wiped the dripping saliva and sticky bile off her mouth and looked down at her dress, now stained with bits of matter that had crept up from her gut. She felt like death warmed over.

"It's all right." Geneviève smiled and tapped her shoulder. "Everyone responds differently. The change can take a few weeks to complete, sometimes months… I've heard of even years for a few… just depends upon the person." The woman shrugged. "If you're already finding your typical desirable foods sickening, then perhaps you're evolving a bit faster. Here, sit."

She pulled out a chair for her, but the woman hadn't touched it. The thing moved on its own. She stared at that chair for quite some time. Perhaps she was hallucinating, seeing things? After all that had happened, losing her mind wasn't farfetched.

I might be turnin' out like Jasper… He started cluckin' like a chicken, went plum crazy after they went 'nd hung his wife and drowned his baby boy in the river.

Venus walked up to the chair and slumped down in it. Old and new emotions stemming from her time on the Miller Plantation filled her, rising to the top just like vomit and acid reflux. The anger burned through her veins. She had a taste for revenge… one so strong, she was fixated on wondering what

Master Miller's body would look like shot full of holes. Geneviève clasped her hands, a somber expression on her face.

"Venus, I can see in your eyes you're changing. It's time to talk. Some things that you wonder about will not make sense to you, even if I answered each and every one of your questions. I am going to tell you what you need to know, at least for now. You found this cabin because you were supposed to. Only people that are meant to see it actually do. However, I made an error in judgment and that caused me to have to move much quicker than originally planned."

"I don't understand." She coughed violently, spewing blood onto the once clean, white plate before her. Geneviève jumped to her feet and floated over to a dresser. Retrieving a handkerchief from a drawer, she handed it to her. Venus continued to cough into it then finally settled. "Am I dying?" She shuddered as her body ran cold, then hot, then cold again.

"Yes and no. You're changing… the old you is dying, but your flesh is so strong, it's holding onto itself, although it's naturally weak. The new you is fighting hard to come forth. You have died and are being born again as we speak."

Venus stared into those cold, light blue eyes of the woman…

Woman… this ain't no woman. She floatin'. She's strong, pullin' me up wit' one arm from that hole… Death is in her eyes. How'd she hide from those men? They couldn't find her, and she ain't easy to miss. She sit there and tell me, 'Died and born again', like baptism… like they declare the Good Book say…

"I ain't got nothin' else to lose. What are you?" Venus sat straight, wanting even straighter answers.

"I am called many things. Your people call me a vampire."

"Vampire? I don't know 'bout that. What's that?" Geneviève stood to her feet and poured herself a glass of that dark red stuff from the crystal pitcher. Then, she poured a second one, too. The glass floated down the table and landed before Venus.

"You will drink it when you're ready. The hunger will become so strong, you will have no choice. Back to your question," The woman took a deep breath. "A vampire, Venus, is what humans call the undead. We feed on human blood… hunters of life essence."

Venus took a deep breath now too as her nostrils flared. The scent of the liquid coming from the glass before her smelled so good and so revolting at the same time. She hungered for it and her stomach knotted from the sight of it, too.

"I've come a very long way, Venus. I've finally found you… I've helped countless slaves to freedom, but never was the one I was looking for amongst them. It's in my nature to not care about anything but what I need. I am not into politics or human rights. I am not an abolitionist. I simply became one to get what I wanted. I had given up hope, and then, there you were…" Geneviève pointed to the glass. "You'll need a sip soon… I can hear your heartbeat slowing. You will hate yourself at first, Venus, but then, you will love yourself. I know it's confusing. It will take time."

"Why were you looking for me?"

"Because you're special." She took a dainty sip from her own glass. "The original plan was to get you to New York so that you could be free and experience the life you so wished to have. However, due to our visitors the other night, it wasn't meant to be... That's my fault, however, and I take full accountability for it. In my excitement, I'd gotten slack. I am sorry."

"I don't know what to say... Nothin' you're sayin' makes sense. You must be crazy and now you're makin' me crazy, too. Are you a witch?"

Geneviève laughed. Her long, pale neck tilted back as she giggled. It was a frightening laugh, a loud, booming sound with high and low pitches.

"I'm not crazy and I'm not a witch, Venus, but your small human brain believes me to be. Why? Well, it's obvious. You need this strange new world you've entered to make sense. I will try my best to explain it to you, regardless. You see, when you cut your hand on the cup, your scent filled the room like a strong, delicious banquet. I had no idea you'd smell so sweet. After I put you to sleep, I returned here to clean up the broken cup but your blood was there, on a piece of it... I tried to ignore it, but I couldn't resist curling my tongue against that rough shard and sampling you. Divine!" She drummed her fingers against the table and her eyes rolled back. "In that moment, I let my guard down and hadn't realized the mask I'd put around the cabin had slipped. You see, that takes concentration. It's my psychic gift, one of a few. I'd put a veil of sorts around it… a bit hard to explain but in time you will get it. As I savored your blood, that tiny drop so intoxicating, I heard the dogs."

"I remember now… That's what woke me. The dogs."

"All of my plans and dreams for you had to be revamped. I couldn't go from plantation to plantation trying to find you. That would've caused undue harm to your family and unlike some others of my line, I do have a sense of responsibility that I honor. I was told years ago that you would surface on your own, that you were built that way. You'd already tried to escape once to no avail. I was pleased that you tried again, this time successfully. Anyway, in order to save you, my Love, I had to turn you right then and there or risk you being killed by their gunfire. I also would have had to kill all of those men, as well as their horses and the like.

"That would only launch a time-consuming investigation due to the scores of dead humans and beasts. Lynchings would have ensued in order to teach you all a lesson and I would have had to burn the entire place down in retribution. They would have stolen what was rightfully mine… *YOU*. I had to do that 238 years ago. Do you know what it's like to have to take out an entire village? It's tiresome, dreadful, and boring. Besides, I really don't like messes," she stated nonchalantly as she rolled her eyes.

"Messes… broken cups…" Venus slicked her tongue against her lower lip. Her skin no longer felt like her own. It was as if she were in someone else's body, simply going through the motions. She felt strong and weak at the same time… dying, while breathing and living. Yeah, none of this made sense.

"I am meticulous about how I conduct myself and my business and I never wish to bring undue attention to my brethren. We've survived amongst you for all of this time for a reason. Most don't even believe we exist and that works in our favor. We work with you, move about the world, smile in your faces, and you are none the wiser. We have high standards, clean our muddles, and avoid big scandals at all costs, unless the opposite is completely necessary. This African slave trade you humans have succumbed to is disgusting." She wrinkled her nose as if smelling a horrid stench. "All humans are sickening organisms… Naturally stupid and lazy, as if one of you is better than the other. You're all mice."

"The white-skinned humans have convinced you all that you are lesser than by removing you from your land, claiming your blood, and force-feeding you lies to keep you submissive. Blood is key! Blood is ancestry. It links you, binds you. You do not realize it now, my Love, but they will erase your history and the good bits of it, claim it for themselves. They will have you turn on one another by instilling divisiveness, using skin tone and color as a weapon. This idiotic notion of house and field slave – when you are all dying slaves! They will have you argue amongst yourselves about hair texture, too. They will infiltrate your music, your dances, your inventions, your artistic expressions, and stupefy your culture and vilify it, too, then make money off your art and have you say and do things that weaken your blood bond.

"There will be broken, bitter families. The parents will be mentally weak, the children emotionally crippled. They will tamper with your education and no one will care until it is too late. They will introduce strange, mind-altering substances into your destroyed neighborhoods that will control you once they see you trying to govern yourselves successfully. You will have no self-worth, no sense of self, nothing at all. The very people that promised to protect you will rob you blind. You will be broken and beaten, but not with whips and chains; it will happen through your own brainwashing and infighting. Your communities will be unsafe warzones. They only need two things to accomplish this and more… the brain and the blood. The disease of self-loathing gets in the brain and eats away at it like a ravenous worm and then it infects the blood, the family line becomes diseased…generational curses.

"They will use religion, false promises, and terror to gain control over you. You will always be on the plantation, even when you are off! They break apart your families, removing the lineage, the blood. They take away the mother and the father, so the original blood line is severed. FOREVER. If you remove the King and the Queen, the village is lost, running around with no direction. It's about blood! They were smart enough to figure that out. They came from you!" she screamed. "Truth they've hidden… but they know! They *always* knew.

"Remove a man's language, you've cut out his tongue! He bleeds to death unless he speaks the foreign words. You can barely read… that's brain control. Blood flow makes the brain work. Reading and writing exercises the brain, my Love! One day, they will no longer have to lift a finger against you – they will have trained you well to do it against yourselves. You'll be a perpetual victim, the mirror forever broken. You, my love, see clearly. They must find you not because another nigger escaped! But because you're a smart, defiant, strong nigger woman with a hot slit between her long legs, perfect for raping so they can spill their rancid seed and force you to bear children for breeding with a man you may never see again!"

Venus gasped, her heart beating nearly out of her chest.

"It has always been about blood, Venus! My kind is just willing to admit who we are... We are proud! It's they who are the *true* vampires. Sucking off of the labor of others, exercising mind control for no other reason than to feel self-important. The jealousy... sickening. How low they've fallen... Descendants of the cast out ones. It amazes me that the God you praise can stand it! Revenge is mine, thus said the Lord. WELL, HOW MANY MORE DROWNED NEGRO BABIES WILL HAPPEN BEFORE THE WRATH OF GOD COMES DOWN LIKE A MIGHTY SLEDGE-HAMMER?! Why doesn't He just destroy them if He is so wonderful and mighty?! BLOOD OF MY BLOOD, FLESH OF MY FLESH!"

She abruptly stood from her seat, toppling it over with a loud thud, and as the woman stood there like some shadowy tower, breathing hard, two incisors emerged from behind her upper lip, bearing down on the bottom one. Her teeth glistened, the ends sharp like knives.

"God!" Venus clutched the edges of the table. Seeing was believing. All the words in the world could never describe how she felt at that moment. How could she understand this? A woman morphing into a ravenous beast, right before her. The woman's eyes shone black for a spell once again, making her look like a snake out in the wild. "God, hear my prayer! Our Father, who art in heaven, hallowed be Thy name…"

"Yes, call Him, Venus!"

Venus lowered her head, clasped her hands together, and kept praying, louder and stronger as hot tears streamed down her cheeks.

"Pray like your mother before she was beaten to death when you were so young! Pray like your father who died from working in the hot sun for twenty hours straight, with not a drop of water to sustain him, no breaks, and then they cast his dead body aside like garbage and made everyone continue working the field. Pray like the first time you were raped, beaten, and whipped. Pray, Venus! Call on God, but not for protection… pray for thanks! God finally did something about your plight. He sent me to save you… Amen. But I tell you something, my dear."

"In Jesus name!" Venus voice trembled as she pressed her eyes shut, trying to drown out Geneviève's words.

"I am incapable of love, but I will come close as possible to treating you as my own, if you allow it, Venus. I will take you around the world, teach you to read and write, educate you, instill in you class and sophistication. And then, my sweet, sweet, Venus, Master Miller and his ilk had better pray, too!

They better pray to the God they don't believe in, that you *never* return. For if you do, it will be for one reason, and one reason only… to burn that entire place down to the ground. And when you do, I will smile and say, 'Well done, my good and faithful servant!'"

CHAPTER ONE

~Modern Day~

Welcome to New York City...

Head of the Throne

JAY Z'S, 'EMPIRE State of Mind' blasted through the gold and black Yamaha speakers of the massive, fifty-million-dollar penthouse on Fifth Avenue in Manhattan, New York. Sitting on his black and red throne with a glass of Kendall Jackson Merlot that he pretended to drink in one hand and the back of a blond bitch's head in the other, he figured he'd be flowing soon, just like the libations. The woman's slippery, wet tongue glided up and down the underside of his rock-hard dick and she occasionally looked up at him, no doubt fishing for clues of his approval and pleasure. He offered few.

Alexandre Marseille sat there studying his surroundings, his home. It was a celebratory party, after all. He'd won yet another case; his client walked away with a $2.4 million dollar settlement. People milled about, eating up the disgusting food they'd surely expected to be served, fucking one another against walls, snorting premium cocaine up their reddened, raw nostrils, flipping playing cards and tossing dice, shoving balls across pool tables and gambling their money away. To his left knelt an Indian woman who sucked his balls in a slow and easy, methodical manner, her expertise with such things quite apparent in the special attention she showed.

The blond lady licking the base of his dick moved to the throbbing head of his nature, lavishing it with needy sucks and slurps, while a short-haired brunette with dragon tattoos up and down the length of her pale, perfect body ate her own pussy before him as she twisted and contorted her seemingly spineless form in the strangest of ways. He took a leisurely sip of his drink, winced, then tossed it down on the floor and snapped his fingers for one of his servants to come pick the shit up.

"Sorry about that, Mason." Alexandre Marseille chortled as his eyes turned to black slits. He forced his true nature to show for a spell, removing the veil of the ice blue pupils he typically donned, which made others feel so much more comfortable. "Someone moved my table." He pointed to the bench that usually rested alongside his throne, now being used by two gorgeous lesbians with leather dog chokers around their necks. One had the other bent over and was fucking her ruthlessly with a long, plastic strap on. Her cries of ecstasy made him lick his lips. He opened his black button down shirt a little more as sticky heat resonated within his slender frame, pouring out to his pale flesh, consuming him from his black hair to his toes. He hated these moments... a reminder that he was a slave to his need to feed, and fast food was becoming more and more commonplace.

Typically, feast time was something he rather enjoyed but as of late, it had become an inconvenience for several reasons. Most notably, his preferred taste of meal was running low on supply, becoming harder to come by. He preferred pure blood, untainted by pollutants such as alcohol and marijuana... When blood wasn't pure, it offered an offputting after taste, and he'd always had a sensitive palate. He could pick up the subtlest of notes in the blood of his prey, able to tell with almost 100% accuracy what nourishment had been consumed that day.

Processed foods and purely vegan diets were disgusting as well... the worst of the worst. He needed the tangy taste of the animals they'd consumed, the subtle bloody flavors of those meats. Those who ate from all the major food groups were the most ideal, but living in a low-carb, Keto diet, drug infested, diseased, cancerous, fast food on every corner, Atkins world made the current blood stock strange and unpleasant, to say the least.

Twisting his fingers tight in the length of the long blond strands of the whore giving him head, he forced her down hard onto the shaft until her nose was pressed against his black pubic hair. He rejoiced in her gagging as he pumped his hips hard and rough, screwing her, driving himself into the roof of her mouth until he flooded her gateway with copious cum. He groaned when the last of him spilled against her tongue.

When she fell back, tears were in her green eyes and a sly smirk on her face as she spit out some of his seed, allowing it to drizzle down her chin like melted vanilla ice-cream along a sugar cone. Swinging his arm, he abruptly knocked the other woman off his nut sack and got to his feet, then stepped over the limber lady who was now squirting and cumming so hard from her self-given cunnilingus, her eyes rolling back as she lapped up her own juices. Tucking his cock back in his pants and pulling his trousers up, he yawned. It was time for a break. He double tracked, bent low between the freak's wide-open legs, and slid his tongue against her pink, sloppy wet slit, then marched away.

His heavy gait echoed over the music, and he didn't miss how people turned and watched him as his dark open shirt swayed from side to side and the necklace around his throat bounced up and down against his chest. Black strands of his hair shifted, covering one eye. He quickly raked his fingers through his mane, forcing the stray locks back in place. Alexandre walked past a series of pure 100% silver wall mirrors, smiling at an invisible reflection, then took the elevator to the second level of his estate.

Once in his private study, he removed his shirt and tossed it on the floor. His shoes and socks followed. Standing in only his pants, he got some much-desired cool air.

Yes, that feels better...

Opening the thick, black curtains, he stood at the large window, arms outstretched, admiring the view of the city.

So much like Paris, but not quite the same. Oh, how I miss you... *J'aime la France...*

He went to the sideboard to pour himself a glass of blood, then made his way to the old record player that rested on a black and gray marble entertainment center he'd had hand-crafted and brought from Italy. Flipping through his old records, many of the covers faded over time, he smiled as he met eyes with Otis Redding. In a matter of seconds, 'I've Been Loving You Too Long' was playing. He moved through the room, dancing, snapping his fingers and singing the lyrics.

I remember where I was when I first heard this song... I was fucking that Spanish woman behind the bodega. Someone was playing it from the apartment above. Then I ate her pussy... made her cum so hard, she thought she was in love. Yes, her pussy was amazingly good. Fat, pink lips that cushioned the blows just right from my thrusts in and out of her tight little wet cunt... It was covered with so much fucking hair, soft, sweet little peach she was... I ate her up... crushed her bones with my teeth even, didn't want to miss one bit of her. She tasted delicious and when she screamed, I covered her mouth and fucked the shit out of her, giving her immeasurable pleasure and pain all at once... The dumpster I tossed her in afterward wasn't deserving of such a prize, but I had no time to place her elsewhere. Besides, the night was still young... There were more bitches to fuck and suck. I was new to the city and out sowing my wild oats.

Raising his arm, he wiggled his ringed fingers about, as if trying to make an object float in the air with a bit of silly Hollywood hocus pocus. He loved American melodies, so rich and soulful... The rhythm of the music pulsed through him. He imagined, if he had a soul, it would feel much like music, drums vibrating through one's spirit, making him dance...

Soon, the double black doors of his office, Chinese designs carved in them, opened, and two of his men entered, gripping tight to a fellow with dark brown hair, his face full of stubble, his appearance disheveled. The man was covered in sweat, and sheer panic swam in his blue eyes.

"Miiiickey!" Alexandre Marseille smiled as he turned the music down. "So nice to see ya again. Please, have a seat."

His two handlers, Bruce and Whiskey, dragged the fucker over. The bastard's legs seemed to have turned to overcooked noodles. Pathetic. He'd lost his will to walk like a man. They tossed him in the chair on the other side of his desk and stood guard.

"Alexandre, please!" the guy babbled, his eyes welling up with the worst thing of all... tears. "I just need two more days, man! I'll have ya money! I was *this* close!"

"Ahhh, close isn't good enough, Mickey." Alexandre circled him like a ravenous shark and tapped his shoulder with a gentle pat. Well, it appeared gentle, sincere, not matching his apathetic nature in the least. "You see, Mickey, it was never about the money. I can make money in my sleep." He shrugged. "My law firm clears millions of dollars a year. I have a waiting list of clients, that's how fuckin' good I am. This is about principle."

He stood behind the man and sniffed the air. The scent of distress was becoming so strong and overpowering, as though the feeling itself had been lifting weights.

"Alexandre, I know... I know! You're the best! You practice law. Please be fair!" The victim struggled, desperate for a little saving grace. "I've been trying to get it, ya gotta believe me! Just one more day, one more!"

"Tick, tick, tick... time has run out, Mickey. If I gave you one more day, what would the others think, huh? Now that wouldn't be fair at all. You had one job..." He put up one finger. "To get me that fuckin' money back plus interest... This is an investment!"

His fangs extended and he found himself licking his chops as he stared down at the man, who was now shaking, sobbing, and pissing himself while Whiskey kept him down in the seat with one hand.

"I told you that failure was no longer an option. I have looked high and low trying to find the woman. It's been quite an expense to track her down. I don't even know how much I've spent for this endeavor, but it's been way too fucking much. I've hired numerous detectives. They all bombed. I've had the help of all sorts of so-called professionals, bounty hunters, you name it, but not one of you motherfuckers can find this fuckin' woman!" He kicked over a nearby chair, causing it to shatter, the wood splintering and sliding in a million directions. "Sure! It's a needle in the haystack. I don't know her name... don't know how she looks, but I know she's here somewhere. That much, I know for certain. I told you what I could, and I knew the job wouldn't be easy... but it's not impossible."

"You're right! It's not impossible! I can do it. If ya don't want the money now, let me get the girl! Gimme another crack at it!"

He began to pace around the man, while rubbing on his chin.

"All the cracks have been sealed. This has been going on for years... The search continues, but I'm running out of time, just like you have tonight." He went around the chair one last time and gripped the arms of it, pressing his forehead against Mickey's and looking the fearful maggot in the eye. The fella's dark eyelashes webbed with liquid, his enlarged pores seeped with sweat. The man's fear stunk like burnt human flesh on an open fire. Weakness made Alexandre want to vomit, especially when it came from the male of any species. "It's life or death... It's the most important thing to me right now, and you failed," Alexandre stated calmly... so calmly.

"Maybe... maybe there's been a mistake, Alexandre! Maybe she died or she isn't here. It happens! Let me... let me find out for ya! PLEASE!" the pitiful bastard blubbered.

"It was clear... there was no mistake. The *Sorcier Cadieux* makes no mistakes. I was told as a boy that she would be here, in this city, at this time." He pointed towards the window but kept his eye on the man. "I do not know much about her, but I can sense her... She's too far away to corner though. It's almost as if she's disguised her scent. It's enraging, you know that?" He narrowed his eyes as his heart beat faster… a reminder of how the mere topic drove him insane, made him want to give chase to a ghost. "It shouldn't be this difficult, but it is. And with all I'm going through, all I did was ask that you repay the loan I gave you after you came groveling to me, begging, pleading like the fragile son of a bitch that you are!"

Snot trailed from Mickey's nose, his words now incoherent as he cried like a fucking baby.

"I hired you to find her. You could not. I didn't slice your fucking throat for that failure. I let you live! And then you returned to me, needing more, promising that you'd find the woman but needed money for some debt. So you asked for an advance… more money. I was told you were the best. You're nothin', Mickey. You're worthless… You won't even taste all that fuckin' great, but tonight, you'll just have to do."

He grinned from ear to ear as he traced the fucker's face with his fingertip, the nail on his pinky extending, growing several inches then curving over. Mickey caught sight of it and winced. The skin around his eyes crimped, almost closed shut as if he were trying to withdraw within himself, like some frightened turtle.

"You're weak… an addict! But you see, Mickey, I know your greatest desires and fears… I know what makes you tick." He tapped the side of the man's head, then grabbed his jaw and snapped it hard out of alignment. The crackling noise echoed in the room. The bastard's eyes grew large and a gurgling sound emitted from the back of his throat… too afraid no doubt to attempt to speak in such a condition. "That must feel awful, huh?" He laughed as he dropped to his knees before the miserable man, yet still towered over him. "Let's see…"

He looked deep into Mickey's eyes, raiding his fears and desires. Tiptoeing in his brain with the greatest of ease, invading his privacy in the most beautiful of ways. "Ahhhhh, there it is. You're afraid of rats… how funny." He laughed. "Fuckin' terrified of 'em! And your greatest wish is to be filthy rich. Makes tha whole sayin', 'gettin' over like a fat rat' come to life, right?"

Alexandre got to his feet. The lights in the room suddenly vanished, and they were drowned in darkness. He could hear Mickey's rapid heartbeat, like a running rabbit's feet in the wilderness. The sound of rats filled the place… chewing, scurrying. Mickey cried out, wailing in fear as the sensation of rats nipping at his ankles and feet soon commenced. Just as quickly as it occurred, the lights suddenly came back on, and Alexandre burst out laughing so hard, he almost choked.

"Oh man! That was great! You should've seen your face…" His smile quickly vanished, and then, he glared up at the ceiling and crossed his arms over his bare chest to take a few deep breaths before proceeding to dislocate his own jaw, making it snap and crack as he extended his fangs. Famished, his mouth watered at the bounty before him.

He could feel his veins throb with his essence, excitement in every fiber of his being in anticipating a fine feast. Mickey's screams blended in with Otis' crooning of 'Pain in My Heart.' In a flash, Alexandre buried his incisors in the prey's neck, while ripping at his flesh with one hand and holding him close with the other. Sweet, crimson blood sprayed in all directions, painting the rugs and nearby wall red. He sucked and drank, draining the bastard dry in a matter of minutes, until all that remained was a ghostly white corpse, dried out to the bone. The body fell to the floor with a heavy thud. Alexandre licked his fingers, lapped at his thumb, then locked his jaw back in place. He returned to his record player while Whiskey and Bruce carried the measly leftovers away, closing his office door behind them.

Alexandre turned up the music, then went back to the window, stepping into a puddle of Mickey's blood along the way. The city lights twinkled and sparkled, glowing like diamonds and colorful jewels...

She's out there somewhere... one of those glowing lights is hers. He inhaled and exhaled hard and heavy, then again, closing his eyes, falling into a trance.

I never give up, my bride. I'm going to find you. But please know, you will be punished when I do. I've grown impatient, and you are to blame...

CHAPTER TWO

I'm Your Venus, I'm Your Fire –
At Your Desire

O VER THIRTY IDENTIFICATION cards, passports, and driver's licenses from various countries and across the US lay sprawled on Venus' kitchen table, in her Manhattan apartment. They were all expired, but at times she enjoyed pulling them out and travelling down memory lane. She picked up one and smiled.

Toronto, Canada – 1943.

There weren't too many places on Earth she'd not travelled to or through by boat, train, or plane. She'd returned to New York a few months prior after living in Rome for three years. She'd bounced around quite a bit, but always found her way back to NYC, where it had all begun for her…

Manhattan was far too expensive, but she needed to stop spending so much time in Brooklyn and Queens. She couldn't afford to be remembered.

Placing her red coffee cup to her lips, she drank, letting the hot liquid slide down her throat. She refused to give up the routine she'd grown accustomed to because a shred of humanity was needed in her life. The usage of utensils, sipping beverages with friends at coffee shops, watching television, shitty YouTube prank videos, and the like was a required protocol she'd demanded of herself. She took another sip and grimaced. Despite the abhorring taste of the brew, she'd maintained the ritual for centuries and refused to give it up.

Notwithstanding her 'condition', retaining these key components of human normalcy proved essential, surpassing even her desire to divorce herself from the past. She smiled as she got a whiff of something sweet… The aroma reminded her of her mistress Geneviève's signature scent. A wall of melancholy instantly consumed her then; her smile melted away like black candles snuffed out by Wiccan priestesses while they summoned the undead.

Geneviève may very well have been a High Priestess herself. She definitely knew magic…

That seemed unheard of in the vampire circles she'd travelled with the woman, though the woman swore they existed. She'd been revered, feared, and admired back in those days. People bowed down to the tall woman, dropped to their knees as soon as she made an appearance. Geneviève had been her freedom, and her imprisonment, too…

I miss her… What's it been? A hundred and twelve years since I last saw her?

The woman had been good to her—the kind of good that was unheard of in such a sick, cruel world. She'd kept her promises to take Venus around the world, educate her, refine her, and treat her well. Venus had never been in a vehicle before, let alone big boats and the like. With Geneviève, she wore expensive clothing, including thick petticoats made by highly-sought-after seamstresses, and slept in beds that were so high off the floor, she needed steps to climb into them. Her hair was done at all times, sometimes braided and adorned with gold and silver beads, and at other times pulled back in a knotted updo. Her now healthy jet-black, kinky mane hit her hips when stretched with the fingers. Most didn't believe it was hers, but it most definitely was... all thirty-two inches of it.

Geneviève had also taught her about her mother's culture, Nigeria, about *all* of Africa, India, and Egypt. The woman had showed her beauty rituals, how to handle money matters, and yes... how to hunt and feed. Though her mistress had been stern and secretive at times, Venus knew it was for her own protection. Their relationship had been at times hard to explain, yet they'd shared a strong connection, one that couldn't be denied.

She was my second teacher... Grandmama was my first. Geneviève taught a slave to read and write. I recognized some numbers, like dates on a calendar, things like that, a few words here and there, but not enough to get by.

She'd immediately taught her to read and write in three different languages as soon as she got her away from South

Carolina. When introduced, she stated that Venus was her assistant, but called her Annabelle in an effort to alleviate the suspicions of those who may have recognized her, despite them living in various European countries during most of their time together.

Geneviève had warned that one could never be too careful about such things, for Venus had a bounty on her head. An escaped slave from a large plantation, one who'd been purchased for a pretty penny and was definitely of child-bearing age was a hot commodity.

Child bearing... breeding... I hate you!

Flashes of the Miller Plantation dashed through her mind.

She gritted her teeth and soon tasted blood. Her fangs had sprung from the gumline and sliced into the tender flesh of her lower lip. The flavor of iron made her pupils dilate; she could feel it, just as she was aware of every single thing her body did at all times. Her every sense was heightened and then heightened some more.

She quickly retracted her fangs, gaining control of herself, and made an earnest effort to shake the repulsive, heart-wrenching memories out of her mind. She turned towards her living room window and noted the bustling sounds of the city were unusually amplified. She glanced at the large black and white clock on her wall, with Roman numerals on its face. It was rush hour traffic. She looked down at the passing cars, yellow taxis and buses going to and fro in bumper-to-bumper traffic. She'd been home for two hours after work and the day had been a blur.

The bright sun was setting, the sky streaked with watercolor hues of candy apple red and cotton candy lavender. Pressing her hand against the cool glass, she took a deep breath, and then another. Her phone rang, jerking her out of her deliberations. She walked back to her small kitchen, retrieved her cell, and answered with a smile.

"Hello, Camille."

"Hi, babe. Do you wanna hang out with me and Deborah this upcoming Saturday? There's a party and—"

"You know I would, Camille, but—"

"Come on, come on, come on! It'll be fun!"

"You and Deborah would have no fun with me, believe me." Venus' lips curled in a grin as she played the modest act. Anything to get out of being at some club or shindig where the lights were too bright and the scent of the people swarming around with ill intentions made her either sick or ravenous. "Remember what happened last time? You both danced the night away while I played on my phone and then got into a Twitter beef with some fucker about the life of Vincent Van Gogh."

"Oh no, no, no… you're not doing this to us again, Venus, okay? Van Gogh defender or not, I need you to lend me your ear, all right?"

"Cute." Venus chortled.

"I will not be tossed aside like last month's assignments. You told us no last week and the week before that and then, when you came out with us a couple months ago, you left after fifteen minutes and caught a Lyft home. Come on, Venus!"

the woman whined in her sweet little way, triggering Venus to smile as she walked out of the galley and back to the window to people watch. "You can't stay held up in that lecture hall discussing dead artists, or jammed up in your home drinking wine alone all the time. Live a little!"

"Oh, I don't know." Her eyes rested on a muscular man donning a black hoodie who was holding a rolled newspaper in one hand and a bookbag in the other before flinging it over his shoulder. She zoned in on him as though her eyes were binoculars. She could practically smell his anxiousness from so far away. That feeling of unease emanating from others made her queasy and thrilled all at once.

Maybe he's running late. His energy is tangible... Shit. Everyone is running late around here, right? Does he have a wife? A lover to go home to?

"Well?!" Her friend interrupted her private thoughts, bringing her back to the here and now. "Are you hanging out with us or not?"

"I have a lot of papers to grade and—"

"We're coming to get you at eight and that's that, Venus. Yashek is having a party and, knowing him, it's going to be incredible. He throws the best bashes! Open bar, too. Look, we've worked our asses off. It's time to unwind for the weekend. I won't take no for an answer. See ya Saturday night."

And then, just like that, the call was over. Camille was a fellow professor at Colombia University. While Venus taught Art History, her friend taught Drama and Theater Arts.

Deborah was part time and taught Film and Media Studies. The three often hung out together gossiping, sharing work stories, growing friendships... This one she actually liked. Camille was fun and beautiful with her short, reddish-brown, bob cut hair and dark tan skin.

She had an asshole ex-husband that she still fucked every now and again for posterity, and a teenage step-daughter who she doted on and spoiled. The woman was a bit too trusting, but she was intellectually astute and worth the time of day.

Venus brought the cup of coffee to her lips once again and swallowed down the awful muck. She observed the muscular man disappear out of a store he'd dipped in minutes earlier and emerge with a plastic white sack in his hand, more than likely containing something to eat for his dinner that evening. She smiled sadly as she recalled picking beans with her grandmother, chewing on uncooked collard greens, tasting the bitter sweetness as she ground the dark leaves between her small teeth. She remembered the smell of soft oatmeal and raisin cookies made of flour and cane sugar, big, pink spongey cakes covered in tart pineapples and syrupy cherries... baked in the big house. When the White folks' dinner was over, she and the other Black children got the leftover sweets.

Her recollections of that time resurfaced, as they often did when she felt all alone in the world. However, in those brief moments, those passing periods of limited joy, she held on to them, like she would onto busted beads from a broken, precious pearl necklace... some slipping through the spaces of her fingers, hitting the floor and rolling away from her on the ground… while others would grow hot from being squeezed so hard in the palm of her hand. She'd hold those few pearls to her chest, so tight, as if her life depended upon it. She couldn't release those coveted jewels, for they were the only thing that remained constant. Memories remained constant, never-changing, like the locked gates of Heaven and broken chains of Hell.

She looked down and shook her head, wringing her hands as her body surged with heat, her muscles tightening and rolling beneath her flesh…

She'd probably have to move again in a few years like she always did. She wasn't aging, so people would have questions. It was the way of her kind. There was no longer any such thing as home. She sometimes left dwellings she'd decorated in her own special way, places she adored, people she cherished, and yet, the gnawing hunger and the pitch black, cold darkness within her would never allow her to fully bond with the outside world. It would be a rare treat to relax, sigh with relief, feel true love for anyone, or to take her time doing anything at all. What would it be like to dip her toes in the water of the stream of life while braiding spiky weeds and tiny white flowers together to make a fine necklace provided by Mother Nature?

After pouring herself a glass of red wine, she sat down at her small kitchen table, going over her students' papers while Kelly Rowland's, 'Ice' played on her Pandora playlist.

A few hours later, when the city was a bit quieter and the crack and heroin addicted whores, the sleepless homeless and mentally deranged swarmed the spit and piss covered streets trying to find a dollar, a fuck, or a fight to pick, she put on her long black cloak, slid on her thigh high boots and black leather gloves, and headed out into the night. Forty-two minutes later she spotted a man asleep inside of his car...

She sniffed the air.

He smells fine...

Over the decades, she'd gotten better at picking out prime prey, the sweetest, flesh-covered fruit. This one had to be in his mid-thirties, well-groomed, and exhausted from a hard day's work. She ventured closer to the car, looked both ways, then tapped on the glass of the driver's side window, startling the man.

"I'm sorry, baby," she spoke in the old Southern accent she'd lost decades ago, laying on the charm. It seemed to make her more endearing to others, and men especially trusted her when she spoke with a twang. "Didn't mean to wake you, honey. I'm new in town. Do you have a cigarette?"

She let her robe fall to her shoulders, exposing her hair and collarbones. Their eyes locked and he began to fall deep into her darkness.

He let his window down. "Uh...sorry. I don't smoke." His eyes narrowed on her breasts.

"Oh, all right. I guess I'll need to wait it out. In the meantime, you wanna fuck?" She tossed her head to the side and giggled as she placed her hand on her hip.

"I don't have any money and, uh, I'm married... but uh, you're fuckin' nice looking... no doubt about it." He sat a bit straighter in the car and sucked his lower lip.

"Awww, you're so cute." She leaned into the car, blinking her long lashes as she slicked her tongue along her teeth. "What your wife don't know won't hurt her, and this one'll be on the house. I haven't had a good hard one in me in weeks, baby."

She winked at him, sealing his fate. Minutes later, she was in the passenger's seat, rubbing her hands all over her breasts as he watched out the corner of his eye. The man was a bit fidgety, as if he couldn't believe his luck, but the offer of free sex was simply one the bastard couldn't refuse.

He drove to an alleyway with an old broken-down motorcycle parked in it, put the car in park, and immediately grabbed for her like some sex addicted beast. The sleeping prince was now a frenzied maniac, pawing all over her, his thick fingers scraping against her skin. His expression went from unreadable to one of pure malevolence and insatiable desire. She smiled through the revulsion… His stench, though undetectable to the human nose, drove her crazy as his body fueled with lust to level FULL. Human pheromones were one of the most pungent odors on the fucking planet. They smelled like wild boars when aroused and the more excited he became, the harder it was to keep her fangs at bay.

"Mmmm, yeah, baby," He buried his head between her breasts and slid his big, hard hand up her thigh. "I like it rough. Don't cha like it rough, too, you horny Black bitch?" He laughed raucously as he pushed his chest hard against hers, his hands roaming all over her. He licked all along her cleavage, tasting her as though he hadn't eaten in weeks.

"Mmmm hmmm, big boy… I like it *real* fucking rough." She rolled her eyes.

"I wanna fuck your used up, sloppy pussy, ya fuckin' whore! Then I wanna fuck ya in the goddamn ass! I'm gonna rip you apart!" He undid his pants and quickly whipped out his short, fat, reddened cock, which lay buried within dense, light brown pubic hair. "Come on, bitch!"

He shoved her cloak roughly up her body and knocked her legs apart, then fumbled along her panties, trying to get the damn things down.

"You can't get a bitch's briefs down? I thought you were a man…"

He grinned then showcased an evil, horrid smile, the kind that made her want to laugh and spit venom and scorching acid in his fucking face. She felt her eyes burning as he wrapped his hands around her throat, squeezed, released, then squeezed again. Her stomach growled and her pussy creamed as he grew impatient… She simply wouldn't black out so he could do his dirty deed in peace… fuck her with no witnesses, not even herself. Fuck her without her judgmental eyes glaring at him. Twisting her head in a 360-degree turn, she wagged her tongue in his direction.

"What tha fuck?!"

She flung him off her with one arm, pressing him so hard into the driver's side window, the damn thing shattered against the back of his head. His eyes grew large, his complexion pale.

"Oh, shit! I was just kidding, baby! Just playin'! I didn't

mean to hurt ya! It was just a game! I got money, okay?! It's cool. Take it!"

She wrapped her hand around his throat and squeezed.

"Do you like that, you sick son of a bitch? Do you like being choked, your miserable life flashing before your eyes? I always pick good ones lately, ya know? Ones like you I lose not one wink of fuckin' sleep over. How many prostitutes have you killed, huh? Five, ten, twenty? I can smell it on you... you're a killer... so ripe, baby!"

She flung her head back and extended her fangs. His bloodcurdling screams echoed and the car rocked back and forth with his futile struggling when she descended upon him, sinking her teeth against the deliciously moist flesh, piercing it hard. Yeah, he tried to fight, but he was no match for her. Soon, he was trembling beneath her, his body succumbing to a seizure as she sucked and devoured the nauseating vessel beneath her.

When he died in her arms seconds later, she paused, blood dripping down her mouth and chin, and turned on his radio. 'Take Me Home Tonight' by Eddie Money was playing on the radio. She turned back to her meal. His dead eyes were looking up at the ceiling of the car, his lips twisted and hanging open. Pieces of glass dotted his hair like tiny diamonds... pretty little jewels. She grabbed him with both hands and continued to feast, making quick work of that before someone came upon them. This fucker would hold her for at least a week, perhaps two if she didn't over-exert herself. She reached for his wedding ring, tore the finger off his hand, and laughed...

'I'm married,' he said... I bet your wife knows nothing about your twisted, secret life. Well, that life is over now. Hanging around areas like this, picking up women and trying to choke them to death while you get off... You son of a bitch!

She tore into his flesh with her claws now, ripping him to shreds with malice, riding the high of her extreme anger. She slid the band off the dismembered finger, tossed the digit in the backseat, and shoved the marital jewelry into his mouth. She unleashed decades upon decades of frustration, vexation, and pure rage on the fucker, used him and abused the bloody corpse in the most obscene ways... Cigarette burns up and down his arms, deep bites and cuts until it had gotten so good to her, she disemboweled him with her bare hands. She roared, dancing between laughter and screaming as her inner evil was let out to play...

She had a second mission now after feasting... When his body was found in the morning, there'd be little to nothing left, except his cold, stiff corpse with most of the blood drained from it, and that damn gold wedding ring jammed between his pearly white teeth...

CHAPTER THREE

Find and Fucking Seek

...Two days later

Alexandre Marseille sat behind his black desk in his
law offices in Manhattan.

"I want to see it."

The manila folder was handed to him and he rested back
against his black and clear acrylic seat, leisurely opening it. He
made a quick scan of the first page, then turned to the next,
only pausing to adjust the gold ring on his pinky finger. Fawn,
one of his many assistants, but most prized, tossed her
platinum blond hair over one shoulder and ran her dark violet

nails against her crossed knee, legs covered in black stockings, as she slowly rocked her red bottom stiletto heel to and fro.

"It looks like you were right."

"Of course I was," he responded.

"Well, you were right if it is her, of course." His eyes narrowed on her. "There's always that possibility that it's not."

"If it's not, you will pay for wasting my time. My only living brother, Victor, is already taunting me like some adolescent who witnessed me fall and scrape my knee while he runs off with my bicycle… childish fucking antics." He hissed. "I have no time for it."

"You both are so very important. Perhaps I'm naïve my Lord but I wish you two had a better relationship. I've only spoken to him once over the phone, but he seemed to be—"

"You know nothing of him. What he appears to be and what he actually is are two vastly different things."

"I wasn't aware that there was hatred between the two of you."

"I don't hate him. I'd have to care about his existence in order to feel that sort of emotion and besides, hatred is weakness spun in the wrong direction, like a spider's web being made in reverse."

"I apologize if this is none of my business, but what is the issue with you and Victor?"

He hesitated for a moment, then decided to answer. He rarely discussed family business, especially with the help, but under such conditions, it may aid him in his endeavors if Fawn understood the true severity of the issue at hand.

"He wishes to replace me, and he knows if this is not re-solved soon, that is *exactly* what will take place. I have a certain amount of time to marry and mate. And even then, it's not guaranteed. The bride has to be of a certain quality, and under the current rules I don't make that determination—the Council does. I'd have to override it, challenge them and that would require a potential investigation and then ruling. If I defy their verdict, I could potentially be stripped of my crown. Due to the fact that my preferred route is to seek a Turned Vamp, it will more than likely lead to a hearing. I see no other way around it."

"I see. I understand now. I will make sure to keep tabs on her, especially since she's such a likely candidate."

"You do that. Now, did you find out how long she's been in New York?"

He paused from reading the materials and glanced at his cellphone. He had court in an hour and a half. He then returned to scanning the information; his heartbeat quickened with possibilities.

This is her... I just know it.

"She comes and goes... hasn't been here that long this particular stint."

Alexandre reached for his glass of water with a few drops of blood floating in it, enjoyed a small sip, then continued turning the pages—chock full of material about the comings and goings of a turned creation by the name of Venus Anderson.

"Let's see... She's a professor. Interesting." He flipped to another page.

"Yes, there are many interesting tidbits about her." Fawn grinned proudly. "I dug up quite a bit, though I'm sure that's just the tip of the iceberg. Nevertheless, no one has gotten this far, except for me." She sat straighter, like a dog who'd brought her master his slippers.

"Don't get fuckin' carried away with your enthusiasm," he snarled. "This report is unacceptable."

"Why is that?"

"*Why?* Are you kidding me?!" He shook the stack in the air, causing the pages to flap. The woman folded in her seat. He hated the way she squirmed. "It's not complete!" He sighed in frustration. "Did I ask for half a bride?!"

"No, sir."

"Then don't do a half assed job! Give me a half assed report! Ask half assed questions! I'll need more information into her background. So far, all of this is material from the last five years, correct?"

"Yes, some things were hard to narrow down, Lord. I believe she uses an alias at times, but Venus may be her birthname... still looking into that." He took another sip of his water and read another page detailing the layout of her apartment.

"I wonder why she went back to the name Venus? I imagine she is more comfortable with her birthname than any alias she used. If I were to gamble as to the cause, I'd bet she is attached to her past spent in the city and enjoys living here, so she tries to be as genuine and comfortable as possible... more

at home, so to speak. That's typical human behavior, unfortunately. They cling to things like that, *especially* the females." He
sighed. "Emotional creatures they are. I'm certain you recall,
well, you still seem to struggle with it from time to time."

Fawn's expression remained placid. He was impressed. Her
sense of entitlement grated his nerves, especially since it was
interlaced with her desire for them to have some sort of
romantic interlude. For her to be one of his concubines. Still,
she was rather cunning, which was why he'd accepted her
proposal when she'd asked to take on the task. That said, he'd
had it up to here with humans, Half Breed vampires such as
dhampirs, turned Vamps, and slothful fellow vampires, too.
He surmised the stress of it all was making his patience
impossibly shorter.

Right after yet another detective failed him, he'd once
again set out to take matters into his own hands. Just like in
the days when he'd been a curious youth in Paris, he headed
out on foot and searched for the culprit that brought him
angst; in this case, his long-lost lover. No horses, vehicles, or
mobs accompanied him this time, like the way it had been
back then. It was just him, the night air, and his senses on all
eight cylinders.

"I've been seeing her in my sleep and in the waking hours,
too." Fawn's eyes grew wider at his confession. "I only had the
tales from my *sorcier* to go by. I suppose I was lucky to get that
bit of information growing up, quite honestly. More times
than not, we know nothing about our future mates. It's all
things we have to find out on our own. The seeking and

catching is consistent across the board, however… This evens up the playing field. Unlike you all, my situation is different because of my bloodline. Your dating and married lives follow the typical human practices and protocol."

"Is that so bad?"

"Yes, it is. We are not the same, Fawn. Each of us has multiple soulmates. We can feel each other, even as children. We can choose which one, from an energy standpoint, we are most connected to. We do the choosing unconsciously. It helps us eventually cross paths but sometimes, complications slow down the process."

"So… there's more than one option? It doesn't have to be this woman?" Fawn's brow arched as she smiled.

"There are options, but I chose a long, long time ago. And I'm happy with my choice." Her smile slowly dissipated. "There are rules for the Royals. Rules that can't be broken. The journey can go on for an eternity."

"What would happen if you married any random vampire, my Lord? I mean, what's the worst that could occur?" She shrugged. "All of this stress you are under could be over and done with if you simply picked a woman, say, right now, and married."

Her tone brimmed with hope. He'd seen her dreams, tasted her desires for him… She was fine fuck material but a Reine she was not.

"The worst that could occur is unrelenting unhappiness, ill health, and the loss of everything. Mating with the wrong one can, well, cause complications…" He exhaled loudly, his forehead bunched in annoyance as he reflected on the countless Vamps that had attempted to prove to him that they were his betrothed. Everyone wanted to be queen. The control and respect that came with that position was seen as a grand prize, but so few of them understood what it truly meant.

"I imagine if you are now dreaming of her, she may feel the pressure."

Fawn was full of curiosity, driven by her own selfish desires. He respected that... couldn't be upset with the woman for trying. He humored her and continued.

"Not necessarily. She's a turned, like you." He waved his hand flippantly in her direction. "Your senses, intelligence, and intuition are never as accurate as those of a true blood such as myself. Some of you are very good, but that's an exception, not a rule, and since most of you are turned by other turned, your skills and gifts are weakened greatly. Physically, you don't even compare. Psychically, you don't come close, either, so the chances of her being my equal on *any* fucking level is highly doubtful. Dealing with you turned bitches is sometimes like trying to teach someone in a perpetual infantile state of mind... It's exhausting, really. I just hope my bride has some redeeming qualities, unlike most of you."

He didn't miss how Fawn's teeth nudged through her gums in annoyance at his criticism.

"Temper, temper now... I've killed for less," he warned with a smile while still keeping his eye on the papers. "I was testing you. I don't quite feel that way about turned women. There are differences amongst you; some of you I even dare say are worthy opponents… but you proved my point about being irrational and emotional creatures. It's sickening. You all must be broken."

"I'm sorry."

"Don't be sorry, bitch. Just be quiet, keep your damn jealousy in check, your overly sensitive nature off of my radar, and do your fucking job," he snapped. "Don't make me regret my decision to have you by my side during this endeavor. Go and get me the razor."

She sprang from her chair and disappeared out of the office.

Now that the room was clear, he could fall into the pool of his private thoughts and drown. For the past several months, he'd felt this Venus woman strongly… knew she had to be close. During one of his nighttime strolls, he settled upon a block in the East Village of Manhattan. He didn't know her name, what she looked like… but he'd picked up on her, a strange yet familiar scent. Intoxicating.

Less than an hour later, he'd narrowed it down to an apartment building. It was a secure structure, with security systems in place and even a doorman, but that hadn't stopped him from fixating on one window in particular, turning into a discreet peeping Tom…

He'd moved fast then. Upon returning to his lair, he rounded up a number of his servants and assistants, Fawn heading the charge, and let them know that he needed the area checked out. And now, here he was, finally holding a blueprint into the life of the possible mate he'd been seeking—one meant for him, and him alone.

"Is she married? Has she mated and borne children?" he asked as Faith handed him the razor and sat back on her seat.

"No marriages on record. No children that I can tell, either."

"Interesting… it wouldn't stop me either way, of course." He shrugged. "I mention it because then that would have to be another inconvenience and waste of time to deal with… destroying a husband and offspring. Since I highly doubt she's a born immortal, those situations of them taking marriage less seriously are not uncommon, they definitely have children without a second thought. Pure Bloods have no accidental pregnancies. Anyway, I like to prepare in advance when at all possible."

"I have a photo of her that I took when she was unaware. Are you interested in seeing it?" The woman reached into her briefcase to retrieve it. He waved his hand in her direction.

"No. As I told you, this has to be handled in a specific way. It's interesting, though." He grinned as he reflected on the whole idea of being handed a photo of his beloved. "Back when I was a youth, we didn't photograph or reflect." He placed the folder down on his desk and closed it shut. "Due to changing technology, the use of aluminum and lack of pure silver in mirrors has allowed us to be seen just like everyone else. There are positives and negatives to that, of course. Especially when one of us goes rogue and tries to blend in with society." He polished off his blood-tinged water and reached for the razor. "Come."

Fawn leapt from her seat, rounded the desk, and knelt before him, wrist extended. He sliced into her pale, creamy flesh, brought her arm to his mouth, and sucked the sweet essence for several minutes. Fawn trembled and slipped her hand beneath her skirt, stroking her pussy as he drank from her. He could smell her wetness, her excitement filling the air. With a curl of his tongue he swallowed one last drop of blood, then pointed to the chair she'd previously sat in. She got to her feet, tugged at her skirt, and returned to her seat, a satisfied smile on her face.

He reached for a black and white striped cigar and lit it with a match.

"No… no picture needed," he said, picking up from where they'd left off. "Just keep track of her. I have an idea. Find out a place she is going to, an event she's attending, somewhere public… like a library or concert… and I will make my introduction. If I'm in the vicinity, I'll find her."

"Consider it done. You will need to be at the courthouse in…" She glanced at her watch. "Thirty-five minutes. Your client is facing a ten year sentence with—"

"I know. We have time."

He reached for the used black bra and matching panties his assistant had managed to confiscate from his fated mate the prior day, when this Venus female was at the laundromat. Closing his eyes, he brought the soft underwear up to his nose and gave a hearty sniff. His dick thickened and he clawed at his desk, fangs partially descended as blood rushed within him.

"She's absolutely divine… deliciously made. I can't wait to

fuck the living blood completely out of her. I've found my Reine Du Sang…"

VENUS HELD THE cold bottle of beer with one hand and rubbed the side of her neck with the other. Her anxiety levels were at an all-time high, and that had been a brand new struggle within the last few months. Not one to wrestle with such things, she couldn't for the life of her figure out why she suddenly felt terrified, almost on par with the angst and anxiety she'd experienced running away from the Miller plantation so many years ago. The sensation came and went, but as soon as she entered the house party with Deborah and Camille, it had made an ugly return.

I just need to get out more… it's all in my head. I only go out to work, run errands, and feed these days. It's becoming boring and far too routine. Maybe it was a good idea to come here, after all.

She took a swig of the beer and plastered on a fake smile as she watched her girlfriends dance and mingle. The Brooklyn brownstone she stood inside was magnificent. It had an open layout; a cozy feel mixed with modern flair. One of her favorite colors, aquamarine, was used as an accent color.

"Hi," A handsome Hispanic man with a bald head approached her, extending his hand. "My name is Benson."

"Hi, Benson, nice to meet you." She shook his hand, admiring his sharp glasses. "I'm Venus." The well-built guy stood about 5'10", and he had an endearing, lopsided smile. His dark brown eyes almost glowed under the ceiling lights. He slid up beside her, his interest clearly marked.

"Venus, like one of the Williams sisters... nice. Ya play tennis?" he asked, as if that were an original question, one she'd never heard before.

She inwardly rolled her eyes, took another taste of the beverage to swallow down a flip response just itching to fly from her mouth, and shook her head.

"Nope."

"Hmmm, you sure seem in shape though... damn!" The guy licked his lower lip then smacked them together. Her gut roiled in disgust. He eyed her like a turkey sitting on the table during the heinous 'Kill an Indian' celebration better known as Thanksgiving. "Nice ass, too!"

"Thank you, and on that note, I don't like the shape of this conversation, and you're the actual ass, so if you'll excuse me, Benson the loser, fuckboy numero uno, I would like to jam my damn head in the toilet and try to drown before I talk to you one second longer."

"Oh, come on, honey!" He chortled.

"My name is Venus, like I already told you. I am not bee vomit, I am not your honey. Guys like you get on my damn nerves. I was having a fine night until you rolled up with your shit. Get the fuck outta here."

"Damn! I'm sorry, baby, I mean, Venus. Really, I am! I didn't mean any harm at all." He looked downright flustered;

his smile vanished and his complexion deepened. "You're just all by yourself over here and I figured, hell…" He threw up his hands. "Maybe I have a shot." He smiled sadly. "I think you're gorgeous, all right? I've had one too many, I tried too hard and it backfired. I'm not usually like this. I know that you're completely out of my league, but if Jay-Z can get Beyoncé, then I thought I might have a chance, too!" She chuckled at his words, her apprehension lessening a smidgen. "Do you accept my apology? Can we start over?"

"Apology accepted. So, Benson, what do you do?"

You're still written off but talking to you may pass the time faster.

"I'm a teacher over at Brownsville Academy High School… 65."

"Ohhh, okay." She nodded, now truly intrigued. "That's excellent… a thankless job to some degree. I'm a professor at Colombia University. I teach Art History."

"Nice! I see we have something in common. I'd like to talk to you more about that, actually. So what made you decide to—" The music transitioned to 'Naughty Girl' by Beyoncé. "If that's not a coincidence, I don't know what is! Let's dance… Lemme be Jay-Z for just one night. Throw a dog a bone!"

She chuckled at his words as he led her to a free spot in the jampacked residence and they began to dance, laugh, and have a good time. The song seemed to come to an abrupt stop and Knoc-Turn'al's 'Muzik' blared through the speakers, starting a frenzy.

She closed her eyes and swayed to the music, screaming

the lyrics, her beer high in the air like some lighter at a concert. She fell deep into herself, the bass thumping through her skull and shattered soul. The air around her seemed to shift then, and a suffocating darkness came over her, but she couldn't open her eyes, couldn't stop dancing, couldn't stop summoning her African ancestors as she spun and moved her feet.

My feet are dancing on air… I am light as a snowflake falling from the sky…

Two strong arms wrapped around her waist and pulled her close…

Benson?

A heavenly scent filled her senses and someone hard, muscular, tall and cold held her tight, his chest flush against her body as if he were about to fuck her right then and there. They moved to the music, in sync, in rhythm. She tried to open her eyes but couldn't; the man was spinning her around and around. The clanking of shackles beat in her ears, applause and whistles from her friends rang in the air as she danced. The beer was out of her hand as if by magic and she twisted and turned, falling into a mental, physical, and emotional vortex. She felt high on something strong, drunk and happy. Her pussy grew instantly wet as a deep, guttural moan echoed close to her ear…

"I'm going to suck your soul, the bit that's left of it… swallow you fucking whole."

Her eyes fluttered open and she gasped, her heart beating painfully in her chest. She was looking into icy blue eyes… Dead eyes, yet so full of life. A tall, broad shouldered mammoth of a man with a slender, hard build towered over her. His clean-shaven face showcased high cheekbones over an angular jawline, a deep chin cleft, raven black hair, thick brows, plush pink lips, and flesh so pale and flawless, it reminded her of the morning's first snowfall.

"Who are you?"

He ran his large hand against her face and shook his head.

"You know who the fuck I am, my Love." His tone was demeaning, hateful, passionate and dreadful all at once. He narrowed his gaze on her, still dancing, then spun her around once more for good measure. She had no control of herself as he waltzed her across the room and pressed her flush against the wall. Her friends cat called as if she were having the time of her life, as if this monster, this feral beast, was what she'd asked for, what she wanted, what she needed.

"Get off me!" She said through gritted teeth. He grabbed her wrist and kept her steady. The music seemed to drown her out, and all the laughing, smiling faces grew distorted, morphed as if melting, stretching, falling apart.

"Well, look at you, pretending to still be human!" He lightly laughed. "How adorable. You're a Turned Vamp in denial. Jesus." He rolled his eyes. "What in the hell was I thinking when I chose you?"

"I have no idea what you're talking about!"

"Sure you do. You just don't remember yet. I felt no need for pretenses. I've waited far too long for this moment. You're more beautiful than I ever imagined... and your smell! Mmmm, soooo sweet, baby. I could just eat you up!" He suddenly released her and stepped back, looking her up and down with seriousness in his eyes. Opening his long black jacket, he revealed an expensive black suit, paired with a black and white damask print tie. "Do you like it?" He did a 360, a haughty smirk on his face. "I wore it just for you."

She moved around him, surveying the place, trying to find the main bedroom where she'd locked up her purse, along with Deborah's and Camille's. She raced away, trying to keep her distance, while refraining from attracting too much attention to herself. To her surprise, he didn't chase after her. Once she entered the room with the key the owner had given her, she grabbed her purse, slung it over her shoulder, then speed-walked to the exit, headed for home.

But when a shadow blocked the light by the closed door, nausea filled her.

"Why are you afraid of me, Venus? I finally found you... You should be happy."

"Leave me alone!" She clutched her sweater, panic striking within. Her fangs descended as her heart pounded hard within her chest. Flashes of running through the wilderness, the dogs hot on her tail, came flooding back. "I don't know you!"

"That's correct. You don't know me, but you soon will. Open the door. Let's talk."

"I don't want to talk! I don't want to get to know you. I don't want to dance! Now please, go away!"

"I'm sorry, I can't do that, Venus. You see, I came here to get something that belongs to me and I refuse to go back home fucking empty handed," he said with a hiss.

"I am going to call the police!" She reached into her purse with a shaky hand, only to be met with laughter from the other side of the closed door.

"And tell them what, baby? A man danced with me… aaaahhh!" he teased, cackling. His deep laughter boomed and shook her insides, her ribs rattled from the low-pitch of his tone. "Oh, what about this one? 'Officer! There's a vampire here. Help! Oh, wait… I'm one too, never mind.' Click." He laughed even harder that time.

She sighed, took a deep breath, and slipped her phone back into her purse. They both were silent for a spell… only the thumping of the music reminded her that she was still amongst mixed company as she slipped in and out of a dreamy state.

He's doing this… he's messing with my mind! I've got to find a way out of here!

"I've dreamed of tasting your lips—both sets, baby. I've fantasized about licking the splatter of your blood when I sink my teeth into your inner thigh, biting into your pretty brown skin, yanking your hips towards my hard thrusts, wrapping your thighs around my neck. I've dreamed about you arching your body, rising to receive me as I make you take every nasty and hard thrust until you orgasm. And then I've dreamed of watching my big cock disappear inside your mouth after fucking you day and night, baby… never turning you loose."

She could hear him scratch against the door, doom, dread and lust filling her like a goblet. She walked closer to the entrance and pressed her palm against the wood. A strange kind of electricity shot through her. She imagined his hand on the other side sending that current within her; it certainly must've been there.

"Do you feel that, Venus?" His dark, deep voice echoed, as if they were in a chamber all alone together. "It's the energy between us. Come home with me tonight, Venus. We need to get to know one another. Don't fight this... don't drag out what is destined to be."

"I will kill you or die trying." She worked hard to free her mind from his control, then swung the door open, her nostrils flared. She looked up at the tall, threatening figure but didn't flinch. She worked through her fears. She saw something in him that almost made her piss herself, but she had to pretend, to make believe that she wasn't afraid... that everything would be okay if she could just get out of that apartment and get back home. "Move."

He smiled at her, stepped to the side, and bowed, and she walked fast down the hall, away from him. Everything seemed to be a blur as her heart beat like a snare drum. The front door loomed straight ahead. She looked behind her and gasped. He was gone. When she turned back around, there he stood, directly in front of her... only a few inches away. She opened her mouth to scream, but he plunged his tongue inside, squelching her protests. Extending his pinky finger, the maniac scratched the back of her neck in one fell swoop. Then, he was gone before she could take another step, before she could form another word, before she could fall apart...

Angry tears welled in her eyes and yet, her body betrayed

her. Her pussy throbbed with need, her nipples hardened, and her chest ached with desire.

Who was that?! What the hell just happened?!

CHAPTER FOUR

Serving Two Masters...

From the Cradle to the Grave

PERCHED ON THE roof of his penthouse at 3:07 A.M., Alexandre crouched down, resting on the balls of his feet, hunched over like a gargoyle. Arms dangling between his legs, he gazed at the flickering lights of the city. Fresh blood dripped from his fingertips, and he slid his tongue along his lips and upper teeth, chasing the fading flavor of his earlier feast. It hadn't been a planned kill, but trouble had come knocking and he'd delighted in giving it a damn good answer. Standing to his full height of 6'6, he sucked his fingers one by one, then rubbed them on his black leather pants, cleaning off any excess.

He'd been out partying at the Mad House Club, one of his favorite dives where mortals liked to play cocaine games and toss their bodies around to techno music under spinning, vibrant lights. He rarely went there to feed; usually, he'd be interested in a fuck fest. The women who frequented the place liked to flirt and all he had to do was sit for five minutes before they gravitated towards him likes bees to honey. Tonight, however, wet pussy hadn't been his mission. He'd simply needed to clear his mind.

As he'd left out to venture home, a guy had trailed him, hoping to shake him down for a bit of cash. He glanced at his blood splattered watch and smiled…

It must've been the jewelry and the clothes that made him think he could rob me…

In seconds flat, he'd had the man in his ironclad grip, crushing his larynx. Then, he'd dragged the fucker to an alley and finished him off. The bastard had got himself a one-way, nonrefundable ticket on King Alexandre Marseille Airlines… final destination, death on Bloodbath Island. After slicing into the son of a bitch's neck with his claws, he'd sunk his teeth into his collar and dragged, pulling and tugging at the tattooed flesh. The man had still been conscious, which had made the experience all the more enjoyable. After he was good and done with him, he'd tossed him onto the pebble covered concrete and stomped on his head a few good times. His brain matter had oozed out of him; funny, there hadn't been much of it…

Now here he was, ready to retire for the night.

When he returned home, he lit the first-floor fireplace, along with several lights around the vast, open living room. Turning on his stereo system, he selected 'Chosen One' by Valley of Wolves, playing it at high volume as he marched to his master suite bathroom.

Surrounded by clear walls and black tile, he stripped down, his bloodstained clothing falling at his feet. He turned on the cold water and slid inside the cubicle, rinsing away the filth and sticky blood.

"Ain't nothin' gonna stop this fire!" he sang along while the water beat against his muscles and back. He took much pride in his strapping yet lean physique, going over his body with an African soap bar, ensuring every drop of shit that fucker may have gotten on him was gone for good. He caught his reflection in the doors of the large enclosure. His light blue eyes sparkled and he smiled at himself, loving the wicked thoughts that raced through his mind at that moment.

I'm still hungry… I'm tired of playing these games with her. I've been more than understanding…

When he was done, he dried off and wrapped a cream towel around his waist, then brushed his teeth, gargling with baking soda. He returned to his bedroom, where he turned the music off, then lay down on top of luxurious black and gold sheets. He picked up his landline phone and dialed. He heard the first ring, then the second…

"Don't call me again." The dial tone soon followed. He redialed, and dialed once again, this time, leaving a voicemail.

"Venus, you beautiful fuckin' thorn in my side… I may rip you to pieces after all," he said with a sneer, getting back to his feet. He wrapped the cord around his hand and began to pace. "I've given you three days to get your shit together. I've called, you've ignored. I've sent flowers, you sent them back. I don't take rejection well, baby… but on second thought…" He shrugged with a smile. "I never get rejected, so I guess there's a first time for everything, right? Your time is up."

He slammed the phone down. His incisors emerged from his gumline, and anguish flooded his heaving chest with its searing heat. Fisting the covers, he hissed and snarled, arching his back as his anger reached an all-time high...

...Minutes later

She could hear two heartbeats... Only one was hers...

VENUS CRUSHED THE water bottle in her hand and tossed it in the kitchen trashcan before the lights went black in her apartment.

"You've struggled from the cradle to the grave. I don't *do* struggle love. I'm so tired of this..." The deep voice boomed through every wall of her place. She felt as if she were spinning, the words echoing around her in stereo. The squeal of tires, the roar of a motorcycle engine made her jump. She looked toward the windows, the front door, then back at a closed closet. Clutching her robe to her body, she turned in all directions, confused, hurting, petrified, pissed.

"WHAT DO YOU WANT?!" she screamed at the top of her lungs.

His strong, musky scent filled the air like a thick fog. It was intoxicating, overpowering, passionate and vile.

"You."

The lights turned back on, flickered, then settled. There he stood, in the middle of the room. Cool air brushed against her skin; the bastard must have jimmied a window to get inside. He cocked his head to the side, his pinky fingernail extended; a flame danced upon it as he lit a cigarette he'd slid like some long, white snake out of his black leather jacket. A thin chain hung around his neck, nestled on his exposed chest with an eight pack in plain view. He made his way to her radio and turned it on.

'House of the Rising Sun' by the Animals began to play through the speakers.

"Amazin' song, isn't it, baby?" He paced back and forth with heavy, laced-up black boots. "It's a classic." Blowing thick rings of dense smoke in the air, he moved about as if he were a trapped tiger—muscles tight, restless. "Where were you in 1964?"

"Minding my own damn business."

He chuckled at that.

"I asked for a reason. You're hard to piece together. Background checks are either full of fabricated information or misinformation about you. Funny thing though, big pieces of your fuckin' life have just... vanished! Like you'd never been born." His eyes grew large in faux surprise. He chuckled and threw up his hands. "Well, we know that's not true... here you are. I want to know what the fuck you've been doing... how you hide so well... who the fuck you *really* are!" He tossed the cigarette in the air, caught it between his teeth, and swallowed it whole.

"Get tha fuck outta my house." She fisted her hands.

He inched towards her, and she took several steps back.

"You stink of fear," he sneered. "Talking big, saying nothing. Tell me your secrets... or I'll take them from you. The choice is yours."

Before she could blink, he was upon her, his arm around her waist and his hand cradling the back of her head. He yanked on her thick, curly black hair as she squirmed and hissed. She refused to let him see the pain in her eyes. He caressed the side of her neck with his fingertips, horrid lust swimming in his pupils as she bared her teeth. Her fangs extended when he brought her closer, flush against him, and made them rise together several feet off the ground. He was so tall, his head nearly touched the ceiling.

"I'm not afraid of you!"

"Fake news!" He cackled. "Awww, I wanted to make ya wet, baby, not piss your pants." She refused to look him in the eye... that was where trouble lived. He leaned in impossibly closer and sniffed her neck, and then again. His eyes rolled back like balls spinning on a pool table. "Fuck! You smell so damn good. What blood type are you? O? B! You're B, aren't ya?" He sniffed again. "Yeah... definitely B. Mmmm... vintage year, too."

She kept her head down.

"Look at me, you turned bitch!"

She screamed when he wrapped his hand around her neck

and pressed his forehead against hers. They glared at one another and she felt sick inside. His eyes danced from blue to black, making her dizzy. His jaw tightened as he tried to invade her thoughts, to enter her private sanctuary.

"Let me see your fucking desires and fears… Let me see them, NOW!"

She held steadfast, her resolve not slipping, but she could feel his power. It was overwhelming, like nothing she'd experienced before. She'd had her share of vampire suitors. Many had been just as egotistical as this one, but none of them had even come close to his physical strength, she could've gone toe to toe with them easily and she was certain he was still merely toying with her. There was no telling what he was capable of, but this was the type of vampire Geneviève had warned her about. He enjoyed killing, yes indeed, but his greatest joy stemmed from mentally breaking down his prey.

This time, it was her…

"I won't let you in! I don't want you!"

He let go and she fell hard. Flashes of the time spent in that dark hole in the floor flashed in her mind. The angry White folk and their dogs, the barking, the curses, the black feathered raven flying to and fro…

He floated back down from the ceiling.

"Venus, this has gone on long enough. I could break you in two with a mere thought."

"Then do it." She gritted her teeth and crawled away from him, stumbling as she got back on her feet. "That's right, you won't… because you want to fuck me."

"I can fuck you regardless of whether you're dead or alive. I've already had cold pussy. I prefer a hot snatch, but hey, I'm not totally against it if it's a bit on the uptight and frigid side." He shrugged. The truth of his words made her shudder. "Where were you born?" She inched further away from him and began to climb along the wall, in the direction of the front door.

"South Carolina."

"Who are you parents?"

"What does it matter? They're dead and I'm turned. They've nothing to do with this." She shrieked when a blur of light flew past her and he was suddenly against her door, sliding up along it, upside down. His eyes glowed bright as he hung there like a fruit bat on a tree.

He was so fast... the kind of fast that made her head spin...

He spit out the cigarette he'd swallowed earlier onto the ground... it was relit and dry as a bone.

"I'm not fucking playing with you, bitch."

"I never believed that you were." He grabbed her wrists and snatched her from the wall, flung her to the floor, and mounted her. He was so heavy, she felt as though a high-rise had landed on her, or a mountain had tumbled and crumbled over her, leaving her with no chance of escape. Raising her arms above her head, he pinned her down. His hard body felt cool against her hot one. He grinded his massive hard-on against her pelvic bone, and her heartbeat quickened.

"I have been looking for you, for years. I have gone

through drastic measures to find you. I'm sick and tired of your games. Either you're extremely cunning, extremely intuitive, or extremely stupid. You've done everything in your power to make this difficult, as if you knew I was coming. Who's been talking to you about me?"

"No one."

He cocked his head slowly from side to side, as if sizing her up, trying to find a kernel of truth in her words. When he grabbed her chin, dull pain radiated throughout the bones of her skull as he looked deeply into her eyes. He snatched his hand abruptly away, forcing her head to swing far to the left, then moved away from her, allowing her to finally breathe again. She coughed a little as she sat up, but kept her eye on him.

"What year were you born?"

"…1813." She got to her feet and dusted herself off.

Pulling a flask from his jacket, he tilted it to his lips and drank, then slipped it back in its place. She could smell that it was filled with blood.

"South Carolina… 1813… you've survived quite a while. I believe you've lived here in New York several times." He plopped down on her couch, sighed, and looked at her from over his shoulder. "Am I right?"

"Yes…"

"Bring your fuckin' ass over here." He snapped his fingers, his brows bunched in annoyance.

She took a few steps, paused, then retreated. He shook his head, his face contorted in a grimace, then burst out laughing.

Suddenly, the ceiling began to peel and splinter. Bits of white paint chips and debris rained down onto her head. The walls pulsed as if alive and the high-pitched noise of shrill, disembodied screams ensued…

"Stop it!" She covered her ears and rocked. The noises made her brain hurt, and her heart felt heavy.

"I don't feel like fucking dragging your stubborn ass over here," he stated carelessly, his tone not matching the words. "If you make me, I will make good on my threats tonight, Venus." She made her way over and sat across from him on the loveseat. As soon as she was there, everything stopped abruptly, going back to normal. "Now, where were we?" He raked his long white fingers through his jet-black hair and leaned back, his alluring eyes hooded. "I asked you about New York… You return here again and again. Do you know why?"

"I love it here… It was my first taste of true freedom."

He nodded and crossed his arms.

"Who turned you?"

"I've been sworn to never tell her name."

He exhaled loudly, but much to her surprise, didn't push the issue.

"So… it was a woman. Was that your preference?"

"My preference?"

"Pussy-to-pussy power. Professional clit licker. Strap on queen. Carpet muncher. Dyke. Kitty puncher. Bean flicker."

"No." She hugged herself as the air grew cooler in the room. "I'm not gay… it wasn't like that."

"Hmmm, I see. Well, it's not uncommon for a turned one

to be told to never tell the name of the person who changed them…reveal their master, or in this case, mistress. As I'm sure you're aware of, that is one of the few things I can't *make* you do. You have to tell me willingly who sired you. I have my ways of finding out these things though, no worries. Something isn't right with you… you rub me the wrong way." His neck clicked and made odd twisting and snapping noises as he moved his head left and right.

"You wouldn't be rubbed by me in *any* way, if you'd just do us both a favor and leave. Can't you find someone else to bother? I don't want you here, don't you get it?! I don't want to talk to you and I don't want to look at you. GET OUT!"

"Who the hell do you think you're speaking to?! I'm Count Alexandre Marseille. I've killed thousands of men, so what would make you believe I give one fuckin' care about you or your silly, infantile feelings? Do you honestly expect me to keep showing you mercy?"

"Mercy? This isn't mercy!"

"The only reason why your tongue hasn't been ripped out your fucking mouth, you little smart lipped cunt, is because I would prefer to have a bride who can suck my blood *and* my dick! No tongue… no sucking. It's just that simple. You're my mate! I want you to understand the severity of this situation. I don't think you—"

"I don't give a shit what you want, Count Alexandre Marseille. The feeling is not mutual and whoever told you that we were destined was wrong. You are *not* my mate! I pick and choose who I date, screw, and eventually marry. You have no say over the matter!"

He smiled at her... the type of smile that made her blood move all the slower within her. A black smile, an empty smile, a death-will-become-you smile.

I've already started fighting back... no need to stop now. He's gonna kill me either way...

"I find you entertaining, to say the least." He paced back and forth, seemingly working various angles in his head. "I didn't expect this." He chuckled loudly... then abruptly stopped. He floated quickly over to her, and she screamed out, her heart beating so fast, it hurt. Picking her up by the neck, he lifted her high in the air, turning her roughly from side to side.

"You're so beautiful, Venus... what a waste it would be to destroy you. Sure, there are others I could make my mate, but they'd always be second best and a gamble. I find you interesting though. Truly, I do. Like a brand-new toy that no one else has."

He slammed her down onto the couch.

She rubbed her sore throat and coughed up blood, kicking her legs as she tried to gain oxygen in her lungs once again. This had to be it... her last breath would be taken before he'd turn her loose. A royal maniac with an axe to grind was going to put an end to her once and for all. He was feral and wild, yet refined... even his features demonstrated the duality of it. He'd never offered a genuine, warm smile, and yet, he was oddly beautiful—too beautiful to look at for too long...

"No one tells you no. I get it and I don't care. Yes, I'm afraid of you! You like that, I know."

"I do… but I suspect that you're not just afraid of me, Venus. Your fear lies in the truth of my words. You've been playing make-believe for far too long. You've slipped away from reality, far from the truth about yourself. Venus is dead. You playing the kind, gentle human is getting old, by the way. Accept what the fuck you are. You've been this way for over 200 years!"

"I *know* what I am, Count… and that's what hurts the most."

He drew closer to her and she shivered.

"Do you want to live?"

"Yes, I want to live, but I've been through too much in both of these lifetimes to allow the likes of you to break me. And yes, I understand that this may mean my death. So be it."

She felt like she was on some witness stand, giving testimony to the man. He kept digging and trying to drill into her mind, to pick apart her fears and aspirations, her deepest desires.

"You're different. Turned Vampires aren't as defiant as you. And yet, I can sense that you're turned, not Pure Blood. You're resistant to me, very tenacious, something almost unheard of. Your kind is usually thrilled to be in the presence of a Pure Blood." He sat back down on the couch and studied her.

"Thrilled, huh?" She narrowed her eyes on him and tucked her body, resting her chin on her knees. "I'll try to remember that next time you choke me out."

"I don't fucking trust you, Venus. Something is so off with

this shit. I'm going to get to the bottom of it." He sneered. He got to his feet and put his hands on his hips. "Take your clothes off."

Her eyes widened, and she quickly weighed her options. He sucked his teeth and his fangs extended ever so slightly... though he said nothing further. Did he have to?

She slowly got to her feet and removed her robe, then her nightgown, until all she wore was a pair of panties. He looked her up and down, then started to walk around her, in a circle. She closed her eyes, feeling like prey, while he was a ravenous wolf, snarling, growling, nipping. She shivered when he ran his finger down her spine, but he kept moving, round and round.

"You're fucking remarkable..." he whispered... "What an amazing body. You've never had children, it's true... Amazing. How could any of my brethren resist not marrying you then impregnating you at the first chance they got? Sooo delicious." He ran his tongue along the side of her face. She winced in disgust. "How have you kept your numbers so low? You're a seductress after all. Your feminine energy is off the charts. Certainly you must use it to your advantage."

"My numbers? Are you talking about the men I've slept with?"

"Mostly the vampires... You've not fucked many men since you were turned. I can pick up on the difference."

She sighed. "I move around a lot, try to keep a low profile. Sex isn't the first thing on my mind. Surviving is."

"But sex *is* survival, baby. It's all interlocked. Now, by surviving I am assuming you are referring to your feeding, first and foremost. How have you been handling that?"

"Here in New York, I go out and pretend to prostitute, mainly. Sometimes I let them fuck before I eat, it depends on my mood and how I feel about them… one last dying wish. Before that, I was ripping off blood bank supplies but that became too risky with the new security camera systems."

He nodded. "Your Sire, the woman who changed you didn't give you any other alternatives besides theft and prostitution? Wow… what a bad governess. Your mistress left you ill equipped."

"You leave her out of this… and I suppose cold blooded murder is better?"

He smirked.

"Look here, Ms. Harriet Tubman with your righteous indignation, pretending to sell your pussy for a pint of blood, risking your life with men who would slit their own throats to pretend to be something they're not is not only risky, it's stupid. If you get arrested, you may not be able to feed for days, weeks, months! You'd die. You are unable to shapeshift, so you'd be stuck in that fucking cage indefinitely! Secondly, stealing the blood from a blood bank, though original, I'll give you that, is also a bonehead move and I'm glad you realized that sooner rather than later. I will teach you how to hunt and feed in a more discreet, safer way. I enjoy a good hunt; you obviously do not. There are provisions that can be made if you do what you're supposed to."

"What provisions?"

"There are hosts… hundreds of them in any location at

any given time. Us Pure Bloods have them at our fingertips. We hunt because we want to, not because we must."

"Who are these hosts?"

"Humans and fellow vampires alike. Just think, baby... No more crawling the streets looking for johns to kill, no more gambling with possibly getting blood sick from essence that isn't up to par, and no more not feeding in timely intervals... it would all be over. Everything would be taken care of for you."

"...And all I have to do is be your mate... be by the side of a menacing, evil maniac." She fought back tears as her stomach growled. She was two days overdue for a feed. She hated it so. It had become complicated, dangerous, and her conscience, which she could never shake, caused her pain that no one would ever understand.

"I'm not a maniac." He grinned from ear to ear. "You definitely have potential."

She could hear his breathing now as he ran his hands along her bare breasts. Her eyes watered when she suddenly felt his warm mouth surround her nipple. His soft hair brushed against her chest as he held on to her and nursed like a baby. She winced when he bit into her flesh, then drew gentle circles against her areolas with the tip of his tongue. She pressed her eyes closed when she felt him jerk her panties down, tearing them to shreds, then cast them aside. The heat of his mouth and nostrils soon surrounded her pussy as he inhaled and exhaled, over and over again...

"Dear God." He shook against her as he gripped her ass

and brought her impossibly closer, as if he were trying to drown in her aroma.

She waited for it to happen… Waited for him to throw her down and fuck her nearly to death. She waited to feel the wet invasion of his tongue against her folds… to scream as he jammed his cock inside her ass… She waited to be forced to swallow his cum…

But none of that happened.

Seconds turned to minutes, and he simply stayed there, kneeling at her feet, holding her tight, his mouth and nose still jammed against her pussy as if she were some altar.

When he'd had his fill, he slowly got back to his feet, whipped out a knife, and sliced his wrist open. She looked at the spilling blood, the scent of it sending her into an erratic frenzy. Grabbing hold of him, she brought his flesh to her trembling lips and nursed from his wound. Her body warmed with delight, and flashes of being with her grandmama entered her brain… pleasant memories of her singing and smiling. He tasted like blackberries and sweet honey tea!

He gently stroked her head as she fed.

"That's it… take me in, baby… swallow me whole."

His blood was so rich! The sweetness was delicious, the warmth and the strength! She saw charging black horses and men fighting when she tasted him… vampires flying in the air, shields and swords. But too soon, he cruelly snatched his wrist away from her, leaving her panting, wanting more…

He turned away abruptly and stormed to her front door, undid the locks, and swung it open.

"Meet me at my home tomorrow evening at 10 PM. I will have someone pick you up. You need to be properly trained on many things, Venus. I'm certain the woman who turned you did her best, but the world is quite different now, and you need to do more than survive. It appears you've been on your own for a while. You need not only a mate, but a teacher. I am both. This is your second chance at life. It's time for you to finally live it…"

CHAPTER FIVE

Becoming Fast Friends...

H E BEAT THE glossy, green and black piano keys as if that was where his hatred lay...

Alexandre sat on the upholstered green velvet seat in the middle of the emerald green parlor of his home, his fingers gliding and pounding on the keys of the gorgeous instrument, playing his rendition of 'Faded' by Alan Walker. Fawn entered the room wearing only a bright red sheer scarf draped around her shoulders. She walked on her hot-pink-painted tippy toes, her milky flesh an odd grayish blue color as she twirled under the glowing jade and violet lights above them in the cylinder-shaped room.

She slowed when she drew closer, then stood before him, her pussy close to his face as he completed the song. He took a leisurely glance at the pungent mound. Stroking her long, delicate fingers against the dark blond wavy strands of her cunt, dipping them into the milky white and pink folds, she worked herself into a frenzy as she glared down at him, panting and moaning until she made herself cum. Chest heaving, fangs dripping with saliva, she gave him the once over as she sucked her fingertips, swallowing her juices. She leaned over and stared at him.

"You've been awfully quiet, Lord Marseille... anything wrong?"

"There's a problem." He slammed the piano closed, clasped his hands, and turned to face her.

"Can I help?"

"No." He stood, buttoned up his black jacket, and prepared to retreat to his office.

"Talk to me," she called out. "I've done all that you've asked. I want you to be happy... Please, I've earned it."

He paused, turned on his heels and stared at the woman.

"I determine what's earned and what's not. Nevertheless, to answer your question, Venus is coming by tonight. I've sent for her."

"Why is that a problem? Isn't that what you wanted all along?"

"I can't easily tap into her fears and desires. She's extremely hard to pry apart. She's also quite stubborn regarding divulging information. Either she innately knows how to block me, or someone taught her. Period. Secondly, she is far stronger than she realizes. She didn't attempt to use that strength on me, but only because she isn't aware she possesses it. Nevertheless, I could *feel* it... it radiates off her like heat against ice."

Fawn's eyes narrowed on him as she wrapped her scarf tighter along her neck.

"How do you think this happened? What you're describing is unheard of for a Fledgling. Are you sure?"

"Yes, I'm fucking sure." He hissed in annoyance. "Whomever turned her was not an ordinary, run of the mill vampire. Not even an ordinary mistress. It's also interesting that she's been left on her own in this state. She's not ready."

"Perhaps her Master was killed?"

"Yes, that's possible, but I feel otherwise. She's far too protective of telling who that is, which lets me know that the Master is probably still alive. Thus, she's protecting her." Fawn nodded in understanding. "Anyway, I had to play down the skills of whoever brought her into their fold… didn't want to alert her to the seriousness of the situation just yet. But it is more crucial than ever that I found her. Not only for me, but for her sake."

"So you care about her now?" Fawn jerked her head as if she were a demonically possessed doll trying to move its own neck, head, and limbs for the first time. Her jealousy flowed from her body and hung in the air like cheap, $2.00 perfume. "This goes beyond your Coven now, Lord… I thought furthering your bloodline was the main motivation for finding your mate? But this… Exhausting yourself, your patience running thin… Marital bliss and protection should be the least of your worries."

"It's simple. This has little to do with care, concern, or even fondness, and you're a fool to believe that someone such as myself would not deem it important to protect my mate!'"

"Well yes, to protect her womb, but—"

"You've gotta be fuckin' kidding me, Fawn. I have an interest in her well-being, for my own sake if for nothing else." He pushed his index finger against his chest. "Would you want your bank account to suddenly be drained? Would you want someone to destroy your brand new house by bulldozing it? No! You invest in those accounts and assets, you want to protect them. I understand that a discussion of these matters might at times go above your head, but I am certain you are playing stupid with me on purpose right now, trying to extort more information." She dropped her head, but he knew that was all an act, too. "I'm not some idiot off the gotdamn street! Just ask your questions and stop this shit. It's ridiculous!"

"My apologies, Sir, if I have angered you. I honestly didn't understand. Please continue."

He stared the woman in the eye. Her lips curled in a slight grin, though she fought it. Right then, he realized a few things about her, a noteworthy one being the intricate, duplicitous way in which her brain worked, but for now, he'd keep these little extractions from her twisted psyche for himself. He knew Fawn very well… She was predictable.

Fawn often played stupid in order to get a leg up, to fool the masses. Being beautiful, seductive, a good fuck and astute, she often had others fooled, falling for her games at will. Sometimes, he allowed her to believe she'd gotten one over. He found it entertaining on occasion; she never ceased to amuse.

"Back to what I was saying… my concerns regarding Venus are obvious. She's a walking weapon, and I want her for myself and myself alone. If some…" He looked down at his cuticles, worked a hangnail away with the pad of his thumb, then made eye contact with Fawn once again. "If some individuals, so to speak, knew of her existence and her power, things could get… *ugly*."

"What does she have? What can she do?" Fawn straightened, her eyes glossing over with curiosity.

"Don't worry about the details. That's my job. Her naiveté will be short-lived, now that I have her. I will be training her myself. I am not certain how long that will take; I will need to further assess the situation. But, I need for you to start making the wedding arrangements immediately. They take quite some time to complete, especially since I'll need to introduce her to the Du Sang Society and the Coven eventually, as you know. I cannot afford to waste more time, especially since it has taken me so long to find her."

"Yes, of course." She nodded. "I will begin preparations right away."

He proceeded to walk away, then paused once more as he reached the door to exit.

"Oh, one more thing, Fawn…" He didn't look back at the woman but he gazed straight ahead, a proud smile on his face. "I have shared this information with you in confidence. You are one of my brightest assistants… always wishing to contribute, to help in my time of need. But let me make something perfectly clear so that there are no misunderstandings. I will kill you in a split second and not waste a moment deliberating over your continued existence if you backstab me. I will rip your heart out of your chest and toss it to Whiskey and his thuggish friends to devour if you double-cross me, try to interfere with my dealings with Venus, or attempt sabotage of any sort. I can read your desires, bitch… you're ripe with envy. Don't let your emotions cause you to do something stupid. Have I made myself crystal clear?"

"Yes, my Lord."

"Good. Call the cleaners." He swung back the green curtain of the room to exit through the doors. "I want my home spic and fuckin' span before Venus arrives this evening. You'll find the bloody mess in the kitchen. You're welcome to the leftovers… Bon Appétit."

VENUS STOOD IN the foyer beneath a crystal, diamond and silver chandelier that swung slowly back and forth, the domed ceiling reminding her of a Roman cathedral. Loud thuds sounded above her head, as if someone was hammering away, doing hard labor, but then she heard the feminine moans… Someone was getting fucked into oblivion.

She muted the noise in her head and focused back on the light fixture. She stared at the teardrop shaped crystals, transfixed by their beauty.

A big half-breed named Whiskey hung her coat up. The guy towered over her, his dark brown hair brushed away from his unusual, square face, showcasing faded scars along his right eyebrow and chin. Hooded, slightly droopy dark brown eyes were cloaked with thick, unruly brows. He wore a burgundy suit jacket over broad shoulders, with a gray V-neck shirt beneath it. The man stood staring at her for the longest, not saying a word. She didn't miss the pistol jetting out of the waistband of his jeans.

"Where is he?" she asked.

"Count Marseille will be ready for ya in a few minutes." The man looked her up and down, sniffing the air like some damned dog.

"I suppose we have to wait for him to finish screwing." She grimaced and shook her head.

"That's not him…" He sucked his teeth as he drew a bit closer, his brow raised. "You're a turned?" She nodded. "You don't smell like a turned." He slipped a cigarette out of his pocket and casually lit it. "Want one?"

"No, thank you."

"Come on, he's ready for ya now."

She followed him into an expansive living area. All of the furniture was bright red and black, accented with red jewels encrusted in gold and silver. It was more than obvious that Alexandre Marseille had opulent tastes. The rugs were thick and appeared to be handwoven, some she was certain dating back to the 1400s. Large bronze and stone fountains showcased different statues, from children catching birds to a woman on her knees praying as the water rushed around her.

But it was the artwork on the walls that gave her pause.

That's an original Claude Monet. How'd he get that?

She followed Whiskey up the red carpeted corridor, with the walls painted pitch black. Pewter scones bounced bright, L.E.D. light throughout the area. Anxiety and anticipation made her feel the trek was taking forever. At last, they arrived at two large double white doors, trimmed in gold. Whiskey knocked, a sound that echoed throughout the place. The doors opened, revealing a room that made her pupils dilate and retract. Everything inside of it was bright, white gold. There, in a gold seat, sat Alexandre Marseille…

His lips kinked in a malevolent grin as he curled his long, jewel-adorned finger in her direction, motioning her over. Her feet began to move against her will… as if an invisible magnet was doing all the work. Struggling to resist, as if fighting a current in violent waves, she tried hard to stop the control he was wielding, to no avail. His strength was something like she'd never experienced in her life.

She jumped when the doors slammed behind her. Whiskey was gone. She stood before Alexandre, jittering back and forth like a spun jar before settling on her own two legs.

"You look beautiful tonight."

She wore a black silk kimono top and pants. Her hair was pulled to one side, exposing a red velvet choker she'd snagged from a flea market in Ohio in 1974. What could she respond to his comment? A 'thank you', would be polite, but Venus wasn't feeling it. Especially since she was here not really of her own free will.

"Who sired you?" He crossed his legs beneath a long, white robe, chest exposed with an inverted crucifix on a gold chain hanging around his neck.

"You've already asked me that and I told you I'm not allowed to answer."

He smiled and nodded, tapping the clawed arm of the chair.

"Doesn't hurt to ask again, now does it? Contrary to whatever ideas you have about me, Venus, this is for your own good. Now, whoever sired you was noble... I will give her credit. However, her teachings are outdated. You need an update or it will be lights out for you. You can't compete in modern day." A flame jumped from his extended pinky nail and he lit a cigar—a black and white striped one; so odd, yet lovely. "Care for one?"

She shook her head.

"All right then." He took a long draw from it then glared at her from hooded eyes. "First and foremost, you have a lot of energy and anger, my dear... you're a fuckin' fiend. I love it." He cackled. "It stems from your humble beginnings, I take it... treated unkindly on a plantation in the United States. South Carolina... Miller Plantation, correct?"

"Yes. I was a slave."

"Never refer to yourself as that again. You weren't a slave, Venus."

"I have no problem with it." She shrugged. "Facts don't bother me. They empower me."

"Power, hmmm?" He slid his tongue along his lower lip. "Power is for the making and the taking. There is power in words. You did forced labor, but you were far from a slave… Choose your words wisely." He must have noted her confusion, so he went on. "A slave doesn't fight, Venus. You were fighting all along. I can see it in you… your spirit was relentless. They should've killed you when they had the chance." He took another draw from his cigar, tapped the ashes over his bare foot. They hit the pale flesh of his toes, then disappeared like a ghost. "You went back and burned that whole fuckin' place down, and you're still not satisfied. You want *all* of his descendants dead. I don't blame you." He leaned forward, his gaze piercing.

Her heart raced for he'd exposed her secret. Only she and Geneviève knew of that fateful night…

"I'm not satisfied, you're right. People from his bloodline are still alive, benefiting from what he'd done."

"Revenge is a good thing, Venus… gives us something else to live for. It's a goal, one built on hatred, sadness, anger, lust unfulfilled. We can discuss that more later, especially since my line of work is securing justice for all."

"I guess you're like the Statue of Liberty." She grimaced.

He chuckled lazily at her words, then extinguished the cigar in a glass of what appeared to be water nearby.

"SHIT!"

Suddenly, a sword came barreling towards her. She ducked in the nick of time, the damn thing landing in the wall behind her, splintering the cement. He got to his feet and clapped.

"Pretty fast response, but let's see if you can—"

"DAMN YOU!" Another came out of nowhere; this time she caught the hefty handle in the palm of her hand. The hard impact made her skin burn and bruised her wrist. She looked at the huge medieval weapon, her breaths coming fast. What had just happened?

He clapped again, slow and loud, and took a step down from his throne. His robe flung open, exposing one of the most exquisite bodies she'd ever laid eyes on. Her mouth watered as if she'd just seen fresh blood drip for the first time since she was reborn. She averted her gaze, though her pussy swelled and pulsed with lust upon the sight of his taut abs and long, extraordinarily thick dick. Taking his time, he covered himself once again. They stood face to face, less than three inches apart.

"Listen. I've got something important to tell you. Don't fucking interrupt me. Once I am finished speaking to you, then and only then will I grant you permission to ask a question. Number one." He held up a finger. "A typical Turned Vampire would not have been able to move that fast. Number two, you sensed the sword was coming before it arrived. I am a Pure Blood fuckin' royal elite from France. Top of the line. I am faster than you. Smarter than you. Deadlier than you on my worst day. You have Pure Blood reflexes and I want answers. You are rare, do you understand me? I need you to help me help you. If the wrong fucking people find out about you, they will kill you, Venus. You're a threat. I need you to tell me who your mistress is. NOW!"

"I am sworn to not tell! You told me to come over here so I could be trained. I did as you asked! You let me feed from you. I saw what you are through that… I felt it!"

"Yes, and that's how I saw what you did to the Miller Plantation. The fire danced in your eyes, your heart and your mind. It's an eternal flame."

"We both know that happened for many reasons… and so, to a small extent, I started to trust you but I see now I can't do that. It's ridiculous. You are a ruthless, selfish demon!"

He chuckled then wrapped his hand around her throat, then lifted her off the ground.

"I'm not squeezing hard, and you're fighting… feel that, Venus? THAT'S POWER! What a beautiful find you are."

He placed her back on her feet. Her throat burned. She shuddered when he leaned over and gently kissed her shoulder, then her neck. The pain instantly vanished.

"Now, where were we? Yes… Who is your mistress?"

"Stop asking me who the hell sired me because you know I will never tell you! It would put her in danger, and I will never betray her in that manner. You know the rules!"

He balled his fists at his side and his fangs extended. The monster's eyes turned lighter making it look like he had no eyeballs at all… white on white. After a few seconds, his fangs retracted, his hands relaxed, and his eyes returned to their natural light blue color. She hissed when he pressed her back against a wall, her face dangerously close to the sword jammed in it. She looked at it from the corner of her eye then turned back in his direction. Heat rushed through her when he pressed his lips to hers… the iron-rich taste of royal blood, a sweetness out of this world, filling her. Her eyes rolled when he wrapped his strong arms around her waist and slid his tongue in her mouth.

Their bodies grinded against one another in a passionate embrace like she'd never known. But, too soon, he pulled away from her, tied his robe, and left her to make his way to the doors.

"Where are you going?"

He didn't look back as he opened them.

"You've passed your first test. Loyalty. I've tested you four times and you've not waivered. You're a good sire. Faithfulness, devotion and piety is very important to me, especially in my mate. Tonight, through tomorrow afternoon, you sleep in the guest quarters. Tomorrow night, we have business to tend to. I am sending Whiskey and a couple others over to your apartment. They will pack and move your things here. This is where you live now. Welcome home."

CHAPTER SIX

A Crash Course in Survival 101 and Fuckology

ALEXANDRE MARSEILLE TYPICALLY slept no more than four hours a day. Rest, for him, was a necessary inconvenience. He stood at Venus' door in the guest quarters, watching her sleep for the past forty-five minutes. He appreciated that she needed her rest, especially since they had such a big day ahead. After all, she didn't have the same level of endurance he possessed, but he hoped she'd improve with his help. He'd cancelled his meetings and focused completely on her. There was nothing more serious or important going on than the woman lying in that bed before him...

His future Reine Du Sang.

She sat up high, on three thick mattresses elevated with a canopy of sturdy steel chains. Lit white candles lined the top of the headboard perched behind it, all of them dancing with a hyper orange glow, aiding in the warmth of the room.

A part of her frailty… she gets cold easier than most.

He'd made attempts to make her first night's stay as comfortable as possible. A glass pitcher of freshly drawn donor blood was set on her nightstand, along with a matching goblet for her to drink from. There were art books for her to peruse, too.

He'd dug a little more into her success as an Art History professor at one of the local universities and found her repute rather impressive. He'd initially figured it was just a way to blend in with society; her weakness undoubtedly was the desire to still belong in a world she was no longer a member of, and if they were to ever believe in the existence of vampires, she'd surely be exiled. Hell, they didn't even accept their own kind should that person's skin be a different hue, have a different belief system or be attracted to a person of the same sex. Why would anyone want to be human? Their very existence was hypocritical, nauseating, and weak.

He found her wish to be human rather repulsive, but he would address it later. As he dug deeper into her life however, he realized that her choice in career may not have been a path chosen just for acceptance's sake. She'd travelled and taught all over the world—considered a genius in her field. Alexandre wasn't much of an art critic, unless it came to women…

Women are the true art of the planet…as well as heaven and the underworld alike.

He was attracted to art purely for aesthetics, not for the meaning behind it. If something appealed to him, he purchased it. Simple as that. He couldn't care less about the man or monster behind the slung paint or marble sculpture; only necessary details of life concerned him. Venus, on the other hand, was rather particular about infinitesimal details, it seemed. He noticed it in the trappings of her apartment...

There was no way he was going to allow Whiskey and his crew to ransack the place without him close by. He was certain there would be secrets to uncover in that hole in the wall she felt so attached to. As soon as Venus was squared away and sound asleep at 5:17 A.M., he accompanied them to her apartment, the men dressed in white movers' jumpsuits and equipped with large cardboard boxes and heavy-duty tape. They pulled up in a truck, looking the part. He was heartbroken yet simultaneously impressed to discover soon thereafter that the lady was two steps ahead...

Most of her personal possessions were gone.

"She's not as stupid as I'd hoped she'd be." He chuckled as he glided towards her, wishing to get a closer look at his bewitching prize. His dick swelled and strained against his pants as he caressed the side of her face with a feather touch. His heart raced; there was nothing he wished for more than to take her right then, to hear her screams of pleasure and pain. Now that would be sweet music to his ears.

I'm going to break you to remake you. I'm going to recreate you, so that no one takes you.

Her eyes fluttered but it took her a moment to rouse. He leaned closer, inhaling the air around her... so deliciously sweet. Each breath she exhaled was like a dark lullaby. Each inhale a bright sonnet without end.

Long, thick black hair lay sprawled all over the red silk pillow and across her shoulders and arms. Her copper colored satin gown hung dangerously close to exposing a set of full, supple breasts that he missed from the first time he'd seen them. Long legs were pressed together as she lay on her side, as if protecting her precious pussy even in her sleep. The pitcher of blood sat half consumed and it looked like she'd been flipping through one of the art books for it lay open. He looked closely at the book, curious as to what had drawn her eye.

Dante and Virgil (1859), painted by William Bouguereau. He pulled the book from the nightstand and looked at the image.

"It's one of the earliest depictions of vampires being portrayed as humans, and not as some bumpy-skinned gnome or hideous creature skulking around in the middle of the night." She stretched and yawned. "Very nicely done. Brutal, but nice all the same." He looked at her for a spell then eyed the page again.

"You're a real work of art yourself. Everything of potential interest to me you've moved to some secret fuckin' hideout or tossed out in a dumpster, no doubt. How'd you know I'd go through your things in your apartment?" He flipped the page.

"Because that's what *I* would've done in your position."

He smirked at her response, then took her hand and helped her out of bed. Not that she needed it.

"Thank you for the feed last night."

The color had returned to her cheeks; it had done her

good.

"The blood came from one of my most popular donors. Did you enjoy it?" He pointed to the glass with only a drop or two left in the bottom.

"Yeah, it was nice. Very smooth."

"The donor is a fruitarian, has been for over ten years. I prefer a bit of a less sweet taste, but it seems that many enjoy him. He's great as a dessert I suppose if for nothing else."

She nodded and smiled ever so slightly as they looked into each other's eyes. He could hear her heartbeat increase, and sense the pulsing of her brain as she thought things through, worked them out in her mind.

I've got to get inside of her...

He pushed, she pushed back as he once again attempted to break through her cloaked thoughts to discover her fears and desires. She was still a bit groggy from her slumber. Perhaps her resistance was down. Her brows dipped and her lips gaped open. The woman hissed and extended her fangs, her eyes turning to slits.

"Get out of my head!" she roared. "I don't like how it feels!"

He was wrong... she was always on guard.

"Let me get inside of something else then... How does your pussy feel?!"

She gasped when he shoved her up against the side of the bed and buried his head in the crevice of her neck. Working his hand up her thigh, he jerked the edge of her satin night-gown up around her waist as he sucked and scraped his fangs against her delicious flesh.

"Yes…" she hissed, grinding against him, rotating her hips back and forth, inviting him for a taste.

The woman swallowed hard and moaned as she clawed into his back, the sting of her nails as she tore away at his flesh like a wild animal feeling so damn good. Her plush, wet pussy lips flattened against his touch as he stroked her drenched zone. Slipping his finger deep within her heated, wet canal, she pressed into it, although she also hesitated in moments, offering some resistance. The pull of their black souls, of her pussy, of their minds and broken hearts was like a game of tug of war.

Yes, war… A wicked war waged between them, one so strong neither was certain how it began or how it would end. He finger-fucked her harder, at a ferocious speed, his digit driving in knuckle deep and sliding out of her, over and over.

Orgasmic tears streamed down her cheeks. She tossed her head back, fangs glistening in the light, and trembled against him, jerking and falling apart.

Pulling his hand out of her tight sheath, he sucked his index finger, his heart nearly stopping at the taste of her. A sticky, honeyed essence, a natural aphrodisiac that lay between her thighs. It was like nothing he'd ever known. He turned to walk away but she flew towards him as if she had wings and wrapped her hands around his neck, violently jerking him in her direction, forcing him to face her.

"Why are you leaving me like this?!" He crossed his arms and looked at her. "You chase me, I'm here, you tease me and you leave! This isn't a part of training. I thought you wanted me?"

"But you don't want me yet, Venus... not with all of your being, my Love. Just two nights ago you detested me."

"But I—"

"Listen. It's simple. Your body wants me now, I want your mind and heart to want me, too. You reject me based on fear. I want it all, your undying devotion, before I fuck you. I'm a proud narcissist, and you are a reluctant one. One day, we'll meet in the middle. Until then, no fucking dick for you." He smirked and caressed her cheek, and her eyes darkened. "Not only that, I have to prepare you before we go any further. I am not like *any* of your previous lovers."

He ran his thumb lovingly against her chin. There was no possible way he could make her understand. All she wanted was to feel his power and taste his blood; it was evident she needed more time. He hoped it didn't take much longer. His desire for her was off the charts.

"I know how to fuck." Her fangs retracted. "I hate you, but I desire you... the least you could do is put me out of my misery."

"I enjoy misery, remember? You said it yourself." A chill ran through him and he welcomed it—anything to stop the woman from tempting him any further.

I can't give her what she wants just yet. She'll have more control then. She has to be kept in her place.

"You're just playing with me, just like you told me beforehand." She turned away and waved him off, disgust in her tone. "You've completely disrupted my life. I was just fine without you. I'm a toy to you, a plaything." She began to pace back and forth.

"Playthings can be cared for, Venus. But if you must know, you're more than that to me. Would I go through such measures for *just* a plaything?" She looked at him curiously. "I don't want to be hated by you, and though I know you're capable of love, I am not. Don't ever forget that."

"I didn't ask to be loved. I asked to be fucked!" Her fangs slid out once again. Her anger had a heartbeat, one that he found disturbingly beautiful.

"Venus, if you prove yourself worthy, I will treat you better than you ever dreamed possible." He groaned when she reached for his dick and yanked. Hard. Piercing pleasure and pain radiated through his cock as she squeezed it. Licking her lips, she winked at him, then released him.

"You're a real piece of work, Count Alexandre Marseille." She turned to the bed and climbed up it with great speed. "Let's start training today, ASAP, so I can get out of here and find a *real* Count to fuck me," she said with a smirk while reaching for the pitcher of blood. She poured more into her glass and took a sip. He smiled at her words, knowing the horny woman was talking shit, trying to get under his skin.

And she was successful in her efforts.

A wave of possessiveness bore down on him, buried itself deep within and promised to remain put. The thought of someone else pounding her pussy to pieces sent him into a jealous tailspin. Their strong connection was just that, resilient, and she knew it, too… It made him recall what his *sorcier* had told him long ago… that soulmates existed. Though the woman was a sensual being to her core, she had unbelievable self-control. Just as she'd stated before, to her, survival overruled sexual conquests. He, on the other hand, was unable to separate the two. And he meant that.

Perhaps this desired fuck was to her mere survival, a manipulative tool. After all, she'd sometimes used it to feed. She'd learned early on the power of her pussy…

That power made slave masters do unbelievable things…

It caused men all over the world to fight, steal, and kill…

She knew the power between her legs, and that very knowledge made her a walking piece of fucking art. She was her own art history, an unnatural relic. She was an art present to him, artistically futuristic with a painted, rich darkness all across the canvas of her soul, one so black he wished he could up and drown in it … then be framed and hung out to dry.

"I'm your last lover." He pointed a finger in her direction. "Your days of fucking others are over." He didn't miss the sly grin that crept across her face as she wrapped her body in the sheets. "You belong to me now."

"I belong to *me*, now…" She cocked her head to the side and winked. "I've held freedom in the palms of my hands, only a slave now to my *own* thirst. No one owns me, not even someone with a lofty status such as yourself… But I wouldn't mind feeling you deep inside of me. That's as close as you'll ever get to possession."

She had a knack for speaking out of turn, showing constant disrespect. She bucked authority on a continuous basis, becoming the true definition of a survivor.

"Right now, Venus, you wouldn't be able to withstand a fucking from me. I'd break you in two." His eyes narrowed on her as her smile faded away. "After your training, I will have you... again and again and again. I *will* possess you, Venus. You will be my pet, my lover, my bride. We will share this home. You will share my bed morning, noon and night. I will fuck you relentlessly for an immortal lifetime, so get your rest now. You're going to need it..."

HE HOVERED ABOVE her and struck again.

Sweat ran down her face, stinging her eyes as she tried to see where he'd gone. They'd entered the third hour of hell in the enclosure, boxed in by a cobblestone and concrete wall. The space was cold and dank like a basement, only it had to be the size of a damn football field. It was hard to tell in the darkness.

BOOM!

Her nostrils flared as she stood defensively, waiting for the fucker's next move. He was unbelievably fast; a mere blink and she'd miss him.

Loud banging and clanging noises made her sensitive ears ring. She'd been there for God knew how long. She'd lost track of time. The smell of dampness and earth all around her made her shudder with memories. She was disoriented, uncertain if she was even still in the Count's home. She surmised she was beneath it, some hidden place he'd created for his relentless craving to torment, injure, and destroy. Blood trickled from her various wounds. The arrows he'd managed to sink into her flesh had made more than a dent. They hurt like hell, but now it felt more like a series of bruises as her body worked fast to heal.

"Where are you?!" she screamed as she searched all around her, trying to pick up his scent.

"If the darts are dipped in silver, imagine what that will feel like, Venus. This is nothing! Show me your survival skills. So far, I'm not impressed. You have to listen... hear the air around you. Your human instincts aren't enough. Taste your surroundings, feel the stillness! Now pay the fuck attention!" the Count's voice boomed.

She pulled the last arrow out of her arm and hobbled over to a corner to catch her breath. Just then, she heard the whizzing of another arrow. Unlike the swords which carried more weight, these were light and faster, messing with her reflexes.

"AHHHHH!" she screamed as she raced across the other side of the room, deflecting arrow after arrow.

Listen.

Taste.

Feel.

She stopped, flicked her tongue out to taste the air, then

spun around and caught one destined for her back between her teeth.

"There you go, my Love…"

When she rolled onto the ground, what felt like sharp broken glass sliced into her arms, but she kept listening for the arrows until she'd caught them all and placed them at her feet.

A dim light emerged in the darkness, revealing the man himself, dressed in thick armor. She hated how her body responded to him, even in her state of immense physical pain and the mind games he played with her. Her pussy throbbed inside her cotton panties and jeans, her nipples hardened, and her mouth salivated.

"You could have killed me. What if one went into my head?" She spoke in a loud voice, ensuring he heard her though he was still a distance away in the vast room.

"It wouldn't have killed you. You'd have been quite uncomfortable and probably in need of a little reconstructive cosmetic surgery, but you wouldn't have died." His voice was slightly muffled beneath the helmet.

"How'd I do overall?" she asked as he now stood before her, towering like a metal mountain. "I know it started out rough, but I think that was pretty good, right?" Oddly enough, she found herself wanting his approval. It was the strangest thing.

He said nothing for several moments. What a getup he had on—the attire of a knight. A long, sharp sword hung on his right hip and he clutched several arrows in his hand. He set them down at her feet and removed his bascinet.

"You did all right."

"All right? Yeah, okay." She chuckled as she slumped down on the floor, taking a much needed breather. "Alexandre, I have some questions I need you to answer." He looked as if he were not interested in her inquisition, but he sat down beside her. "What is all of this training about?" She threw up her hands. "I'll admit, I came and agreed to stay here in your home because you promised discrete feedings, from donors no less. I was going to eat and run. I am still here though, because something inside of me is telling me that you are telling me the truth... that I *need* this. You said I could be in danger, that I'm not up to date to protect myself. What's going on?"

"You're not like many of your kind. That's intriguing. I am not exactly certain why you're not, Venus, but what I *do* know is some will want to experiment on you, while others will want to kill you out of jealousy or fear. Some will want to steal you away and claim you for their own. Others will want you dead because *I* want you...because you've caught the attention of a Count of my status."

"You love bragging about yourself, don't you?" She smirked as she flicked a piece of glass out of her flesh.

"I'm not bragging." He had on a stern expression. "What I think about myself is irrelevant when it comes to public perception. This is how I am regarded in our world, Venus. I am one of the last of my kind, a dying breed. Not dying due to weakness, but due to stubbornness. I am trying to break that curse. With *you*."

"Why are you so obsessed with me? I know about you

now…"

The man leisurely leaned back, his eyes glowing. He lit a lantern and turned back to her.

"Let's take this one step at a time. What do you think you know about me now?"

"I know that you're highly sought after by women but have not committed to anyone, though it is expected of you. I know that you were supposed to be married over three years ago, and now the throne is in jeopardy. I know that you're from France but have refused to leave New York. Why?"

"There are certain connections, a certain spark, as humans would say, chemistry, that a vampire of my magnitude looks for when selecting not a fuckbuddy, not a concubine, but a bride who will also be his mate. I have had fulfilling trysts with many females. I love to fuck, as we all do… Show me a celibate vampire and you will have found a needle in a haystack. I love a woman's company. It began early on. When I was a young boy, I was assigned a *sorcier*."

"A wizard…"

"Yes, you know French?"

"Some."

"Good. That means teaching it to you will go much faster. You need to be fluent. Anyway, we'll deal with that later. My *sorcier* was, for lack of a better word, like a caretaker for me… assigned to watch over me while my parents fought and went off to war. All members of my Coven are trained for combat, we're born into it. That's part of the reason why I am training you as well. No Queen marries without knowing how to properly physically defend the throne. Anyway, my *sorcier* told me, in secret, that I would meet my mate here in New York, my bride. He said it was imperative that I wait for her because my bloodline would depend upon it. Time went on, and I never found you. I began to secretly worry that he was mistaken and I'd wasted valuable time. Having an appropriate mate was very important not only to myself, but to my family. I have searched for you for so long, Venus, and now… I finally have you."

His eyes grew lighter as he reached over and glided his fingers softly against her hand. She looked down, intrigued by his gentle touch. "I'm obsessed with you because you are beautiful. You're resilient, smart, at times enchantingly silly, and full of lust. I'm fixated with your stubborn nature, and I can feel your attraction to me… it's so strong. But you don't feel as strongly about me yet as I do about you. That must change. Our connection, regardless of that, goes beyond the physical. I felt it as soon as we looked into each other's eyes for the first time."

"Like love…"

He looked at her as if he didn't know what to make of her words, as if he were confused by such a suggestion. Could vampires love? She knew that she could, though she hadn't felt love since before she was turned. But she remembered the feeling clearly… it was still within her. She did have a connection to this beast, this horrible tyrant. Something in him seemed to soften now when they were around one another. He'd let his guard down. He stopped using every opportunity to pry into her mind, to humiliate her, to make her bend to his whims. It was as if he was trying to sell himself, make her see what she could have and that, perhaps, he'd be willing to be what she wanted, if she agreed to stay with him.

She sensed loneliness… anger… hurt… desertion… pain.

"Alexandre, I was told that you can't mate. You've been confusing me by calling me your mate, since that is a term typically used for those wanting offspring."

The man chuckled then cracked his neck.

"Myths, fairytales, legends…" He shrugged. "Don't believe the shit. The details are boring… like a history lesson."

"I teach history. I'm here for it."

She smiled at him and he smiled back. He stood to his feet and removed the suit of armor, one piece at a time, each part clanking to the ground until he ended up in only a pair of boxer briefs. He walked away, disappearing into the darkness for several seconds. When he re-emerged, he was wearing loose burgundy satin pants. His necklace beat against his hard, muscular chest with each step he took. His bare feet slapped against the cold, concrete ground as if they were made of steel. Sitting beside her once again, he raised one leg and had the other straight out.

"All right, I will explain this as simply as I can. There are many types of vampires, at least five different varieties, but the most notable are Pure Bloods, Turned, and Half Breeds." He counted on three fingers.

"Yes, I know that. My mistress told me."

He nodded. "All three categories go by a plethora of various names depending on where in the world they are located, but I will use the terms I just gave you as reference. Well, for whatever reason, your mistress didn't tell you about the birds and the bees for our people."

"No, she did, but there's always more to learn."

"Okay, here goes nothing: Pure Bloods are able to mate, Venus. You're not the first turned human to believe otherwise. We just often have chosen not to do so since some believe they shouldn't mate with anyone else who isn't pure. That has resulted in centuries of incest, which of course doesn't affect us intellectually, but it made our bonds weaker, meaning, outside genetics tend to make us stronger because we then incorporate their powers and skills versus just recycling our own. Since we are in the minority, there isn't much that is known about us, and misinformation gets spread in our community, but keeping firm to the belief that we should only breed with our own is what caused our numbers to fall even faster. It was a terrible choice if you ask me, but I was a youth at that time, and had no say. My grandfather was king then. Anyway, moving on.

"Female Pure Bloods can mate with another Pure Blood via intercourse, just as humans do. We all have dicks and pussies, ovaries, nutsacks that are fully functional and behave similarly to human and mammal reproductive constructs."

"But I heard that Pure Bloods can't have children with humans."

"Well, that particular rumor has merit. If a Pure Blood mates with a human, a male Pure Blood in particular, the human female has a high chance of dying during childbirth, if the sex act alone doesn't kill her. It happens nevertheless from time to time, though a Pure Blood mating with a human isn't ideal if it's male to female, due to our strength and inability to control ourselves during mating targeted coitus and the subsequent climax. In other words, we fuck and cum hard when mating and the human female body isn't built for that."

"But you've fucked plenty of human women."

"I have. But there's a difference in fucking to impregnate, and fucking to just get off." She nodded in understanding. "Also, there is a difference even in how we fuck human women and fellow vampires. It may look similar to a bystander, but it's not. Also, I'm sure it goes without saying that all vampires, turned or Pureblood, can reproduce, so to speak, by biting a human with intent. Intent means, not biting to kill." She nodded in understanding. "How we bite to feed versus to turn are completely different. To turn, we release a virus as well as a healing serum simultaneously.

"To feed, well… you already know. Another difference is we control our reproduction one hundred percent, unlike humans, Turned, and Half Breeds. Now, we can physically mate with another Pure Blood, and obviously that would have no consequences. In that case, we'd go forward similarly to any typical sexual encounter and conception. Turned Vampires such as yourself can mate with Pure Bloods, too. That's a given or I wouldn't have pursued you. The sex is still rough for the turned if she or he isn't mentally prepared for it." He held his hands up like scales. "It's intense, for lack of a better word. There's also a great power differential. Once you build your strength up, tap into it, which is another reason for this training—despite your basic survival skills which I'll admit are impressive—you and I won't have any issues."

She smiled then burst out laughing.

"Now it makes sense. That's why you haven't fucked me."

"Well, not exactly. You have to be ready, just like I said. You would handle a fucking right now with flying colors; breeding, not so much. I need you to be able to take both because if I fuck you and in the middle of it I sense you're fertile, I can't promise that I'd be able to control myself. To resist the chance to procreate right then and there with my mate, since I've already chosen you for my Blood Queen would be damn near impossible, especially when creating a first born. It's totally biological at that point. Timing is everything though. This needs to go right. The last thing I want is to—" He stopped, unable to say it. Refusing to say it.

"What about Half Breeds like Whiskey?"

She gave him a way out and he jumped on it as fast as he could. God forbid he voice any words of love for her.

"Whiskey is my right hand. He's a Half Breed, which are the offspring of humans and Turned Vampires, thus considered half human and half vampire, can mate with humans or other Half Breeds with no problem. Half Breeds sometimes have an almost uncultivated quality though. We cannot mate with them." He pointed to himself. "We can fuck them, but there's no successful reproduction to date between the two. Turned such as yourself are barely human anymore so the mating is usually successful. All right, glad I didn't have to pull out an old dusty slideshow presentation with a bunch of hard cocks, vampire sperm, and eggs."

He grinned slyly as he got to his feet. He reached for her hand, and she looked at his fingers. They were ghostly white… practically translucent. Protruding, knotted blue veins ran up and down them, and she could almost see the blood flowing through them. She took his hand and stood, kicking the arrows off to the side with a swipe of her foot.

ZOOM!

She fell to the ground, ducking when a bullet came barreling towards her. Racing to a corner, she looked all around her, listening to him laugh as he whizzed around in now complete darkness once again.

"You fucker!" She stood on guard, climbing up the wall in reverse. Her adrenaline kicked in… She was ready to play.

He'd stolen the stingy bit of light they'd had with a mere whisper in the lantern's direction. They were shrouded in black.

"Awww, baby, don't be pissed. All this talk of fucking and breeding got me horny!" He cackled. "Now… let's see how many fucking bullets to the head you can dodge. Show me just how bad ass of a survivor you can be, Venus!"

The gun cracked, and a series of shots resounded all around…

CHAPTER SEVEN

Eat Your Heart Out

…Several weeks later

A LEXANDRE SAT OPPOSITE her at one end of the long white table, watching her indelicately jam her fork into a plate of salad in the dimly lit dining room. The pieces of Romaine lettuce and sliced tomato turned to mush between her gnashing teeth. He slumped back in his seat and glared up at the silver domed ceiling, rolling around a glass apple paperweight in his hand. One of his clients had given it to him as a gift. Seconds turned to minutes, and he was at his wits' end. Her chewing drove him mad. He looked back down the table at her and sucked his teeth in displeasure. He rubbed down the side of his clean-shaven face and rested his hand there for a moment.

"If it bothers you so badly," she stated around a mouthful of food, stabbing the plate to death as if she and the lettuce were in a duel, "put earmuffs or something on. I am eating as quietly as I can." She swallowed, then started again, the horrible cycle continuing. Her full lips twisted to the left then right; her cheeks reminded him of a damn squirrel with a mouthful of nuts.

"You chew like a fucking camel."

"Your mama chews like a fucking cow."

"My mother is dead."

"So is mine and so am I and so are you and your entire crew. Pass the motherfucking peas."

He picked up the crystal bowl filled with peas and carrots over white rice and slid it down the long table. She managed to catch hold to it, even with her bandaged arm. There'd been an unfortunate incident with a black bear the day prior… They made a trip to the Catskills, in New York, for some hunting and camping out. She hadn't fared so well when it came to the animal attack portion of her training. Once the big, beautiful creature sank its teeth into her shoulder and practically snatched the whole damn appendage off, she screamed out in pain and horror. He'd offered to assist, but as she bled profusely, the woman picked up the animal high in the air above her head and ripped it's head off with her bare hands…

…And then she fell to her knees and cried.

These fucking human emotions would be the second death of her.

"Who's your favorite artist of all time?" He clasped his hands together and smiled, while 'Make It Wit Chu' by Queens of the Stone Age played through the speakers. She scooped up a spoonful of the rice and vegetables and shoved it in her mouth, then took her time chewing it all up.

"Faith Ringgold."

He reached for his freshly poured blood in a wine glass, took a sip, and set it down alongside the paperweight he'd been toying with.

"I've never heard of her. Is she a sculptor? Painter?"

"Painter. Quilter. Children's book writer and illustrator. She's from Harlem. She's also an activist and was heavily involved with the African American Civil Rights Movement of the 1960s, with a concentration on Black women's liberation. Much of her work is very colorful and tells a tapestry of stories."

He smiled at her words. "Nice pun. You're naturally corny. It's kinda cute." He huffed, growing a bit bored.

"She's an inspiration to me." The woman dabbed at the sides of her mouth with a white linen napkin then set it back down.

"Why do you feel that you need to be inspired by some-one, Venus? I never understood that about human nature. Why aren't you people able to make your own choices? Move about on your own steam? Why do you need a predecessor? Someone leading the charge?"

"The same reason why your parents were Queen and King. Everyone needs someone to charge ahead, to teach them the ropes. That's the reason I'm here, right?"

"Touché." She kept on eating.

"I like how you think, Venus. It's foreign to me... the way you construct ideas. It's like your brain is full of artistic renderings of life. I'm a more linear thinker. I believe even if I were human, I would have been that way." He shrugged. "It's simply my personality type."

"Maybe, but you'll never know." He sat there for several minutes deliberating on what she'd said. "Let's reverse roles for a second." He grabbed his napkin from his lap and slapped it onto the table. "I want you to train me on how to be a human."

She smirked. "Why should I even bother? I thought you had that already down pat. We're pathetic idiots, right? Just imagine a snail trying to make it down the opposite end of a street in rush hour traffic. That's a person in your eyes... a human being destined for continuous acts of stupidity. One after a-fucking-nother."

"Not necessarily. It's obvious that you still need that connection. You're sitting here eating their food still for God's sake. You hang out with them. You insisted on going to work, even during your training with me, stating that the students needed their tests handed back and you had a duty to teach. I enjoyed watching you, by the way. You seem to have a really good time."

"I didn't sense you there. I didn't see you, either. You were supposed to be in court." She reached for a roll and bit into it.

"I *was* in court. I watched right afterward. I had a camera placed in your classroom to record your lecture." Her lips curled in a tight smile. "You're quite astute. Those students seem to like you. You have a rapport with them."

"Where did you go to law school and why are you practicing law?"

"I went to law school in France, initially. Every fifty years or so, I start all over again, pretending that I am a new student just for the fun of it when I must travel for lengthy periods of time abroad, amongst humans and have extended stays. I pass the bar exam in various countries, I set up an office or firm. That's simply the way it has been. I have plenty of money now so that was never the incentive. I must say this though—this time around has proved to be the most fun and lucrative. There are some interesting people here in New York." He picked up the glass apple, a spoon and a fork, and began to juggle them as he continued to speak. "I practice law because I need to be able to vouch for the how and why of my existence."

He placed the items back down and lifted his arms up and around, pointing to his surroundings.

"So basically it's a cover for explaining how you could afford a home such as this, in the middle of Manhattan."

"Yes! I can't live here undisturbed in these lavish surroundings and not have to provide further justification. Who the fuck is going to believe a school teacher could afford this, huh? Or a nurse? I knew from an early age that one must cover their tracks well. I'm sure it'll go over real well if I told everyone the truth though, right?" The woman grunted and rolled her eyes. "'Hey everybody! No need to worry about little ol' me! I'm just a fuckin' four-hundred-year-old Royal vampire that kills your girlfriends 'nd husbands, and sometimes your little dog, too... sucks their blood outta their damn neck. I don't need your money, so settle your tits! I own plenty of land all over the world, and I have enough money to start my own country and buy anything I want! Including your grandma Bessie!' Nah, that's obviously not gonna fly, now is it?" He picked up the paperweight once again and twirled it back and forth in his palm as he leaned back in his chair. "Not only that, it's a hobby. I enjoy it. Law suits me."

"It feeds into your enormous ego... your need to destroy people, to be their judge and jury."

"Actually, I'm an attorney so me being judge and jury isn't quite accurate," he teased.

She laughed and shook her head. "You know what I mean."

"Yeah, I know what you mean, but you've gotten off the subject. Let me help you get back on. Now, let's talk about you schooling me on the human condition again. Let's see... oh, I've got it." He slammed the glass apple down onto the table and stared at her, a grin spread across his face. "Tell me the top three wonderful things you miss about being human?"

"I was a slave, so my experiences are a bit jaded, naturally." She swallowed a bite of bread, then pinched off another taste. "But uh, I enjoyed basking in the sunlight. Now, yeah, unlike the myth, you and I can go out in the daytime but it gets uncomfortable if I'm out too long. Exposure to the sun wreaks havoc on my immune system. I miss wanting and enjoying food, too... *real* food." She wrinkled her nose at the glass of blood. "So, I sit here, pretending. In the mornings, just about each and every day, I make myself a pot of coffee. I sit down with a newspaper or watch the news… newspapers are becoming a rarer commodity. I work out on my old exercise bike, lift my little weights. I sing, I cry, I dance. I miss love."

He leaned back in his seat and crossed his arms. A heavy cloud drifted in the room. The immensity had no eyes and no feet, it was blind and couldn't walk, but it entered somehow anyway… and it was enormous.

"I can help you with the sunlight issue." He lit a cigarette and blew smoke out the corner of his mouth.

"How?"

"I'm not as sensitive to it as you. Of course, that took my family centuries' worth of evolution to achieve. The first vampires to roam the world could not step out into daylight for even one second or they'd burn, but you and I are advanced… evolved. That was like Cro-Magnon, so to speak. Anyway, there are measures you can take to help protect yourself. We'll go over them. Now, regarding the food, I can't help you there." He threw up his hands. "We just don't want it. We don't crave it and it actually sickens me to watch you doing what you're doing right now to that plate. But I understand that you're a creature of habit and it makes you feel less ghastly, I suppose. Lastly, love is abstract to me, Venus. I understand the basic definition, I'm not an idiot, but I can't grasp the full 3-D concept, if you will."

"Well, what do you want to know about it?" She crossed her legs and rested her hands on her knee.

"How is it different from like? Is it just a more intense

version? I can like people… I like a few. I like *you*." He winked at her.

"No, they aren't the same… not even close. You can like a car. You can like a stranger you just met five minutes ago. You can like one blood type over another. You don't love that car. It's an inanimate object. You can't love someone you just met five minutes ago or a blood type, either. People use the word love so loosely nowadays."

The woman stood from her chair and made her way over to him. He sipped some more on his blood beverage and hooked her gaze. "Explain it to me then. Teach me…" He reached for her hand, his heart racing. He placed her palm against his chest, then lifted her hand to his mouth and kissed her fingertips. It came so naturally, like fucking and feeding.

"That. Did you feel how your heartrate changed? I felt it through your touch. That's the beginning stages of love."

"That's ridiculous." He chortled, snatching his hand away.

"It's not. Have you ever felt that way with anyone else?"

He stared at her for a moment, then looked away.

"No." He sucked air as he felt her take hold of his fingers and place them against her lower lip, one at a time. His breathing accelerated and his eyes glazed over with pure, unadulterated lust. He observed as she sucked each finger one by one. His dick stiffened, twisted and turned in his pants, begging to slip into her mouth, her pussy… any fucking orifice would do. His fangs began to push through the pink, soft tissue of his gums and the veins in his neck throbbed, right along with his dick.

"Love is the way you looked at me when I was being attacked by the bear. You stepped close to intervene instead of being your typical ruthless self and allowing me to fend for myself. I handled the situation, but if I couldn't, we both know you would have killed the beast on my behalf." She sucked another finger, sliding her wet, warm tongue against it.

"Of course I would have..." His chest swelled as his breathing quickened and his heart beat like a loud ticking clock.

"Love is the way I looked at you when you admitted you had cameras in my classroom, knowing you owed me no explanation. You wanted to get to know me better, see me in my natural element, but you're too hardheaded to admit it. It had little to do with control. It had to do with a genuine wish to see what makes me happy."

She sucked his thumb, moving it in and out of her mouth like a cock, taking her sweet time with the fellatio simulation. He fell under her horrible, tantalizing spell... he was doomed. "Love is when you had art books on my nightstand my first night here. Love is when you watched me sleep to ensure I was comfortable and okay. Love is you preparing food that I don't need, that I can't digest, that we both know I will vomit up later because my body can no longer tolerate it, but I still *need* to do it... I need to pretend... I need to believe that I can *still* experience love!"

"Venus, I don't love you." His eyes turned to black slits.

"I don't believe you." She smiled sadly at him as she wrapped her hands around his face.

He looked at her neck, back into her eyes, then closed his own. He couldn't bear to look at her. What was happening? Had he been running from the truth for weeks, perhaps months on end? Had he been trudging through the forest, racing from the reality that stood before him? Was he a slave trying to get away from anything that challenged what he'd been told? What he'd learned? What he believed in? No. It couldn't be.

"That's not love. That's protecting my property... my bride. No, you're not my slave, but you do in fact belong to me. That's vested interest. There's a difference, Venus." He looked her in the eye, making sure he didn't flinch.

"No, Count Alexandre Marseille." She regarded him as if he were some poor sap, a fledgling soul, an unfortunate being. "You're wrong. I don't need your love, so please don't get it twisted, but I have it. I know what I know. And I said what I said." She raised her finger in the air, making her point. "You can deny it all of you want. You know truth from fiction, fact from fantasy. You're an intelligent, violent, vile entity who's capable of love... great, obsessive, fantastic love. I've seen it over my time with you, Lord. You've shocked me. Your kindness and loyalty have taken me by surprise. You don't say the words, you show through action. You've just realized that, too, and it scares the shit out of you."

He swallowed as his entire body warmed with anxiety.

He'd never sent a woman or Vamp flowers. He'd never treated *anyone* as well as he treated Venus. He even cooked for the damn woman... something he'd never done for another.

LE ROI DU SANG

Stood in a grocery store and bought the bullshit that made him want to hurl. When they weren't together, he was thinking about her. When they were together, he was savoring every moment, hoping that one day soon she'd want him the same way he wanted her.

"You've never been in love before." She caressed his cheek and he pulled away, out of her reach, baring his fangs. She wasn't troubled or deterred. "You've bought the notion that you are incapable of passion and compassion, Alexandre Marseille, because that's what you've been taught. You became a slave to the idea that it was to never be a part of your many lifetimes. It takes work to break a mold. You've already done so by pursuing someone your ancestors would have scoffed at. I'm a Turned Vampire... considered beneath you."

Bending down, she kissed his forehead. Nothing had ever felt so sweet... Flashes of when he'd been a youth flooded his mind. He recalled laughing one time while swimming in the Bay of Biscay with his brother, Victor, during one of the few times they didn't have to train for war or fight. It had been a perfect day...

"Don't do this, Venus..."

"How can I not do something that's already been done?" He could barely breathe. Barely contain himself. "Love, to you, is a weakness. And you're right; it is... but it's also a beautiful gift."

She released his hand and straddled him, planting a devastating kiss on his lips.

He eagerly wrapped his arms around her waist and they

137

tore at one another, clothing flying in shreds all around them like confetti. He snarled as his fangs fully descended. Grabbing the glass before him, he broke it on the table and sliced his wrist with the jagged edge. Placing the wound to her mouth, she devoured him, hungrily and viciously. He rocked his pelvis against her moist garden as she sucked his blood. He had to clutch the arm of the chair to keep his composure, but it was no use. He screamed out, a sound that echoed throughout the place, a deep, rumbling growl from the pit of his gut. Wood splintered off the arm of the chair, making sawdust. His face burst with sweat as she swayed her hips back and forth along his erect cock, fucking him over his pants.

"You're going to start something that I won't be able to stop! Shit! You don't want this right now, Venus!" He groaned.

"I do!" Her dark eyes pleaded as she continued to nurse from him. "Make love to me, Alexandre. I can take it! Come on, baby! Let me feel your big dick inside me! Fuck me raw! Hurt me! Please me!" Her fangs descended and her eyes turned pitch black.

"*Tu m'excites!*" he roared.

His eyes rolled back and for a split second, he went blind with lust and desire. He picked her up with one arm and swiped all the food and drinks off the table with the other. Loud crashing ensued when plates and glasses hit the floor, shattering. Slamming her hard against the table, he towered over her. Her eyes grew large with excitement. He undid his belt and discarded what remained of his clothing, including his underwear, exposing his large, rock-hard cock.

He delighted in how her eyes and fangs glistened at the sight of it, her lips, smeared with blood, curving in delight. The flesh of his shaft was paler than snow, lined with blue, thick veins from the base to the top. Tearing her pants from her body, he caught her neck with one hand and shoved her thighs apart. She screamed in a way he'd never heard in his life, an earthshattering sound, when he sank his teeth violently into her neck. Blood spilled into his mouth, its richness so divine. She clutched him to her, shaking from his intrusion. In a matter of moments, he penetrated her again, this time with his needy dick.

"OH GOD! OH GOD!" Her back arched as he thrust deep and hard within her, with no build up, no warning... fully engulfed in her soft, hot passage.

The table broke beneath them, but he heard it splintering and picked her up in his arms, cradling her close as he continued to jostle his mate up and down his shaft, deep inside her pussy, stretching it wide.

"You feel like new death and sweet rebirth! You feel like sunset and full moons! You feel like myths and legends! I can't stop, Venus! You should've never asked for this! Years of wanting you... feeling you feeding off my dreams! I'm going to get what I need from you now. I'm going to fuck you to death then bring you back to life!"

"It hurts so good, baby! You're killing my pussy, tearing it to pieces! SHIT!"

Tears ran down her face as she laughed then shuddered,

going through a gamut of emotions. Her body was fast covering with bruises as he tugged at her arms, pulled her into his deep lunges, balls deep inside of her tight, wet pussy. She gripped his hair with one hand and yelled curses as he made her take every thick, long inch he had to offer. Carrying her over to the other side of the dining room, he laid her on the floor. Folding her legs so her knees rested against his shoulders, he made love to her face to face...

He could feel the strain within him, and he fought letting completely go. He could see his reflection in her dark eyes... it stole his breath away.

There he was, moving back and forth like a fucking rabbit, plunging so deep he could practically feel her womb. The vein in the middle of his forehead protruded—he felt it—as he rammed her over and over again. She held him tight, a smile on her face. Her pussy muscles squeezed the shit out of his piston; it felt so damn delightful, he couldn't describe it even if he had to. Cupping her ass, he brought her impossibly closer and angled himself just so, to get his pelvis to rub against her clit.

He slowed to envelop her right nipple into his mouth. The dark chocolate goodness was smooth and sweet. She sighed with pleasure. As the sound of his balls slapping against her pussy echoed in the room, her sticky essence ran down his shaft and nuts. He gently kissed the spot where he'd bitten her on the neck, taking the hurt away.

He'd claimed her. Their fate was sealed.

Shifting his body, he dislocated his spine, pushed and compressed the muscles in his back. The woman watched in wonder as he contorted and twisted until he was doubled over, his tongue now curled tight against her swollen clit.

"Fuck!"

He jammed his cock faster inside of her, while slowly licking and sucking on her bud. Gliding a finger in her ass, he fucked the small, puckered hole with his digit, lavishing her pussy, clit, and ass with much deserved attention.

"I'm cumming!"

Sweet, sticky goodness trickled out of her pussy, down his shaft, across his tongue… making a beautiful mess. He kept fucking her, needing her, loving her.

With a single kiss to her clit, he sat up, cracked his vertebrae back into place, and peppered kisses all the way back up her body. The woman trembled as if having a seizure. Her eyes rolled until there was nothing but white showing. Her fangs remained extended and her claws were tinted with his blood when she raked them up and down his arms in ecstasy. With the gentleness of a lamb, he slipped out of her sheath, then glided back inside her, much slower this time. Kissing her collarbone and breasts, he fucked her nice and slow, while they held on to one another for dear life. When he looked into her eyes, his body began to shake.

He could see within her…

Her most precious desires! Her greatest fears! She'd allowed him in, leaving no barriers… no more walls between them.

"You want me too now, don't you, my Love?"

She smiled at him and nodded, running her fingers through his hair. "Yes, I want you!"

He possessed her, holding her tight against his needy flesh. He roared, and his seed spilled deep within her, over and over again. Their sweaty bodies collided as he milked the last of himself within her sweet valley… and when it was over, he lay nestled on top of her, holding her close.

Out of the corner of his eye, he saw a shadow exit the room…

Fawn.

She was a notorious voyeur. Perhaps she'd grown curious as to how their first tryst would go. Nevertheless, he pushed it out of his mind and enjoyed a brief rest with his bride-to-be. He clutched her to him, and a new horrid wave of possessiveness overcame him.

She's mine… MINE!

"We have to finish your training, Venus. We're almost there, but not quite. I need you to take off work for at least a week. It's imperative. Do you understand me?" He rose up and tilted her chin, forcing her to look him in the eye.

"Yes, I understand." He outstretched his hand, noting the large, dark bruises between her legs from his forceful thrusting, as well as the redness from his bites and licks that covered her body.

"I'm sorry… They'll all be gone in the next few hours." He helped her to her feet.

"Don't be sorry. It was well worth it." She eyed his wet cock, which swung between his legs, dripping with cum and her essence. The woman dropped to her knees, taking him off guard, and engulfed his dick in her mouth, giving him an instant erection once again. Slamming his back against the wall, she noisily slurped and sucked his length as he grabbed the back of her head and fucked the hell out of her mouth, pumping upward, driving himself in and out of her at rapid speed.

"*Suce-moi la bite*! FUCK!" He shot his creamy load, snatched his cock out, and watched her swallow his velvety special delivery. "I'm not fuckin' done with you. Let's take this to my bedroom and resume."

Smiling, he helped his mate onto her feet and they walked out of the dining room, hand in hand. He imagined they looked much like Adam and Eve at that point, unapologetically naked… after all, he was now joined with his rib. Hopefully the only serpent to come between them would be his dick. On their way past the living room, he spotted Whiskey sitting on a chaise, talking on the phone. He barely noticed them.

"Whiskey," Alexandre called out.

The man immediately placed his phone down and jumped to his feet.

"Yes, Sir?"

"Move Venus' things into the master suite. My bride will be staying with me from now on out…"

CHAPTER EIGHT

Court is in Session...

Everything is a game to be won. I refuse to fucking lose—that's not an option. Please don't let this suit and my smile fool you. Nice guys finish last, and I'm always in first place. I will play dirty to get what I want, for that is the way of a warrior, a master, a Royal Pure Blood vampire, an elite Royal Le Roi Du Sang...

"I 'M NOT HERE for the bullshit," Alexandre Marseille whispered to his client before he casually stood from his seat in the courtroom, buttoned his two-toned tan jacket, and made his way to the witness stand.

Time to put an end to this open and shut case.

"Good morning, Mr. Rutherford." Alexandre placed his hand on the railing of the podium before the older man, then leaned slightly forward and smiled.

"Good morning," the defendant stated without a smile, looking him up and down with an uneasy eye. The older man wore a thin navy blue and pale yellow checkered sweater over a wrinkled white shirt. Mr. Rutherford was no one's eye candy or eye sore. In fact, he looked rather unassuming, with nothing notable about him in either direction. He was the type of man that wouldn't be remembered in a crowd or even on an elevator, among a handful of people. His features weren't keen or exaggerated. He had nothing that made him different, such as a cluster of light brown freckles, an ill placed beauty mark in the center of his chin, or keloid scar above the brow. He was simply existing—a ho hum specimen. Maybe all of this played a role in how the cards had been dealt, becoming partly the reason why they were here today.

Their eyes locked and Alexandre cocked his head to the side and slipped within him, like a ghost through a wall...

What are your weaknesses, old man? What are your fears? Come on, fucker... Tell me... Tell me... Tell me... Oh, beautiful... look what we have here...

He slapped the desk, looked towards the jury, then back at the man.

"Mr. Rutherford, you stated that, on August 11th, Mr. Laurent came to your place of business, Rutherford Furs and Leather, asking to speak to his estranged wife, Mrs. Amanda Laurent, and was refused. Is that correct?"

"Yes. Amanda was in the back taking care of some inventory," the man stated with a thick Brooklyn accent. "I was in the front of my store and he came in there yellin' to talk to her, then threatened tuh shoot me when I told him no."

"Mmmm hmmm, I see." Alexandre smiled and began to

slowly pace back and forth. "So, why did you refuse to let him speak to his wife?"

"Amanda said he'd been doin' strange things, harassin' her."

"Amanda had told you, in her own words, that her husband, Mr. Laurent, was harassing her before this all occurred, correct?"

"Yes."

"She used the actual word, 'harass'?" Alexandre put his fingers in quotation marks.

"Yeah, she said stalked, actually... said he was stalkin' her."

"Did she give you any examples of this stalking that was allegedly taking place?"

"Yes. She said just two weeks beforehand, I believe, he was drivin' on the street outside her house, going back 'nd forth and honking."

"Mmm hmmm, but he still lived there. There was no restraining order and his name was on the lease. However, playing Devil's Advocate, let's say that she in fact said that her husband was stalking her. How do you know for a fact that Mr. Laurent was driving back and forth while honking his horn?"

"Speculation. Amanda Laurent is not on the witness stand," the DA stated from behind his table, the man rolling his eyes as if tired of his shenanigans.

"Okay, please strike the question," Alexandre intervened before Judge Camus got involved. Amanda Laurent's mother was deathly ill, and she was unable to attend court. They were all on their own. "Let me ask this a bit differently... Did your employee, Amanda Laurent, seem afraid of her ex-husband?"

The defense attorney jumped up from his seat. "Hearsay!"

"No, it's not hearsay," Alexandre stated as he turned towards the DA. "This was an active, working relationship, not hearsay. One can infer several observations that lead to credible conclusions from a person's behavior, especially an employee that Mr. Rutherford has had working for him for over two years. Working that closely, day after day, would allow someone to safely conclude whether a behavior or statement was out of character. We are here referring to Mrs. Amanda Laurent's personality, moods, and tendencies."

"Overruled."

"Thank you. So, I will repeat the question, Mr. Rutherford. Did Amanda Laurent seem afraid of her husband?" The man sat there for a moment, fidgeting.

"Well, Amanda is the type of woman who doesn't really express emotion that way, you know? So, uh, she didn't use those words per se but I knew that she was."

"Mr. Rutherford, if you have an employee who has told you that her husband is driving past her home uninvited, is calling her at all hours of the night begging for reconciliation, and giving unsolicited gifts, all of which she told you of in great detail, according to your own previous testimony, why wouldn't she also state that she was in fear?"

"I, uh, I don't know, but I think it's obvious that she was. You could just figure it out."

"It's obvious? You could just figure it out? Mr. Rutherford, I'm not convinced that it is so obvious. I believe you are hiding something."

"I object! Mr. Marseille's comments are pure conjecture and we are not here to get an opinion!"

Alexandre's lips curled in a smile. "I asked Mr. Rutherford if Mrs. Laurent ever stated that she was afraid of her husband. I didn't ask for his opinion, observations, or his own judgment regarding this specific matter. I asked if the plaintiff's wife ever stated verbally to him that she was in fear of my client, Mr. Laurent." Alexandre wore a smug expression as the Judge ruled in his favor. "Okay, let's continue… Mr. Rutherford, I am concerned about some information that leads me to believe you haven't been truthful in this courtroom today."

"Dishonest? I am tellin' the truth! That son of uh bitch had Amanda 'fraid to death!"

"Mr. Rutherford, please watch your language," the judge stated.

Mr. Rutherford nodded, duly chastised.

"Afraid to death? Hmmm… interesting choice of words. No vested interest? Okay. I am presenting into evidence, Exhibit C." Alexandre marched swiftly to his table where his client sat, picked up a folder and returned to stand before Mr. Rutherford. "I want you to take a look at a log of text messages between Amanda Laurent and my client, Gregory Laurent. Please, so that the courtroom can hear you, read the date and the text messages between Amanda and Gregory Laurent."

The man swallowed, picked up the file, and began to read

aloud.

"August 13th... uh, this is Amanda speaking I guess... It says, 'Hi, Greg. We can have dinner later tonight.'"

"And what is Gregory Laurent's response?"

"Um, it says, 'Okay, baby. Thanks for inviting me.'"

Rutherford kept reading the messages for several minutes, the people in the room taking it all in.

"Now, does that sound like a woman who is being harassed or stalked, Mr. Rutherford? Does it sound like a woman who is afraid for her life, scared to death, as you phrased it? Does it sound like a woman who has no interest in her husband?" He began to pace back and forth, looking over at the jury a time or two. "Does it seem as if she believes her estranged husband is bonkers? Crazy? Out of his mind?"

"She was just trying to make peace with him for their daughter's sake!"

"Wrong!" Alexandre swung back in Mr. Rutherford's direction. "You didn't want them back together because you and Amanda were having an affair, and when Mr. Laurent walked into your store to take her out for lunch that fateful day, you became enraged, removed your gun from behind the counter, and shot him in the arm!"

The judge began to violently beat the gavel. "Mr. Marseille!" Judge Camus yelled gruffly.

"Your honor, I have proof that Mrs. Amanda Laurent and Mr. Rutherford were having an affair and that Mr. Rutherford did everything in his power to seek revenge once Amanda called it off between the two of them and tried to reconcile with her husband."

"Well, I suggest you present it right now and stop turning this courtroom into a three-ring-circus!"

Alexandre opened the folder once more, removing a few sheets of paper detailing a series of text messages between Rutherford and Amanda Laurent. He slapped them down in front of the witness.

"Read them." Rutherford's complexion deepened. With a shaky hand, he picked up the paper and began to scan the words. "Aloud."

"We were not having an affair!" the man yelled as he flung the papers down onto the stand. "I cared about Amanda, all right?! That's it! You are trying to pervert it!"

Alexandre pulled out a second copy of the text messages from the folder and began to recite them loudly:

"March 1st – 'Amanda, I love you. It's been a long time since I've felt this way. You make me feel young again.' March 3rd – 'Your body is so scrumptious. Oh, the things I will do to you!'" The jury begun to murmur amongst themselves. "'March 4th – 'My cock is so hard for you. I bet you're wet for me, too. March 5th – I got us a hotel room at the—"

"STOP IT!"

"I got us a hotel room at the Four Seasons… June 8th – 'Why haven't you come into work today?'… June 21st – 'Your husband called. Are you sleeping with him again? After everything I've done for you… June 22nd – 'You fucking bitch. I have sacrificed everything for you and you turn around and—"

"I SAID STOP IT!!!" The man rose from his seat, shaking his fist, full of rage.

That's it… Fall the fuck apart in front of all of these people. Unravel, come undone. I'm going for the homerun, baby. I can't afford for these simpletons to fall for the old man in love and good Samaritan bit, either. There's a lot of money on the line. I want your entire fucking savings. ATTEMPTED MURDER. We've got to make this shit official. Your fear was the truth getting out, that you've been fucking around on your wife with the help.

Rutherford pointed his finger at Laurent, Alexandre's client. "He was abusive to her! She was afraid!" the old man yelled, his voice trembling. His eyes bucked and his cheeks were now bloody red.

"No, you were afraid that you were going to lose access to that twenty-four year old woman! In fact, the day of the shooting was her last week working there. She'd put in her notice. You blamed Mr. Laurent for doing what men are supposed to do when they've lost someone they love, someone they've committed to – fight for her. You pulled out a gun and tried to kill this man!" He pointed to his client.

"No… No! He said he was gonna shoot me! I feared for my life!"

"The evidence shows otherwise. He had no gun on him when the ambulance and police arrived. You shot at him twice. You missed the first time, and the second went into his arm and now he cannot lift it, nor will he ever be able to again according to two different doctors, who've already submitted their medical reports."

"I didn't cheat on my wife!" Rutherford looked out into the audience, his eyes landing on his spouse. "That was just talk! We were just horsin' around. I never had sex with Amanda!" The woman's eyes were crimped at the edges, her lips downturned, and a mixture of confusion and hurt was etched on her ruddy face. Alexandre pulled out an envelope filled with receipts and dumped them onto the podium before the witness.

"Let's see here…" He picked one up from the pile. "Apparently you like to write off just about everything for your taxes, Mr. Rutherford. No worries, your secret is safe with me. We've got dinner receipts at Per Se on Colombia Circle. Funny, for cross reference, there is video footage of you and Mrs. Amanda Laurent entering the establishment on the exact same date! What a coincidence, don't ya think?! I don't know about you, but I would never spend that sort of money on someone I wasn't getting any honey from."

"Mr. Marseille! This is your final warning."

"I apologize, Judge Camus. My point is, there is more where this came from. Mr. Rutherford. My question is, 'Were you having an affair with Ms. Amanda Laurent?" He glared into the man's eyes… lulled him towards his trap, caught him in a snare.

Say it… say it… say it. Tell the truth. Tell the truth or your wife will leave you. Look at me, motherfucker. That's right, keep staring into my eyes. Your wife will divorce you if you lie. She'll take the rest of the money you have, find out about the accounts you think no one knows about. Tell the truth, Pinocchio. Tell it ALL. You were fucking

Amanda. You were taking Viagra and your wife thought it was for her, complained it wasn't working, but it worked all right... you were fucking that pretty young thing... spending all that money on her. And then, she took that sweet, tight pussy away and tossed it right back in her young, brawny husband's face. Get out of this while you can. You won't even serve much time, old timer. TELL. THE. FUCKING. TRUTH.

Rutherford's eyes glossed over and he slumped back down in his seat, looking utterly defeated. He said nothing for several seconds.

"Mr. Rutherford, can you please answer Mr. Marseille's inquiry?" Judge Camus questioned.

"Yes... Amanda and I were romantically involved."

The entire courtroom buzzed with raised voices and outbursts. The judge grabbed the gavel and slammed it.

"Order!"

"She told me that she wanted to get back together with her husband..." The man's eyes watered as he looked over at his wife, then at the jury. "I was upset about it. Her husband came into the store to take her out to lunch... and then... and then I just... I just lost it." He ran trembling fingers through his thin salt and pepper hair. "I reached for my gun and I shot him. I didn't mean it! I just... snapped!"

Several minutes later, Alexandre was standing beside his client, giving him a hearty handshake. Mr. Rutherford was being placed in handcuffs and the courtroom was abuzz. The local news was going to have a field day with this...

Old man with lucrative fur and leather business falls prey to some young beaver... It'll getcha every time.

Alexandre exited the courthouse, making his way to his car after seeing his client off. His cellphone rang, and he smiled. He opened his white BMW car door and slid inside before answering it.

"Venus... what can I do for you, my Love?" He turned on his stereo to hear the sounds of Jane Birkin and Serge Gainsbourg singing 'Je T'Aime, Moi Non Plus.'

"I am in between classes. I wanted to thank you for not making a big deal about me wanting to visit my friends yesterday. I needed the break," she said on a sigh.

"You're not a caged bird, baby. Besides, you've been doing quite well with your training. I trust you... well, to some degree." He smirked as he pulled out of his parking spot.

"You don't trust me at all." She chuckled.

"What would make you say that?" His brow rose in curiosity, though she was right.

"Because the night we met, at the party, you sliced into the back of my neck with your finger and it still hasn't fully gone away."

"Ahhh, yes, the tracking mark so you'd be easier to find in case you got any grand ideas of running away." He laughed. "After all of that time, I couldn't risk not finding you again, Venus. You were afraid of me. What did you expect me to do?"

"I want it removed. You have what you want... I'm not going anywhere. We're together, *willingly*. You know that I care about you."

"Yes, I know that you do." He deliberated over her words

for a spell. "I tell you what, I will remove it after our trip to Paris. Once you meet the few remaining members of my Coven, you may try to leave me. You think I'm a piece of work? You really haven't seen anything yet!"

She chuckled at that.

"How did court go today?"

"Fantastic! I got a full confession."

"Right there on the witness stand? Wonderful. Good!"

"Yes it is… That old man is going to pay me and my client quite well. Funny though, my client and his wife think they're smart… I've been on to them from day one."

"On to them? What do you mean?"

"Sweetheart, remember this if you never recall *anything* else I ever tell you. Question everything, and then question it again. My client and his wife set this guy up."

"What?!"

"Once the old, horny bastard showed interest in the wife, they realized they had a golden egg. I doubt they believed it would go this far, but she figured she could squeeze some money out of him, and she did… over $40,000 in gifts, loans that have never been paid back, trips, you name it. When she got tired of fucking him for the funds, she pulled out of the arrangement and the guy blew his top. Case. Fucking. Closed."

"You have got to be kidding me… and how did you figure this out?"

"I asked my client on our initial meeting about the case what his greatest fear was. His answer? 'Being broke…'"

Alexandre slowed his vehicle when he spotted a familiar man

standing in front of his car as he sat at a red light. The two locked eyes. He clutched his steering wheel hard and revved the engine. His fangs descended and sank into the flesh of his lower lip. "Baby, I have to go. There's some roadkill in the middle of the street." Before she could respond, he ended the call, then rolled down his window.

"Alexandre!" the man said with a roguish grin, his long white hair blowing in the wind. Two men joined the fucker by his side, seemingly coming out of nowhere. "Powerhouse attorney! Man on the move! And from what I hear now, vampire in love... So, are you just going to sit there, or will you invite your dear, younger brother Victor for a ride?"

CHAPTER NINE

Brothers and Buddies...

A LEXANDRE'S LIPS KINKED in a vexed smirk as he maneuvered his shiny white BMW over to the side of the busy road and parked it, ignoring the incessant honking and curses of passersby. Hopping out of his car, he locked it and approached his brother with his two rapscallion Turned Vampire slaves that stood on either side of him like a pair of broken-down French bookends. Slicking his hand into his jacket, he retrieved one of his favorite white and black striped cigars, brought it to his mouth, and lit it with his fingertip. Smoke eddied from his parted lips as his eyes hooded, regarding a motherfucker named Victor.

"Well, to what do I owe the pleasure of getting an impromptu visit from my one and only living sibling?"

"*Ne t'ai-je pas manqué?*" Victor chuckled. His platinum white hair fell past his shoulders, a deep contrast with his black leather trench coat. The man's dark violet eyes twinkled with evil… the kind they were both made of.

"Sure, I missed ya, little brother." Alexandre took another draw from his cigar and tapped the ashes onto the sidewalk. "Missed you as much as a lion misses an antelope."

"Ahhh!"

One of his brother's bookends screamed when Alexandre flung his coat open to shroud him as he jammed his fist all the way down the bastard's throat. The idiot's skin around his thin, pink lips split open on both sides, ripped apart. The man's struggles filled Alexandre with satisfaction.

"Let him go," Victor stated calmly.

"You know I can't do that, Victor. You came looking for trouble. Well, now you have it."

Victor's smile slipped away as he watched him pull the minion's throat muscle out from his body, and twist the tendon covered mass. When Alexandre released him, the weakling dropped to the ground like a heap of trash being thrown from a six-story window.

He could only imagine the extreme pain the fucker was in, and that pleased him to the point of laughter. Alexandre looked down at the man who was bleeding from the mouth, lying wild eyed, unable to talk and focus. People moved about along the sidewalk, barely paying them any attention. They carried on their way, probably assuming he was drunk or high, going through withdrawals. New Yorkers for ya…

"I am Count Alexandre Marseille." Alexandre spat on the man and sneered before tugging at his coat collar with bloodied hands. "Don't you *ever* stand that close to me again, acting as if you're going to do something… lay a hand on me!" he roared. "I am your king, and you stand here with my brother in defiance! Treason!"

He pointed to the other one who had now moved several steps away, but it was too late. He was not a forgiving Lord…

Alexandre narrowed his eyes on the coward and in a flash, he forced the vampire to glide close to him. The weakling tried to resist, but he had no power… it was far too easy.

"Scream, and I will murder you. Make even one noise, and I will cut your head off and shove it up your ass."

He grabbed the fucker by the gut and twisted the taut flesh, crushing the stomach muscles and intestines, causing the man to grit his teeth in pain. "I would disembowel you right here, right now for your lack of devotion; however, I need for you and your now voice-box-less friend here to return to Paris with the good news that Count Alexandre Marseille is alive and well."

He pushed the man down onto the concrete, walked around him, and opened his car door to get back in.

Victor glared at him. "Your time is up, big brother. We cannot use the old laws to rule the new nation and then make new ones only to fit our own agenda!"

"Isn't that called intelligence?" His brow arched. "Getting rid of what doesn't work and keeping what does?"

Victor grimaced and hissed, his already naturally flared nostrils elongated. "I heard she isn't a Pure Blood. I heard she will destroy the little we have left!"

"I have plenty and will gain more than New York's finest wolfing down donuts. You have practically nothing and will lose the little you possess if you ever pull something like this again."

"She's. Not. Fit!" Victor's eyes glowed with rage, and his pale flesh flushed in shades of blue.

"Whoever I chose as my mate is none of your fucking concern. My judgment is trusted for a reason. As far as everything else, unless you hear it directly from me, brother, it's only a rumor. I'll see you back in Paris soon. Until then, play nice or I will play dirty... actually, I won't be playing at all, but whatever the game is, I am certain to win."

Victor turned his back to walk away.

"Oh, one more thing before you fly away like the southern cockroach that you are... If you ever do this again, you know, try to bombard me and act as if I answer to you, I will kill you on the fucking spot, in front of the Coven and the Council. I will then go to our family mausoleum and dance on your grave. Perhaps the clouds will cry in your honor. Call me Gene Kelly, I'll be singin' in the motherfucking rain on that tomb. Rest in a millon bloody pieces." He winked at the bastard, slid into his car, and took off down Broadway...

WHISKEY SAT ACROSS the restaurant with a thick, charcoal gray skull cap pulled over one of his furrowed brows. His big muscles were wrapped around his wine sweater, not the other way around. He was a big brute of a man with warmth in his eyes. A black barbed wire tattoo surrounded the considerable circumference of his meaty neck.

Venus had had about enough of the man following her. He hadn't even tried to pretend he wasn't. The day before, his big ass was there, behind her, pushing a shopping cart full of shit she was certain he didn't need. He lurked around the university campus, even followed her to her old apartment where she went every now and again just to have a moment to think things through. Her mate's home was beautiful, but with all of the servants, grandiose décor and what not, at times it was simply too much.

She brought the martini glass to her lips and took a sip of the red liquor as she glanced briefly at her laptop screen. She looked up at him again, and the fucker had the nerve to smirk and wave.

That's it. I've had it.

"Whiskey!" she called out, slamming her computer closed. "Come here, please."

The big guy slid off the barstool and came to the booth

she was sitting in by herself inside the dimly lit eatery. He stood before her, his hands clasped over his gut. He would send chills down people's spines from the very sight of him. Whiskey was huge… tall and wide, like some brick wall.

"Why are you here?"

The guy grinned and twirled a toothpick in his twisted mouth as he looked leisurely to his left, then to his right. "I like uh good steak… nice bottle of wine. You know, the usual bullshit one says when they're babysittin', but *not* babysittin'."

"Sit down, please." She pointed to the seat across from her. He took his sweet time doing so, then folded his huge hands along the table. "Why does Alexandre have you following me?"

"For protection." He twirled the toothpick back and forth between his lips, like a pendulum.

"Protection from *what*?"

The man stopped playing with the little stick and glared at her.

"From yourself."

She glowered at him, not in the mood for riddles. "Look, Whiskey, I've got a lot of work to do. I am way behind because of the time I took off from work at my… I don't even know what to call him." She rolled her eyes.

"Your mate. He's your husband-to-be."

"Alexandre is his name, and that's what I'll call him."

The guy lazily rolled his eyes and shrugged. "Women are dramatic sometimes… whatever. You know what this is… he's your lover. Your man. Your king. And you are his queen."

She ignored the man and continued. "Alexandre has kept me tied up—"

"In more ways than one…" The guy grinned in a naughty sort of way, then chuckled as if the joke were hilarious… but it was true. The two had been fucking like jack rabbits. Alexandre was a beast in bed. He transformed pain into pleasure, and pleasure into pain… She craved him like opium; it was a matter of self-control, and at times, she struggled with it. "We can hear you two fucking every morning and night. Good for you." He applauded. "You make him happy."

She flopped back in the booth and crossed her arms over her breasts.

"What's your story?" The guy slid his knitted hat off and placed it on the table. "Come on, Whiskey," she pleaded. "I need help! I'm free, but also a prisoner… I'm lonely, but people are all around me. Alexandre has all of these individuals at my beck and call. He is spoiling me, but I'd rather have my questions answered and he spend time with me that doesn't include screwing and training. He has a one track mind!"

"He's taking care of you, and he's taking care of business. You'll just have to trust him."

The man's loyalty to the crazy king was unreal.

"I'm in love with an insane zealot and half the time I have no idea even where the hell he is! This isn't right. I'm trying to help Alexandre, Whiskey, but if he doesn't talk to me about everything, how can I? I need to know more about him so I can be the best mate for him. Help a sista out."

He looked at her through half-lidded eyes. She wasn't certain if she'd convinced him to give up the info or not—but she was leaning towards the negative.

"He's not insane…" the man said, drumming his fingers on the table. He glimpsed at the burning candle out the corner of his eye. Licking his fingers, he extinguished the flame with wet fingertips, then leaned forward, his eyes turned blood red. "Lord Alexandre Marseille is one of the smartest, most rational men I know," Whiskey began, looking down at his hands for a second, then back into her eyes. "He saved me. I was on the streets."

He stared at her as if trying to burrow within her very soul. Sorrow and pain swam in his brown, syrupy eyes. "Nobody wanted me… He took me in. He saw potential in me. He trained me. We became friends. He's the father I never had so when he says 'Jump!' I say, 'How fuckin' high?' Yeah, he's a control freak… he's a predator, but all of us are. You'd be like him too if you *ever* had to live one day of his life."

Her heart beat faster at his words. She turned away and raised her hand for a waiter to return and give her something to make it go down smoother.

"Hi, can I get another martini and… Whiskey, what do you want?"

"What type of whiskey do you want, ma'am?"

"Oh no, sorry." She chuckled. "That's my friend here's name."

The waiter nodded in understanding. Whiskey laughed a little, the first time she'd ever seen him do such a thing. He had a nice smile.

Whiskey was a Half Breed. He had the luxury of drinking blood and consuming food, and enjoy it as well. The flavors didn't nauseate or make him sick; he had the best of both worlds. Her jealousy of the man was born right then and there, but she respected and admired him all the same.

"A glass of Blue Moon beer would be cool, thanks."

The waiter disappeared with promises of bringing their drinks from the bar in no time at all. They sat there for a spell, neither of them saying a word.

"Whiskey, I'm in a strange predicament."

"What's that?"

"My entire life has been turned upside down. Things are happening that I never believed possible. First and foremost, I moved in with a man after knowing him for only a short while... totally not my style. But there was fear, promises were made, as well as an undeniable attraction and connection, regardless of how many times I tried to convince myself otherwise. I knew it from the first moment he whispered in my ear... my insides screamed. He felt so familiar, and I felt so frightened and safe, all at once. I'd seen him in one of my dreams! It didn't make sense." She took a deep breath. "Secondly, he is teaching me things, incredible things... not just fighting techniques, but information about my kind, our history, that I never knew."

"He's an excellent teacher."

She nodded in agreement.

"I realize now though, all of this time later..." She lowered her gaze for a moment. "That I am not who I thought I was!"

Her voice trembled. "Imagine thinking you are one way, only to discover it's only half true? It's devastating."

Their drinks came and Whiskey took his quickly, wrapped his thick lips around the rim of the bottle, and gulped down the liquid. His tan flesh flushed with color as the alcohol filled him.

At first, he seemed uncertain how to respond, then he said, "I think none of us are who we believe we are, Venus. I think, ya know," he said with a shrug, "we're always evolving."

"Yes, I suppose that's one way to look at it. Sorry to bombard you with all of this, but I have no one to talk to, Whiskey." She rubbed her head. "I can't talk to my friends at work, obviously. They'd have me committed in a mental hospital if I ever contemplated telling them what I *really* am and what I've been up to for the last 200 years. I have no family, my mistress is gone, I hop from place to place to place... I feel... I feel lost."

Something about Whiskey made her feel comfortable, like she could spill her guts with him. But the way he was looking at her had her second guessing her instincts about him.

"You can talk to your mate about it." He exhaled loudly as he looked down at her.

"No, I can't. Alexandre is full of secrets. I ask him something and if he believes I don't need the answer right then, he says I'll know in time. He keeps telling me I'm different, but I have no idea what that even means." Her eyes glazed over. She felt so unsure, so silly. "Sorry." She smiled nervously as she dabbed the napkin against the corner of her eye. She had so many emotions within her—secrets, lies…

"Nah." He waved her off. "It's all right. Look, Venus, I trust Marseille, okay? If he tells ya that he will tell ya what's going on when it's time, then trust that he will. Just do what he says and don't cause any trouble."

"But I can't be that way, Whiskey. That's not who I am." She shrugged. "If Alexandre says or does something I don't agree with, I tell him. I am not a 'yes' woman. No offense to you and the rest of his assistants and guards, but I just can't do that. Right is right, and wrong is wrong."

"Nah, rules are different in our world, Venus. See, the Count thinks you're playin' with your food." She looked at him curiously. "You talk about your friends ya can't talk to. Well, maybe they aren't really your friends then?" He threw up his hands. "Maybe you need to make new friends, all right? Humans, like my mother for one, are not on your level. I cared for my mother, don't get me wrong, rest 'er soul, but she couldn't understand things the way I could, the real way of the world. It went over her head, despite her havin' a sexual tryst with a vampire one day and gettin' pregnant with me. Now, I obviously have nothin' against mankind in general—my existence depended on it—but I can tell you this much, humans have treated me the worst outta anybody. I don't wanna be friends wit' them. Not now, not ever!" His eyes grew dark.

"I see you've been reading from a page in the Count's playbook." She grimaced and shook her head. "He's a bad influence on you, Whiskey. He's made you see this as all or

TIANA LAVEEN

nothing. Not *all* people are bad."

"He hasn't turned me against anyone. These are my own beliefs." He pointed to himself. "You're gonna have to learn the hard way if you're not careful. If you can't be yourself with someone, all the parts of you, how can you say that they're your friend? You have to pretend to be one of them, Venus, in order to be in their world. Can't ya see how fucked up that is? With Alexandre, you can be yourself! In his house, you can feed in plain view. You can do whatever the fuck you wanna do. You might be a smart cookie to the humans you teach." He pointed to her laptop. "But you've got a lot to learn, Venus. You're too trusting; you believe in the goodness of humanity and that's a fairytale. With the Count, he is true to himself. He doesn't give uh shit what anyone thinks about him. He's just doin' what he has to do. He didn't become king just because... trust me, he earned it."

"Earned it how, though? That's the problem. Killing all day and night! I know that I'm no saint. What I've done was a matter of survival. The cravings must be fed but my mate has donors and still stalks prey!" She rolled her eyes. "Look, I understand where you're coming from but to take pleasure in suckling from newborn babies and the elderly is going too far. Vampires are evolved and yet we hold on to this wicked way of life! We should be—"

"Lady, you gotta let this go. That good heart, give peace a chance bullshit ain't real! From what I know about your background, you of all people should know better!"

His words stung. She was suddenly flooded with images of

168

her racing about on the plantation, hating her life, hating the pale fleshed people who looked down upon her. He was right. She'd been tricked by her own delusions. These people didn't give a fuck about her. They hated her when she'd been a Black slave girl; they'd hate her if they found out she was a vampire. She'd been looking for love the entire time; perhaps the people she'd expected to provide it to her were incapable of doing so…

"You're wakin' up." He smirked. "Welcome back, baby. You've been a survivor and got caught up in the matrix, almost forgetting who you were. That Sunken Place is a bitch. Put the teacup down and listen to me, Beautiful." She blinked back angry tears. Pushing the laptop away, she took a taste of her drink. "Who's out here startin' the wars, huh? It's not us. Who's out here starvin' their own children, not givin' healthcare to the needy and takin' care of their Vets? We take care of our war heroes. We give honor to our seniors and we make a big ass production about our offspring drawin' their first breath.

"These motherfuckers can already be billionaires but they're so greedy, they want more and more and more, and for what?! It ain't us, Venus. It's *they* who are the monsters!" He pointed around the restaurant at all the humans sitting at the tables drinking, laughing, and messing around on their phones. "They're not civilized. They're fuckin' pests pretending to be superior! The government ain't nothin' but a bunch of vampires – suckin' off the workin' class and lyin' about it. These big corporations are vampires, too, payin' people pennies while the ones makin' minimum wage do all the hard work, and then all the big wigs gotta do is show up to a meetin' or two, cut their employees' bonuses in half, raise their own salaries, and go home to their mansions.

"Me and the entire fuckin' crew got money! Count is out for himself—it's his nature—but he keeps it real. He's smart enough to know that if he doesn't keep us satisfied and our pockets lined, we'd be more apt to turn on him, do somethin' messed up. It's all about loyalty. It's earned! Not one of us would dare speak outta turn against him 'cause he deserves our trust, so before you down him and put your human friends on some pedestal, know something…"

The man downed the rest of his beer and stood to his feet.

"He cares about ya, all right? He's done the impossible for you. So if there's something you don't like, he might not care right then to change it, but he'll remember what you said. You've got more pull and influence over him than you realize. You really think he searched all over this fuckin' city for you 'cause of some damn wizard's predictions when he was a kid? No… he wanted to experience the one thing humans had that his people don't: Love. He was driven to find this so-called soulmate of his, and once he saw you, he came home and told me about it. He looked me in the eye and smiled, and he said, 'I've found my Queen … *Ma Reine Du Sang.*' That was the day his life changed forever. A king ain't shit without his queen. Now, with you, he's complete."

He grabbed his skull cap, slid it back over his head, and turned to walk away.

"Whiskey!" she called out, getting to her feet. "Please! How do I talk to him? How do I break through the wall?"

The man stared at her for a spell.

"You show him that you're loyal. You pay attention to everything he tells ya and you learn from him. Then you'll become the teacher, and he'll be your student. He's not too proud to learn from you. In fact, you haven't heard this from me, but that's what he really wants…"

CHAPTER TEN

The Rules of Engagement

"**L**ET ME TASTE it." He skulked toward her, over the raspberry silk sheets of their bed, wagging his tongue. The sun was rising over the horizon, its beams filtering through the large arched window behind their bed, showcasing the city skyline.

"No." Venus grinned as she backed up from him, crawling in reverse, daring him to come chase her. "You've done nothing but talk shit about what I drink and eat. I'm not wasting my precious wine on you." She tilted the bottle to her lips and drank.

He lunged forward, but she moved out of his way just in time.

"You'll hate it."

"I've drank liquor before, wine too; just not that brand or

type before. Maybe it'll be different. Maybe this time it'll taste good."

"No. I kind of like it now, but it's an acquired taste. You're not man enough for it anyway," she teased, poking the bear.

Alexandre snatched the bottle of wine from her grasp, making it splash all over the damn sheets, and brought it to his lips. She chuckled as he gulped it hard, his Adam's apple moving up and down, the poor bastard wincing a few times along the way. He tossed the bottle onto the floor and vigorously shook his head like a dog fresh after a bath.

"It's fucking repulsive!" He grimaced and made all sorts of funny noises, acting as if he'd been poisoned. She chuckled at his antics, then paused. His beautiful naked body called her name.

"I warned you." She cooed when he wrapped his muscular arm around her waist and drew her in for a deep kiss. The sound of tearing fabric ensued as he destroyed her dark purple negligée, exposing her nude form. She shuddered when he leaned in close, sniffed her... then sniffed again.

"Mmmm, you're so wet for me, baby..."

In lightning speed, he turned her onto her stomach then buried his face between her ass cheeks. The heat of his mouth sent shivers up and down her spine.

"Venus, I have a confession... I'm hooked on your crack."

She squirmed against him and laughed when he dragged her up the bed towards the headboard like some brute, the tip of his wet, long, stealthy tongue gliding along the delicate crack of her ass. Her muscles tensed when she felt coolness along her flesh…

He was gone within the blink of an eye.

"Alexandre?"

She looked over her shoulder to catch a glimpse of him releasing the thick metal chains from the ceiling. It appeared many of the bedrooms in his estate had them. He grabbed her left ankle, then her wrist, shackling them both, and did the same on the other side until she was spread-eagled, swinging above the bed, face down, as if hang gliding. The chains sighed and rocked loudly, blending in with the sounds of Tank's 'Dirty', which played through the decadent space, with black and red candles burning all over the room. Dangling helplessly in lust, she moaned and bit into her lower lip when his big hands covered her breasts and squeezed.

Her eyes watered with anticipation. Wanting him… Needing him…

Trailing kisses down her spine, her shoulders, he delicately teased her feminine temple with his fingers while he positioned himself beneath her. As she swung and strained, he playfully flicked his tongue against her nipples like some viper vying for a taste.

Back and forth she swung, and he matched her movements, rocking his exceptional body to the beat of the music. Her hair hung down, some of the strands gliding against his chest. She groaned in ecstasy when he inserted his long, thick finger within her pussy, and then another, and another. He slipped them out just as leisurely, sucking her juices off his digits. Her thighs quaked, and the way he looked up at her stole her calm, turned her insides into lightning and torrential rain. Her fangs extended as she eyed his large dick, which pulsed right before her eyes with a life of its own.

"Mine… give me the dick that belongs to me." She hissed, her desires for him making her love struck and lust sick.

The man floated closer, his body now lifted off the bed, until he was directly beneath her facing backwards, their bodies caressing one another like black and white feathers floating past each other. The chains swayed faster as he disappeared between her legs. Holding her hips steady, his fangs and tongue gliding against her pussy, he played with her, tortured her so.

"Shit!" She hissed when he bit tenderly along her inner thigh, over and over, each bite more painful than the last. He returned to her saturated zone, licking and sucking her pussy as if it were his last meal. He made a loud mess of it; wet noises filled the room as she melted against his oral embrace. His cock was deliciously close to her face now… she simply couldn't resist. She took hold of the thick shaft with both hands while he ate her pussy, and took him into her mouth, devouring his nature, claiming her throne. Precum and saliva mixed together as she savored her mate, unable to get enough of the way his cock felt and tasted.

She ran her fingers along his large balls, massaging and caressing them, then sucked hard on the tip, giving the throbbing head special attention. She paused and hissed when his tongue snaked within her pussy, wiggling and shaking inside her nature like a fresh, battery powered sex toy.

He pulled her impossibly closer, his muscular hips compressing and relaxing while he fucked her open mouth. The chains rattled as they swung back and forth, their bodies swaying like ribbons in the wind. Like pendulums marking time that now stood still. Suspended. She took him further down her throat, gagging on the monster between his legs.

His loud moans made her pussy cream with anticipation and appreciation until she came against his roving lips, raining down her nectar. He slurped up her moisture, licked every drop that trailed between her sticky thighs. When she calmed, he slipped away stealthily, and she clenched her teeth when the weight of his body rested against her back. Swinging back and forth, the chains bore their combined weight as he guided himself inside her. Her hair blew in the air as they rocked, and her body convulsed when he started to pump hard and fiercely within her, his chin resting on her shoulder. He pounded her pussy with ruthless determination.

"I will have you multiple fucking times a day… just like I promised. You will be beautifully abused, my Love. Your pussy is mine… It's raw and dripping. Your body is beaten and exhausted, and I don't care. I want what I want, and that's you. I will have you whenever and wherever I want you, even when you can't take it anymore. You'll cum all day long; your pleasure is my duty."

Her body shook as she had another orgasm, overcome by his words and the feel of his long, fat dick working overtime within her hot canal. He brought his mouth to the side of her face and she turned her head toward his. His fangs glistened;

blood tinged the side of his mouth from when he'd bitten her thighs. "You think you can handle me now, my sweet, nasty *ma Reine Du Sang?*"

She narrowed her eyes on him, gnashed her teeth, then chomped the air… trying to get a piece of him.

"You're the one who can't handle me, *mon Roi Du Sang…* Ahhh!" Her body swayed hard when he fucked her fast, becoming a mere blur. He went in so deep within her, she could feel the bastard in her gut and her body cried out in complete indulgence.

Soaked with sweat and desire, he unceremoniously released her, forcing her to fall clumsily onto the bed. The restraints clanked together when she was set free. Never did she feel enslaved by him… helplessly captive. She felt liberated, more than she ever had, free to be her true, original self. He fell down alongside her, but like an angry cat set on revenge, she pounced on top of him, grabbed his dick, and slid her slippery valley onto it, riding him hard and ruthlessly. She bore her fangs and dug her nails deep into his chest, raking them down and drawing trails of blood. He rose and met her movements with his own brand of merciless, pounding thrusts—delivering them with apt and violent precision, the maniac making her lose her breath.

Spirals of her hair tumbled before her eyes, blinding her, as the stickiness of their bodies, the scent of their sex, and their nasty words lay thick in the air. He gripped her throat, a tense expression on his rigid face. Lips parted, gritted teeth, he jammed his dick within her as she rode him, killing her cunt with his cock, each harsh stab at a time.

"Cum!" he ordered as he traced her clit with his free hand, delivering perfect strokes with his finger, like the pianist that he was.

"No." She balked, refusing to give him what he wanted.

He smirked at her dismissal, seemingly pleased with her refusal to follow the rules and play fair.

"You'll cum… whether you want to or not." He stroked her faster and lifted his ass off the bed, pumping within her with ruthless abandon. Their bodies knocked against each other, louder than the chains that previously kept her in control. She struggled to keep her orgasm at bay, fought to not give him his desires… She wanted to play with him a bit longer but then her body betrayed her…

She hated the smile that broke across his face.

Her pussy showered him with honey, her legs shaking as she had a full body orgasm, losing complete control. As she closed her eyes, she felt the heat of his mouth around her erect nipples. She screamed from the piercing, delicious pain of his sharp fangs sinking into her breasts, then sighed at the soft, delicate kisses that soon followed. Moments later, he had her face pressed hard into the pillow as he wrecked her body, her swollen pussy a prisoner to the hungry beast between his legs. The monster never let up… never grew tired. He'd been right—she'd never had a lover like him.

She shuddered when the warm gush of his climax flooded her. He bellowed loudly as he came. Holding tight to her hips, he forced the last of himself within her. He collapsed against her body, almost cutting off her air supply with the weight of him. Rolling off her, he gazed at the ceiling of his bedroom, his expression content, his chest rising and falling. The sunlight now beamed across his striking, ghostly white face.

He lit a cigar, and his deep voice drifted like a lullaby to her ears…

"When I was a youth, my parents taught me many things, Venus. Both of them are gone now. My mother died in battle; my father was attacked by our enemies. He died fighting, as well. Right before their passing, I went through a period of confusion… feeling lost… trying to understand the world in which I lived. One day, I met a human boy in the woods." Her eyes widened. "He was wounded, had fallen and was badly hurt.

"Instead of feasting upon him—he would've been easy prey, naturally—I felt badly for him for some strange reason. Perhaps because we appeared to be similar in age, and I helped him out of the trap he'd gotten caught in. I didn't know any better, Venus. I was too young, too naïve… I ignored every-thing my parents had taught me in that moment. My brother Victor and I never really got along. We only tolerated one another and my other siblings were in training, just as we had been as small children. So, I clung to this boy… my new friend. One day, after we'd been doing what boys do for a long while, playing with sticks, jumping in the ocean and fishing, I told him what I was."

His lips curled in a hideous, evil smile. She knew now, that was his way to hide trauma, true unadulterated pain. She caressed his neck, leaned in close, and licked the side of his face as she reached for his hand and squeezed it.

"He never met me in the woods again after that. I could handle that. It was fine. But what happened afterward was not."

"What happened?"

"The fires... men with guns and lit torches showed up, bombarded us and burned our lair down. They grabbed many of the women in my family, stripped them naked, and then burned them alive. They shot several of the men and sliced some up with swords, claiming we were all witches... because of what the boy had gone back and said. I never told my parents the role I'd played in that massacre, how I'd inadvertently invited this mayhem into our lives... but they knew. They looked at me, and they definitely knew. My family went the following night, prepared this time, and killed all of those men and women who'd caused so much pain and loss to my family. And then they killed the boy who'd been my friend, too. I never trusted humans again after that, my Love."

He brought her hand to his mouth and laid a gentle kiss on it. Time passed with them lying in silence and she ached for him again. Perhaps it was her way of trying to wash his pain away, make him forget all about his tortuous past. Before she could mount him, he disappeared from her sight, soon returning with a single black rose. He handed it to her, opening the petals just so, and ordered her to look down into it.

In the center of it sat a blood red jewel, pulsing and glowing. Her heart pounded in her chest when he slid the ring along her finger.

"Today is the first day that I've ever trusted again, Venus. I understand that you will always need a part of your past to hold onto, regardless of what I think about it. I accept you as you are. I… love you, deeply. I have no desire to change you, simply to prepare you, to make sure you're equipped to defend yourself should trouble arise, as well as the throne. I feel now that you can."

She leaned down, joyous tears in her eyes, and kissed his soft, succulent lips. He gripped the back of her head and kissed her in return until, before long, he was back inside her, shaking the bed with his timely strokes. Fingers clutched, sweat and swear words abounding, they made love endlessly. The sun set, and he carried on, fucking her beautifully, making her believe him, trust him, love him, well into the night…

CHAPTER ELEVEN

It Feels Good to be King

B ENEATH THE MONTPARNASSE, Paris cemetery existed a series of elaborate tunnels dating back to the 12th century. The walls were lined with gold, the floors created from the crushed and discarded bones of those who'd given their lives for a blood sucker of Imperial heritage to be fed. This was Royal Headquarters, a lengthy network of homes that had at one time housed over 2,000 vampires in the Royal Family, the Marseille Clan. It was sacred ground, and still not easily accessible, barely known about to outsiders.

It was cold and abandoned now; most of the remaining members and their offspring lived above ground in modern day, blending in with society like ferns and trotting foxes. The bloodline had weakened—an embarrassment for certain. They worked as merchants, bankers, teachers… some were even in the entertainment industry, accused of such things as being a part of some trumped up bullshit the humans referred to as the 'Illuminati.'

A feeling of melancholy consumed Victor at the sight of a fine, set dining room table that had remained untouched for ages. Golden goblets sat layered in dust, empty bowls devoid of blood at each setting… He raised his arms in the air and spun around, taking inventory of an image of his childhood, the memories soaked in days gone by.

"This was supposed to flourish! We were the warrior Royals! We were the fiercest clan to ever rule, not only in France, but Europe, period! It all went terribly wrong… We should have never trusted anyone else. As soon as we let our guard down, our walls crumbled, our families were decimated. My eldest brother, King Alexandre Marseille, was supposed to be here ruling France! We still have a stake in all this, and he is pissing it away.

"Instead of leading the flock, he abandoned those that depend upon him the most. Many years ago, he took off on a voyage to the States, one he told none of us about, stating it was for the betterment of our kind. He promised to rule from a distance, and he did at first, but then he became distracted." His slaves moved about quietly, listening, not daring to interrupt. "My brother, though was always quite secretive ... I trusted his judgment. The problem was, he never quite trusted *mine...*"

Victor's eyes narrowed as he spotted an old, torn white cape... similar to the one their father used to wear during important ceremonies. He made his way to it, ran his fingers along the thick fabric, and shook his head. Memories accosted his mind, taking over.

"Perhaps my brother knew my true intentions. I was helpless against my true nature... just as he is. He was born to build, I was born to destroy anything and everything that threatened the throne. We were to work in tandem." Victor picked up a black sword from the middle of the floor and dusted it off against his black and crimson cape. It glowed bright, and he smiled when he couldn't see his reflection in it. "Quality, pure dark silver."

He marched out of the desolate space and made his way above ground, he and his men trudging up twenty flights of steps to one of the many locked and bolted exits. Flinging it open, he shielded his face, the sudden sunlight blinding him. He stood there for a spell, adjusting to the harsh sunrays, then pulled himself the rest of the way out. He then sent his slaves away to their home. For this next journey, he wished to be on his own.

His driver pulled up to take him to the train station for his trip to Carcassonne, a hilltop town in the Languedoc area of Southern France, infamous for its medieval sanctuary, La Cité, a structure with plentiful watchtowers and fortifications. It was also the site where the Council resided. Where the laws were upheld and judgments were made. It was time they became enlightened about the king's comings and goings. He got comfortable in the back of the vehicle, clutching a flask full of warm blood.

My brother has an amazing way of making everyone feel comfortable, right before the kill. He keeps his true dealings in the dark, holding tight to their ignorance... he banks on it. Alexandre Marseille makes his decisions from afar, signing contracts and papers, pretending everything is under control. I am second in command, and yet he tells me nothing; he makes decisions without consulting me... and now he's gone too far... in New York City, promising over thousands of years of royalty, power, honor and prestige to a Turned Slave Bitch!

He spit out the window, his fangs descending as he hissed, his hair flying in his face. A violent surge of energy rose within him.

He has no honor, no sense of tradition... trying to turn a servant into a queen. How ridiculous!

My brother was born on a full moon. Deception and animalistic behavior consumes him, like the malodorous wolves we've had to battle from time to time. But I am not fooled... You have gotten your hands on a precocious Turned Vamp. She would be the first non-Pure-Blood to become Queen, La Reine Du Sang, and I cannot allow that. We're pure, and that's how we'll remain.

He leaned in the back seat, fist on knee, and seethed. His cellphone rang.

"Bonjour..."

"Hello, Victor. I am calling you back per your request."

"*As-tu des informations…?*"

"Yes, I do have new news. The Count has agreed to meet with me about the situation. He proved a bit, shall we say, testy when I approached him previously about the matter, but he appears to be in better spirits as of late, so I will try my hand at it." They'd had a previous video chat that he much enjoyed once the female in his brother's camp alerted him of her concerns regarding his dear brother. She was a fine specimen indeed.

"Perhaps you shouldn't, Fawn. You see, your beauty and intelligence are a rarity in this day and age, but it appears my brother is blinded by an idea that should have been abandoned centuries ago. I think we'll need someone with a bit of a, shall I say, bigger influence in the fight?"

"What do you suggest? That I contact the Coven directly?"

"They are enamored with him, it would be useless. I have a better idea. My brother has a few close associates, I understand, one of whom is named Divo Bianchi, goes by Whiskey. Trained him himself. Are you familiar with this man? The big Half-Breed that he entrusts with everything?" He smirked, already knowing the answer.

"Yes," the woman stated dryly. "With all due respect, I am not sure that's a good plan. Whiskey is, shall I say, not very refined, Victor. He's a bit of an idiot, really. I think that—"

"No. I want Whiskey. Convince that man to talk my brother out of going forward with marrying her. It will be a disaster if this isn't stopped."

"Why don't we just kill her?"

He smiled at her words. "Because my brother would blame you, me, and everyone in his midst, which I don't too much care about either way, but it's the aftermath of that which would wreak havoc with my peace of mind. You see, Alexandre is notorious for engaging in unbelievable acts of revenge, Fawn. He's like our mother…" He took a deep breath. "He will slaughter five hundred people just to eradicate one. He's a walking timebomb. I prefer to use a bit more strategic planning for this event. Killing her will be our last resort, but it's not completely out of the question."

"May I ask you a question, Victor?"

"You may ask." He chuckled. "I may choose to not answer. Try me."

"Is your issue with Venus regarding the fact she is a Turned? Or is it her character? Maybe something else altogether. Honestly, if you ask me, her beauty is rather average." The woman's jealousy was so thick, it rivaled a brick. "Alexandre deems her as special for some reason, somehow different. I don't see it." She laughed. "In fact, she would be classified as bottom of the line. I can't blame her though, she obviously wishes to have a Cinderella story."

And so do you…

"I think Turned Vamps are equals." He grinned as he ran his finger down his cheek and contemplated. "It's this *particular* Turned Vamp that is the problem, Fawn… one that is completely unsuitable. You, my dear, come from good lineage. Your education is impeccable. I understand that you fell on hard times at one point in time and had to work at a tavern as well as danced, but you found your way out of that rather quickly. I believe with proper training you'd be an exceptional fighter, as all Queens should be and you'd provide fine offspring."

He could practically see her grin on the other end of the phone. Damn it, her witlessness was entertaining and delightful. She'd make such a nice toy. Too bad she was so far away… an excellent sex slave at the very least.

There was a long pause.

"I will see what I can do."

"No. You will *not* see what you can do. You will *do* it, and you will be successful or our arrangement is off the fucking table."

He ended the call. Outside, as they drove on, the trees turned into branchy, gray blurs. His lips curled in a smile as he imagined the Council's response once they were alerted of Alexandre's latest conquest…

This is your last chance to turn this around, Alexandre, but we both know you won't. In fact, I'm banking on it. From my end, it will appear as if I was fair and forgiving, wanting what was best for my brother, my Lord, my King. I have to do this, however. I must give the appearance that you've been provided plenty of opportunities to get your shit together. I came by to speak to you in person in New York and you assaulted my men. Now I have alerted your team to run an intervention, to make you come to your senses by any means necessary, and we know what the outcome of that will be—you'll scoff, you'll fight, you'll dare anyone to speak against you. Perhaps some heads will roll even, literally. You'll be proven unfit. Finally. You'll dig your heels in as you always do, and then, you will be stripped of your title and put down like a mangy dog with rabies… and I will settle into my rightful place…

Lord of France… King Victor Marseille has a nice bloody ring to it…

I NEVER LIKED this bitch…

Whiskey stood outside the office building where his boss was speaking privately with a new client. It was two in the afternoon, and he'd just finished a large lunch of crispy fried fish, hot sauce soaked French fries and a blood smoothie that passed as beets and wheatgrass. He people watched, enjoying the fresh air. The Count had had a busy day and warned he'd be working late, but Whiskey didn't mind hanging around. Besides, he could always go to the back of the building and get his dick sucked by a Vamp while watching his boss with an eagle eye.

"Gotta prioritize," he said with a grin. The woman he loved to hate drew closer. He was hoping she'd turn down another street, but instead, she kept her trek steady, gunning right for him. "Maybe she's just going inside…"

"I need to speak to you, Whiskey."

Fawn wore a short plaid skirt, showing off her long, snow-white legs and feet clad in a pair of six-inch stiletto heels. He crossed his arms over his chest and twirled the toothpick around in his mouth.

"I'm not eatin' your pussy again today." He smirked.

The bitch was a good lay, that was for sure, but lately she'd gotten lazy and came to him for tongue lashings, then ran off before returning the favor. Selfish cunt. Besides that, he couldn't stand her. He hated her voice, the way she moved. He hated practically every damn thing about her. She was a convenient fuck every now and again, usually when he was intoxicated, though he had others he much preferred. Fawn rolled her eyes and sucked her teeth.

"I'm not here for that!" she said between gritted teeth. "Look, we need to talk. You and I both know—" She paused to stare at the closed door behind him that led into the opulent Law Offices of Alexandre Marseille. "We both know there's a situation that needs to be discussed. We need to help Alexandre."

"Help Alexandre with what?"

"Step over here with me, please."

"What? Afraid of the boss' bat ears? He can hear ya thoughts before you even think 'em," he teased... well, only partially. Count Marseille's hearing was unreal.

"I just need two minutes, Whiskey." The woman didn't wait for an answer. She entered the building and pointed to a sitting area decorated with modern wooden furniture and white, fluffy furs draped across the sofas. Christina Perri's, 'Human' played in low volume as he walked to one of the couches and sat down. Fawn sat across from him and clasped her hands, then crossed her shapely legs and smiled.

It was the fakest thing he'd seen in weeks.

Whore. Cunt. Bitch. Tramp.

"How much do you care about Alexandre?" He grimaced and sighed, rolling his eyes in the process. "All right." She put up her hand. "Fine. I'll just get to it. Look, Venus is trouble, okay? She's bad news."

"Are you sure you're not talkin' about yourself?"

"This is serious, Whiskey."

"Okay. Why do you say that?"

"For starters, she's not on Alexandre's level."

"And *you* are?" The vixen twitched about in her seat. "I don't have time for this shit." He yawned and stood to his feet. "When you have a *real* reason that I need to jump in and fetch, you let me know."

"There's money involved and you will finally be put in a position you deserve! Don't you hate being his lap dog?! Jesus!" She stood, too. "You just used the word 'fetch', for God's sake! Grow some fucking balls, Whiskey. Be a man!" He rubbed along his chin. "You and Bruce are treated like Venus in her pre-turned life! Slaves!"

"I'm not treated like Venus. He's not fuckin' me... he's not turnin' me into his Queen," he teased as he batted his eyelashes in a girly way. The woman hissed. "All right, what type of money are we talkin'?" He crossed his arms over his chest and rocked back on his heels.

"Millions."

He swallowed. "And what do you want me to do to get it?"

"Get him away from Venus. Get her completely out of the picture."

"Kill her? Have you lost your fucking mind? Do you have any damn idea what he'd do to anyone that touched a fuckin' hair on her head?"

"No, there are other ways."

"You're crazy." He cracked his knuckles. "No one can do that. They're all into one another now."

"Oh yes you can, I have faith in you. Alexandre listens to you, Whiskey. He *trusts* you. Work on him. Slowly. There's something I've noticed over this time that they've been together, something I've never seen him exhibit before."

"And what's that? Less time fuckin' around with the likes of you? In fact, I bet he hasn't even let you kiss his hairy ass since he took her to his bedroom and set up shop. That must eat cha up inside, huh?" He swished the toothpick to the other side of his mouth and chewed on it some more before spitting it out onto the nearby table.

"I don't give two fucks about who he is sleeping with. If I wanted to fuck him again right now, I could. That is beside the point. You have to use the man's weakness, Whiskey."

"He doesn't have many."

"That's true, but he's *extremely* jealous when it comes to her. Why do you think he has you chasing behind her all the time? He's insecure when it comes to Venus… doesn't want her even *looking* at another man."

Whiskey ran his tongue along the inside of his mouth, tasting the lingering flavor of the tangy blood he'd consumed earlier.

"You've got it all figured out, huh?"

"Yes, because I care about him so much, Whiskey." Her sad expression was almost believable. "Alexandre is brilliant! I don't want to see that all go to waste. A true friend sometimes does things they don't want to do… for the greater good."

Her lips curled in a slight smile. Sickening.

"So what's your plan?"

"Tell him you've seen Venus with others. He'll believe you. You watch her, you follow her, act like you're all broken up about it, you know, devastated to have to tell him that the love of his life is still out in the streets fucking random cock for her feeds. Be detailed… describe the dicks plunging down her throat, the way her pussy gaped open from the multiple fucking, all taking her at once… tear him up inside. You know what to do." She smiled as her eyes grew dark. She lessened the gap between them and looked up into his eyes. Taking his black shirt collar into her hands, she gripped it tight, coiling it around her nimble, long fingers. "You can finally be free, Whiskey…" she whispered before pressing her lips to his.

"I owe him, Fawn."

"We're not faithful, you fucking idiot!" She stepped back from him, fire in her eyes. "We're not fucking wolves! There is no pack." She waved her arms about. "Each and every vampire is out for himself and if you think the Count wouldn't throw you under the bus for someone he deems more efficient, then you are a fool! We're all expendable to him. You're not special, and neither is *she*!"

He mulled her words. "All right, you've made your point. I'll talk to him."

The woman's features relaxed and she sported a pleased smile.

"Good, glad to hear it." She turned to walk away. "Do it soon, though. We're on a tight deadline."

"How much money, Fawn? I want an exact fuckin' figure if you expect me to put my neck on the line like this." He jammed his hand into his pants pocket.

"$3,000,000… enough for you to start fresh on your own, and never have to answer to anyone again."

"And where are you gonna get it from? I mean shit, he pays well, but not *that* well."

She slipped her purse over her shoulder.

"Don't you worry about that. I'll handle it." She winked before sauntering away.

Whiskey slumped back down onto the wooden couch, while the sounds of Daniel Powter crooning 'Bad Day' played through the speakers. He had to burst out laughing at that.

"Isn't that the fuckin' understatement of the year…"

CHAPTER TWELVE

Farewells and Bombshells

IT HAD BECOME increasingly harder for Venus to keep her secret under lock and key. Her friends insisted on information, and they demanded answers to the point that they could no longer be ignored.

'Where the hell have you been?'

'Did you move in with that guy from the party?'

'Someone said he's a cutthroat attorney. Is it true?'

She decided to invite the ladies out for a weekend lunch. For Camille and Deborah, it would be a typical girls' day, a routine good time. But for Venus, it would be a cruel goodbye...

Over the past few weeks, she'd come to the difficult decision, one of the hardest of her life. It was time to come completely into her own and take Whiskey's wise words, that he'd said to her weeks prior, to heart... though she didn't for one second believe that Camille and Deborah were evil incarnate. No, her motivations were a bit more complicated than that. These women needed protection.

She didn't want them involved in this mess. There were consequences to being a Queen to a man like Alexandre Marseille. Anything and anyone she cared about could be in the crossfire should things go awry. Her lover had never admitted to her that anyone in her circle was in danger, but she could read between the lines. He expected her to use common sense. He'd never told her outright how to move, what to do, and how to think. He expected her to figure it out on her own and this was no different. It was best not to have anyone she cared for too close, someone who could be used and abused for blackmail, threatened, or taken apart, limb by fucking limb.

She tossed on a big smile when she spotted her girlfriends walking into Russ and Daughter's Café on Orchard Street to join her. She'd already secured their table, and the bustling place was filling up fast. It was one of Camille's favorite spots to get authentic Kosher comfort food. She had to admit, the fare wasn't half bad. The hell with the fact that Venus would be vomiting it up soon thereafter, she was now used to that being part of her eating process—a minor hiccup. They sat down beside her at the table, both with sparkles in their eyes, no doubt ready to get the dirt on her new life. After engaging in a bit of small talk, discussing the weather, the new professor who always wore galoshes, things of that nature, they all ordered their food.

She took small sips of her water. "All right, I know I was

out sick last week and we've barely talked."

"What's going on, Venus? You haven't called us back. I've personally left numerous voicemails," Deborah chastised, her expression a mixture of irritation and true concern. "Did you move out? I stopped by. Your neighbor said you were gone."

Venus took another sip of her drink and put her cellphone face down.

"I am in a relationship." She didn't miss how Camille's eyes landed on her ring. "My boyfriend's name is Alexandre Marseille…" Her lips curled in a grin. "I moved in with him, and we're together…living together, that is."

Camille gasped, slapped the table, then burst out laughing.

"Ms. Impulsive suddenly?! Oh my God!" The woman tossed her head back and cackled. "I could time a clock to your actions. This is soooo not you, lady! You've got to tell us, Venus. What brought this on?"

"I met the one." She shrugged. "What can I say?" She tried to curtail her smile to no avail. It was true… of course there were details they'd never understand, ones she wouldn't dare mention, but that was the damn gist of it.

"So, when do we get to meet him? I mean, yeah, we saw him at the party but—"

"Who *didn't* see him?" Deborah chuckled, the woman's cheeks reddened as her eyes sparkled with mirth. "He was quite attractive. Lucky you, Venus."

"Yeah, I imagine many noticed him. I, uh, I think we can all meet up soon." She swallowed down the lie.

"Well, I can't wait to talk to him. I wonder whose friend he was? Who invited him to the party? I asked Yashek and he said he thought I had invited him." She shrugged. "I asked Norman, too. He was clueless."

"Well, there were so many people there, he could've been anyone's friend," Deborah added. "So, whose friend was he?" Both of her friends looked at her, waiting…

"Uh, he said a friend of his, Tom, invited him."

"Tom who?" Camille picked up her coffee and took a sip.

"Brady." SHIT! It was the first thing that popped into her mind… How silly!

"He's friends with Tom Brady?!" The two women burst out laughing. "Doesn't he play for the New England Patriots? What was he doing in town, for a little party at that?"

"Not *that* Tom Brady. This guy is an attorney… just like Alexandre."

The conversation went on and on, and Whiskey's words continued to haunt her. The lies, the made up tales, all to cover a story that should've been easy to relay, one she wasn't ashamed of at all. But these women were not from her life; they were not even from her world. She sat back for a spell as the two talked and laughed amongst themselves…

They have no idea what I've been through, my struggles, my true joys… This is all superficial. This stuff isn't real. Yeah, my concern for them is, but Whiskey was right… I have to be like them for them to TRULY like me, accept me. Who is standing around wanting to be more like ME, so I can accept THEM?! No one…

She'd seen the devastation of a nation. She'd survived several wars, the Great Depression, and more. So many things her mistress had prophesized had come to pass... Crack addiction in the 1980s, one of hundreds of examples... She recalled not being able to drink from the same water fountain as White people in the 1940s, '50s, and part of the '60s. She remembered dancing in Europe and meeting Josephine Baker... She'd been practically around the world and seen things most would never dream imaginable. This was her life, a special life, a hard life, a miserable life, a rich life, a poor life, an incredible life.

"Well, if you can clone him, do so," Deborah teased.

"I know, right? Did you see how damn tall he was?!" Venus sat back and watched her friends continue to talk amongst each other, the two falling into their own private world that she was a mere spectator to.

"Are you kidding me? The first thing I noticed was his height... and those eyes. Wow. What is he, a Viking?" Deborah joked.

"His last name is Marseille. That's French," Camille interjected, leaning back in her seat and crossing her legs. The two locked eyes. Camille's smile slowly faded... as if she knew something was up, that everything wasn't as it seemed. Venus grew warm with self-consciousness, and the looming death of her love for these women hung over her head like a black cloud...

Despite it all, some things were just undeniable. They'd been there for her, welcomed her into their fold. She could not dance in two worlds the way she had been any longer though. Things were more complicated now, far more problematic.

Their entrées arrived. She'd ordered some lox and bagels, cream cheese on the side. It looked absolutely delicious but her stomach churned, and a need to vomit came in hard, violent waves. It wasn't the food that disgusted her, but the friendship funeral she was now in the midst of, front and center...

At that moment, she realized something. Venus wasn't choosing Alexandre over her friends; she was choosing her freedom over them... and what a price to pay.

The three drank and ate, and the place was abuzz. Venus laughed so hard, her face was hot. She shared stories, opening up as much as she could, for she knew, this was it... the final countdown.

Next week, I am going to turn in my resignation letter to the college...

One day soon, neither of these women will see me again. My phone number will be different, my last known address will be changed... I will be untraceable. I have done an amazing job of divorcing myself from my emotions, just as my mistress and mate have tried to instill in me. But if that's the case, if I have turned off those human responses to pain, then why does this hurt like hell?!

REDMAN'S, 'I'LL BE DAT' blasted in the Darkness Club as

Alexandre sat back in the VIP section of the bar and dance lounge. Sitting comfortably with his legs open, his arms resting across the back of the black leather booth, he took in the sights. Naked Vamps twirled and twisted their beautiful bodies all around him, their mouths gleaming with blood, their pussies glistening with girl juice. Smooth flesh was all around him, women with long purple ponytails, redheads with humongous, natural breasts—a wonderful buffet of female energy.

He brought his cigar to his lips, tilted his head, and laughed. In the distance, he could see Bruce and Whiskey, and the rest of the crew, too. The dizzying red lights spun around them as his boys drew closer, Whiskey leading the pack. Alexandre waved his arm, a signal for the wet pussy all around him to scatter and get lost.

The four guys flopped down around him, all of them smelling like weed, cigarettes, and alcohol. It had been a rough two weeks... but all one could do was smile to keep from screaming.

Whiskey twirled the toothpick in his mouth, his eyes hooded as he smirked.

"You've been gone several days. Usually I'd say no news is good news, but when it comes to my brother, not so much. How'd it go?" Alexandre blew out smoke from the corner of his mouth as he stared at the man.

"I know I'm not in any position to ask you shit, Count Marseille, but I gotta... just this fuckin' once."

"Excuse us." He waved the other guys away, picked up a

glass of wine, and took a taste. "What is it?"

"Why in the tabernacle tambourine Holy Ghost Hell did ya let Fawn get this fuckin' close to ya, huh?! Do you have *any* idea the shit she's been up to? The trouble she's caused? Maaaaan!" The big beast balled up his fist. "I warned you about that fuckin' bitch!" Whiskey's voice rose, something Alexandre rarely witnessed from the guy.

He shook his head, then burst out laughing. "Whiiiskey, Whiskey, Whiskey... I can answer you in so many different ways. I will do it like this... Here's my question to you: Do you know what a fucking house cat does?" The man's expression turned curious. "I'll tell you. It slinks around barely able to be heard. It meows, fucks in alleyways, drinks milk from a bowl on the fucking floor, devours fish, and licks its own fur and ass. It's domesticated, comfortable with itself, and believes itself superior to others, unlike its wild ancestors in the jungles and deserts.

"You know what to expect from a fucking cat... we've known, since our vampire ancestors in Egypt worshipped them, that they were magnificent, self-important creatures. But there's a dark side... there's always a dark side, Whiskey. You must anticipate some fuckin' claws, some begging, some hissing and absolutely no loyalty. So, you ask me, why did I allow Fawn to make moves? I was playing chess. She was playing checkers."

Whiskey's lips curled in an understanding grin.

"When you know your opponent, it's much easier to manipulate them, make them do your bidding when they have no idea that their treachery has aided you, not harmed you. I like knowing *exactly* what to expect. I set her up to fail. If someone is going to use a weapon against me, I prefer to be the one that designed that missile... so that I know how to dismantle it, then destroy it when it's aimed right at my face. That chosen weapon was Fawn. She is my strongest chess piece, but also my weakest link. I gave her just enough information about my private life to do what she needed to do. I am controlling my own destiny. I'm about to embark on the fight of my life, Whiskey. My brother is not small potatoes. He's my biggest opponent. Victor is emotionally and mentally unbalanced, a fucking nutcase, but quite intelligent. He's brilliant, actually. But because of his true nature, an insatiable need for power, he didn't dig deeper. He was in too much of a hurry. This time he made a fatal mistake... trusting a cat, who was hired by a dog. WOOF."

Whiskey burst out laughing, slapping the table hard before he pulled out a joint and lit it. His eyes changed from dark brown to olive green in a flash.

"BAT FUCKIN' EARS! You heard her talkin' to me! Hilarious! I had no idea. You didn't even tell me you already knew when I turned around and came in your office, tellin' ya all the bullshit she said... all of what she was tryna get me to do."

"It was fun." Alexandre shrugged. "I didn't hear everything, but I smelled it on her. I'm not even upset with her, and she's none the wiser that I know what's going on. She even already had a Plan B in case you did what you did, ratted her out, and I confronted her about it. This is her *true* nature, and she follows those urges, no matter what. Would you rather fuck with someone who's unpredictable, or someone who falls right in line and brings forth the inevitable?" He could practically see Whiskey's mind working…

Whiskey shook his head. "Venus got cha drinkin' wine, now? No fake drinkin' like at the parties with the food, I mean, the humans. Jesus…"

Alexandre grinned and nodded. He studied his glass.

"It was my own choice. She loves this shit, though. You know what? It's not half bad. You know us French are known for good wine, Whiskey. I never dared try to find out until now, but I'm starting to get used to it. I'll have to piss out razorblades in about fifteen minutes, but it's worth it."

Whiskey burst out laughing and lounged back in the booth. They both drew quiet for a few minutes.

"I was right, wasn't I? I told you to watch Fawn after my brother popped up into town. I told you that he was going to go back to Paris to report me to the Council. I told you that he was going to use those who were close to me to get back at me. He's still pissed about the 'love tap' I gave his favorite slave… the fucker still can't talk." Alexandre shrugged and rolled his eyes. "Not my fucking problem. He should be grateful that I didn't cut all three of their heads off right there on the sidewalk."

"Yeah, true, but you didn't tell me that the bitch would be so bold as to approach me and say some shit like that to me. Why didn't you tell me that, too? A warnin' would have been nice. At first I thought the bitch was shittin' me, testin' me. Then I realized she was fucking serious. I take it you knew before it happened."

"I wasn't sure how she'd do it, but see, Victor can be very persuasive, Whiskey. Fawn wants to be Queen."

"No shit."

"If she can't have me, which obviously she can't, she'll take second best, my brother. Let Victor get everyone on his side. That would knock me out of the picture; then she'd have a second chance at bat."

"But why in the hell did she agree to find Venus in the first fucking place then?! She's the one that found her. Well, *you* found her, but she did all the research and everything."

"Because once she realized Venus' background, she thought I'd definitely reject the woman. Then, when she saw her, she thought surely I'd scrap the whole plan and it would be over."

XXXTENTACION's, 'Guardian Angel' played loudly through the speakers. The room began to spin in reverse, upside down all around them. The walls turned blood red, pulsing, dripping, smelling like the sweetest sliced vein...

"Looks like we've had some donors enter the premises... We don't have much time. Let me show you something before it gets wild in here..."

Alexandre took several deep breaths, his cigar in hand, and began to bob his head to the music.

"Close your eyes, Whiskey..." The man did as he asked, and he pushed him into an instant dream state. "Picture a little

Black baby born in the middle of a field... Blood is every-where, pooled in between her mother's trembling legs. Her mother screams out and cries under the full moon lit sky, then laughs as she picks up that baby, covered in the milky bloody wash of birth, and pulls her close, cradling the infant to her swollen, bare breasts. It was a hot night in South Carolina when that very thing happened. She was a slave woman, now the mother of a slave baby.

"That baby, like her mother, would be beaten, lied to, ma-nipulated, raped, tortured, all day and all night. She'd be worked nearly to death, forced to live like an animal. As that baby grew into a little girl and young woman, anything she dared show that she enjoyed would be used as leverage or snatched from her, never to be seen again. Imagine your life is not your life... you were just born into it.

"Laughter is all around you, but it's not coming from your mouth... It's coming from other people, laughing at your expense, enjoying themselves because of your sacrifices... Is that not evil?" In the distance he could hear the gnashing of teeth and screams. "Is that vampiric? Is that not... bloodlust? But you're special; only nobody knows that you're special, except your mother.

"She looked at that baby and said, 'You're going to be different, Venus. You're going to break the chains, get out of these shackles. I pledge your life. I give my life, for yours. In exchange, you shall have power, riches, but most of all, freedom. I promise you to the Gods. I give you to the sun and the moon, so you can escape this life. I turn you over; your soul is sold. Never forget your ancestors…"

The sound of heavy, hard beating drums vibrated through the spinning club over the Rap music, blending in like rain drops on a watercolor painting.

"That little baby's mother knew the old ways of her tribe. They didn't worship Jesus Christ. They gave homage to the dark and the light of the world. That woman knew of witch doctors, spells, blood sacrifices. That mother pledged her baby to someone else, and someone must've heard her and taken her up on her offer…For here the fuck I am."

He blew out thick clouds of haze. "So, Whiskey, to an untrained eye, those bastards with the whips and lies that they used to influence those stolen people from Africa and used as an excuse to continue their misdeed, missed the fine work of art in their midst. How fitting that she teaches Art History… Fawn did much of the same. She is no better. All Fawn saw was a tired-looking professor doing her laundry when she came upon her… Open your eyes."

The man before him slowly opened his eyes and they looked at one another, like father and adopted son.

"This woman, my sweet, delicious, dark-eyed Venus, didn't have much money. She was Black. She was out using her pussy as bait to feed… to survive, then destroying man after man after man, sometimes having nightmares about it… because she still has a fucking heart. She still cares. But even with all of that, she was happy. Even with all of that shit in her life, she was complete, whole… She was Venus, Goddess of Love, and I was Mars, God of War, before I met her.

"She was standing there in an old gray oversized sweater and jeans that flared at the bottom. Her hair was wild and all over her head that day… just beautiful. Her skin was this rich, bronze color as if she'd been sculptured from the finest minerals. Her cheekbones, lips, and almond shaped dark brown eyes were magnificent. Her ass, lovely and soft. Her legs long and her voice incredible. She hummed as she dumped the laundry powder into the machine. She drank from her can of soda while watching videos on her phone, then she called her friends and later, she fell asleep for a few minutes in that laundromat. She's always trying to get clean… always trying to wash the blood away, but it never fully goes away. It's there to stay, because she's one of us…"

"Yeah, she's definitely one of us now…"

"She does what she does not just to blend in, but because these were things her people were never supposed to be able to do. To live, to be free… And she fucking wants it. She wants to enjoy it. Now my queen can mingle amongst other races. No more slavery, no more segregation… but she's segregated herself from her vampire side for as long as she could, and now, that's over. She needs this sovereignty, *too*."

"I can't believe this. You saw her when Fawn did, too? I thought that had been a solo act."

"Never trust the help who possess ulterior motives." He took a puff from his cigar and grinned. "Why would I send a cat out to chase my mouse?" He handed Whiskey the remainder of the bottle of wine, and the man tilted it up to his lips and took a swig. "But who is better to catch a mouse than a cat, huh? She was the perfect woman for the job and Fawn led the way. I knew she'd find her because she was driven and so arrogant to believe that I was wrong, that her discovery would cause me to drop this matter at once. So, I had to plan accordingly. The beauty of it all, Whiskey, is that Fawn mistook my bride for a rodent... easy prey.

"She believed I'd agree with her, so she was eager to show her report. She wanted me to see the photo of this downtrodden woman who didn't wear designer clothing and clung to her human past. But oh, no." He shook his head adamantly. "That's not the true reflection in the mirror. Venus is *far* from what meets the eye. Whoever had heard her mother's prayers is her mistress. There has to be a reason why my mate was so easy to train, heals so quickly, and when we fuck..." His eyes rolled and his fangs descended. "Just the thought of her body near mine gives me a contact high. And that reason is tied to her past... the last night she spent on that plantation."

"Do you know who turned her yet?"

"No, but someone was thinking ahead. Venus had to have been marked as an infant. Whoever turned her was patient, methodical, and did an incredible job, to say the least. I barely had to do anything, in the grand scheme of things. Venus is like no one I've ever spoken to or fucked. She's taught me so many things..." He swallowed and hung his head. "And I know there's so much more to learn."

"Venus still won't tell you who turned her, huh?" Whiskey picked up the bottle of wine and licked the rim, fighting for the last drop. "She's a stubborn one."

"No, she hasn't told me. I am no longer obsessed with trying to make her tell me. Now, I want to find out on my own. See who this vampire was... because I know now that not only did they plan all this out, there was far more to the story. When they were done with her, they sent her my way..."

CHAPTER THIRTEEN

They Come in Threes...

TEACHING ONLINE CLASSES did not prove as bad as Venus had once believed.

Alexandre appeared genuinely surprised when she announced she was leaving the university job, though she explained her contingency plan, at least until the dust settled. Perhaps one day, she'd return to the brick and mortar scene. The thought of owning an art store, or perhaps, a museum of sorts was appealing, too. If she were honest with herself, that was where her passion lay, but things had gotten incredibly complicated; it was time to make the tough decisions.

She parked her new blood red Mercedes at the number 9 pump at the Mobil gas station on E 10th Street in Manhattan after spending some time at the public library doing a bit of research and enjoying a few hours of retail therapy, too. It had been a while since she'd shopped for herself, taken a pure pleasure trip, and a sales clerk had complimented her on how gorgeous the colors blue and taupe looked against her skin tone. It was time to freshen up her wardrobe—a new start on all counts.

She stood outside under the glow of the gas station lights, enjoying the cool night air. Clad in her blazer, bright high-low top, black leggings and boots, she pumped gas and watched the numbers go around and around, racking up the coins. As she stood there, she took in the sounds of people chatting on their phone, tossing trash in the bins, slurping loudly on straws filled with fizzy drinks, walking in then out of the small one-story store holding bags of beverages, snacks, cigarettes and beer. All of this overwhelmed her, made her distracted.

This is overload.

She could even hear people around her breathing or picking up change from their car console with the door closed some five pumps away. Everything came through in stereo. It seemed, since her lover had bitten her during their first time making love, he'd given her a gift—heightened senses like she'd never known.

Almost full…

She noted how much gas she'd pumped as her mind whirled from absorbing all the different sounds around her. Loud, crazy … but why was this affecting her so right at moment?

Her cellphone rang. She answered the call with a smile on her face.

"Hi, baby."

"*Bonjour, où es-tu, mon amour?*"

She could hear what sounded like a printer in the background. He was probably in the home office, burning the midnight oil as he worked on another case.

"I'm at the gas station. You should know where I am though, nosy ass. Don't you still have that tracker on my phone and Whiskey following me somewhere around here?" She chuckled as she looked about the lot, half way expecting to see the big guy's Harley and him leaned over it, jamming a hotdog in his mouth.

"No, no, no… I told you that I understood it made you uncomfortable and honestly, you need to be able to handle yourself without intervention. Please remember that, in three days, we are leaving for Paris and as soon as we arrive, due to my brother's report about me, they are asking to first see me alone. I attempted to speak with them on the phone but that, according to the Council Cardinal, was not sufficient. It's no big deal though. I would've had to go anyway to speak to them regarding our nuptials."

Her heart beat a bit faster, her blood pulsed in her veins. It was time she asked the man about something she'd had on her mind.

"Alexandre, what if… what if they don't approve of me?" Her heart sank at the thought of this. He was king, so there were just some things they would not allow. She may be one of them.

"This is a process, my Love. Look, each part of the world, every country, is run by a vampire monarch. Each monarch has a Council, which is, for all intents and purposes, like congress here for the U.S. government. I essentially have to answer to them and go through them for certain decisions, but, unlike the U.S. government, I have final say and can overrule many of their judgments *unless* I am ruled unfit due to mental or physical deficiency. I am the monarch for France, naturally, via the royal bloodline of the Marseille Clan, which has ruled for centuries, but I had to fight in order to prove myself worthy."

"So you're telling me your opinion can't be just over-looked, swept under the rug."

"Exactly. My opinion does more than hold water… it *is* the water. This isn't something that is simply handed to my family due to our lineage. Under my governance, we've won the majority of our wars with other countries, and trust, there have been more than a few, triggered by everything from land to money. Our trade deals have been airtight and any problem that is brought to me, I have handled expeditiously and effectively. The only thing that has not been done in what would be deemed a timely fashion according to tradition is—"

"You getting married." She grabbed the pump once it stopped then placed it back in the holster.

"Correct. There is a certain time period during which it is expected for a king or queen of any jurisdiction to be married and mine had expired long ago. I've had several extensions, but those have run out as well." He sighed loudly. "I have explained to the Council the reason for this and requested their patience. They relayed that they understood how important this is, especially with me being one of the last survivors of my bloodline. Unfortunately, that has caused some people to try and infiltrate themselves into my love life with an overzealous preoccupation in regard to old traditions, and the idea of keeping the family intact, genetics wise. I told them that I was looking for my Bloodmate and refused to settle... I have finally found her. YOU." She smiled at his words. "So, now that I've explained in depth how this works, you should be at ease."

"But I'm not." She chuckled as she slid back into her car and sat there for a moment with the radio playing 'More Than Words' by Isabella. "They can still make an issue about it and cause all sorts of problems... and I knew most of what you told me, baby, but I also know they want all monarchs to marry another Royal, especially one that is a Pure Blood." She started up her car and began to make her way out of the station.

"There aren't enough of us left... the Coven is quite small. We have to diversify. I've been saying that for decades and as long as we find a suitable mate with a strong mind and heart, a Vamp that understands and respects the Council and the monarch, and can produce quality offspring, then that is a good start. My Life..." She grinned... loving when he called her that. "Please leave this up to me to worry about, okay? I'm not what?"

"Sloppy, stupid, or one to be fucked with..." She smirked. It seemed to be his favorite thing to say as of late.

"That's right. I keep abreast of *every* fucking thing. Now come home to me... I need to fuck you." He abruptly disconnected the call, leaving her there with her cheeks hot and her pussy swelling with desire.

"I hope you're right about the Council," she mumbled under her breath as she got on the road. At times she worried that Alexandre wasn't cautious enough, but that also could be due to the fact that he kept so many damn secrets. "He must know more than I do, just hasn't said anything… of course he does."

She reached for her radio and turned up the volume on 'Automatic' by The Bonfyre. Snapping her fingers to the beat, she flowed into the city traffic, blending into the bright, flashing lights and action, the pulse of the place. She was absorbed by her surroundings, so much so, her head began to spin.

Suddenly the hairs on her arms begun to rise, as if she'd caught a chill. She swallowed and looked in the rearview mirror, seeing nothing out of the ordinary. Shaking the hint of fear out of her head, chalking it to exhaustion, she kept on driving.

That was short-lived. Less than a few blocks away, that chill came upon her once again, this time worse than the last. She got a whiff of something off-putting, a stench, like rotting meat. As if there was a tape recorder in her head, she heard the words, '*Look. Taste. Smell. Listen. But don't speak…*" It was her lover's words, the ones he said to her multiple times during training, awakening her senses to a level she never deemed possible. They were words he shouted when they fucked… each time was like the first time. She looked alongside her at the various cars and buildings. Again, nothing appeared out of the ordinary. Yellow Taxi Cabs, honking vehicles with annoyed drivers eager to get to the bar or home, people moving about here and there along the sidewalks… She swiped her tongue quickly through the air, then grimaced.

Something was off. Something strange, unfamiliar was peppering the air around her, blending in with the expensive perfume her lover had bought her. Sickening. She listened closely, then turned the radio off when her heart started to pump faster.

Two heartbeats… one far more erratic than her own…

"SHIT!" The blade of a knife was shoved in front of her, at her neck, while a grimy hand wrapped tight around her throat. The blade scraped against her flesh. "What do you want?!"

"Keep driving, bitch," said the gruff voice from the back of the car.

"Driving where?" She wrapped her hands tighter around the steering wheel, then looked through the rearview mirror once again. Her heart dropped. A man with a sunken in face covered in fresh and old scars, mossy green dead eyes, and straggly light brown hair sat behind her, hunched over like an ogre. "Ahhh!"

"Did I tell ya fuckin' ass to look at me, huh?! Did I tell your ass to look at me, bitch?! Now shut up and just keep drivin'!"

He grabbed a fistful of her hair and tugged so hard, she was certain her head was bleeding, the scalp now instantly tender from the torture. She could hear him sniffing the air, then pressing his hooked nose into her hair, inhaling, exhaling. The warm breath from his nostrils made her sick to her stomach as it tickled her scalp. She looked back at the man and realized he was a damn Bottom Feeder... the type of vampire that was turned by another Bottom Feeder, one who wasn't trying to salvage or help him. It would have been a mistake, a wreck job, an accidental 'pregnancy.' It would have been a vampire who'd simply messed up on their feeding and thus created their version of a derelict monster...

Then, said vampire would have abandoned the carcass of their creation. One had to raise their 'turned'; there was a sense of responsibility, but not with Bottom Feeders...The problem with the majority of the Bottom Feeders was that they were often crazy due to the poison they ate. Because of this, they were habitually used and sent to do higher ranked Vamps' work with no questions asked. This she knew from being on the street during her feedings. These grotesque creatures moved about like rats, pretty much staying out of her way, but they were always around, begging for things, threatening and making a ruckus. They killed not to just eat, but for the sheer joy of it.

She kept on driving and swallowed, knowing damn well that if he got her alone somewhere, pulled over in a dark, desolate place, he would not only attack her, he'd do vile, unspeakable things. Things so grotesque, this would bring her the type of end that she simply couldn't accept. No... this is not how her story would end. Her lover's bite had pumped some of the bastard's personality into her as well, and this was the wrong time to resist it. Her veins throbbed with Alexandre's brand of audacity, arrogance, pride. The beautiful bastard's massive ego was deep within her.

Fuck this shit! She jerked the car crazily through traffic, almost running into a bus. The honking and cursing of nearby cars ensued.

"What tha fuck are you doin'?! Keep the car steady!" The guy sliced deeper into her neck and she hissed when she felt his sticky tongue lap up the flowing blood. She jerked the car again. "Stop it or I'll jam this fuckin' thing all the way into your neck! Crazy bitch!"

She kept one hand on the wheel as he dug deeper into her neck. The knife was dull and jagged, creating an excruciating pain that radiated throughout her adrenaline-filled body. Over the next few minutes, she managed to inch forward as she turned corners, rocking her body in natural movements. When the time was right, she reached beneath her seat and pulled out the silver blade. Snapping her neck around as though it lacked muscle and tendon restriction, she smiled at the fucker then jammed the silver dagger with all of her might into the middle of his forehead.

"AHHHH! FUUUUUCK!!!! FUCK! FUCK! FUCK!!!"

The bastard fell back into the seat, writhing about, wiggling like an electrocuted worm. His own knife fell onto her seat. She grabbed it and tossed it on the floor by her feet, then turned her radio back on to drown out the motherfucker's high-pitched wails. Alabama Shakes crooned 'Sound & Color' at the highest volume, which suited her needs. She laughed as she looked back through her rearview mirror. Her killer within was awakened… and it would not take 'no' for an answer.

The glint of the beautiful silver dagger her Love had given her shifted around in the car as he rolled back and forth, his misery a thing of beauty. The blade was imbedded so deep, his head looked almost split down the middle. He cried out, trying in vain to remove it. Minutes later, she pulled into what had been one of her favorite alleyways to take a john and feed back in the day… Ahhh, the sweet fucking memories. Fangs fully descended, nostrils flared as she sniffed the pungent air, she pulled the fucker from the back of her car with one hand, dragging him with the greatest of ease. He looked up at her, his complexion growing ashen and pale.

"That's that *good* silver, motherfucker!" She cackled. "They don't make them like that anymore. Made in 1592 during the French Wars of Religion. A little history for ya there, in case you were curious. Now let's get down to business, you smelly piece of shit. Who sent you?"

He offered an evil, nasty grin before coughing up black, coagulated blood. She sniffed the air around him, listening closely to the wind around her… There was a thud, and then another. In record speed, she kneeled over the fucker, pulled the knife out of his head, and slashed it across his throat. He gurgled and his eyes rolled until there was nothing but white, but he still tried to smile. Her heart beat like a damn drum…

I've got company…

She sniffed the air again and smelled the stench of more

Bottom Feeders. They often ate bad blood, making them rotten from the inside out. She could hear their footsteps crushing on broken glass.

This was a set up! They followed me here!

Suddenly, a tall, thin one emerged, popping up from behind a dumpster like a willowy tree growing at rapid speed. A crooked grin spread across his face like poison ivy. His trench coat swung open with each step. The glint of a gun peeked out from his inner pocket.

"You're going to be fun!" he roared.

"Heeey, Saturn, Venus, Uranus, Ur-fuckin' anus! We're going to fuck you in the ass before and after we kill you, bitch," came a raspy female voice. Its owner emerged, sporting shoulder-length, wavy, light blond hair and dead black eyes. She had on a dark, knee-length dress, and her legs were covered in dirt.

"Who sent you?" Venus demanded as she kept sniffing the air, listening to the heartbeats, tasting her surroundings.

"We don't have to tell you shit." The willowy one spat as he drew slowly closer. The girl stayed close behind him, her eyes filled with craziness. "We just need to do our job, get paid, and uh, oh yeah, have uh good time with you, baby! Mmm, aren't you a looker! Isn't she pretty, baby?"

"Mmm hmmm." The female showcased a black smile, only brought to light by the whiteness of two extended fangs tinged with what appeared to be old blood.

"They never told us how cute this bitch was, Lilith! Three-some for fuckin' sure!"

"And you know she got money. Look at her car, and 'er clothes. Look at that ring…that's gonna look nice on me. I wanna eat her pussy so good! I heard once you go Black, you never go back." The woman cackled as she wiggled her long, pointed tongue in her direction then squeezed on her tit. The bitch shimmied her left breast up and over her bra, brought it to her mouth, and began to suck on her own reddened nipple.

"That is a nice car, isn't it? I bet we can take it for a spin. It's the least she can do after killin' Anthony. YOU STUPID FUCKIN' CUNT!" The man's fangs descended as he pointed to their dead friend, the one who'd been waiting for her in the car.

Venus burst out laughing; she simply couldn't help herself. Oh, this was going to be sooo good.

Both of them stared at her in confusion.

"It looks like your dead pal here didn't have time to tell you the conversation he overheard right before he tried to slice my throat open. I've got some blood flowin' through me that is so rich, so vibrant, so deadly, so beautiful that there isn't a fucking thing you can do to me!" she roared, then jumped on the nearby brick wall, crawling in record speed across it, her silver dagger with sick Anthony's blood still on it wedged between her teeth. The music from her car kept on playing. Iggy Azalea's 'Bounce' gave her motivation as she raced around them, weaving from side to side like a ping-pong ball.

"What tha? What tha fuck is she doing?!" the one named Lilith exclaimed. "Where is she?!"

"Stealing your motherfuckin' soul! Eat *this*, bitch!" Lilith let out a groan as the silver dagger struck the back of her head, piercing all the way through until it protruded out of her forehead. In seconds flat, the bitch had been cut through her thin, pale flesh, half way decapitated.

Venus jerked the blade, slicing downward, splitting her head in half. The tall one roared and raced towards her, his long, thin fangs descended as he lunged for her, while Lilith hit the ground like the bullshit that she was. Venus darted away, scaling the wall once again, chasing shadows and marrying the night.

"You stupid bitch! You killed my friend and my woman! I'mma make you pay!" He took his gun out and begun to shoot into the darkness, lighting up the alleyway—but nowhere close to where she was. She slid down against the same dumpster from which he'd emerged when she first laid eyes on him, and tracked his movements for a spell…

He's slow as shit. This will be a piece of cake.

"AHHHHH!" His yell was short and choppy as she came up behind him and snapped his neck. He fell to the ground, still very much alive, his eyes wild.

"Hi, motherfucker." She towered over him, then crouched down, snatching his gun away. She quickly opened the chamber… silver bullets. *Well, I'm not a fucking werewolf; this shit isn't lethal, but these bullets still pack a hell of a punch. They'd slow me down for sure.*

Yeah, they came prepared. Someone definitely sent them my way but this was in no way good enough. None of this would kill me now… Maybe they didn't actually want me dead? Or perhaps, they have no idea what I am actually capable of…

Removing the bullets, she slid them into her jacket pocket then stabbed him in the heart, twisting it hard and rough. His moan warmed her soul… but he held on to his miserable life, refused to die just yet.

"My name is Venus Margaret Anderson. I was born in South Carolina over two centuries ago. I am the Turned daughter of my mistress. I am the betrothed wife of King Alexandre Marseille of France."

"I don't… I don't give uh fuck who you are." He coughed. But she knew better… When she mentioned her Boo's name, fear coated his face, even as he took his last dying breaths.

"Whoever hired you didn't tell you the full scope of the job, did they? And ya boy over there smelling like five-week-old boiled cabbage didn't have a chance to inform you, either." She laughed as she hovered over him, getting into his face. "Yeah… you just tried to off the wroooong bitch. Ya grew up a fuckin' screwup. Rest in Peace, Biggie!" She cocked her head from side to side, then drove her fist into his gut, all the way through his body and out his back. He gasped and began to convulse as she withdrew her hand, bringing out his entrails with it, and stood to her full height, his stinking guts and blood dripping off her knuckles.

Moments later, she was inside her car, breathing fast, her fangs out and her furor taking her asunder. Bloody tissues and wet wipes lay strewn across her passenger's seat as she attempted to tidy herself up a bit. Her cellphone rang while she made her way back home. Her chest still rising and falling faster than the speed of light, she snatched it up, uncertain what she was going to say.

"Why were you in an alley so fucking long?"

"I knew you were lying. I thought I'd told you to stop fucking tracking me, Alexandre? You said you had less than forty-five minutes ago." She was halfway amused and pissed all at once.

"I lied. Sue me. I took Whiskey off your trail, but left the tracker. I'm not stupid."

"And neither am I, but I am pissed the hell off! I just had to kill three Bottom Feeders, Alexandre."

"Bottom Feeders?! Are you okay?"

"Yeah... as okay as expected. It was an ambush."

"Three? Where?! In the alley?"

"One of them snuck into my car at the gas station while the other two must've followed in a car behind us. They're all dead now... in that alley. I'm on my way home."

Alexandre was quiet for a spell.

"Are you certain they're dead? If not, I need to come and finish the job."

"Of course they're dead. You trained me to kill far bigger prey than this. They were small potatoes but I tell you what, I plan to take the longest shower *ever* when I get home. Damn, do they stink!" She sniffed her car and winced.

"Yeah, they drink inferior blood... like from dead cows, rotten meats... They'll eat any fucking thing, like vultures. No real discretion. I told you something like this may happen, that people would come for you once they were aware of your existence. A shower sounds good. I will join you... do you need to feed?"

"Yes. Are you offering yourself?" She smirked. She knew

that whenever he allowed her to drink from him, they'd get into a sexual frenzy and fuck for hours on end.

"Of course… but in the meantime, I have a few calls to make."

She knew what that meant. Call was code word for someone's spine being ripped from their fucking back.

"Don't keep me in the dark, Alexandre. I've earned my damn stripes." She looked down at her bloodstained clothing and grimaced. "I just bought this outfit! Damn it!"

"Incinerate it. You'll never get their smell out. I'll have the clothing replaced in the morning."

"Who the hell sent these bastards after me? I know that you know, Alexandre!"

The man hesitated for a spell.

"I will level with you. I honestly suspect my brother is involved, Venus. Victor would never directly hire a hitman. He leaves that to others, despite him being a skilled marksman. The fact of the matter is that he doesn't want to get his hands dirty."

She sighed and shook her head. There was dirt, filth, grime everywhere. No amount of bleach, detergent, soap or elbow grease would scrub it away. Things were getting ugly, and fast. She prayed she'd be able to keep up…

CHAPTER FOURTEEN

脚踏实地 (jiǎo tà shí dì)

...To step on solid ground.

A LEXANDRE'S GOLD MEDALLION swung against his bare chest as he climbed down the steps to his parlor on the first floor, clutching his phone in one hand and his car keys in the other. His white silk pants caressed his legs with each stride. Noting the time, he surmised he had about thirty-five to forty minutes tops before his Venus returned home from her evening with the three Fucketeers.

That should be plenty of time, with a few minutes to spare...

Seconds later, he was barreling down Interstate 86, sucking his teeth and blasting 'Sour Mango' by Gabriel Garzón-Montano. His thoughts raced, and he wanted nothing more than to gouge his brother's eyes out. Perhaps then, the fucker would finally be able to see the truth. That happening was definitely a *real* possibility, for it appeared that his brother was so blinded by his own needs, he'd even convinced himself his actions were all for the greater good of the Coven and Paris at large.

Soon thereafter, he stood at the apartment door of a particular Mr. Latham. He hadn't spoken to the man in quite a while, but his visits to the bastard were never friendly in nature. He rang the bell, then beat on the large chocolate brown door with the side of his fist. Soon, the sleepy-eyed fifty-five-year-old man swung it open, rubbing his weary eyes with rather small hands.

"Alexandre, oh goodness... it's late. Uh, what are you doing here? Anything wrong?"

Alexandre marched inside, slammed the door, then helped himself to the man's fully stocked liquor cabinet. He grabbed one of the bottles on the bottom shelf, filled a small shot glass, and downed something atrocious and old fashioned called vodka.

"Is anything wrong? Does a fuckin' bird go 'tweet tweet'?" He smirked. "Is your wife here, you piece of shit? I'd hate for her to have to see me jam a cattle prod into your fuckin' guts... then she'd be next. What a shame, I kind of liked her."

Latham's eyes grew large as he gasped and threw up his hands.

"What in the world is going on here? No, she's not here. She's out of town on business but—"

"Why didn't you tell me my brother had contacted you in order to get some assistance for his little misdeeds?"

The man looked dumbfounded, threw up his hands once again and shook his head vigorously.

"Alexandre, I have no idea what you're talking about. I haven't spoken to Victor in over five years, maybe even longer."

"That's interesting, I believe otherwise." Alexandre crossed his arms and glared at the man. Interrogations were his thing. Certainly this fucker didn't think he could get off the witness stand so easily.

"Would you, uh, like something to drink more to your, uh, liking?" He pointed to the now empty glass dangling in his hand.

Mr. Latham was one of the few human beings on Planet Earth who not only knew of the existence of his kind, but he often conducted business with vampires, taking care of shady financial tasks that were done under the guise of stocks and trades. He also helped orchestrate a bit of gambling and last but not least, killers for hire. Mr. Latham was first and foremost Victor's friend, someone who helped keep check on things while Alexandre was away from Paris. He was a rather savvy accountant; however, Alexandre had deemed him a bit too intrusive and severed the cord. He no longer trusted him, like he did anyone tied to Victor.

"Let's get right to the point. Victor Marseille orchestrated an attack on my fiancée by not one, not two, but three blood-sick fucking hyenas!"

"Bottom Feeders? Jesus…" The man rubbed his wide chin, worry etched across his face.

"Thanks to the fact that my fiancée is naturally daring, is now highly trained and was already familiar with their kind, she handled the situation. However, if she'd gotten bitten by one of these motherfuckers and he was diseased, well, I highly doubt things would've turned out so well." The man's complexion deepened. "I suspect at least one was sick because she described the putrid odor. I also know that it is no coincidence that not one, not two, but three were sent. There's a message in that, about vampires standing on solid ground. We must move in threes, always three steps ahead... This has been part of the Marseille warrior training from the beginning of our existence."

"It's also a mockery of the trinity." The man seemed astounded at his own words, even going as far as to bring two fingers to his lips while taking several steps back.

"Trinity? You liken me to demons, Latham? You self-righteous pretend Christian! Demons work for Satan, you ridiculous frightened fuck. I am a slave to *NO ONE!* Don't fucking play with me, Latham!" Alexandre threw the glass of vodka across the room, making it shatter with an almost deafening sound before picking up the man by the throat and raising him high up in the air with one hand.

"Alexandre! Please!" He shook the bastard like a pair of underwear being waved about on a long stick. "I know nothing about this! I swear!" Latham's thick, dry fingers clawed at Alexandre's as he fought to catch some air, to breathe, to not black the hell out.

"I tell you what. Call my brother on the phone. If Victor knows nothing of this, I will let you go. If he admits to a plan to send out three losers onto my woman, well, I think you know the consequences. I'd suggest a closed casket."

"Marseille!"

"NOW."

"But I know nothing about this! Like I told you, I haven't spoken to—" Alexandre extended his fangs—a clear warning that, in a matter of seconds, he'd be drained dry and his skeletal remains left in a heap by his fireplace. "Okay, okay!" Latham was shaking like a leaf as Alexandre stood a mere few inches away, watching his every move.

He glanced at a clock on the wall. *She'll be home soon... she'll have questions about my whereabouts.*

"Hurry up!" He shoved Latham in the back, sending him to his knees in a prayer position. The guy scrambled about like a spider dodging a foot, adjusted his glasses across the short bridge of his nose, and picked up his cellphone, which he'd dropped on the floor. He dialed, placing it on speakerphone.

"Hello... uh, Victor Marseille, please." Seconds later, his brother came on the other end of the line.

"*Bonjour*, Mr. Latham! And what do I owe this honor?"

Alexandre smirked as he ran his tongue along his teeth. Victor was too smart for his own good... covering his tracks.

"Um, it appears that, uh, some Bottom Feeders assaulted your brother's fiancée, to my understanding."

A brief silence ensued.

"Bottom Feeders... aren't they delightful?" Victor chuckled. "Did the slave live?"

"Uh..." He looked at Alexandre for direction. He nodded. "Yes, um, apparently she did but she's rather shaken up."

"I see... Well, that's too bad, now isn't it? What a pity. If that is all, please send Alexandre my regards until I see him soon. Also, please tell your lovely wife that—"

Alexandre snatched the phone from the man.

"*Mon frère*, it's obvious that you know I'm here, and that's how I planned it. You fell right into your typical con artist, lying ways. Deny. Deny. Deny. I'm here in person to look Latham in the eyes and let you know there is no stone I won't un-turn to get the goods on you. I am a man of violence. I am also a man of proof."

"You are a man hellbent on destroying everything our parents, their parents, and their grandparents built!"

"Let me tell you something, you inept, selfish son of a bitch. I know you had something to do with what happened to Venus this evening. Directly or indirectly. I will fix you, dear Victor. Fix you after I break you into a million pieces."

"Are you threatening me?! You're insane." Victor chortled.

He could envision his brother sitting there in his black velvet chair, all smug and grinning, his white hair pulled back.

"You fucked with someone I have affections for, so I am going to fuck with someone you control and I will do it so well, you won't know what hit you until it's far too late. By the time I see you in Paris, you'll—"

"I had nothing to do with this, Alexandre. I didn't contact Latham to arrange a hit and if that happened, then it seems this energy of yours would be better used in exploring ways to get your ass back to France and find a suitable, Pure Blood wife! Your paranoia has reached critical mass. This is further proof that you are becoming psychologically unwound."

"We both know the truth, and you're allergic to it. You chose three to come after my Reine Du Sang. I will choose three to seek my revenge!" he hollered out so loud, a window burst, the glass crashing onto the wooden floor.

"I shall report this to the Council as well, Alexandre. You're unfit to be king."

"Yes. Report me. You do that!" Alexandre chuckled. "Hey, report this, as well, Mr. Snow White! I have a special surprise for ya! Please share that, too!" He ended the call abruptly. Suddenly, the lights in the apartment dimmed until they were both shrouded in black. He could smell the fear on Latham; it eddied off him like steam from a grill.

Leaning in close, he whispered in his ear, "My brother will have an endearing present from me soon. As for you, I have good news. I am letting you live. This is only because I have come to understand that my brother didn't involve you in this particular scheme, but he wished to make it seem as if he had, so you could be sacrificed to ensure he looked squeaky clean. He was banking on me killing you, eye for an eye... but oh, no, that will never do." Latham swallowed. "The second option is he honestly doesn't have any involvement in this, but is still somehow the cause. You come across as completely unaware, but I hate you... still not a reason enough to snuff you out I suppose. Just yet. Either way, I will be getting to the bottom of it. Now, as for you and I, I need for you to arrange something for me."

"What?" the man asked, sweat rolling down his face, his

breathing erratic.

"I need true killers by my side... not soft, wimpy punks." He sneered at Latham, whose time was almost up. You don't mingle with the undead, make secret, lucrative deals, and leave in one piece. "Contact Zhang Wei."

"But King Zhang Wei is not available! He could be any-where! He also—"

"I don't give a shit if he's tap dancing in a grass skirt on the third floor of the bowels of Hell singing, 'I Will Survive'. He's an associate of mine and from time to time, we help one another out. Plus, he owes me a favor. I know you've worked with him several times. I have no idea where he is right now and don't want to waste valuable time when you already have his most recent contact information."

"Okay." Latham grabbed his phone and began to dial.

"You make sure he comes to New York. Tomorrow. I need his assistance with this matter. Things have gone too far, and yet, I know Victor is nowhere near finished." The lights flashed and came back on full strength. Latham swallowed hard, as if relieved. His complexion turned red and sweat kept oozing off him as if he'd just been dunked in a pool. "If you fuck this up, I am going to return here to your home and peel your skin from the muscle and bone, all while you are still breathing. And tell him to bring his mate, Syà. It's power couple time..."

ALEXANDRE WAS IN the master suite bathroom, standing under the massive waterfall shower, decorated with gold and plum lights. The water flowed down his tall, broad shouldered frame. Phony Ppl crooned 'Why iii Love the Moon' through the surround sound speakers.

Venus had only been home a few minutes, but it was more than evident he was vexed. He barely looked at her, as if needing a moment, a sliver of composure to hold on to…

His intense anger perfumed the room. His arm muscles appeared tight, stiff like casts, and the way he'd walked about earlier, fast and hard, made him look like an enraged war general. At last, he turned to her and curled his finger in her direction. Instead of waiting for her to come to him, he pulled her towards him, dragging her bare feet with his mere mind. She glided past her shed clothing coated in feral blood. A light breeze blew through her hair as he summoned her; the music grew louder and the room began to spin in shades of red. In mere seconds, she stood before him, his erect dick, framed with midnight black hair, flush against her pubic hair. He wrapped his strong arms around her and claimed her lips in a kiss.

"My Blood Queen… my precious *Reine Du Sang.*" She shuddered when he squeezed her tight against him, his worry for her palpable. His cold, hard yet comforting flesh felt so good pressed to hers. Picking her up in his arms in the shower—which was as big as a bedroom—he had her wrap her thighs snug around his waist. She rested her head against his shoulder, their bodies surging impossibly closer to one another in a wave of magnetic attraction that could never be broken.

He ran one hand through her hair and, with the other, he helped her down onto her feet in the enclosure. The warm red water felt like life, liberty, and blood for all as it beat against her body from the massive double showerhead. She sighed with delight when she felt his body behind her. He positioned her against the wall, in the stance of one about to be strip searched. Interlocking their fingers, he delivered sensual and rough kisses to the back of her neck, his mouth sliding down her wet flesh, his fangs nipping at her sensitive skin. He paused to run a tender finger over the healing puncture wound of where the dull, dirty knife had raked across her neck.

"That filthy son of a bitch! I should resurrect that fucker and make him suffer for all of eternity!" he roared in a way that had the words vibrating within her soul. She winced for her pain became his, and vice versa. He cupped her shoulder and turned her around. They locked eyes. His glowed like cobalt diamonds… icy blue. The red water gave him a purple glow; the navy undertones of his flesh had never looked so beautiful.

"I'm fine, baby. My mama didn't raise no fool." She smiled up at the man, trying to tame the enraged beast as she stroked his cheek with the palm of her hand. He held her fingers tight, as if his very life depended upon that act. Closing his eyes, he brought her hand to his luscious mouth and placed a petal soft kiss on it. She sighed when he hoisted her up again, draping her on him like a backwards robe. Wrapping her arms around his neck, she brushed his lower lip with her own, their noses touching as he rubbed and squeezed on her breasts.

Her dark nipples hardened under his touch. Pure ecstasy filling her, her head fell back and her hair became saturated under the intense current of the powerful red stream. Her eyes hooked on the pulsating blue vein in his neck. It called to her; she thirsted for him so badly, her stomach growled at the sight. She lunged at him, mouth gaping open, but he stopped her, pressing his finger against her mouth without offering a word. His eyes said so much... yet her body was crying out for him.

"I'm hungry," she pleaded, needing his blood, his essence, his love.

"And I'm going to fulfill all of your needs and desires. Just let me hear your heartbeat for a while longer... before it races out of control, before we lose ourselves and there's no turning back."

He bent down and pressed his head against her chest, holding her tight. She breathed in... then out... then again. Falling into a trance, a lullaby echoing inside her, flashes of her life flipped inside her mind like pages torn from a worn, black and white comic book of yesteryear. He was deep inside her... looking at her life, picking her apart, piece by piece! She gasped, almost losing her footing as he dug deeper, then deeper…

"I see all of your fears and desires. So brave, baby… so many fewer fears than even a month ago."

"You mind fuck me but don't fuck my body?! Help me!" she screamed and scratched at his back as he lunged hard upward within her, taking her breath away. Her fangs lengthened as he grabbed the back of her neck with force and brought her close to his throat. He groaned when she pierced his delectable flesh. His exquisite blood poured like wine from the artery, more precious than a 1947 bottle of Château Cheval Blanc. The liquid pooled into her mouth like the nectar from a juicy strawberry and she hungrily swallowed his flavor, streams of it dripping down the sides of her mouth and chin. He rocked hard inside her, and her pussy compressed around his long, fat cock as he knocked her fucking walls down one harsh stroke at a time.

"Take my love. Take my blood. Take every blow of my dick! TAKE IT!" he barked forcing his cock as far as it could go within her. Her back bumped violently into the wall, so much a few of the tiles around them cracked, pieces falling to the ground just like the days of her lives, since she was born. She grew dizzy with lust and love, an intoxicating cocktail. Gripping her ass cheeks with both hands, he forced her into his ruthless lunges.

"I can feel you so deep inside me!" She sucked his neck where she'd laid her claim, licking her plate clean. He stirred his hips wildly, his movements so delightfully rough and flawless. She screamed when the man suddenly turned her upside down, hitching her to him like an apron. She dangled like grapes on a vine. Knees resting on his shoulders, ass in his face, he slid his long, wet tongue along her slit as she reached for his hard dick and enveloped the large, thick head into her mouth.

She sucked the length with all that was in her, savoring his flavor, and they came together, his cream filling her oral cavity in relentless spurts while she dropped her honey pot against the curl of his quicksilver tongue. When she was good and satisfied, he stood her back on her feet, facing away, bent her at the waist, and entered her from behind like a frenzied brute. She clawed at the walls, screaming his name, cursing him as he viciously drove within her tender walls. Holding her hips, he worked her like a pump, sheathed inside of her and showing no signs of fatigue. And she didn't want it to stop... she *needed* it like her next breath.

Reaching behind her, she grabbed his rocking hips, drawing him impossibly deeper. Soon, he shuddered, filling her pussy with a few final hard thrusts. In moments, he was carrying her in his arms, out of the water and into their bedroom. Laying her wet body over the gold and red sheets, he climbed to her side, lifted her leg, and slid inside of her once more.

Their voices echoed as they moaned, fell under each other's spell, and he brought her close to feed once again. She took her time, suckling from his skin, sipping him one precious drop after another. Minutes turned to hours, and they were still in the throes of making love... deep in an epic marathon. The last thing she recalled before shaking from a massive orgasm was her legs bent far back close to her head while he drilled her with his massive cock, his balls slapping violently against her fat, swollen pussy lips. She fell in and out of fantasies as her orgasms came one after the other, mere dominoes knocked over from the slightest touch. Hours later, they lay entwined, resting, legs wrapped around one another, sheets hanging half off the bed, bright red blood splatter across the pillows...

She fought sleep but soon lost, only to be awakened by the sound of a knock at their bedroom door. Her lover got to his feet, wrapped his black robe around his body, and went to open it. Whiskey stood at the threshold, with two people she'd never seen in her life...

The first was a bald-headed Asian man, standing about five eight but muscular as fuck, and a beard that fell in a thin braid to his navel. An enormous sword was strapped to his back, heavy black boots covered his feet, and a series of intricate tattoos lined his arms. On the man's right stood an Asian woman, a bit shorter than he. She was beautiful, her skin the color of Egyptian papyrus, her cheeks holding a peachy glow. Her long, raven black hair was shaved on the sides and pulled up in a high genie-type pony tail that appeared to reach down to her ass. A large gold septum ring like that of a bull's pierced her nose and her body was covered in a liquid leather black jumpsuit.

Venus sat up to get a better look. They were intriguing to

say the least. She could hear her mate speaking to them in Chinese, then in French… and a few words of English in between… merely small talk. Suddenly, Alexandre chuckled, a sound of relief, and extended his hand for a shake.

"We came as soon as we heard you needed us," the man said in a deep voice, his Chinese accent thick. The woman stepped around him and approached Venus, walking fast towards her with a smile on her face. Venus stared her up and down, her defenses heightened. She slid her hand beneath her pillow, clutching the handle of a dagger, just in case.

"Relax, honey," the woman stated in Mandarin Chinese with a chuckle. "We all need friends and now I'm yours. You're standing on solid ground, queen-to-be. Welcome to the sisterhood…"

CHAPTER FIFTEEN

Blood Brothers

H E EXPECTED HIS brother's arrival in forty-eight hours…

Victor's chest rose slowly up and down as he stood in his home. The quiet wasn't quite normal; his sensitive hearing could pick up little with the exception of his servants' breathing. His cold, hard flesh drew even colder for he stood in the midst of a full-scale bloody massacre… in the privacy of his own mansion.

Three of his servants' bodies were laid out neatly on the floor of his visiting area, all of them with their arms criss-crossed, serving as a platter of sorts to hold their own severed heads. He opened his mouth and roared.

"NOOOOO! DAMN YOU, ALEXANDRE!!!!!!"

One…two…three. Just as he promised.

Celine… blood oozed out of every pore of her body, her skin partially ripped apart.

Raphael… one would think he were sleeping if it were not for the massive red ocean beneath his body.

Arthur… one of his favorite servants by far. His eyes were still open, a look of utter horror on his face, flesh burnt to a crisp.

Several windows broke as he unleashed his demons, his anger deeper than words could ever describe. The carpet beneath their bodies was soaked with dark red essence, and the place smelled of bloodshed, terror, and pain. All he could hear now was his own racing heartbeat and the concerns of several of his other servants as they stood around, their mouths no longer sealed.

"Sterilize this place and put the remains in the furnace. Clean out their rooms, and I mean *every*thing! Clothes, furniture, personal effects… I don't want to see any evidence of their existence in my home!" he barked at one of his servants before storming off to his office and snatching up his desk phone. He dialed and waited for her to answer.

"*Bonjour!*"

"What have you done?! WHAT THE HELL HAVE YOU DONE?!"

Fawn was quiet for a spell, then spoke matter-of-factly, "I did what you asked."

"I *never* told you to send three Bottom Feeders! At first, I believed Alexandre was trying to frame me, test me… but I see he was telling the truth! You sent BFs after the slave. You've ruined everything!"

"BFs? Oh, the Bottom Feeders? Relaaax, Victor. Trust me, things are going as planned, even better! She was shaken by it all and Alexandre ranted and raved for hours. I bet they even argued about the incident, too. The timing was perfectly planned. He'd pulled Whiskey off of trailing her and sniffing her ass because she'd complained about it and—"

"Damn you! We were still in a negotiation phase… now all leverage will be lost! My brother is out for blood and if you believe for one fucking second that he will let this go, even after killing three of my most prized servants, you are mistaken! A code has been broken and now he will stop at *nothing* to exact revenge. Threefold!"

"How could he kill them? He's not even there."

He wanted to reach through the phone and choke the bitch with all of his might, see her black out, come to, then choke her again! Certainly, that would wipe the smug expression off her face that he was certain she had right at that moment.

"He doesn't have to be here to kill them…"

"He sent someone to do it? That doesn't really seem like his style."

"It's not! Wake the hell up. You are not in Kansas anymore, Dorothy! Let me break this down for you…" *Fucking Turned Vamps…* "My servants are low tier on the totem pole. They aren't that powerful. They come from poor lineage, low lying fruit, if you will. Easy targets… easier to control that way. All my brother has to do is know their names, tap into their fears and desires, and he can manipulate, torment, and destroy just about anyone he wishes. He heard their greatest fears, scared them to death then had them believe the only way out was to cut off their own fucking heads! He's a perceptual prestidigitator! A sadist! Just fuck it!" He waved his arm about.

"Well, seems to me then that *you* should be the one concerned, Victor…"

"How do you know I'm not capable of the same? You flippant bitch… It doesn't even matter at this point! He is proficient at things you have *no* fucking clue of!" He heard her swallow on the other end—the first sign of the foul vixen actually giving a damn. "My brother has destroyed complete towns in a matter of minutes with his mind alone! Why do you think he does so well in law?! Do you honestly believe it's just because he's such a swell motherfucker?! Perhaps it is due to our genetic good looks? He has kept his gifts from you and everyone because not knowing makes him all the more powerful. Who the hell goes to New York City and after only three months owns practically an entire block of real estate, wins every fucking case he touches, and no one questions him about his strange comings and goings?!

"The orgy parties, all of it! Everyone is paid off to keep their fucking mouths closed and even if they tried to explain, 99.9% of the population wouldn't even believe them. He has a cartel of fucking human donors who think this is just some kinky fantasy roleplay, some crazy costume party shit that they get cut a check for, not even realizing they are dealing with *real* vampires every time they empty their veins for his erotic revelries! This isn't Halloween night in a suburb in Wisconsin! THIS IS OUR LIVES! THIS IS REAL! It happens because of who he is, the gifts he possesses… It's his supremacy!"

He pounded his fist on a nearby statue, so hard it shattered into a million pieces.

"Victor, please calm down. You're becoming emotional and it's rather… well, unbecoming. Furthermore—"

"Your fucking body chopped up into twenty equal pieces then delivered to your whore of a mother would be unbecoming as well, correct?" He was met with silence. "I'll calm down when my brother is stripped of his fucking title that he no longer deserves. I need that crown! I need his position and no one will stand in my way. I can't believe this…" He began to pace back and forth, his nerves a wreck, trying to think of something, anything. "Why in the hell would you do something like that without consulting me first? I know my brother better than *any*one. I thought you were actually intelligent, despite being a Turned!"

"Victor, you are losing sight of the big picture. Also, your insults as to my status and astuteness are duly noted," she stated haughtily.

"I wanted you to prove me wrong. You failed."

"You are so blind with hatred for Alexandre that you don't even see that it actually worked." She chuckled. "Venus was afraid. She'll be looking over her shoulder now and reflecting if this is a good idea to proceed with him and—"

"Have you lost your mind?" His long, curled nails dragged

down the side of his desk, tearing at the wood. "If we were discussing an ordinary vampire, you'd be right, but we are not! Due to this new information, I am no longer convinced that Venus is a Turned Vamp." The woman grew quiet, her confusion more than obvious.

"Of course she is. Why would you think that?"

"I don't know what is going on, but she managed to survive an attack by three Bottom Feeders, Fawn."

"Big deal. Bottom Feeders are slow and revolting. I could fight ten with no issue."

"How naïve of you. Where did you find these BFs, Fawn?"

"I asked for a referral from the Underground Network."

"Ahhh, the good ol' black market. Well, guess what? They gave you one of the best. One of them was no ordinary BF. His name was Skelton, and he was notorious for slaying Turned Vampires and other Bottom Feeders for profit. He's a bounty hunter. Well, *was*… She slaughtered him and two of his friends in a fucking alley in less than thirty minutes… left him rotting for all to see. That sends a message out there in the streets. Do you *honestly* believe that is normal?" He was met with silence. "How did she not get bitten? How did she fight all three of them at once, despite your oversized bravado in believing you could do the same or better? No, they're not the strongest, definitely not the fastest, and certainly not the brightest, but they have a vicious, infectious bite if they are diseased. And many are, having a sickness that often requires medical intervention in a short amount of time, or death is soon to follow.

"Due to their poor eating habits and other factors, they have a poison in their blood that once it enters the bloodstream, it attacks all of the cells of their victim, killing them. Bottom Feeders are dying, slowly! They are like zombies; the virus eats them alive. They now use it as a weapon to get their way. That's why we have the constabularies out and about—not there to round them up, but to—"

"Exterminate them."

"Exactly! That terrible bite is their claim to fame. I don't know what the hell Venus is, but she should have been dead." He took a deep breath and closed his eyes, trying to regain his composure. "I also have no doubt now that my brother trained her. This isn't good. This isn't good at all. She's a threat. Something must've spooked them. They hesitated perhaps? I need to see this Turned Vamp for myself, but at this point, it may be far too late."

"I am sorry, Victor, for not asking for clarification and permission before carrying out my plans. I thought I was following your instructions to put a little fire under her since Whiskey reported back to me that his conversation with Alexandre went absolutely nowhere. I am to accompany Alexandre in Paris, but a day later, after I finish up a few things. You and I can meet in secret and discuss what to do. I want to make this up to you. What can I do?"

"What you've done, Fawn, is irreversible. However, we can still try to salvage this." He took another deep breath then lit a cigar. "I need for you to testify against Alexandre here in France, in front of the Council. No more interventions, no handouts, no sneak attacks, no hiring hitmen, nothing. We are dealing with this head on."

"Testify? I can't do that! He'll kill me!" she said in a shrill voice, the first time he'd heard her behave in such a way, demonstrating any shred of sentiment. "Right now, he has no idea that I'm involved, Victor! He even hugged me two days ago and gave me a diamond necklace, thanking me for my hard work organizing his wedding."

"Well… I think you need to calm down. You're becoming emotional. That's so unbecoming." He cackled. "Now you listen to me, and you listen good. That is the *only* way we can remove him from power and if you think I give one strip of a shaggy shit about you being out of my brother's good graces, you're sadly mistaken. If you want to be by my side, you have to earn it! That is what a Queen does! She sacrifices her comfort for the greater good! Now prove to me that you're worthy. This is your last chance."

"Don't you understand? If this doesn't work, being out of a job will be the least of my worries…" She sounded so pitiful, so pathetic.

"You're in too deep now. If you don't do it, dear, I will make you regret it for the rest of your days. And trust me, those days will be short-lived. Doesn't matter if you're killed by me or my brother, each death will be especially heinous and painful. This way, you'd have my protection, or you can always go out on your own and take that gamble. You're so fucking smart, right? The solution is obvious. *Au revoir.*"

He disconnected the call and stormed back out of his office...

ALEXANDRE SAT AT his dining room table, sipping dark, rich blood from a black and crystal wine glass, while Whiskey and Bruce loaded up the van with their luggage to head off to the airport. He twirled the glass slowly back and forth, watching it wash up on the sides like the ocean upon the surf and sand. At the other end of the table sat his Bloodline, Venus, and across from them both was King Zhang Wei and his bride, Syà, from China.

"Syà, I fear, though my soon-to-be wife has not stated it, she is lonely and in need of friends such as yourself." The woman nodded and smiled gracefully. "I will not speak too much on her behalf. She is fully capable of articulating her own thoughts." He winked at her, and Venus winked back. "But she's had a difficult time, and I want to make this as stress-free for her as possible. Thus far, it's been everything *but* that." He took another sip of his drink then placed it down.

"That's understandable. It's difficult to make it alone," Syà stated. "Venus and I spoke last night. She's lovely, inside and out, has a good head on her shoulders, and a strong grip... quick reflexes. I think she will fit in just fine."

"Thank you." Placing a ringed hand over the other, he continued with his spiel. "Thank you both for coming all of this way." The couple bowed their heads and nodded. "I hope that you found your room comfortable and that all of your needs were tended to last night."

"Your facilities and munificence were more than sufficient. My wife and I are happy to assist you, Lord Marseille. Under your leadership, France has been quite generous with us, an adversary during times of strife, but now a consistent ally." The man stroked his long, braided beard. "It was the least we could do. When I was alerted that you needed my support, Syà and I dropped what we were doing and immediately arranged the speediest way to arrive. May I be honest?" The man placed his glass down and gave him a serious look.

"Of course."

"Alexandre, there have been rumors floating about for over a year that you had been neglecting your duties. I never believed that; your service spoke for itself. Regardless of whether you were planted on Parisian soil or not, your leadership was topnotch."

"Thank you, Zhang Wei."

"I am at a loss for words that Victor would betray you in this way. In China, the consequences for his actions would be swift. However, after you and I discussed it in further detail this morning, I understand that you must tread lightly or you will fall right into his trap... to make you appear crazy, incompetent."

"He is banking on my fiancé's temper," Venus spoke up, shifting her weight in her seat. "I've been working on my mate regarding that, helping him remain as calm as possible in times like this. He is waiting for Alexandre to explode." Syà nodded in agreement. "He continues to do many, many things behind the curtain. This last episode apparently was the final straw."

"Victor is a bitch," Syà stated matter-of-factly, causing several bursts of laughter. "It's true. He could *never* run a Parisian boutique, let alone the entire country of France. In Paris, he was walking around pretending to be in charge… He's been driving everyone crazy. Victor was initially elated when Alexandre left; we all saw it. No one wanted to say anything, it was seen as disrespectful to come to you about your own brother… a noble Pure Blood and second in line to the throne… especially since there was nothing he'd done per se, to put the country at risk. Yet."

Alexandre nodded in understanding.

"The Russians, Japanese, Cambodians, Turks, Egyptians… we all talked." She waved her hand lazily and rolled her heavily-lidded eyes. "Here is my theory. He never believed Alexandre would find what he wanted here." The woman glared at Venus, then at her husband. "Making jokes about the prediction of your *Sorcier Cadieux*, as if it were some fairy tale. Venus, Alexandre has the gift of desires and fears… a very powerful gift." Venus nodded. "And he uses it wisely. I believe Victor was jealous of that, though he has his own talents, but Alexandre was the one that seemed more highly favored by your constituents. Honestly, we took to Alexandre's personality much better."

"Victor was enjoying his time there, throwing his weight around, telling everyone that since Alexandre wasn't there physically, everyone had to answer to him… as if you were dead," King Zhang Wei interjected, shaking his head in disgust while his wife cocked her head to the side and her pupils turned amber, her fangs partially descended in repugnance.

"When he found out that you had possibly found your mate, he was concerned that you would return with her to Paris, I believe," Syà stated. "And then when he was told she is a Turned Vamp, he became enraged… but just that fast, he realized that was his way to take your place, that perhaps a blessing of sorts had fallen into his lap."

Queen Syà slowly got up from her seat and rounded the table, approaching Venus. Placing her hand on her head, sliding her long, sharp fingernails along his sweetheart's arm, she sized her up. Then, Syà caught Venus' chin in her grip. Venus' fangs extended and she hissed, a sound that reminded Alexandre of a hundred rattlesnakes suddenly appearing in the room.

"Easy, baby… she's not trying to hurt you." Alexandre sat back, crossed his legs, and watched.

"Alexandre, this is remarkable…" Queen Syà stated with a toothy smile and lighthearted chuckle. "Have you seen the stars in your bride-to-be's eyes?"

Alexandre's brow rose and he got to his feet. He made his way down to join them. Venus stared at Syà, then at him, confusion and curiosity in her expression.

"I … I've looked at this woman a million times over in our short time together." He fell to his knees beside her and peered into his mate's eyes. "I've never seen that before, until now…" It was true. Very small, white dots gleamed within her pupils, not oval or round, but shaped like five-pointed stars.

"Sometimes it takes someone else to point it out. You do know what that means, right? This is amazing!"

"I don't understand? What's amazing?" Venus questioned.

"Venus, you're pre-chosen." Syà turned to Alexandre. "She was sent to you from a prayer, a curse and a dream. Three, by three, by three." His heart began to pound in his chest.

King Zhang Wei got to his feet. "How exciting! A true Bloodmate!" he exclaimed, his voice booming.

"What are you talking about?" Venus asked. "What does this all mean?"

"It means that your mother was into some powerful stuff! That's what it means! She sent out the prayer, and you were already cursed due to being in bondage… that was two down, one to go! Alexandre, did you have a dream?"

This was not how this was supposed to happen… He'd been planning to tell Venus in his own time, but now the door was wide open, and there was no turning back. He dropped his head for a spell.

"Yes and no."

Venus snatched herself away from the woman's grip and popped up from her seat. "What is going on, Alexandre?! What is she talking about?! What do you know that you've been keeping from me?!"

"King Alexandre, you must tell her!"

"Syà, please!" King Zhang Wei ordered. "You are overstepping the boundaries! It is not our place!"

Syà hissed, but said nothing further.

"Alexandre!" Venus backed away from them all, fire in her eyes. "What does this Chinese Pure Blood vampire, who has never seen me a day in her life, know about my mother?! What is going on?!"

"Your mother practiced Hoodoo!" he explained, not even certain how to make it make sense, how to make it plain to her.

"My mother dabbled, but she was no witch!"

"We never said that she was… and even if that were true, would it have been so bad?" Syà stated coolly before returning to her seat.

"She didn't *have* to be a witch, Venus. This has nothing to do with sorcery or spells, it has to do with the power of her faith, Venus… Prayer—the *original* incantation. Your mother believed wholeheartedly in the prayers she uttered, my Love. I did not dream it until recently. Right before we met in person, I dreamt of you, but someone saw you *years* before that. My *Sorcier Cadieux* did, at least a century before you were even born! He saw you in his vision!" Venus' chest heaved up and down. "He saw your mother and the brief life you had with her. She gave her life away, exchanged it, so that you would have a future. He told me that my mate, the one promised to me, the one that would help me rule all of France and bear my children for future generations, was born from rich Carolina soil that her mother toiled herself and then was dipped in the Hudson river, baptized beneath the standing, large green woman with the torch.

"He said her skin was the color of fire-hot bronze, her hair a vast wreath of tight, dark curls, her heritage the oldest of the entire land, and her bloodline rich. He said you were brave, resilient, beautiful… and you were something I am not: kind."

Venus' eyes watered. He knew her heart was breaking, but what could he do? Only the truth was acceptable now; he could protect her from it no longer. The woman paced back and forth, running her hands along her black leggings, turning in various directions as if trying to collect her thoughts. No one said a word for several minutes. They all respectfully gave her space.

"My mother prayed that I'd be… turned? How could she? How could she do something so… so cruel?!" She looked them all in the eyes, her gaze bouncing from face to face, searching for an answer.

"No, that's not what happened. She prayed that you'd be free, my Love…" Alexandre approached her and wrapped his arms around her. He kissed the top of her head. "I was going to tell you, but I held back because I knew you may not understand yet. I know how you felt about your mother, about her tragic death. I didn't want to bring you any more pain. You've had enough." His eyes watered and out poured a bloody tear. Venus' lips trembled as she reached upward and wiped it away with a gentle swipe of her knuckle.

"Venus, *Sorcier Cadieux* predicted your arrival. Your mother gave your soul away to save your life. But you earned it back," Syà explained. "In my culture, prayer is important, too. It is strong. Powerful." Her eyes turned dark as she balled up her

256

fist. "Your mother was a warrior. When she could no longer fight with her hands, she fought with her prayers, her words, with the fresh blood of your birth. While you were covered in that blood, she said those verses. That new lifeblood of a newborn baby and her mother could be felt, heard, smelled, tasted in the air and almost touched by our kind. Someone heard your mother's prayer. Someone who respects blood, someone who understood her pain. My dear."

Syà approached her and gripped her chin once again, looking into her eyes. "Who turned you? We must know. You're not what you think you are and your husband-to-be, your king, could lose everything if his brother, who is also powerful and cunning, gets his way. This is about more than leadership. It's so much deeper than that…"

"Syà, I wish I could, but I cannot tell you! I swore! I made an oath. It could put her in danger."

"Syà, I've already spoken to Venus about this. I've accepted that she made a promise and I am no longer pushing her to reveal it. She is loyal, as she proved time and time again, and I wish to have no part in making her anything other than that. Especially when it comes to *me*."

"Very well then, we will simply do the best we can." Syà released her, clearly disappointed, and went back to her seat. She drank from her glass and looked around at everyone. "Venus, do you know why Alexandre called us specifically? Of all the Pure Blood monarchs in the world, he called us… Have you questioned why?"

"Yes, I want to know why." Venus walked back over to

the dining room table and took her seat.

"Because Count Marseille was there for us when few others were. A little under a century ago, our monarch was under attack from the Japanese Emperor over a deal gone bad. Our nation had fallen ill due to a local poison, a disease that only affected us, and it wiped out over half of our army. We were outnumbered. We were being slaughtered by the Japanese due to not being able to properly defend ourselves. We just didn't have the manpower. Alexandre came in with his army that his family had trained themselves, and fought right beside us. The war ended three days later, with few casualties on our side. Japan retreated. Decades later, we made peace with Japan, in part due to Alexandre's negotiating skills.

"It's time we assist him in his time of need. Despite that setback, we are some of the fiercest warrior Pure Bloods in the world. The Marseille Clan has an established reputation of being the strongest and fastest in all of Europe. Alexandre comes from a long line of soldiers who ruled with their brains and their brawn. My husband, King Zhang Wei, also has a similar background. My maiden name is Huang. The Huang Clan was also known to be ferocious, even to this day. I was fighting from a very early age.

"Our parents arranged our union, but we work as a team, and care for one another. With this merger, our bloodline is now the fiercest in all of China. Our children are soldiers, all seven of them. We fight to the death!" In a flash, she snatched her sword from behind her back and hit the table with the tip of it. At first, all seemed well… until the damn thing split in two, falling apart as if it were merely a stack of cards.

"Damn it. I just had this shit replaced!" Alexandre burst out laughing, half teasing. "Fucking on the table… broke it. Invite friends over, now this! Are you going to fix this shit, Zhang Wei and Syà? Or is this just a magic trick that has an unfortunate, unclimactic ending?"

They all burst out laughing, a welcome reprieve from the pain his blood bride was certainly feeling. Syà placed the sword back where it belonged.

"My wife likes to show off, Venus." Zhang Wei grinned. "But she can back it up." He patted Syà's hand. "We are here to help you both. We will be travelling to France together as character witnesses and whatever else you need, Alexandre."

"Thank you."

"Due to these new circumstances, I propose we also have the wedding as soon as possible while in Paris." Syà stated with a smile. "Leave everything to *me*."

Just then, Bruce and Whiskey walked back into the room.

"You're all settled, Boss. Oh and uh, Alexandre, I hope you don't mind, but I called a few other of your friends too and explained the situation. They are prepared to meet you in Paris."

"Thank you, Whiskey, for thinking ahead." The truth of the matter was that Alexandre detested asking for assistance, but Victor could not be taken lightly. There was no telling what other tricks he had up his sleeves.

Moments later, they'd all changed into more befitting attire, the weapons cast aside, and piled into the SUV, on their way to LaGuardia Airport. He took Venus' hand and kissed it. The sight of her made him breathless. She was the most beautiful creation he'd ever seen, and the stars in her eyes shined bright.

"Maybe you can be a light in my dark tunnel." He looped his arm around her and brought her in for a kiss. "I produce no light. I was born from cold, dank darkness... but you're the sun, Venus."

"I'm not the sun, baby. I'm Venus. I am the second farthest planet from the brightest star in the universe. Being second isn't bad. I'm second in command, like a mate." He smiled at her words. "Venus rotates in the opposite direction of all the other planets. She does her own thing. That's called independence, making my own choices, going my own way. Fearless. Never followed behind nobody. Venus was the Roman goddess of love and beauty, but being beautiful is only skin-deep. It's what's in here..." She pointed to her mind and heart. "Your strength, your courage... all of that makes you truly magnificent.

"I adapt to the conditions around me, no matter what comes my way. That is what makes me a survivor. I see now that I was held up in prayer." She caressed his face as he trembled from her touch. "And I'm not mad at my mother now that it's all sunk in... now that you and Syà have explained it to me. My mother did it 'cause she loved me... but she was afraid for me, as many mothers were for their children during that time. Being afraid is being a slave to your own emotions... living in fear. Phobias make you a slave. Anxiety makes you a slave. Fear of giving and receiving love makes you a slave, too. It's a terrible thing; it slows you down. My mother gave me a gift. She had no way of knowing that slavery would ever end. It lasted over four hundred years. She did it so I'd *never* be nobody's victim *ever* again. I love you, Mama!"

One clear tear escaped her left eye, and a blood red one from the right. Her humanity refused to die, and her vampirism refused to not fight until the bitter end...

CHAPTER SIXTEEN

All in the Name of Love

When good Americans die,

they go to Paris.

— Oscar Wilde

A LEXANDRE TUGGED AT the collar of his black trench coat and stared at Venus' reflection in the full-length mirror. It had been a long trip, and he'd spent most of the flight planning out various scenarios in his head. His beloved was sleeping, her chest slowly rising up and down. She looked so peaceful...

He hadn't been in his Parisian home in such a long time, he'd *almost* forgotten how beautiful it was. The Renaissance style architecture definitely caught many people's attention; his property had appeared in multiple interior decorating maga-zines and the like. Impeccable landscaping, lime and ivory statues created by some of the most noteworthy Parisian sculptors, as well as two double meandering blacktopped driveways that led to a garage housing a multitude of classic cars, all in impeccable condition. The property was always manned with armed security guards working round the clock daily.

Inside the mansion were multiple winding staircases, many fashioned out of pure gold and granite, as well as numerous floors and wings that hosted a variety of needs, and of course, undeniable desires. One room was stocked with glass bottles of blood from preferred donors, a place where one could sit and feed, and listen to music surrounded by historic books and art in the privacy of a small gallery.

Yes, I can keep some property in New York, run my law practice there but live back home. I think Venus will like it here… it's beautiful. Fit for a queen.

He took a deep breath and put on his cufflink. He smiled at the memory of the two members of his Coven who'd welcomed him home with open arms—his cousin, Theo, and his dear uncle, Henri. With such a small Coven left, Alexandre treasured the members of his family, of his sacred bloodline that still lived. It was time to continue building… to have offspring of his own.

"You look incredible." Her voice broke into his inner thoughts and he spun around in her direction.

"Ahhh, I see the special sleeping pills I gave you have

worn off. You're awake." He glanced down at his Rolex. "What was that? A forty-two-minute nap? You're sleeping like me now, just a bit here and there." He smirked.

The woman yawned and stretched, her nude body displayed for his lustful pleasure. He stroked his erection over his pants as he took her in. She clutched the edge of the mattress, acting as if oblivious to his perverted thoughts, her thick mass of black tresses spread around her like a storm cloud. He made his way to her and pushed some of the soft bushy coils out of her face, then bent down and kissed her lips.

"I don't want you to go alone." She ran her hand up and down her arm. He could feel her eyes following him as he returned to stand in front of the mirror.

"It shouldn't take terribly long."

"That's not it… I don't want you there with no support. It will feel like one against eighty." She stood from the bed and walked to him. Reaching for his zipper, she tugged it down and ran her tongue against his scrotum.

"Actually, they're not against me, or for me. They are for our people."

"Allegedly. I don't trust anyone anymore."

He said nothing in response, though he agreed with her.

"Secondly, the Council is comprised of thirteen members… Ahhh…" He hissed when she enveloped his erect dick into her mouth, sucking slow and hard along the length.

"Unlucky thirteen… fabulous." She chuckled dismally before popping him back into her mouth, the tips of her fangs scraping across his flesh. He ran his fingers through her hair and pumped his hips in a hard, jerky motion, chasing his climax. Closing his eyes, he fucked her mouth until he exploded… Relief felt like a cool, refreshing breeze, his entire body now relaxed, almost sedated. Slipping his cock out of her mouth, he tucked it back into his pants and pulled up the zipper.

"Venus, I need you to do something for me."

"Yes?" She swallowed, then slicked her tongue across her lips, collecting the last bit of his cum.

"While I'm meeting with everyone, I want for you to go with Syà into town and do some shopping. Take your mind off things."

"How can I shop for purses, lingerie, lipstick and curling irons while you are being investigated, unfairly I might add, Alexandre? How damn shallow do you think I am?" She twisted her lips and put her hand on her hip, attitude officially launched.

"That's not it. I don't think you're shallow in the least. You're still on your humanitarian kick, and that's just who you are. In fact, I wish you were *more* shallow, since you see self-preservation at times like some curse."

"Self-preservation *always* comes first, but you can care about others at the same time. It doesn't have to be all or nothing."

"Let's make something clear: this isn't an attack on your character." He leaned her down onto the bed, lay beside her, and slid two fingers within her pussy. She sighed and grinded against his digits as he finger-fucked her slow, then hard, then slow again. "I told you that I accept you and love you as you are. Just as you accept me, too." He leaned closer and ran his tongue along her neck, kissing and sucking, nipping at her delicious flesh. "I am who I am, you are who you are, and that's just how it is."

She smiled at his words then shook against his touch, cumming undone.

"The bottom line is, Venus, that I would feel much more at ease if I knew you were having a good time." Her eyes rolled as another orgasm hit her... He wanted to be inside her in the worst way. "Now, can my fiancée please go the markets and shop? Buy whatever you wish, and bring me back a gift, too."

He got off the bed, slid on his suit jacket, and checked himself out in the mirror once again.

"Alexandre, come here."

He went to lift her from the bed and hug her close. Soon she was wrapped around him, her warmth a salve to his troubled soul. Running his hands up and down her body, he wished they had more minutes to spare, just enough time to fuck her back to sleep, but he had to be on his way. With reluctance, he stepped back from her, still holding her hands for a little longer, then slowly released.

"I will see you later today." He blew her a kiss, then exited out the bedroom door...

THIS WASN'T WHAT Venus had expected…

Venus thought she was being hauled off to Carrousel du Louvre mall, or perhaps the bustling and beautiful Beaugrenelle. Instead, she was deep below the ground surrounded by strung flashing lights, red lanterns, and the scent of fresh kills filling the air. Her eyes grew large with excitement as she moved about among other Vamps with their glossy shopping bags and expensive attire. Some of the men were dressed like Dapper Dan, a few smiling in her direction, or exposing themselves, offering their cocks for a quick romp. Some yelled lewd things in French as they rubbed on their dicks.

It's New York all over again…

She smirked and shook her head, feeling a bit more at home. *Fucking bastards.* Moonchild sung, 'Cure' through speakers she couldn't see. She followed close behind Syà who appeared quite familiar with the area—an intricate vampire network underground teeming with artists, singers, magicians, trinket sellers, and the like.

Fragrant perfumes, hand dipped candles and incense lined several tables that caught her eye, as well as seamstresses peddling their wares for the most elaborate and elegant gowns. As she and Syà moved side by side, shoulder to shoulder, the woman pointed out a stall with shelving showcasing various glass bottles of blood, letting her know what vendors to trust and who to steer clear from. A few Bottom Feeders had tents and tables set up, chock full of stolen jewels and other odds and ends.

Venus paused and pointed to her right, spotting a performance taking place on a golden stage. She tugged on Syà's arm, urging her to get closer. Three nude dancers, all of them with bright red straight hair, moved like the air and the sea itself, twisting and turning to some of the most haunting music she'd ever heard.

"Look at that… They're great."

"The Duranceau Sisters," Syà explained with a smile. "Well known, very talented." Venus nodded in understanding as they walked on. "These are beautiful." The woman took a silk scarf into her hands, running her fingers over the deep dark wine material. *"Combien ça coûte?"* she asked the vendor, a rather short Vamp with long, spindly fingers, her eyes a strange dark orange color.

"Je les fais moi-même. 342.00 Euros."

"It's nice that you make them yourself. However, I think 300.00 Euros is a fairer price."

"330."

"325." They shook on it and the vendor placed the silk scarf in a soft, pink bag and handed it to her. *"Merci!"*

"Merci!"

Along their way, Venus spotted a deep burgundy silk tie and gold cufflinks shaped like daggers that she simply had to get for Alexandre. They continued on until Venus nearly lost her breath. A young man in a gray smock sat at an easel painting a beautiful portrait of a young African woman. Syà stood next to her as she eyed the piece.

"Looks just like my mama… just like her." Venus trembled with emotion, her heart pounding with elation and a rush of memories.

The artist regarded her. He was a young Turned Vampire, his youth evident, his eyes still warm. He pointed to the painting and told her in a thick accent, "Almost finished. You like?"

She nodded.

"How much?" Syà questioned, her tone serious. The young artist looked at Syà, then at Venus, then back at Syà. He didn't speak for several seconds, cocked his head to the side and stared into her eyes.

"*Gratis.*"

"Free? I can't take this for free. Here, you have to take something for it." Venus dug into her wrap-around satchel and pulled out some money. "Damn it. I forgot the money Alexandre left for me on the vanity. I have mine, though. Um, sorry, all I have are US dollars, is that okay?"

He nodded and graciously took the cash. "Come back, five minutes?" He held up five fingers. "All done."

"Of course, yes. I'll be back."

"Looks just like your mother, huh?" Syà asked as she looped her arm around hers, just as a best friend would.

"Yes. It is a remarkable likeness." Venus felt a sisterhood with Syà, just as the latter had promised when they first met.

The Vamp was a Chinese Pure Blood from a highly respected family, she was physically strong and assertive, but she didn't act superior or put on airs. In fact, she'd been so gracious and kind to her, showing her the ropes, it touched Venus in ways she couldn't describe. Sure, Syà said things at times she probably shouldn't, but that just made her all the more authentic. Minutes later, Syà was introducing her to a host of Parisian Vamps, all of them reminding Venus of 1950's Hollywood movie stars, clad in dramatic, expensive attire, all with exquisite taste. Their attitudes were practically tangible.

"And this is Constance, that's Emilia, Angèle, Hélène, Véronique and Madeleine." Syà went down the line of women, all of them seemingly in the throes of a shopping spree.

"Nice to meet you all." Venus extended her hand but the women instead nodded, looked her up and down, and smirked amongst themselves.

"*Bonjour*, Venus." One of them, Hélène, finally extended her hand, wrapped in a black satin glove. The woman's hair fell in soft platinum blond waves to her shoulders. Her skin was ghostly white, her eyes an incredible rich violet and her lips, a deep purple tone. She wore a black blazer jacket with a sea shell and pearl pendant, matching pencil pants, and black pointy stiletto pumps. "Excuse some of my friends." The Vamp shot the other ladies a side glance. "It's wonderful that Syà brought you. I look forward to getting to know you better. Maybe we all can visit one of the blood bars later for drinks and vaping." The woman's English was flawless.

"Thank you, Hélène. I'd like that." Venus felt a tap on her

shoulder. She turned around to find the young vampire painter. He handed her the work of art.

"*Je vous ai trouvé.*"

"Thank you so much for tracking me down, I lost track of time. Beautiful! *Magnifique!*" She held up the painting, still a bit wet in a couple of spots.

"*De rien!*" The guy nodded and headed off.

"He tried to give that to her for free." Syà shifted her weight and regarded the women with hooded eyes. They seemed to be having a silent conversation Venus wasn't privy to, and even if she were, she probably wouldn't understand. "It means he sees the stars in her eyes, too."

All of the Vamp women's fangs extended at the same time as they leered closer, peering into her eyes. They oohed and ahhed, as if she were some freak on display. Suddenly, one of them tossed her fur over one shoulder and huffed.

"You're pretty, Venus. Too pretty for America. I see why Alexandre wants you. Stars in your eyes... How could he pass that up?" Jealousy dripped from her tone, and perhaps a bit of confusion, too.

Syà's cellphone rang. She dug into her designer purse and answered.

"*Nǐ hǎo,*" Syà was speaking so fast in Chinese that Venus missed practically everything that was said after 'Hello.' "We have to go." She jerked Venus's arm, but tossed on a fake grin at the ladies before taking off. "*Zàijiàn!*"

"What's wrong? What's going on?" Venus questioned as they both moved swiftly through the crowd.

"My husband is spying in on Alexandre's hearing. He feels as if things are not going well and suggests that they meet you before this goes any further. Thing is, we're not supposed to be there—it's a private hearing. We'll need to improvise. Shit! This is all Victor's fault... I wish I could eat him alive... son of a bitch! We need to do everything we can to stop this from going the wrong way. Victor being in power would be a disaster, Venus. It would destroy centuries of alliances. He's just not diplomatic enough. He doesn't know how to play the part."

Venus hissed as she kept up with the woman, and a surge of rage heated her core. The two pushed their way through the lines of merchants, street performers and patrons.

She looked down at the painting in her arms and forced a smile.

Mama, please promise me everything will be all right. I am taking this painting as a sign of faith, a sign of hope. An answered prayer...

VICTOR GRIPPED THE podium with both hands as a cool breeze moved throughout the vast, vaulted room. Framed paintings of their forefathers and foremothers lined the walls in the domed basilica and in the center, his brother sat on a wide gold chair with intricately carved legs and arms, the bastard looking so debonair, as if he had not a care in the

272

world. In times past, King Alexandre Marseille had been the one running the show, but now, the Council, all thirteen elders in their red and black robes sat behind a long white marble desk, prepared to issue judgment. Everyone in that room spoke in French, including himself, as was the custom.

"So that is why I, reluctantly and humbly, have made a case against my very own last living brother, Alexandre Marseille."

"*King* Alexandre Marseille," the fucker corrected.

They locked gazes, engaging in a battle of wills. Alexandre's ice blue orbs blazed in the darkened room. The pale flesh of his face, neck, and hands practically glowed. Long limbs covered in an expensive black and gray pinstripe suit—typical of his sibling, as well as the black trench coat that fit as though tailored for him. He wore several rings, which gleamed when he moved his hands. Alexandre extended his pinky nail, making it grow long and curved. It was a clear warning...

He'd been marked.

The threat was real, and his dear brother, regardless of the outcome, had made a promise to get him. Victor wasn't the least bit surprised; in fact, he rather looked forward to it.

"King Alexandre." One of the elders cleared his throat and leaned forward, only his lips visible from beneath the hood of his thick black and red cape. "Victor Marseille has presented sufficient evidence to bring this matter before us. Can you please explain, in your own words, your position on the circumstances that are in question?"

Victor took a seat, but didn't take his eyes off his brother.

This motherfucker is going to try to be slick. But your tricks don't work in here, Alexandre Marseille. None of us are susceptible to them!

"Most definitely, Judge Autin." His brother clasped his hands together and acknowledged everyone in the room with a nod. "I left for America, New York City to be specific, in order to find my mate. This is true. I was upfront about that, especially after dragging my feet for so long due to public outcry, the needs of the people, and pressure from my Coven, most notably my brother Victor, to marry someone who also was Pure Blood.

"Though it is always my mission to be the best leader that I can be to my subjects, the issue of matrimony is one of our most sacred and important binds, not only for our people, but for our very own happiness."

Several of the judges nodded in agreement.

"The Marseille Clan has been rapidly dwindling due to the ideology that we must mate and marry only fellow Pure Breeds. Even if I were in agreement with that, the selections are quite limited. In my case, for instance, I would have to go outside of France to find a non-family member who would be eligible for marriage. I am not homosexual, so pairing with a male is not desirable for me. Furthermore, I wish to have my own offspring, which is expected. Though incestual relationships have been widely accepted historically and even encouraged among vampires, in this new day and age, we've discovered certain genetic mutations that make it less desirable, due in part to a loss of power. When a Marseille mates with another Marseille, they will produce weaker offspring. However, were I to go out and mate with, say, a Vamp from

Italy, a Pure Blood, my chances of having mentally, physically, and emotionally strong offspring would increase.

"Recent information in our own scientific studies also suggest that if we take it one step further, and procreate with Turned Vamps, as long as they are of good pedigree, we not only receive the talents and gifts of our own bloodline, but we receive others that would have otherwise been previously unobtainable."

"Excuse me, King Marseille, with all due respect," another Judge of the Council intervened, his long black fingernail pointed directly towards the ceiling, "a Turned Vamp was once human, and that actually weakens the Pure Blood bloodline. Humans are less intelligent, less physically adept, and definitely have no gifts such as psychic abilities, mind reading, telekinesis, rapid reflexes, fast healing, dream jumping, heightened senses and the like, which negates what we've worked so hard to secure and advance since the beginning of time. Though we've welcomed Turned Vampires to some degree into our family, to marry and consequently procreate with them is still looked down upon for the aforementioned reasons."

"Yes, I understand your concerns, Judge Carbonneau. Yet, evidence points to the fact that a Turned Vamp, once she reaches age 100 from her rebirth, is more vampire than human. In fact, her human traits and characteristics have faded by at least 65% by that time. Thus, Turned Vamps of good pedigree are a viable option to continue our fledgling bloodline, which is now only in the hundreds; and most of those are no longer able to bear children, barren due to chromosomal disorders, physical deficiencies, or injuries suffered in battle, which forfeited their ability to reproduce. I am a viable, fertile warrior male who has saved my seed for the right Vamp. I have not even attempted to breed outside of matrimony but now, the search is over. I have finally found her."

Whispers abounded amongst the judges.

"Please, tell us the specifics about this candidate for queendom, King Alexandre."

"Certainly. I wish you would have allowed her attendance today, so you could meet her for yourself, but I understand that is against the rules." Alexandre stood from his seat. "She's incredible. She's—"

"An imbecilic Black slave woman from South Carolina with unkempt hair. She teaches Art History to a bunch of bleeding heart humans... She's not good for the bloodline. I've seen pictures," Victor interrupted, folding his arms over his chest.

"Victor Marseille, there are to be no further interruptions from you during this proceeding!" one of the Judges chastised.

"Yes, my apologies." He smirked, his mission already accomplished. When he met eyes with his brother, Alexandre's fangs were slightly descended and his eyes hooded.

Nice. Perfect. Fall apart. Attack. Show them what a fucking wreck you are over Turned pussy...

"King Alexandre, please continue."

"Yes, I was saying that she is everything I would ever wish for in a queen…" Alexandre went on a lovely, dramatic spiel about this beautiful specimen, how well she took to training, her intelligence and love of art. He discussed her unusual physical strength, lovemaking skills, and how several of his assistants had taken to her. It went on and on and Victor stifled several yawns. *A vampire Blood King in love… how wretched!*

Finally, the question and answer session about the Turned beast was complete and Alexandre took his seat. Twenty minutes later, the judges returned after having finished deliberating.

Judge Couture stood from his seat. He placed his emerald chalice down, the sides of it glistening with blood. Removing his hood, he let his silver and black tresses flow outward. His hair was bone straight, parted down the middle and reaching to his waist. The elderly Vamp's eyes where pure black, like onyx jewels.

"We have reached a decision." Alexandre nodded and looked the judge in the eyes. "We have concluded, King Alexandre Marseille, that you violated many codes and rules of the throne."

"What?!" Alexandre's fangs fully extended. His eyes burned with hatred… it was so beautiful!

"We are in agreement that due to these encroachments and the preponderance of evidence against you, that you be stripped of your title and position. King Alexandre Marseille, you have violated the code of full disclosure, refused to come to the Council and update us in a timely fashion regarding the matters at hand, murdered three of your brother's servants by psychological and psychic abuse and intimidation, then ordered that they commit suicide, attacked one of your brother's servants so severely that he will never regain the ability to speak again, and violated codes 5A, 7H and 2C-R."

"But you didn't even ask to meet her! You haven't even finished hearing my side of this! NO! This is wrong! I won't accept it!" In a flash, Alexandre levitated, his body rising in the air. The flames of the candles all around swayed violently as he hovered above, moving practically at the speed of light.

Show them how crazy you are, brother of mine... Temper, temper, temper. There'll be no coming back from this... See? You're a loose cannon... King Alexandre is dead.

The judges remained fairly calm, but Victor knew better. Alexandre could go on a killing spree in a split second; he was just that volatile.

"You have three days to clear your personal belongings and evacuate your property at the Marseille Mansion, Alexandre. The next in line for the throne is Victor Marseille, who will be sworn in one week from today."

The gavel sounded like sweet, thundering music to his ears. His eyes burned with blood, tears of joy. Victor sat there, stunned, overwhelmed with bliss. It seemed at times during the hearing that Alexandre had them eating out of his hand but that last bit of evidence from Fawn must've worked after all. The woman had done everything she could to wiggle out of getting on the stand, but she'd offered a fair compromise—something even better. She'd supplied a video of him ranting and raving, then going on a murder binge in his own home over some unpaid debts… Mayhem.

Alexandre lowered himself back down to the floor and turned his head in a stiff manner, as if it were attached with rusty nuts and bolts. His lips curled in a grin before he spoke in such a low tone, the sound of his voice vibrated through his body like an organ.

"My dear brother, Victor, you've gotten what you've come here for. My sweet, sweet, brother, I'm coming for what's mine, *too*." Alexandre placed his hand over his heart and grinned. Before Victor could respond to the threat, Alexandre was upon him!

"SHIT!" The judges moved from their seats as the table toppled over from Alexandre's speed in closing the fifty feet of distance between them.

Pandemonium broke out when Alexandre wrapped his strong hands around his neck and squeezed.

"Die! Die! Die!"

Victor's head became foggy, the air cut off from his lungs. He could hear the commotion all around him, the bodies hitting the floor, the screams. He reached up with a shaky hand and managed to twist and break Alexandre's wrist—the crack was almost deafening. Alexandre barely flinched. He kept one hand securely around his neck, popped his wrist back into place with a vigorous shake, and continued to choke the living shit out of him.

"Alexandre!" Several of the judges rushed to his aid, but Alexandre pushed them aside as if they were made of cotton balls. The hatred in his brother's eyes astounded Victor. The brute strength he possessed was like nothing he'd ever experienced before, and yet, something within him knew that Alexandre was holding back, for if not, he'd already be dead.

"Someone call the constabularies before it is too late! He's going to kill his brother!"

"STOP IT! THERE'S A MOB AT THE DOOR!" came a booming voice that he didn't recognize.

Suddenly, it sounded as if the doors burst open and the cathedral went completely black.

A bright light shone, and Alexandre slowly slipped his hands away from his neck. Victor got to his feet, rubbing the heated flesh, and looked in the direction of the commotion.

At least twenty-four monarchs from all over the nation stood present with their spouses, all of them with weapons drawn. Massive silver swords, bows and arrows, guns probably loaded with silver and serrated bullets, gleaming axes, and two witches with stark black eyes glaring at him holding odd little velvet bags in their grip. The crowd parted, and in the middle walked a beautiful barefoot Black woman with a cloud of black curls framing her face, her skin like brown satin. She donned a vibrant green gown that brought out the richness of her skin color. Victor could no longer deny her beauty. It was impossible.

She extended her fangs as she glared at him, then her eyes glossed over when her gaze fell on Alexandre, his brother, her lover…

"No worries, my Love."

"We demand an opportunity for appeal!" the Dutch monarch, Lord Van de Velde, stated. "Any king stripped of his title has a right to an immediate appeal within twenty-four hours! This is a travesty! A miscarriage of justice!"

An uproar ensued and the room vibrated with rage. Victor's chest rose up and down like an accordion being played and tinkered with at full speed. There was no way these bastards would leave peacefully! Where had they all come from? How had Alexandre convinced them to leave their posts and speak up on his behalf? Alexandre was cruel and ruthless… he had no friends. Or did he?

"I AM KING NOW!" Victor roared. "You can't come in here and—"

"Be quiet!" Judge Carbonneau yelled, one long, bony finger pointed in his direction. "We've already made a decision, but Alexandre is entitled to an appeal. King Van de Velde is correct."

"WE WANT IT NOW! WE WANT IT NOW! WE WANT IT NOW!" the mob began to chant.

"May I speak?" The slave's voice was strong, yet her eyes held a desperate plea. Judge Couture studied her from the podium. The room remained fairly silent for what felt like an eternity.

"State your name."

"Venus Margaret Anderson."

Judge Couture stared at her for so long, seconds turned to minutes. He came down from the judges' stand, taking his time, until he towered over the Turned Vamp. He sniffed. Then sniffed again. His fangs descended, causing a hush and whispers in the room. His long piano-key-striped white and black hair blew about, as if caught in a whirlwind.

"You smell... familiar." He slowly walked around her, then again. After several moments, he stopped, staff in hand. "Before you volunteer any information, I want you to answer this one simple question."

"Yes. What would you like to know?"

"Who turned you?"

The slave stood there, and her body began to shake as she looked down at the floor. After several excruciating moments, Alexandre wrapped his arm around her and pulled her close.

"Pathetic!" Victor could not stand one more second of this. He leapt from behind the table that had been turned right-side up but before he could advance any further, someone tossed a silver throwing star at his head. He ducked in the nick of time, and took note of fucking King Zhang Wei and his slanty eyed Chinois bitch, Syà, standing there, their peepers and smiles black as night.

"Who turned you?!" the judge demanded once again.

"I will tell you if it will help Alexandre." The slave woman held her head high, though it was obvious she was overwrought with emotion. "But first I must explain that I love Alexandre and would do practically anything for him. I ask in advance for forgiveness from my mistress, for breaking her trust, for breaking our secrets… My mistress' name is…"

CHAPTER SEVENTEEN

The Queen's English

THE WALLS PULSED and caved inward. A sound like a bomb going off in a volcano erupted the entire place, forcing everyone to take cover. Dark smoke spread like a suffocating gas, the basilica windows burst and shards of black glass flew around, slicing into skin and landing on every surface—as if the sky had frozen and broke to pieces right above their heads. Chaos, vampiric shrieks and curses ensued, many taking cover and shielding their eyes.

When Alexandre removed his arm from his face, he spotted Venus on the floor several feet away, her head tucked and her body covered in debris. He stormed over to his woman and immediately picked her up in his arms. After dusting her off, especially her head and shoulders, he covered her with his coat. Clouds of gray dust drifted about like a caravan on a mission, then finally settled, and all was quiet.

Someone may be dead...

He looked over at the judges—all of them appeared to be fine, barring their confused expressions. Two guards, who'd arrived on the scene after the mob arrived, began to assist in clearing up the area.

All around him, the pews were covered in glass and dust. Behind him, the kings and queens from around the world were all on bended knee, their eyes still shielded...

The mood had shifted. The Earth was alive with a force yet to be seen.

Where the fuck is my damn brother?

He looked in all directions but didn't see Victor. For a split second, he figured the coward had run off, but that couldn't be. He could smell the bastard lurking close, keeping a keen eye on all that was around him, scoping him out like Alexandre was attempting to do with him. After a deep breath, he rose to his feet.

"Is anyone beside you down? Is everyone accounted for?"

All the kings and queens murmured their assent as they lifted their faces. One by one, they stood and swiped the debris from their bodies. The distinct sound of crunching glass underfoot could be heard now, reminding him of vampire spines cracking under tremendous weight. A robust feminine energy filled the place—strong... sweet... awful... beautiful. Through a dense cloud of dark gray dust appeared a tall figure in a blood red cape. At the base of it peeked out black tie up boots as she walked. He could not see her face, but the hands were bare... pale white with blue undertones, the veins large and knotted. Thick, curled, long nails adorned each hand, one finger donning a large diamond sapphire ring that looked all too familiar.

Alexandre's chest heaved and his eyes burned from the haze, but his brain began to pulse and throb, to hurt in a way humans would describe a hangover.

No... no, this can't be...

The woman paused in the center of the room, gathered the material of her hood with both hands, and allowed it to fall away from her face. Venus screamed out. Jerking away from his embrace, she flew to the newcomer like a lost baby to a mother! His bride's feet lifted off the floor, and in a blur of love, life, and loyalty, she wrapped herself around the figure, squeezing, holding, embracing with all of her might, all that was in her, all that she'd hoped to become....

Venus' desires were rich and open. He read them like pages in a book. She admired this vampire, respected her, *loved* her...

The vampire wrapped her arms around her, too, and a smile split across the figure's angular face. Long, thick black strands of hair flowed from the Vamp's scalp like dark ropes. As the two clung to one another, the woman's blue eyes changed to a piercing shade of red, reflected upon him and her smile vanished... Alexandre tapped his foot then cracked his neck. He smiled, anything to keep his limbs moving, to make his mind not drift into a darkness that he could never come back from.

"I'm sorry for betraying you. I didn't see any other way!" Venus explained, her voice cracking.

"I am not upset with you," The traitor stroked Venus' hair. "You did exactly as you were to do... what I prepared you for, so long ago."

"Geneviève, this is my mate. He—"

"Oh Venus, my Love, please don't waste your breath with silly introductions! Geneviève! Wow!!!" Alexandre bellowed, the veins in his body throbbing with anguish, or perhaps it was pure pain.

Victor materialized then thrust out from the smoky shadows like a white piece of dog shit from some tight, puckering asshole. The fucker's eyes nearly popped out of his head as he made his way over the rubble, tumbling towards them like a drunken idiot.

"This is outrageous! This is obscene!" Alexandre cackled at his brother's words and turned in a circle, his arms in the air as his fangs descended from the gumline. "No... I don't believe my eyes. How?" Victor murmured, his voice barely audible.

"Shut the fuck up. This is between me and Geneviève," Alexandre ordered as he shot up in the air, his movements causing the broken fragments of glass and dust to sway in a counterclockwise vortex. The woman ignored Victor, gently nudged Venus out of her way, and floated towards him quickly, her fangs descended as she hissed. They spun around one another, dancing in midair as his rage turned blacker than black.

"*Quelle surprise!*"

"Geneviève? Alexandre? What's going on?!" Venus asked, her face a mask of confusion, her hair sparkling with dust, her eyes full of light and darkness.

"My Love, Geneviève is no mistress! This is my mother!" Fire burned in his eyes as he bit into his lower lip, drawing out his own essence. It dripped down his chin as he tried to restrain himself, tried to make sense of the ultimate betrayal.

"But... you died!" Victor called out. "You died during the war!"

"I did not die. I was captured! At the time, we were fighting the Fernández Clan. It was a brutal battle... so many of our own met their demise! It was either stay away from my family, give up my throne, or you two would be in danger. You'd perish! They'd already killed your father and stolen your sister, Alainne! She killed herself soon thereafter to prevent from being their slave. I couldn't have my only two living children murdered as well!"

She flung her cape around herself and floated back to the floor, covering part of her face. He hadn't heard Alainne's name in centuries...

"This is a personal matter. Let's leave and give them time alone," Queen Syà Wei stated in Chinese.

"No!" Alexandre hollered. "Everyone stays! You all have shown more loyalty to me today than *this* woman that birthed me!" Mother's eyes glowed with wrath as she glared at him. "Let me tell you *all* what type of Vamp she is! She left me and my brother to fend for ourselves. We were not infants, but we were young, still in need of guidance and preparation. I had to teach myself how to survive… and teach my brother, too. We had to fight and kill all day long to prove ourselves worthy of staying in our own home. And then, I had to fight again and again to claim and secure the throne once I'd made it to age! I was an orphan… no one here to pass down the sword and the crown."

"And you survived! That is what counts, Alexandre!"

"Survived? Do you have any idea what we endured?! The torture was endless, despite being of Royal blood! Some of our own family members, our own Coven, tested us, called our father weak for being killed in battle, and called our mother the same! They said we were not of good stock, that I wasn't fit for the throne! I slaughtered day and night. I did it in part to clear my family name! To prove that the Marseille Clan was all that we were said to be in the glory days and more!"

"I HAD TO DISAPPEAR TO SAVE YOU!"

"YOU'RE A WARRIOR QUEEN. YOU DON'T HAVE TO DO ANYTHING BUT DEFEND THE THRONE!" he roared so loud, her hair blew from the sound of his voice. "You're a Marseille. I don't believe you… everything has been a lie."

He reached into his pants pocket, pulled out a cigar, and lit it with his fingertip. The dark smoke billowed between them, forming foggy depictions of desires and fears… scurrying rats… vats of blood… silver swords… lust. All the fears he'd dined on for his entire existence, those he'd eaten up one after another like a delicious blood buffet. After a few moments of silence, his mother began to pace the floor. She appeared far less at ease, but that was fleeting. She cooled down quick, and her expression smoothed out.

He could hear her heartbeat, and her steps matched its rhythm. Her breaths echoed in his ears. Her demeanor was something he loved, something he hated. She looked at Venus and paused, stopping dead in her tracks.

He couldn't deny that there appeared to be affection in her eyes towards his Bloodmate—the same way she used to look at him and his younger siblings, and their father, too.

"Alexandre, you were born to rule." She snapped back in his direction, shoving her cloak out of the way as she made her way forward. "You were born to be okay, no matter what became of me and where I went. It is in your blood, it is in your training. It is your choice whether to believe me or not. I did what I needed to do to protect my family!" He slid his tongue down his right fang, licking it, picking up the remnants of his bloody breakfast. "A warrior protects their young offspring, even if it costs us everything! I was banished. It was made clear by the Fernández Clan that, should I attempt to come back to Paris, I would be killed and everyone else, too. At the time, they outnumbered us trifold! They wanted our resources. I watched you from a distance, my dear son." Her voice quaked. "You defeated the Fernández Clan less than one century later!"

"You could have returned then! Where have you been all of this time?" Victor's eyes darkened.

She kept her back straight, her fangs descended. "MY GREATEST MISTAKE!" She pointed at Victor. "You have no right to question me after the treacherous, treasonous acts you've committed against your own Coven member, your king, your very own blood brother! The eldest brother who protected you in your time of need!" Mother moved swiftly to stand before him, her milky bosom heaving up and down in her corseted gown, now partially exposed as her cape hung off her body. His brother didn't flinch, but his anxiety coated the air, thick with burden. She slowly lifted her arm, then smacked him so hard across the face, it echoed throughout the place and brought him to his knees. He stayed down, his face averted.

"I curse you…" Victor stated with steel in his tone.

"And I curse you, too." Mother turned away, her eyes now upon Alexandre.

"I want answers as well. Why are you here now, Mother? After all of this time?! Why didn't you return after the war was over?" Alexandre took Venus in his arms, needing her close… something to stand between him and the woman he'd once revered but now detested.

"I was bound. It didn't matter if millions of them existed or just one… and you being king made you even more of a target! I fought; believe me, I did. I would come in the dark of the night and watch you… but you rarely sleep, so my visits would always be far too short. So many times I wanted to kiss your cheek, soothe you when you were enraged, mad at the world. I ruled from a distance, my dear son. Something you do

well, too. I had to come today. I found out what was happening… I always know what's going on." She narrowed her eyes
on him. "Not only is Venus free, but you are free now, too…"
Mother approached slowly, the crunch of broken glass under
her feet now amplified. She sounded like a million men
walking… the strength… the courage… the respect.

"Now I know why Venus is stronger and more powerful
than the average Turned Vamp. Your blood runs through her.
It's almost unheard of for a Pure Blood to turn a human. I
only have part of the story. I need the rest. Why did you turn
her, then spend all of those years fostering her?"

Mother ran her hands over one another, pacing a bit, then
stood still.

"The one way I could ensure that our bloodline stayed
strong, resilient, was to ensure that you, my first born son,
next in line for the throne, had the proper mate." Venus
looked at his mother, love in her eyes. "I was exiled, but still
Queen, Alexandre, despite what the Fernández Clan had done
to me. I endured years of torture as their captive! And I still
defeated them, with my mind! I escaped and immediately took
up my throne from a distance. That is how a *true* Queen rules,
Venus." She regarded his mate then turned back in his
direction. "But I was fueled also by sweet revenge.

"My mate was dead, your father, the king. My kingdom
was in disarray, but I knew I had taught my sons and daugh-
ters all that I could. With only two of my spawn left, it was up
to *them* to rule France in a way that would make me and their
father proud." She turned to the Council. "I needed to take

heed of what my son's *Sorcier Cadieux* had predicted. It was no fable or tall tale. *Sorcier Cadieux* was one of the most powerful in all of Europe. He was rarely wrong about such things. He was born of a 7th witch mother from a power Coven in Ireland and 7th born warlock from Romania. Those are powers we do not possess; full psychic strength eludes us. So I did the next best thing: I befriended some sorceresses and necromancers who *did* have the power of the 3rd eye. I split my throat and *Sorcier Cadieux* took my blood, and I took his. It's how I heard that prayer from an African slave woman secretly practicing Hoodoo... what her mother called rootwork conflicted with her newly found Christianity, but she wanted her baby to live!

"I did the unthinkable. I broke the pattern of what was once a contentious relationship with our indigenous occultist community, and created comradery. The right mate can mean life or death! And Venus is life, while we are the undead!" She turned to the Council. "Can't you see? Being Pure Blood is irrelevant! We must adapt to the changing times and take advantage of anything that can benefit us! My grandchildren will be stronger, not weaker!" She turned to Venus. "I needed to find you... you were the key. Come to me. Let me see you."

Alexandre released her from his grip, and Venus walked promptly up to his mother. She looked over his bride from head to toe, running her fingers through her hair, smiling.

"You've gotten incredibly prettier and stronger since I last saw you... since I turned you loose, let you go. I know you were quite upset when I vanished, but it was time that I allow you to fulfill your mission, the very thing I'd educated and trained you to do… to be my son's mate. I never told you that was your assignment. I needed you to find out on your own. Come, sit with me." Mother took Venus' hand and sat in the chair he'd been assigned during the court hearing. The seat was so wide, the two sat in it side by side, their fingers intertwined like loved ones do.

"I see your mother in your eyes." Venus offered a sad smile. "Your mother was a woman of faith, Venus. She'd mixed Christianity, witchcraft, and a multitude of other belief systems, learned from her ancestors, so she could survive and have something to consider, something that would make a difference."

"Did you hear her praying over me, just like I was told?"

"Yes. Right after you were born, when she first held you in her arms, she said a prayer under the full moon where she delivered you all by herself. I had been looking for you for what had felt like an eternity. I had no idea when you'd be born, if you were already born, nothing. I believed *Sorcier Cadieux*, though many believed I was foolish to do so. And then, just like that, he was proven right, long after his death. Once your mother said that prayer, I could sense you, Venus. I could smell your fresh blood of birth… I had *finally* found you. I had been living in South Carolina for longer than I ever wished, just to ensure that I wouldn't miss you.

"I decided that since you were a slave, I would be a part of the underground railroad, and that would attract you to me once you became of age. But, I could not take you away from there. No, just like all the Marseille Clan Coven members, you

LE ROI DU SANG

had to *prove* you were worthy. You had to demonstrate that you were the one, that you were different. I felt you attempting your first escape, and you didn't make it. I then sensed you making your second one, and you had to go the distance... You did. I could smell your fears, taste your desires. The closer you got to me, the harder it was for me to contain myself. I could not intervene. I had to allow you to make it all on your own.

"And I did." Venus smiled before kissing his mistress on her cheek.

"Yes, you did. I was hard on you because I knew what you needed. I had to toughen you up. After all you had been through, the horrible violations and devastation of your family, your mind, your heart and your body, you remained far too compassionate and understanding. It boggled my mind to see how you could care for others still, and not be hardened. I can see in your eyes that that is still a problem, but you've improved." Mother ran her hand along Venus' chin. "You were destined to be my daughter-in-law, to give my first born strong, resilient, intelligent offspring. I—"

"You fools! What complete bullshit!" Victor stood to his full height as he approached Mother, this time, with a long sword in hand. "All of this to help save some Turned Vamp! As if there was no one else in the land that would qualify to fuck my brother and bear his seed! She's *not* special! She's an abomination, thanks to my mother and my brother! My mother turned her, giving her life, a rebirth, a baptism of Pure Blood! My brother has strengthened her even more by cumming inside of a slave Turned Vamp, training her for combat and feeding her from his neck and wrist repeatedly! Now she's had not one, but two fucking Pure Bloods give her their essence! SHE'S A MONSTROSITY!"

Alexandre leisurely dropped his cigar and snuffed out the smolder with a mere blow of his lips. He bent down to pluck a piece of jagged window pane from the floor. He turned his back and tossed the glass over his shoulder. When Alexandre turned around, Victor was clutching his chest, his eyes bright red. With a grunt, he pulled the piece out of him and dropped it to the ground.

"You missed. Fucker." Victor chuckled.

"I didn't miss. Despite my anger, I refuse to kill my mother's son in front of her eyes. I marked you… That's to ensure that I can smell you better when you go into hiding and I go hunting. We both know deep down you're afraid to fight me, a complete coward."

Victor sliced the air with his sword, daring him.

Alexandre shook his head. "I'm not fighting you here. That's what you want."

"Who's the true coward?" Victor cackled.

"You're so naïve to my *true* nature, little brother. You think you know me, but you've barely scratched the surface. You felt my hesitation when I was choking you a while ago. It was only because I could sense Venus was close by. You were spared because I didn't want her to see that, and not for the reasons you may imagine. But that was only temporary, a thing to settle once I could get you alone. Now, you want the insurance that I will not take you down in front of the matriarch should we battle and you lose."

"You can't beat me in a sword fight, Alexandre. You never could."

"You're a very good swordsman, Victor, but the hatred I have for you now will ensure that nothing you do or say from this point on would *ever* be enough to keep me from guaranteeing that you die, and die excruciatingly. I would kill you now," he said with a shrug, "in front of all my friends. They'd enjoy it, I'm certain, but again, since Venus is here and she loves her mistress, doesn't want to see her in distress, I will not. Venus has no love for you; it would hurt her to see you killed only because of our mother's pain! Venus has saved you twice now. She cannot save you a third time." His eyes narrowed on his brother. "I will see you later… you can count on it, *mon frère.*"

Victor disappeared back into the darkness. Soon, Alexandre heard a door open and close. He turned towards the Council members who were sitting in their seats, observing the scene.

"Judges, I understand that it has already been ruled that I am to lose my crown, title, home and position. I have not had an official appeal per se, but due to the—"

"Alexandre Marseille," Judge Autin began, "this is highly unorthodox. Your family has, for years, kept France protected but today's activities have been harrowing."

"I understand that. My apologies. I was unaware that my mother was still alive."

"As were we." He looked over his shoulder at the woman, and his chest surged with heat. "An appeal within the next twenty-four hours will not be necessary." Waves of applause and cheers could be heard. "One of the charges against you was in regard to your chosen mate... The fact that Venus Margaret Anderson was turned by a Royal Pure Blood, the Queen herself, overrides any ruling. It is more than evident at this time that Venus was pre-chosen, as seen by the stars in her eyes, the mark on her neck—your lover mark, claiming her as your very own, which has never fully healed—and the scent of her now mixed blood. Yet, we are presented with another issue. Now that the Queen is alive, there cannot be two Queens of France. Therefore, we suggest—"

"I officially relinquish my title and duties in favor of my soon to be daughter-in-law, Venus, once they are wed."

Murmurs and gasps filled the air.

"Very well, Queen Geneviève. You will be noted as Queen Mother Geneviève after the marital ceremony between Alexandre and Venus is completed and the marriage has been consummated. In regard to the three murders of your brother's servants, as well as the de-throating of his slave, there will be penalties. As a man of law, though those are not the laws that we follow, I am certain you can appreciate and understand this."

"Yes, I understand that a crime against one's spouse, slave or sibling, in our belief system, is a punishable crime."

"Indeed. However, we are ruling that those actions were committed *after* Victor Marseille baited and beleaguered you and your mate... there was provocation. It is evident from his behavior after the ruling that his intentions were not pure, despite the evidence. He came to us earnestly, with a preponderance of evidence, and was quite convincing. Obviously, this new information changes our views regarding this matter and we are ruling accordingly."

"What about Victor's punishment?!" Venus hissed, marching towards the table. "All this time, you've condemned Alexandre even though his leadership was practically flawless. You took the word of his brother, a jealous and heavily hated man who'd not done a good job of hiding his true intentions at all, if you ask me!"

"But we didn't ask you," Judge Autin stated, a smug expression on his face.

"Well, I am tellin' you anyway!" Alexandre heard Syà snicker. "You all sit up there like somebody is supposed to be scared of you and then when you've messed up, you won't even apologize. Instead you opt to use big words to try and cover your shit! You can call me a freak of nature, a slave, a silly human, Turned Vamp bitch and all of that shit, I do not care! All of this time I waited, and I still have not heard *any*thing in regard to dealing with the son of a bitch that almost ruined my fiancé's life: his brother! What about him having me almost killed by three Bottom Feeders, huh? I know he is to blame for that. Is what Victor's ass did not punishable by your laws?!"

Judge Autin's eyes hooded.

"Venus, please sit down," Mother urged, but Venus appeared rather pumped up, hot and bothered. Alexandre wasn't even certain she'd heard her mistress, or cared enough in that moment to reel herself in. She had the floor, she'd earned it. He certainly wasn't going to stop her, and should they attempt to do something to his mate, he'd turn that fucking place into a blood bath.

"Young woman, you are to *never* approach this table without permission. You—"

"You all sit there and judge everyone in here all day, every day! We're blood suckers! Killers! I admire my mistress and my mate because they both know what they are and make no excuses for it. You are no better than Alexandre or Victor or anyone! You are no better than the bleeding heart humans you snub, see only as food, or the Satanically ruled Demons that work the grounds beneath your lair!" A wave of murmurs surged in the room, then quieted down so she could continue. "You took my fiancé's crown away without even allowing me to speak on his behalf—hell, on my own behalf, and without digging further! It's almost as if you wanted this to happen!"

"Remove the Turned Vamp from the courtroom until these proceedings are over," Judge Couture stated dryly. Two guards approached and placed their arms on her. Alexandre slid another cigar out of his pocket and lit it. He wished he could wipe the fucking smirk off his face, but it was damn near impossible. As soon as both guards had her by the arms, Venus hissed and began to spin around, turning into a virtual volcano, erupting from her core. The glass, debris, and furniture were caught in her violent tornado, but Alexandre stood his ground, still quietly puffing on his black and white striped cigar. When she slowed, the guards went flying, their backs slamming against the walls, then slumping down into piles of ash.

"I'm goin' to have my say!" Judge Couture shook his head, and his lips curled in a grin... how could he not? Venus was indeed a monstrosity—the most beautiful kind of all. "You better do something about Victor and if that isn't the law according to this place, then it *should* be! Look at all this time and energy that's been wasted! I'm supposed to be preparing for my wedding. Instead I am here standing on broken glass. Look at all these queens and kings here!" She turned and pointed behind her at all of his supporters. "They have left their thrones and appointed others to take their place in their absence, all because of their loyalty towards my mate! They knew he'd do the same for them if the shoe was on the other foot. I told Alexandre when he left out this morning not to trust you all, and now I am sure he sees I was right. Now, what are you going to do about Victor? I want an answer before I leave!"

Judge Couture cackled. He laughed so loud, it rocked the entire place, as if it wasn't already in shambles.

"Silly, silly Turned Vamp! Your humanity is both entertaining and disgusting! Your physical strength is incredible and a thing of beauty." The entire Council burst out laughing and nodded. "You're fun... Hopefully your mind will catch up with that mouth of yours!"

"I bet my fist and foot up your ass will—"

"Venus!" Mother warned. His mate stopped speaking.

"There is *nothing* we need to do about Victor, dear," Judge Couture explained. "He's already done it to himself. There is zero that we could do to him that would compare to what your mate will do to his brother… and we will not intervene or punish. For in our world, that is the rightful conclusion, starry eye for a starry eye, fanged tooth for a fanged tooth… As you humans would say, 'One reaps what they sow.' The Council has spoken."

CHAPTER EIGHTEEN

Fawning Over You...

FAWN TOSSED HER monologued cream and umber Louis Vuitton luggage onto the quilt of the Queen size bed in the hotel, then toed out of her raspberry colored heels. The flight had been incredibly long. Some pretentious teenage human girl kept going on and on about her college prep classes, as if anyone on that flight gave a final destination fuck. Another gentleman decided he could handle his alcohol. He was wrong. He projectile vomited all over his seat and a bit on the woman in front of him. Ghastly.

Thankfully, that's all over...

She wrapped her hand around her neck and worked out a kink... even sitting in first class she'd grown uncomfortable, her long legs having barely enough room to stretch. She sat there on that plane sipping a glass of water the majority of the time—the only thing on offer she could drink that she could keep down. Though she rather enjoyed the flavor of a

Margarita from time to time, missed them from her life before she was Turned, it simply hadn't been worth the risk. She reached into her luggage and removed the thick black binder where she kept work related stuff, including relevant contact information, venue, catering sources, the works. She'd been using it on the flight, too.

Flipping through it, she landed on a page that almost gave her a panic attack, she detested it so much. It was a design of the custom-made crown Venus was to wear on her wedding day. An exquisite creation in gold, black onyx, and covered in diamonds and rubies... Her fangs emerged from her soft pink gums and sliced into her lower lip as jealousy like she'd never known filled her. Most in her shoes would fuck up such a task as payback for not being the chosen one. Instead, she'd gone ahead with her job, as if the thing was intended for her... just in case Alexandre changed his mind. But he hadn't; in fact, things had gotten worse.

This was supposed to be MY husband! My man! The father of MY children!!! You stupid bitch! Why did he have to find you?! Why did he not reject you and see you were nothing! She kicked and hit the air, her entire being a bundle of nerves. After a few moments, she regained her composure and turned on the television to a music station.

A nice bath will do me some good. Let me relax for a moment first.

H.E.R. sung, 'Focus' on the musical channel. Fawn took several deep breaths, trying to push her disappointments out of her mind.

She slicked her hand into her purse, grabbed her cell, and

dialed his number once more. Straight to voicemail it went…

She hung up. "Fuck."

Alexandre hadn't been answering his phone. Why? She'd called Whiskey and several others asking if they'd heard from him. No one had, or they didn't seem particularly alarmed at his lack of a damn response. Getting anything out of Whiskey lately was like pulling teeth. Perhaps he was miffed she'd asked him to talk some sense into Alexandre, but hell, it was for their own good. He was a slave to the man, just like Venus had been. Didn't he want his self-respect back?

Her phone buzzed and she sighed with relief… but that was short-lived. It was a detailed text message from Victor, who described the shitstorm that had blown in like tumble-weeds in the wild West. She sat on the edge of the bed, rubbing the balls of her stockinged feet. The fucker called, but she didn't feel like talking, so another text came through, this one more pissed than the last. He made it quite clear, all bets were off. No longer was his focus on Venus; it was now on the head motherfucker in charge.

He wanted his brother dead. End of story.

She hissed when she slumped down onto the bed. Closing her eyes, she wished she could rewind the clock to better times. Those nights and mornings spent cuddled up next to Alexandre, his white hard flesh like steel and spikes against her curves. The way he fucked… he did it like no other… the way his thick, fat cock pumped inside her pussy, ass, and mouth tore her apart with ecstasy.

She'd watched that time he fucked Venus in the damn

dining room... it was different.

The way he moved, the things he said, the way he look at and held the woman... it sickened her. She'd watched from the doorway, stroking her pussy, fucking herself as Venus came over and over again. Alexandre had fucked the slave woman as if he had to, as if he needed it in the worst way. He'd devoured her, his eyes rolling, his body hungry. He'd pumped hard and nasty, his form a blur as he'd given it his all. A new seed of jealousy had been planted and now, she had an entire green garden of envy that flourished in the bowels of her dark heart. No sunlight needed...

Everything is a disaster! His plan backfired... Victor! I'm sure he'll find some way to blame me for this. Her phone rang once again, but she ignored it. It was him... The Non-Victorious One. She wasn't in the mood to argue. *What I need is a good nap. This bed sucks.*

She hated that she wasn't at the Parisian mansion with all of the high-class servants, surrounded by opulent décor and being waited on hand and foot. What was the point of being in the city of love and not having a delicious, hard body to curl up to and drain dry?

She was supposed to stay at the Marseille Mansion with Alexandre per the itinerary, but when her taxi pulled up, she was denied entry due to her name not being on the guest list. What utter bullshit! She was his assistant. Surely, there was some mistake! She snatched her phone up once again and dialed the fucker's number, ignoring the missed calls from Victor.

COME ON! ANSWER!!! She grabbed her dark tortoise-shell sunglasses from atop her head and flung them on the nightstand next to the 'Welcome to the Hôtel Ritz Paris' Sign, the room service menu, and the complimentary chocolate.

"You've reached Attorney Alexandre Marseille." She sucked her teeth and rolled her eyes, drumming her black nails against the nightstand. "I am unable to take your call at this time. If this is an urgent legal matter, please contact my assistant, Fawn Nettleton, at 212-843-4321. If this is concerning an urgent non-legal matter, please contact my assistant, Whiskey, at—"

She quickly ended the call. She'd already left three messages. A fourth wouldn't change any damn thing.

Did Victor tell him I was involved? She wedged her stiletto shaped nail between her teeth and nibbled. *He said he didn't, said the Council didn't ask about who filmed the tapes and if they had, he had a name for that, too. Maybe Alexandre knows it was me? I mean, I set the camera up secretly in his office… I had to do something! There was no way I was going to sit there and testify against him! I was pretty discreet though. No, he definitely doesn't know. If he did, I'd be dead by now. I mean, he didn't seem to know. He was too busy with HER.* Her heart beat a bit faster as a surge of hot envy flushed through her entire system. *No, I doubt he knew… I covered my tracks. It could've been anyone. He has hundreds of people walking in and out of his penthouse in Manhattan at any given time. All those damn parties, orgies… hell, it never ends.*

She jumped when someone pounded at her hotel door.

"Who is it?" Her paranoia kicked into high gear until she

thought it may be her *true* desire… The king she deserved.

Maybe it's Alexandre. Maybe he played my voicemail where I said I was here at this hotel and needed to be brought back to his estate.

There was another hard pound at the door.

"I said, who is it?!"

No one answered. She made her way to the hotel door and looked through the peephole. Two vexed violet eyes, lined with silvery white lashes, peered back at her from a face framed by thick layers of platinum hair tossed over one shoulder. The tall man wore a luxurious navy suit and silk ivory tie. His nose was just like Alexandre's—long, pronounced, with a bit of a bulge in the bridge.

The fucker on the other side said nothing. He simply stood there, his chest heaving. They stared at one another, or at least it felt like he was staring at her.

"I know you're in there… I can smell you. Open the fucking door and let me in," he stated calmly while looking up the hall as if he were expecting someone.

He sounds a bit like Alexandre, too.

"Ahhh, I know who you are now. You must be Victor." She chuckled. "You look a bit different than you did on the video chat. Why didn't you tell me on the phone that you were stopping by?" She removed the chain and lock and he burst in, brushing past her as if he had to use the john in the worst way. She closed and locked the door and made her way towards the fellow, who stood with his back turned, hands on hips. He looked out of her 6th floor hotel window for several moments before he turned back in her direction, looking as pissed as he'd been moments prior.

"Kill him. This is not up for discussion. If you want *any* chance at all at being Queen, you must kill him, Fawn."

She crossed her arms and paced back and forth.

I'll play this nutjob's game… but I'm not going to attempt to kill Alexandre. The stakes are far too high…

"Why don't you kill him yourself, Victor? Why would you need a Turned Vamp that you despise, that you feel is beneath you, to do your handiwork?" She gleamed. His eyes narrowed on her as if he were surprised she was onto him. The fucking jig was up. The rose-colored glasses were off and broken under the weight of a spiky heel… Things had gotten out of hand, and she was done having him as a puppet master. Strings were cut like veins with razor blades. How beautiful it felt to be free.

"Because everyone expects me to try 'nd kill him now!"

"Cain and Abel, modern day…" She laughed as she walked over to the dresser and pulled out a nail file, then began the detailed, tedious work of sharpening her right fang. It had gotten chipped during her lunch. Brittle bones of an old bitch… "How do you plan to pull this off?"

"I'll have an alibi. If you do it, no one will suspect you. Once he is dead, all of our problems are solved!"

"I don't have any problems." She shrugged. "Well, I take that back. If you're havin' brother problems, I feel bad for ya, son. I've got 99 problems but Alexandre ain't one. Hit me!" She cackled. "Oh, not a Jay Z fan? Hmmm, your musical tastes are questionable then."

"Stick to what we're discussing, Fawn. This is serious."

"Oh, it's serious all right. I wanted him, he chose someone else, but I'm still eligible for fucking and sucking." She did a little shimmy dance, shaking her assets. He curled his lips in disgust… how cute. "My paycheck is pretty fucking fat, too. Why would I give that up? Besides, I'm curious to know if Venus is interested in a sister-wife," she teased.

"For the final fucking time, this isn't humorous. You have a job to do. I suggest you prepare for it."

"And what if I refuse?" She smirked. "I think you better sweeten the fucking pot, you male version of Storm from X-Men. I'd fuck Halle Berry in a heartbeat. You? Hmmm, I dunno." She shrugged. "I've been catfished… you look nothing like I thought you would, boy, you must've used a filter on the phone. I mean, you're attractive and all but hey, it must be tough brakes being the younger brother of a practical sex God while you stand in the background looking more like Einstein after a Brazilian blowout. E = mc2."

Victor kept silent, his face unreadable. He leaned against the wall and crossed his ankles and arms, as if waiting for a date to finish getting ready for their night on the town.

"What a son of a bitch you are! Wow!" She threw up her hands. "Did you *honestly* think I was going to keep doing your bidding with no payback? Keep putting myself on the line? I'm not Whiskey and I'm not Venus! I am a slave to *no* one!"

"You have not properly done what you've been instructed to do by me. NOT EVEN ONE DAMN TIME! If you had not sent Bottom Feeders after Venus, he would have been more amenable to engage in negotiations, you fool! I know my brother! He and I still had a decent enough relationship at that point where I could have gotten through... I just needed someone to open the door for me and you blew it!"

"There is nothing less sexy than a grown ass vampire blaming a woman for his own errors. If you truly knew your brother, then you would have known that since that bitch came into his life, he has changed! He is still uncouth, conceited, dreadful... but there's something different about him now, something I can't put my finger on. I didn't blow it, *you* did. In fact, I did you a favor by even orchestrating that attack! You should have taken that opportunity to come and try to console your brother, and offer to help! That's how you get in close, little brother! You throw a bomb, then slide in and offer protective gear. You let everyone know that attacks against your family won't be tolerated, while all along you were the mastermind. It's an airtight plan! But it's too late now... You're clueless." She rolled her eyes in disgust.

"If you had testified instead of using that damn tape, he'd be convicted right now! It would not have been overturned! Your bumbling and fumbling caused him to be able to gather others and take over the entire basilica. If you—"

"It's everyone's fault but yours, right, Vic? The idea of being Queen to the likes of you no longer seems so lovely to me, Victor... I am annoyed by how you always fail. Gross." She laughed dismally and rolled her eyes. "My precious pussy is only for winners... or at least those that can pretend to be. I mean, really... being fucked by you on a daily basis would have to be terribly disappointing, boring, and ho hum to the 5th power." She grimaced.

"I like *strong* men, okay? Alpha husbands, men who can handle whatever life throws their way and then some. I like *nasty* men. Men that take what they want and don't accept no for an answer. I like big-dicked men." She glanced at his pants, wondering if he was as blessed below the waist as his brother. She doubted it. "You're smelling more and more like an imposter, a Beta Pure Blood pathetic piece of shit. Give me more… because right now, just looking at you makes me want to vomit."

In a second flat she was off the ground; the fucker had his hand wrapped tight around her neck. Her pussy cried, her heart pounded, her lives flashed before her eyes… both of them. He raised her high in the air like a lantern, squeezing her life away. Her legs kicked back and forth in all directions and she struggled to breathe. Heat rushed to her cheeks and her vision became blurry. She came as she almost lost consciousness…

"Do you like to be choked while you're fucked?!" he roared.

She heard what sounded like him slipping his belt through loops and the distinct sound of a zipper being yanked down. Hard. He threw her across the room, tossing her on the bed like some plaything. When she looked over her shoulder, his long, snake-like, pale cock was out… throbbing with need. The bastard's chest rose and fell as he stood before her.

"I don't know what type of game you think you're playing,

Fawn, but you just lost. Now, I am going to tell you *exactly* what to do, and you follow my orders to a T." He sneered, showcasing sharp, glistening fangs as his eyes glowed like car lights in the dead of the night. She hated herself for being so aroused, loathed that the maniac made her pussy hot and wet as he stood there exposing himself and making perverse demands... Perhaps he was better than she'd initially thought...

Slipping her hand against her nature, she stroked her slippery cunt over her black pants, the moisture soaking through, then got on her knees and took his dick into her hands.

"Suck it, bitch." He gripped the back of her head, wound her hair around his fist, and shoved himself within her mouth. "Show me how a Queen swallows a sword."

She greedily accepted him, rolling her tongue along his length, slurping and tasting him as he wasted no time fucking the hell out of the back of her throat with ruthless abandon...

Victor would do in the meantime, but in a moment she was certain her question would be, *"Motherfucker, what have you done for me lately?"*

DONNY HATHAWAY CROONED 'Love, Love, Love' in the dank cellar furnished with two old card game tables, a collection of historical vampire novels, cases of rare cigars, and a lit oval fireplace, the flames within glowing a vibrant orange. Whiskey tossed the pictures onto the glossy, diamond-shaped red table in the center of the room where Alexandre sat. The place was located deep within the recesses of Marseille Mansion. Alexandre looked at the photos with a lazy glance and ran his fingertips down his exposed chest. His sheer, button down white shirt hung open, and a light breeze from a ceiling fan gave some reprieve in the stuffy private room, created just for conversations such as this. After a long silence, they looked at one another and burst out laughing.

"It's a bullshitty thing, ya know? Bull-fuckin'-shitty, but I like it." He grinned as he brought an emerald green and silver cigar to his lips and leaned back in his chair. "Right at this moment, I am just about certain that Fawn has already seen Victor. They've probably even fucked by now. Victor has a voracious sex drive, similar to my own, and there's no way he's going to let that tight piece of ass slip on by. Right now, she thinks I don't know that she bugged my office, contacted the Council on my brother's behalf, and is oblivious to the fact that I am the one that ensured she wasn't allowed into my home... Some places are just off limits to her."

"Shit, that was ballsy of her, the camera, ya know?"

"Yeah, but desperation makes one do shit like that. I wasn't surprised. As soon as the Council said they had tapes, I knew who'd done it."

"If Venus knew what the bitch had been up to all of this time she'd probably kill 'er on the spot."

Alexandre nodded in agreement.

"Definitely. See, this is what I was talking about, Whiskey. Fawn's arrogance is so outrageous that she believes she is smarter than me... than anyone, actually." He rolled his eyes and grinned as he plucked a photo off the table of Fawn going into the hotel, a scowl on her face. "She and Victor are so much alike, it's sickening. I can time each of them by my damn watch."

"What is crazy to me though is that she probably actually believes he is going to marry her, even after all of that has happened."

Alexandre shrugged and propped his legs on the table, ankles crossed, and began to swivel back and forth in his seat.

"She doesn't believe that." Whiskey's eyes turned black as he shook his head. "Again, she's a cat, remember? Always on the fucking prowl, loyal to no one. Beautiful seductress, witty, devoid of anything you can hold in your fucking hand..." He picked up a small gold vase in the middle of the table and crushed it in his palm. Sparkly dust particles fell between his fingers onto the floor. "You have to know her next move before *she* does, Whiskey." He tapped the side of his skull with his fingertip. "But her creature comforts keep her predictable. That's why I was thrilled when Victor chose her for his scheme, believing she'd be the rat, instead of what she truly is. He could never read women like Fawn well." He yawned. "She goes wherever the power, money, and lust are... just leave breadcrumbs and she'll follow."

"Follow the sardines and yarn balls..."

"Exactly." Alexandre chuckled, reached for a smoky black

cup with white billows of smolder floating from it, and took a sip. "Shit. This isn't so damn bad."

"I told you it was good! It's that, uh, ice shit, with the warm water below, giving that nice mist… and then they add a little dab of lamb blood, gives it sweetness. And some goat milk. Just a drop, nothin' to make ya sick or hurl or anything."

"They're getting creative, aren't they? Blood lattes on the rocks 'nd shit!" He and Whiskey burst out laughing again… though his gut turned with rage. He wanted to taste his brother's pain.

Patience…

"Well, either way, she has to know she's in way over her head now. She's in deep shit. How is she going to try and get out of this? Victor is outed; the Council now knows what he did."

Alexandre tossed his lit cigar from one hand to the other, rolling it around between his nimble fingers, doing tricks before bringing it back to his mouth and taking a hard draw.

"One of two things will happen. She will attempt to do whatever Victor asks her to do then turn on him, or two, she will pretend to be in agreement and as soon as his back turns, rat him out to me, absolving herself of all guilt. Either way, I'm going to play along because she's my key to getting him just where I want him. He won't make this easy for me. He knows I'm after him so he is preparing."

"What about the Queen mother?" Whiskey removed a cigarette from his pocket, lit it, and took several puffs. "I heard she's pretty upset about all of this."

"I cannot speak for her, but I am certain she expects me to do just as I am doing because I can't stop being *what* I am…" Alexandre looked down at the blood red table, catching his reflection in shades of crimson. Venus had unraveled him and given him strength like he'd never known, all at the same time. Jorja Smith's 'Beautiful Little Fools' played through the speakers. And now, he also felt something for Geneviève besides a sense of betrayal…

He couldn't deny how seeing his mother hold his Blood-mate, stroke her hair, and press her close to her chest broke him down inside.

Mother was not affectionate. She was not sweet. She was not loving. She was a callous warrior Queen with a heart made of pure black cracked ice. But he saw another side of her now, one that showed protection and warmth.

Had Venus somehow infected both of them, too? Had she turned his mother, as his mother had turned her? Did her kiss and her pussy get inside of him, rewire him, make him see things in a way he never had before? He no longer had tunnel vision; he felt more in the know, wiser. She had to have done this to him… it was a reciprocal poisoning… Venus was in his system. It felt good. He didn't think he wanted to be cured.

He gritted his teeth and slowly got up from his seat. Grabbing his leather jacket, he slid it on. He and Whiskey didn't say a word—it was understood.

The show must go on… dead or alive…

SYÀ WAVED A black cape in the air, letting it fall around Venus' nude body as she sat in the glass chair. The woman tied it securely at her nape like a barber cloak.

"I'm in charge of your wedding planning from now on. Fawn the Fucktress is fired. Forget whatever she told you, whatever you two had planned. This is *my* show now," she stated with a stern expression as Gary Clark Jr. sang 'Bright Lights' in the small, cave-like room with cobblestone walls. They were somewhere in the entrails of Paris, near the catacombs. Red lights swung from silver ropes and chains hung from the low ceiling, swaying from the hard and heavy dancing from above. There was some party going on, a gory fuck fest that Venus wished she could spy on. The French were fabulous freaks!

The room was full of Vamps, most beautiful and half na-ked, sliding their tongues along each other's bodies, their necks adorned with fresh bites and shiny chokers and dog chains.

"These bitches will do what I tell them to do," Syà snapped as she pulled out a drawer full of sharp needles, bottles containing what appeared to be black ink and other strange odds and ends. "They are your wedding party." A couple of them nodded then turned right back to one another, feeling on each other's breasts and sucking on flesh. A lovely Haitian one with skin like black glass, a crown full of dark brown soft curls, winked in her direction and puckered her lips, as if to say, 'You're next.'

"Your hair, your makeup, your dress, jewelry, all of it has to be done a certain way, Venus. Did Alexandre tell you about any of this?" Syà paused, looking at her as if she were a mere confused child in need of assistance.

"Uh, no. He just said that—"

"Typically your mother would do all of this for you, but you have none, so here I am."

"Thank you. I love you, Syà."

"You're all right, I suppose." Venus giggled at the woman's words. "Okay, let's get this bride something to drink, get her body prepped. Now!" She loudly clapped her hands, causing several of the young Vamps to scurry away. When they returned, they brought platters of small glasses filled with blood. Venus reached for several of the drinks and downed them quick. She had a feeling she was going to need it. Syà kneeled before her and snatched her knees apart.

"Yeah… this will never do. I'm going to widen your pussy."

"What?! What for? I'm not a virgin and Alexandre and I fuck all the time. I know what to expect."

"You've never been married to a King Pure Blood Vampire, Venus." Syà rolled her eyes, as if she didn't have time to explain. She grabbed a speculum from the tray and slid it within her. Venus' eyes widened as she clutched the arms of the chair. Dull pain radiated throughout her body. "How men like Alexandre fuck on any given Sunday is far different from how they fuck when they're trying to knock you up.

"The intent makes all the difference. King Vamps are pussy killers when it comes to making their spawn, babe. It's serious business for them... they do not plan to fail. It's a beautiful time, fun, deliciously good loving, but it's rough, baby... *real* rough. Now, let's see here..."

Venus swallowed hard as the woman worked her busy fingers between her legs, pushing and pressing.

"Be glad I can help you. In my mother's day, whoa! What a big surprise." Syà cackled. "Okay, all done... and what a pretty pussy you have, Venus." She felt the air from the kiss the Chinese Pure Blood Queen blew towards her vulva before getting back on her feet and standing straight, her fingertips tinged with blood.

"Tonight, you will be tattooed... your king's initials on your inner thigh. It's tradition. Right now though, we will pick up your gown from the seamstress. She alerted me, let me know she was finished."

"Huh? How'd you get my measurements?" Venus asked with a smile. She reached for another drink and downed it, wishing there was a way to get high off of blood alone.

"I can look at you and see what you are. 36D, 26 inch waist, 37 in the hips."

"Well, shit! I'm impressed." Venus rose to her feet, then sighed from the stinging between her legs. "What the hell did you do in there?"

"You'll be fine in about ten minutes. You got up too soon." Syà grabbed her jacket and handbag. "We've got places to go. Stand, sit, whatever, for a few seconds… and then we're off. We've got limited time to pull this all together. I have an entire team working with me to get this done."

"Does Fawn know she's fired?" Venus asked with a smirk. "I don't like her anyway, so trust me, it's no love lost." She reached for her satchel and placed it over her shoulder, crossbody.

"Oh, she'll know soon enough." Syà winked and headed out the place with Venus following close behind…

CHAPTER NINETEEN

Would you be mine? Could you be mine?
Won't you be my neighbor?

VICTOR'S NEIGHBORHOOD WAS nothing like Mr. Rogers'. Alexandre, Zhang Wei, and Whiskey stood on an underground street deep below Rue Saint Denis. For this venture, he had to go small in numbers. The less of them the better—more inconspicuous. They'd passed the groups of heavily painted human prostitutes wearing little more than a lacy thong and sick junkies looking for a fix, right before opening up the manhole and worming themselves into Victor's private sanctuary, a world within a world. A horrible place, populated by the dredge of their society—the stuff of nightmares. His brother was known for this sort of shit, for favoring the bizarre, over the top, appalling and foul creations, all a part of the world he created with his demented brain. He presented himself as well put together to the public, articulate and artful, even. But, behind closed doors he had a secret. Alexandre knew the fiend's true fears and desires—and at times, they were one and the same.

"This kinda reminds me of the place you said you grew up in, Alexandre," Whiskey whispered as they trudged through the muddy, tight space wedged between the human realm and his brother's carefully carved out abode.

"Yeah, my family lived under ground for centuries... Historically, we didn't start mingling with humans on a consistent basis until our bodies could take the sun. We just hunted at night. Now, we blend right in with society... as it should be."

Victor, however, seemed to have an affinity for the 'old school' ways. His heart was tied to their rich Marseille heritage, living beneath the radar, dancing on Hell's ceiling just like their ancestors, going way back. Those old aristocratic homes filled with jewels and money, beautiful thoroughfares and elite districts had been long abandoned, but many years ago Victor had created a *new* one, in his own name.

Alexandre slid a gold cigarette out of his jacket pocket and lit it. Bringing it to his mouth, he took a hard draw. The light from it illuminated the strange area they'd stepped into—a surreal place inhabited by frolicking freaks and deranged deviants. Here was a fitting home to the desperate, rejected, and mentally unhinged.

Small Victorian style houses lined each side of the lopsided, cobblestone street, all of them fairly similar in color and design. Posters were placed here and there, some curled at the edges. All of these consisted of paintings, glossy blown up photos, and various artistic renderings of Victor Marseille, often depicted with a crown on his cranium.

"Son of uh bitch," Whiskey mumbled under his breath as he drew his knife, taking it all in. Even to a Native New Yorker such as Whiskey, who'd had to fend for himself on the hard streets of the city, this shit had to be somewhat over his head. "Egomaniac, much?" Whiskey chuckled dismally observing his surroundings, while the vampires walking around were lost in their own little worlds.

Their footsteps echoed as they kept going in the dead of night—the best time to have a chat with Alexandre's dear old brother. Though they were Daywalkers, nighttime was still preferred to mingle, handle business matters, and of course validate a timely kill. At that time, they had the most energy, feeling high off life.

Victor had a rather strange set of rules for the residents of his three-road village—one of them being that, at night, the houses were required to have open curtains. Voyeurism at its best. Victor enjoyed perusing the streets late in the evening or early morning from time to time, peeking in on the residents, watching them in the throes of violence, feeding, and fucking. Vampires weren't modest; no one seemed to give a damn, but he made it worth their while. If they allowed themselves to be viewed at all times of the day, lower rent and mortgages were guaranteed.

They kept moving, ignoring the arguments between some of the residents, the racing cars and neglected youth roaming in the night. Alexandre and his skeleton crew walked past one home in particular that caught his eye...

A greenish-gray-skinned bloated Vamp was lying on a bed, prominent red veins, purplish bruising, and angry welts covering her body. Patches of dark hair, knotted and wet, lined her hairline. A bright light shined down between her open, thick thighs, revealing a pulsing, swollen pussy while a surgeon kneeled before her, cradling a heavily deformed Vamp child, its barrel chest covered in paper-thin skin, the heart clearly seen pumping beneath. The baby's head was abnormally large, the dark eyes far apart and the limbs limp. Those small, spacy eyes stared back at him... He stiffened, feeling frozen in time for a moment, then, snapping out of it, he motioned for them to continue.

Another home a little farther down the road had on the wall an American poster of some campaign against drug usage with a Black preacher and an athlete shaking hands. French graffiti, mostly swear words and slang for body parts, practically covered the whole damn thing. It was strange how it just hung there, tattered, as if some vintage living piece of art, something to be treasured.

"Hold on," Whiskey stated as he moved a few steps ahead of them, his hand on his gun.

Standing in the middle of the road, about twenty feet away, was a naked Pacific Islander vampire, a middle-aged, confused male. He moved oddly on the cobblestones, on his tippy toes, like an animal on its hind legs. He then paused, like a rabbit caught in the headlights of a speeding car. He had sparse, poker-straight, short black hair, flaccid chest and limbs, a thin frame with the exception of his gut, which looked like a water balloon filled to capacity, as if he'd just devoured a large meal. Blood was smeared across his chest and chin, dark, as if it had been there for quite some time. The bastard blinked hard, then moved quickly away, dodging into a building, and slammed the door behind him.

"What in tha fuck is going on here?!" Zhang Wei asked, holding tight to his sword. "Your brother is... I don't even have the words."

"I do. Victor is royally fucked in the head. That's about as Royal as he is," Whiskey teased as he ran his hand along his gun. The man was serious though, despite his light tone.

"Fellas, this is my brother's playland... his toy world." Alexandre shrugged and took another drag of his cigarette. "I don't believe he sees anyone here as real. It's all a game to him. He made his own tiny biosphere to rule over, I suppose. I didn't know about it until one of the residents complained to the Council Magistrates, filed a grievance that he'd doubled her rent because she closed her blinds when she and her lover were fucking one evening. I knew he'd been working on some private sanctuary for less fortunate vampires to live in, but I never knew it was actually a place like... well, like *this*."

"He pretended to do charity work, provide low income housing, huh?" Whiskey smirked and shook his head. "Un-fuckin' real. These fuckin' people are totally screwed up... just like him. I had no idea your brother was such a basket case."

"He moved in here, had a big house built and demanded to

be praised. He made up rules as he went along, gave incentives to get everyone to do what he wanted, things like that."

"They call it a God complex," Zhang Wei stated as he swiped the back his hand across his forehead.

They all drew quiet when they heard faint music coming from a small car parked on the side of the street… the sounds of a French song, '*Ne me quitte pas*', by Jacques Brel.

The car rocked violently as they drew closer, like a washing machine on the fritz. Once close to it, Whiskey rolled his eyes and hissed, fangs extended, nostrils flared as if he were horrorstruck. Zhang Wei's nostrils flared too and all Alexandre could do was flick his cigarette onto the ground and crush it under the thick soles of his black boot. A Turned Vamp was inside the vehicle fucking a long dead vampire with all of her might. The stench alone from the decomposing body made Alexandre want to hurl.

Her moans began to echo over the music and she only paused to toss them a glance from over her shoulder. An eerie, crooked smile danced along her face as she rode the corpse hard, her small, milky ass rising and falling on the ashy, stiff body that was nearly skin and bone. Tendrils of strawberry blonde hair hung down her tattooed back. Tears welled in her light brown eyes and wilted red rose petals were strewn all about, some of them spread between her thighs.

"If I keep fucking him, he will wake up for me! He will come back to life!" she said in French, her pupils brimming with insanity. The woman suddenly shrieked, a deafening noise, extending her fangs before turning abruptly away and riding him all the harder.

Having seen enough, they kept on their way until he saw the gold and white house up on the hill.

"This is it, boys." Taking careful steps, the three made the trip up the steep hill. It was strangely serene compared to the 'attractions' on the journey over. In fact, from the outside, Victor's house looked normal—a nice plot of land with a massive home that didn't display any out-of-the-ordinary madness on its façade.

Minutes later, they'd arrived at the large white doors, knowing full well they were in view.

"You want us to stay out back or, uh, maybe wait to the side?" Whiskey asked as he loaded a few bullets into the chamber of one of his many weapons.

"No. We're going to walk the fuck in. Like men."

Suddenly, five guards lunged at them with guns, screaming in French. "PUT YOUR HANDS UP!"

Zhang Wei turned around like a spinner top and released five poisonous Chinese stars from his fingertips, flicking them faster than bullets could fly. All five guards wobbled on their feet, the stars embedded deep into their foreheads like toothpicks inside of a cube of cheese. Zhang Wei dodged between their bodies, knocking them about with a swift chop to the neck, then forcing the stars farther in until they popped out on the other side. All the guards fell to their knees, one by one, dead in a matter of seconds. Wasting no time, Alexandre kicked the front doors in; they crumbled to the ground in a pile of wood. Immediately, an alarm sounded, but the three took their sweet time entering the place, checking their surroundings.

"He knows we're here. There are cameras everywhere."

"Where do you think he is?" Whiskey asked as he looked to and fro, his senses heightened.

"He will go to one of two places: down into his basement or his bedroom. That's where he keeps the majority of his artillery. I looked at the blueprint files before we got here."

"I'll check upstairs!" Whiskey announced before flying half way up the staircase, but when he was a few steps in, a guard raced towards him with a firearm and shot three times. "Shit!" Whiskey dropped down on his haunches and shot the bastard twice in the chest, and once in the head. In a matter of moments, the big man was standing over the officer, his knife raised high with both hands. Blood sprayed on the floor below and all around, including Whiskey's body, when the man jammed the blade into the side of the fucker's skull, then wiggled it back and forth from side to side. When he was done, he rushed the rest of the way up the staircase until he disappeared from sight.

"Let's go!" Alexandre and Zhang Wei headed in the direction of vault. They moved about along a red carpeted corridor. Paintings of their deceased family members hung on the walls. All of a sudden, the power went out and the sound of a generator being shut down could be heard. Trapped there for several seconds, they attempted to gain their bearings. Cool air filled the area, and a stiff foggy vapor rolled against their forms like a sleepy lover in need of a gentle touch. They looked at one another in the darkness and their eyes immediately adjusted, the sclerae turning infrared.

"Ah!" Zhang Wei hollered out. His eyes bucked as he bent forward, holding his gut. Alexandre jumped on the wall closest to him, hanging from it like a bat as he tried to gauge what the hell was going on.

"Zhang!"

Zhang Wei screamed out again and again. Something zoomed around in the air—something heavy and hard, flying at rapid speed.

Zhang Wei's eyes pressed shut and he wobbled on his feet, barely able to stand. He succumbed to his injuries and fell to his knees. Alexandre could suddenly hear heavy footsteps storming toward the man. Crawling closer along the ceiling, he sized up the prey, then jumped down from the wall, picked the battered king up, and spun him around in full force, knocking the predators right off their feet. They too fell to their knees in a praying position. Tossing Zhang Wei onto the ground, he did a back flip, his arm outstretched, hand out in front of himself, and sliced it through the mist, decapitating the two guards that drifted in the floating fog with swift chops to the sides of their heads. Then, he landed softly back on his feet. Zhang Wei moaned and rolled about until he was able to stand again. Screaming with rage, he tossed the sharp stars into their domes, driving them deep within as an act of ultimate reprisal.

"Are you all right? Let me help," Alexandre said.

"No. Let me do it myself..." Zhang Wei nodded as he grunted in agony. "I can feel where to take it out... must do this carefully… hold on." The man's back twisted and cracked as he reached around himself, groaned in pain, then dug into his spine. In a matter of seconds, he removed the thick axe blade now covered in his own blood. The damn thing had been deeply imbedded, leaving a hell of a hole.

"You need time to heal. Here, sit down." Alexandre helped him over to a wall and sat him down on the floor.

"No… I can't let you go down there by yourself." The king winced and slumped over. His hand trembled as his body made haste to right the wrong.

"You have to stay here… you're in no shape to fight. Look, Zhang Wei, you've done your part. You've done more than enough. You came to my home and met my mate. You came to France and spoke on my behalf. You helped me get in here by getting rid of those guards with the potent poison from your stars. Just stay out of sight. If you see Whiskey and he still doesn't know the whereabouts of my brother, tell him to stay put, too. This fight isn't yours, anyway. It's between Victor and me." Alexandre turned to walk away.

"Alexandre. Wait. Take these." Zhang Wei coughed, dug into his pocket, and tossed him several stars, one by one. Alexandre caught all of them between his fingers, slipping them into his jacket. He smiled at the man and headed into the basement, the smell of freshly drawn blood stinging his nostrils as he climbed down the stairwell.

"Oh Brother, Where Art Thou? Ahhh, there you are. I can smell your fears and desires. Big Brother is watching you…"

VENUS EXTENDED HER leg, her diamond anklet gleaming against her skin, her eyes barely open as naked bastards moved around her, covering her with jewels, kisses, feeding her blood, dancing and singing at the top of their lungs, their tongues and lips tinted with gore and essence...

It was a crazy bachelorette party, the kind that one would only read about. Syà stood a few feet away with six other Chinese Vamps, holding a needle dripping with blood in one hand and a soaked cotton ball in the other. The Chinese women cackled and laughed, all of them dressed in red silk gowns, their gorgeous sleek black hair pulled back in various elaborate styles. One held a long, thin amber pipe between her pale fingers.

"Syà..." Venus called out to her friend, unsure if she was going to pass out. Syà had been working on her tattoo for what felt like an eternity. The Queen appeared to be easily distracted, noshing on frozen sweet blood cubes, purchasing a slew of elaborate clothing and intricate sex toys from peddlers. The woman even had the audacity to get into a physical altercation with a man who she believed had insulted her in some way. Syà was savagely stunning, for that same man now lay in a messy heap, his body cut in three pieces of equal size. She'd tossed him at the foot of the door, partially shoved to the side, where he was bleeding from every orifice. "Syà!" She called out again, her inner thigh stinging to death. Oh, what a night…

"Oh yes, here I come, you big baby," the woman teased as she left her den of hens, sat back on her pedestal chair, and assumed the position of tattoo artist. "What a bridezilla you are… so impatient. At least your dress looks nice, right? Beautiful. After she finishes those few adjustments, it will be incredible!"

Venus glared at the bitch as she began to jab and jam the crooked needle into her flesh, treating her temple like an embroidery stitch.

"Do you have to be so rough, Syà?"

"This is nothing compared to your wedding night."

"Oh, stop trying to scare me! It's sex! No one said we were going to breed right away anyway… breed. God, I hate that word." Venus swiped her hand across her forehead. "Why can't you just say have children?" Syà shrugged, clearly not giving a shit. "You all say spawn like it's a creation of the Devil! I am not saying it anymore." Venus crossed her arms mulishly over her chest.

"Doesn't matter what fancy word you want to use, Professor. They are offspring, spawn, viruses… the vampire fetus is a horrible leech. Us mothers never forget that… depletes you of everything. The more powerful the parents, the worse the pregnancy they say." Syà's brow rose as she regarded Venus, shook her head and grinned. "Alexandre is *very* powerful, like my husband… said you're very powerful, too. I believe it after watching you in the Basilica. Those guards never knew what was coming. Now we know that you were turned by an original Queen Mother Pure Blood then mated with her son. Girl... your first pregnancy is going to zap you dry... turn you to salt. You'll be at your second death's door."

"It's so nice speaking to you, Syà. You're always full of good cheer." Venus grimaced and rolled her eyes, causing the woman to burst out laughing.

"If it helps, each pregnancy after the first is much easier... body used to it then. The first baby is like an invasion... so greedy... eating up everything like Pac-Man." Venus burst out laughing, winced, then laughed once again. "Toru Iwatani invented Pac-Man... he was from Japan. Should've been from China."

"Thank you for that trivia... it's riveting." Venus smiled, appreciating how Syà was trying to take her mind off everything, cool her nerves. Fact of the matter was, it had been an odd day from the start. Alexandre drank breakfast, fucked her against the wall of five different rooms in his mansion, then went for a leisurely jog. He and Whiskey returned for only a few moments, then disappeared without another word. When she called him, the calls went straight to voicemail. She'd texted asking if he was okay and he simply wrote back: *Yes, don't wait up.*

It was then that she knew what he was doing.

Hunting.

... Seeking big prey, familiar prey, vengeful prey.

"Ouch!" Syà shook her head at her, but kept right on.

"How long does it take to tattoo two damn initials, Syà?! What are you doing? Writing King Alexandre Marseille in Chinese five times over?!"

"I am adding a special gift for you. Shhh…"

"If it's a little picture of a dick squirting cum, we're going to fight. I could see you doing something silly like that."

"Shhh!"

Venus drew quiet and took big, long breaths. When she looked to her right, she noticed such a pretty creation… A little vampire youth, her storm-cloud-colored eyes unusually large and doe-like, raced around the area laughing and getting into mischief. Venus had no idea where the little cutie had come from. She moved about like a tiny whirlwind, her short, kinky chocolate brown hair pulled in an afro puff and adorned with a large jade green bow. Wearing a gorgeous tulle matching dress, she danced about with a glass bottle of bubbles. Jungle sang 'Casio' through the strangely surreal place, creating more of an atmosphere. There were no bed times in the underworld of her mate's people; there was no peace and quiet except in one's mind. She was now a member of this strange society. The rules and bones of their enemies were meant to be broken.

She smiled at this revelation as the pain got good to her, the needle piercing her flesh, drawing out carnal agony married to delightful pleasure… penetration like no other. Her eyes rolled and she laughed lightly as she realized she was high. What kind of ink was that? What had her new Chinese sister spiked her drink with? Venus laughed harder and harder as her eyes pooled with tears of celebration and death, rebirth and resurrection… all while lavender and pink bubbles floated in the air over her head, promising to never be popped…

CHAPTER TWENTY

Heaven Rained Hell Upon Their Heads...

THE SOUND OF dripping water mixed with the delicate beats of the classical music…

Beethoven.

Alexandre took a careful step, and then another down the dark brick staircase that leaned slightly to the left. He paused and laughed as he placed his sword against his thigh, resting it in the sling attached to his pants. Pulling his phone out of his pocket, he searched through his playlist.

"As usual, little bro, your musical taste sucks. I mean, I like Beethoven, but uh, for this, we need a little more flavor. Let's put on something a bit better for the special occasion…" Alexandre turned on one his favorite playlists. $UI-CIDEBOY$' 'Paris' began to play from his phone. He turned it up full volume, placed his cell back in his jacket, and continued on his trek. Swaying to the beat, his lips curled in a smile, he inhaled his brother's sticky emotions floating in the air like particles of times gone by. His sword made a swoosh-ing sound as he took hold of it and kept on his way. Out of the corner of his eye, he spotted a black raven fly by. He sniffed the air then snarled. The foul stench of a diseased Bottom Feeder…

Descending farther down, he took note of someone dressed in a white, bloodied gown. Her dark, disheveled long hair covered part of her scratched and bruised face and her neck appeared broken, strained and covered with old ligature marks. The Bottom Feeder snapped and twitched, some of her movements quick and jerky, others slow and drawn out. And then, she just stopped and smiled. He quickly ducked when she suddenly raced towards him in lightning speed, her mouth wide open, bellowing broken curses, her yellowed fangs bared. Alexandre burst out laughing and shook his head.

"The ol' sick ass Bottom Feeder in need of a feed trick, huh, Vic? Here we go again! Only, I'm not my mate… I've been killing these fucking bitches for centuries!"

He climbed the wall to the ceiling and dared her to ap-proach.

Flying backwards, her body twisting and wiggling in the oddest of ways, she came at him, her head thrown backwards as she eyed him. And then, she paused, as if something within her recognized who he was… that he was king. She tried to retreat, but it was far too late…

"Oh no, you don't! I can't let you try to double back later or have you out here biting citizens. You wanted a piece of me, right? Well, it's time to get served!"

He quickly caught her by the ankle, swung her around, and sliced her head off with his sword. Her body remained floating, as if on an invisible cloud, while her head hit the ground in a blood-spattered crash. For several seconds, her eyes roamed about in her skull as if unaware of what had just happened. He blew ever so lightly on the suspended body, forcing it to fall down in a thud and join the rest of her, then continued along the path. The pounding of booted feet could be heard. Moving speedily to his right, he glanced up the staircase and saw Whiskey holding three heads by the hair, all dripping with blood, the eyes within the faces dead and wide open and the skulls freshly removed.

"Whiskey! I didn't want you down here. Did you see King Zhang Wei?"

Alexandre got out of the way in the nick of time when a sword swung right towards his face. He sliced through the air as another guard moved about, taking full advantage of his distraction. "Shit!" Jumping down and landing flat on his feet, he knocked the first guard over with a swipe of his hand, then stomped his brains with his heel. He fended off the other with his sword as he continued to stomp the shit out of the guard on the ground, then jammed the sword in the bastard's mouth, jerked it out, and removed his head.

Whiskey was suddenly out of view, and he could hear screaming and bloodcurdling cries for help. "Fuck! Whiiiskey! Can ya hear me?"

Moments later, Whiskey re-emerged, his body dripping with blood... but it wasn't his own.

"Yeah," he said breathlessly, his chest rising and falling hard. "There's a shitload of guards in this house, boss. We've been killin' them. King Zhang Wei is strong as hell; he's been fightin', but he doesn't have a lot of energy left. He isn't getting any time to heal 'cause of this."

"Get him out of here... take him back to his wife, Syà. He needs to feed and he needs rest."

"But what about—"

"Ahhh!" His arm stung as he felt the piercing pain of some projectile entering his flesh. "Don't worry about me! GO!" he ordered when Whiskey started to rush down the stairs. Zhang Wei needed him far more than he did. He refused to have the death of his fellow king and friend on his watch. He looked around in the dimly lit, colossal cellar, unable to see who'd shot him. He flung off his jacket and shirt to the ground. Forcing his baby fingernail to emerge, he dug into his arm, his fangs descending as he grimaced through the sharp pain. Mining out the bullet, he tossed it into his pocket. Alexandre tossed his head back and chuckled, slowly going insane with each moment. The music playing from his phone through his jacket pocket fueled the anger and madness as GHOSTEM-ANE yelled the rap lyrics to 'Mercury.'

"Just like I said! You're a fuckin' coward!" Alexandre screamed at the top of his lungs as he stomped through bloody puddles on the ground amongst the maze of carcasses. "Quit sending your cronies after me and fight like a fuckin' man!"

Suddenly, he was surrounded by five cloaked entities,

blackness instead of faces, their eyes glowing bright red. Heat like he'd never felt rushed through his body. "Oh... you motherfuckers wanna play?" He smirked. "My brother sent you. You've come for the king's head."

One of them moved ever so slightly, a buzzing sound emitting from its nonexistent mouth. The noise grew louder when all of them were doing it simultaneously. The ringing burned his senses and he began to spin about, covering his sensitive ears with his free hand while holding tight to his sword in the other.

The deafening noise pieced through him like miniature swords, jabbing until he completely lost his mind. He yelled out in agony and stumbled about, trying to keep his composure. His mind turned to a fog and he felt as if he were revolving like the Earth, seeing only a dizzying display of reddened eyes, black capes, and leaping, angry flames. A sudden searing heat radiated along his leg. He looked down and took notice of a fiery skeletal hand clutched to his knee, slowly climbing higher. One of the cloaked fuckers was holding onto him, trying to debilitate his ability to move altogether. Alexandre took in a deep breath, mustering all of his strength to snap out of the extraordinary, incapacitating trance they'd put him in.

"Ahhhh!" he yelled out as he did a hard roundhouse kick and knocked the bastard off him then flew like a phoenix up into the air, his head inches away from the ceiling. "All of you will die!"

Opening his mouth, he breathed out a cold breeze that

surrounded the demons, silencing them. Flying back down, he cut the air with his sword and removed all of their heads in one swoop. Their bodies tumbled to the ground, but when he landed and kicked their cloaks open, there was nothing but broken bits of bone and heaps of gray ash. The hooded heads no longer had eyes, only smoke billowing from the black cloth.

"VIIIICTOR!" Sweat dribbled down his bare chest as he stomped around the place, smiling wickedly, his mind broken and scattered like fallen puzzle pieces. Adrenaline rushed through him in full drive, his heart pumping fast and hard. Nostrils flared... he was not leaving without his pound of flesh, even if he had to pay with his own life, too. "Don't you think we're a bit too old to still be playing Hide and Go Fuck Yourself? Come out, come out, wherever the hell you are!"

Alexandre entered a small enclosure with mirrors for walls. He took a breath, and then another.

He's so close...

A purple and gold jewelry box sat on the floor in the center of the small chamber. The notes of 'Candle in the Wind' by Elton John, played and a tiny, black ballerina moved around and around—only she was upside down, her legs extended in the air and a strange, off-putting expression on her tiny, painted face. Alexandre reached into his pants pocket and attached one of Zhang Wei's throwing stars onto the tip of the blade, securing it with the bloodied bullet that had been inside his arm. He blew heat upon the ammunition, making it pliable, like gunmetal colored clay, then blew cool air to make it hard once again.

"That's what has come between us..." Victor's voice boomed. "A pretty little upside down, wicked monstrosity... a *thing*." His brother's image appeared in a mirror, and then another, and another. The man was dressed in black from head to toe, a ruby inverted cross hanging from his neck. "I will never forgive our mother for creating her... and I will never forgive you for nurturing her degeneracy, making her stronger, then turning your back on the Coven, deserting Paris. You've shamed the throne."

"Oh, Victor." Alexandre groaned. "We both know this has little to do with the Coven, Mother, Paris, or Venus... My Bloodmate was just a tool, a matter of contention for you to get yourself a way in. You played upon that. She was a ticket to ride, something you could abuse to try and get your way."

He threw up his free hand. "But you failed. You've created an insane, nightmarish Disney World of sorts here, but I suppose even this simply wasn't enough." Alexandre looked about the place and grimaced. "No, you needed the *real* thing... the realistic sex dolls with wet, tight, plastic pussies, the nonstop hand jobs, masturbating yourself to unconsciousness weren't doing the trick. The vibrating, battery-operated silicon mouths were no longer doing the job, either." Victor stepped slowly around and around, as if moving up and down on a carousel. Where was he? "No, dear brother... you'd grown bored. You needed a woman of your very own... a *powerful* one. Dominance is infectious and addictive all at once. Power is *definitely* female. We crave it like blood, the fearful, choppy breathing of prey, and the last thump of a strong heartbeat coming to an end." Alexandre slicked his tongue into the air, tasting it. Anger and fear from a fellow vampire were salty... like human tears.

"After your death tonight, Alexandre, I will endure a grueling hearing. My alibi will prove that I was thousands of miles away. I will tell the Council how wrought with grief I am over your death, especially since we'd ended our relationship on such tumultuous terms."

"Your delusions are always rather entertaining, Victor. Where'd you get such a creative, twisted mind? Perhaps instead of living off your inheritance, you should have become a magician? You keep tricking yourself after all... perpetual sleight of hand and mind."

"Oh no, I can see things quite clearly, big brother. I understand that your wedding is being planned, the final steps, as we speak. In fact, you're due to be married in the next few days, right here on Parisian soil. What a pity that Venus will lose her lover, and what a sad realization will come upon her when she understands that it will be I, who is next in line, to make her my sex slave and fuck her ruthlessly, relentlessly, mercilessly, until she perishes from the pleasure and unimaginable agony...."

"AHHH!" Alexandre moved back as a large, shiny black sword swiped by his head. Victor came after him with his sword drawn, but only in the mirrors... he was fighting a mere ghost. Alexandre wielded his weapon, swinging it wildly to the left, then the right. He winced when he felt moisture. Blood trickled down the right side of his face. He reached up to catch bits of black glass that were stuck along his cheek and temple, scraping and cutting, no idea where they'd come from.

The flickering shadow of something fluttering about could be seen out the corner of his eye. He could hear a heart thumping like ancient drums within the chest cavity of the depraved entity better known as Victor. Shards of glass burst from one of the mirror panels as his brother leapt from it, slicing him across his chest. A perfectly formed cut started to bleed, dripping and pooling with red essence. Victor's nostrils flared as he cut the air again and again. In a flurry of motion, Alexandre dropped to the floor and rolled a safe distance away.

Victor levitated off the ground as if in slow motion then swooped down like a famished eagle after juicy prey. The tip of the blade almost jammed in Alexandre's stomach as he rolled to and fro, kicking and sliding, trying to get back onto his feet. Propping his shoulder against a corner, he quickly propelled himself upward, making a mad dash towards the other side of the area. His brother chased him about, lunacy in his eyes.

"I'm better than you, Alexandre!" Victor roared as he paraded back and forth like a snow leopard in a cage. "We could've been a team! BUT NO! You had to go and ruin it!"

"You've come undone… you're fuckin' insane!" Alexandre breathed slow and hard, mentally measuring the distance between him and the man, calculating his next move.

"I am a genius! I had the brains, you had the looks and appeal. We could've ruled the woooorld! But no… Everything is gone now, but I will gain it back!"

"You want to be king, Victor? You can't even run this crazy municipality you've created, let alone an entire country. Definitely not the world!"

Victor burst out laughing.

"You idiot! I was born to be king. I am not so consumed with fables from a whacky wizard assigned during my youth, who died centuries ago, predicting that I would forsake my Coven and my country in the future. You think I'm not personable, you believe no one likes me? That's ironic!" He laughed, a loud, harsh sound. "The people you trust, the very ones you hold dear, now *despise* you!"

"Hmmm, really?" Alexandre grinned as he slid a cigarette he'd been holding onto for Whiskey out of his pants pocket, and lit it with his fingertip. "Like who? Since you believe the jig is up for me, maybe you can, uh, ya know, humor me... tell me as my last dying wish."

"Right now, I have your very own Fawn at my fingertips. She'll do as I wish!"

Alexandre leaned against the wall and drew on the cigarette, smiling from ear to ear. Victor's smile faded ever so slightly, but it was more than apparent that he was determined to hide his confusion at such a reaction.

"Do you know what traitor pussy smells like, Vic?" Alexandre swallowed the cigarette whole and began to toss his sword in the air, catching it like a ball going up and down. "It's piquant... it's intoxicating. It's a flavor you never forget. See, it's usually attached to a temptress, the kind of bitch that most men, vampires, wolves, you name it, would go loco over. I met Fawn in a bar one night. She worked there, barely making ends meet. She was only a couple decades old in her Turned life… fresh, so very young, and ripe with desire. On the side, she stripped. I'm sure you know that part, though. You make sure to find out weaknesses. She was a black hearted, cold blooded slaughterer… fed her hunger like no other, with not an ounce of remorse. She was amazing… you know, the kind of woman we like.

"I knew immediately that a lot of guys would love her, take to her. She was smart. She was beautiful. But I never trusted her. Yet, being the man I am, with the way my mind works, I knew that she'd be a perfect addition to my law firm. You know the old adage, 'How do you know when a lawyer is telling the truth? He stops talking.'." Alexandre chuckled loudly, then turned in a flash. He quickly karate chopped an attacking guard in the neck, then tossed one of the extra throwing stars into the bastard's skull. The fool slumped against the wall then fell to the ground. He casually turned back to his brother who was still pacing, his sword high, his eyes dark.

"I hope you don't mind… I'm just gonna let him bleed out for a sec, then I'll finish him off in just a little bit." There's a special poison on this blade from this star now, but what's in it is an ancient Chinese secret." He winked at his brother and grinned. "It focuses on the brain… what little you have left that hasn't been devoured by madness. Shhh… you hear that? He's gasping for air. I like the sound of his suffering… it calms me. Anyway." He coughed back up the cigarette he'd swallowed earlier and puffed it a few good times. "As I was saying. Fawn was bought and purchased with the intent that she'd do all that she's done and more. You fell right into my trap. If someone is going to use a deterrent against me, I prefer to be the inventor of that weapon. Congratulations! You win the, 'I fucked myself up' award!"

Victor lessened the distance between them, his black sword still drawn.

"Lies. This is what you do. You're a lawyer by trade. You're a mind fucker, but I know you well, brother. I'm not falling for it, Alexandre." Victor's fangs gleamed from beneath the curled lips of a wicked smile. The bastard wore a proud expression, held his head high.

"Oh really? I'm full of shit? Where is she at then, Victor?" His brother's smile faded. "You asked her to do something, right? Yet, she isn't where she is supposed to be. She left you to handle it all by your damn self. Again. She will *never* come directly after me. She still sees me as the prize. You honestly think she ever wanted you?! You can't use my own bitch against me. I *made* her."

"I… I don't believe you! You'd never have anyone in your midst that you didn't trust… you're far too paranoid."

"Oh, I trust her… I trust her to do *just* as she did. Stab me in the back!" They raced towards one another at full speed, and yet it felt like everything was quiet… still… barely moving. Alexandre held his sword high, aiming for the bastard's head. Victor mimicked his stance. The slicing pain of the black blade ran the length of his body. He hollered out, the moans of his ancestors echoing in his mind. Black feathers and bits of shiny glass fell from nowhere; the heavens rained hell upon their heads. A roaring call, a whiny moan, and an ungodly heat surrounded him. His body shook as he looked down at the black knife embedded deeply into his chest.

He slowed down, the radiating pain stealing his breath, his chest dripping and draining like a sink faucet. His brother laughed, his voice echoing throughout the abysmal, funhouse-like chambers.

"Look at the king!" Victor taunted as he scaled the wall, teasing and toying with him. "That sword in your body is one of a kind! It belonged to our great, great grandfather, King François Marseille. I found it in the abandoned ruins of our childhood home... left like trash in the dust and rubble!" the madman went on, taunting, talking, laughing... It was obvious he wished for him to die a slow, agonizing death.

Alexandre looked about, his eyelids heavy as his energy drained. He kept his sword up, stayed on his feet... but for how long? He wouldn't live by the sword and die by the sword; he'd simply bleed and bleed and when he was weak enough to the point where he was unable to lift a finger, he'd need to be fed... but his brother would starve him. Perhaps worse, feed from him while he was dying, taking his last bit of life... the ultimate disrespect.

Out of the corner of his eye, Alexandre spotted the half dead guard he'd jammed one of Zhang Wei's throwing stars into. The guy breathed harshly, gasping for breath. Alexandre took slow steps back, pretending to stumble more than he needed, until he was practically standing on top of the body. In his mind, he counted slowly as his brother screamed, telling him what a fuckup he was… how he hated him so… how he and their mother destroyed the French Pure Blood legacy.

He counted in his head…

3…

2…

1…

"AHHHH!" He fell back onto the body until he landed face down on the guy, the guard beneath him wailed. Using the fucker as a shovel, Alexandre moved his torso against the half dead bastard, until the sword began to move, pushing outward.

"What are you doing?!" Victor screamed out.

Gritting his teeth, blood dribbling from his mouth down his chin, he worked the tip of the blade out of his back. He got to his feet, both blades in hand now, then knelt down and cut the guard's neck, putting him out of his misery. Victor attacked again, screaming as he raced towards him, vengeance in his eyes. With both blades raised, Alexandre yelled and impaled his brother in the chest with the black blade from their forefather. At the same time, he drove the silver Chinese star into his forehead.

Victor stopped in his tracks… swaying back and forth… a look of lost hope, forsakenness… and brokenness in his violet eyes. He opened his mouth to speak, but only bright red blood pooled out, garbling his words.

"K...Kill... me..." Victor uttered, his eyes filling with watery crimson tears.

Alexandre snatched the sword out of his brother's head, knowing it would be a short time before he succumbed to the poisons that would directly attack his brain, eating it up like ravenous worms... Raising the blade high in the air to cut off the fiend's head, he prepared to do the deed that begged to be done until large, silky black feathers fell from all directions and a moan that rattled the world vibrated his soul. The black raven swooped low then disappeared into the shadows. Half a second later, his mother emerged from the darkness.

Queen Geneviève...

She slowly approached, her long black hair flowing like a boat sail behind her, her nude body covered in pieces of shimmering black glass. She floated, her bare feet not touching the ground. Long strands of thick hair covered her snow-white breasts and her pupils turned jet black right before his eyes. She took her wayward son into her arms. Victor's lids fluttered open and his mouth opened once more, but he was simply speechless... succumbing to his destiny. His body became limp in her grasp as she brought him close and kissed the wound on his forehead. Victor's eyes rolled and he began to shake, the brain poison taking effect, a bit at a time...

"My sons..." Mother's face was now streaked in red as her bloody tears fell from her eyes. She rocked Victor against her body as she knelt to the ground with him in her arms, holding him close, like a baby. "You cursed me, and I cursed you," she said with a smile as she looked down at him. "Your curse to me has been fulfilled. I have lost my boy… you're dying. My curse to you begins *now*!"

Mother sank her sharp, long teeth into his neck, brutally ripping and pulling at the alabaster skin. Victor's eyes grew large as his body shook, his limbs going in all directions. Mother paused and looked at Alexandre, death and heartbreak in her eyes, the terrible pain visible. He could see it… *feel* it…

Her greatest desires and fears had come true in the exact same night. She wiped her mouth with the back of her hand and roared in agony as she held Victor's dead body against her own heartbeat.

"Sometimes, a mother has to eat her young…"

Dear Reader,

Her Royal Highness,
Genevieve Marseille
requests the pleasure
of your company

At the Marriage
of
His Royal Highness,

King Alexandre Marseille
With
Miss Venus Margaret Anderson

RSVP as soon as you
read this to Tiana Laveen on
Facebook.

CHAPTER TWENTY-ONE

The Bride's Blood Bath

She exhaled… coughing up the thick sludge of the past, swallowing the sharp flavor of the future…

Her eyes turned in her skull as her back arched in orgasmic delight, colored in shades of supreme being…

Roaring, she yelled at the top of her burning lungs as she emerged from the copious, scarlet fluid, then disappeared back beneath the soft layers of blood…

V ENUS COULD SEE no one... but she heard them, felt them all around her like black raven feathers brushing against her soul...

It was her bridal blood bath, a sacred ritual for all fiancées of Parisian Pure Bloods that took place before their wedding ceremony. PVRIS sang 'White Noise' through the speakers of the place. Her hearing was so sensitive, even the sound of a vamp's breath from a mile away was amplified. The music helped blend the noise, made her a bit more comfortable.

"Thaaaat's it," someone said. She assumed it was Syà. "Breathe." The blood splashed out of the massive gold and ivory tub and soon, her eyes began to focus again. Syà moved before her, standing in a black silk gown, her long dark ponytail wrapped around her head, pinned up, and adorned with a jeweled hair pin. She held a reflective glass before her and smiled. "Be still, Beautiful. Look at how stunning you are... how clean... how shiny and new." Venus regarded herself, took notice of her eyes, their natural dark brown now a light amber. Though they'd return to their natural color eventually, she knew this wouldn't be the last time she'd see herself looking this way.

Her black hair was slicked back and saturated with the blood. An ornate black collar of sorts, resembling a lace choker, was wrapped around her neck. Syà stepped away. To her right, the room was huge, stark white, glowing like the footprints of crushed, fallen stars left behind. Vamps lined up on that side, wearing sleek black dresses, barefoot, holding red roses. On the left side stood the vampire men, all of them impeccable, wearing three-piece black suits with neat white shirts beneath. They were barefoot, too. In their hands they held black roses, their fragrance filling up the area. Slowly, the vampires began to float towards her. She closed her eyes, her heart beating so fast…

When she opened her eyes once again, the roses had been dropped all around the tub like a floral frame, some inside the blood bath with her, christening her. The vampires returned to their posts against the walls, all of them wearing smiles as they regarded her.

Syà begun to speak in Chinese, then French, and after that, English.

"Now, your Bloodmate must officially approve you. King Alexandre Marseille, please enter…"

The room, which had appeared doorless, suddenly opened up, exposing a long rectangular void across from her. She sat up in the bath, causing the blood to slosh about, and clutched the edges of the tub as everyone looked on, waiting. Billows of white smoke came from the entrance, and soon, her mate… her gorgeous groom… the lover of her soul entered. The Vamps dropped to one knee, heads down, in honor of King Alexandre.

He was dressed in a fitted, slightly shiny black suit, paired with expensive-looking shoes. His steps echoed as he approached, his hands clasped in front of him, his fingers adorned with fine rings. His silky ebony hair was combed away from his face, exposing his exquisite features—the high cheekbones she'd kissed a million times over, his full, succulent lips and dark eyebrows. She was biased, but damn... the man was fine! Finally, he stood before her. Such intensity swam in his ice blue crystal eyes. He bent down and looked her dead in her eyes.

She shuddered as she got a whiff of him. His scent was exquisite. Her pussy pulsed and her fangs descended in pure lust...

Slowly closing her eyes, she waited...

And then, she felt it. A soft kiss placed upon her lips. When she opened her eyes, he'd turned and began to walk away.

Something caught her eye.

Floating on top of the bloody waters was one white lotus flower.

"King Marseille has given the gift of the white flower. He has approved his bride," Syà announced with a smile as soon as Alexandre disappeared back from whence he'd come. The room lit up with cheers and dancing. Venus' lips curled in a smile. Juice Newton sang 'Angel of The Morning,' fitting music to her mood. She hummed the lyrics: 'And though we're victims of the night, I won't be blinded by the light...'

That moment was the oddest, yet one of the most beautiful in her life. What a ceremony... what a life she was embarking upon with the man she loved. It felt intimate, even with all of these people, now *her* people, cheering her on and delighting in the carnal sensuality of their existence. Syà stepped close and extended her hand to help her out of the tub. Venus felt a little cold as the Vamp wrapped a lush black towel around her body.

"Here you go. Now, you will take a shower of spring water and place the white lotus flower inside your pussy overnight. No sex until the morning. Tomorrow night, you will be wed. We have more preparations to make until then." Syà hugged her, taking her off guard. It was quick. It was fast. But it was a hug, indeed.

"Wow, what was that?" Venus teased. "A sign of affection… I wish I had this on camera."

"If you tell anyone, I'll deny it." Syà laughed, but then, her smile faded. "The more I'm around you, the more thoughtful I feel… not just towards you, but everyone. I don't like it." She chuckled, though Venus knew she meant what she said. Smiling, Venus ran her bloodied hand across the woman's soft cheek. "My husband was hurt, and he has since healed, but for the first time, I was worried about him. This is your fault, Venus. You infect all those you care for. A little bit of you rubs off on us, and we are never the same. A dreadful yet lovely poison runs through your veins. There is something wrong with you, beautiful Blood Bride, but we accept you anyway. How could we not, when it feels so right?"

"YOU BIG, DUMB ass, stupid motherfucker!" Fawn hissed as she packed her things to leave her hotel and return to New York. "You're his closest friend! You knew I had been looking for him! I fucking hate you!"

Whiskey chuckled as he pulled his pants back up. The place smelled of expensive perfume, and the scent of her pussy was all over him. This time, he'd made sure he got his blowjob *first.*

"Who called who, bitch? You were the one wantin' your back blown out. I figured I'd let you have me, but you being you, of course, you thought you'd be able to manipulate me, get some information on Alexandre, find out if he's been avoiding you. Don't get angry at me because I made sure I busted a few good nuts and you got nothin' in return but cum down your fuckin' throat."

"You come over here to tell me this... you think it's funny?"

"Nope." Whiskey cracked up again as he pulled his fitted white shirt over his head. "I gave you what you wanted and got what I wanted, too." He shrugged. "Look, he's busy, all right? The world doesn't revolve around you, Fawn."

"This is ridiculous! I was supposed to be planning the wedding, and now you tell me that some Chinese half-bald-headed warrior princess that is older than time is in charge?! Why didn't Alexandre tell me himself?! I still haven't heard from him!"

"First of all, she's a queen, highly respected worldwide, so you better watch your mouth. I've heard Queen Syà has had people killed for even looking at her wrong. She's also not someone you are going to fight with and win. She was born and bred for that shit. Secondly, Alexandre is really busy with a lot of shit that got messed up due to his brother, Fawn. You have no idea how bad it is..." His words seemed to pique her interest. She turned and faced him. "So, he's gotta get that all squared away. There are ongoing meetings with the Council in regard to Victor, the municipality he established and ran... his property, all kinds of shit."

"He had his own town?" Fawn had the audacity to sound sad, as if she'd missed out on something great.

"Yeah, if ya wanna call it that. It was a fuckin' freakshow, and not the good kind. Anyway, it's being taken over by the mayor, they'll try to keep it intact. More importantly though, Alexandre and Venus are having the wedding here in Paris instead, so that's why your plans were scrapped, all right? Stop takin' shit so personal. You Turned Vamps can be so damn sensitive." He didn't miss the horrid scowl on her face. She quickly turned away and jammed another pair of shoes into her luggage. "I've barely seen him myself... It's just like that. I'm sure he'll contact you eventually, though."

The Vamp said nothing more as she angrily snatched clothing off the bed and floor and stuffed it in her bag.

"You can leave now," she spat, her back to him.

Sliding his belt through the loops, he smacked her on the ass, making her jump. She hissed, but kept her gaze averted as he made his way to the hotel room door.

"See ya later. You should stick around for the wedding though, Fawn. I'm sure he expects you to be there."

"I doubt it! Obviously, Alexandre is too busy thinking about himself and Venus. The hell with me, right?!" She threw up her hand. "After everything I've done for him! Alexandre is ungrateful! I'm done, that's it!"

"How many times do I have to tell ya? It's nothin' personal. In fact, he said you'd done a great job! Oh, and don't forget about his brother's funeral, too. The bastard double-crossed him, but ya know, Pure Breed Vampire memorials are a big deal, so that still has to be handled." He didn't miss the way her body stiffened at his words. "Well, see ya back in New York in a few days. There's a bachelor party in a little bit I refuse to miss. Vamp pussy galore!!!"

"Just get out. You're getting a kick out of this. I hate you, Whiskey."

He laughed then blew her a kiss and stepped out of her room. As he walked down the long hotel hallway, the buckles from his black leather jacket jangling with each step, he slid his phone out of his pocket. After he'd gotten on the elevator and made his way down to the lobby, he dialed.

"Boy, I love you, but do you know what time it is, Whiskey?!"

"Yo, is he there with ya?"

"Alexandre just left to only Lord knows where. Why?"

"Need to tell ya something."

"This better be good," came the sleepy voice. "You know I have to get ready and there are hundreds of people pulling me in a million different directions. They do it big here!" Venus laughed, and he couldn't help but follow suit.

"I know, sister-in-law," he said affectionately, "But, uh, has your mate told you about Fawn?"

"What do you mean? Is she okay?"

Whiskey took a deep breath and grinned. It was time for that bitch to get what she had coming to her. From his understanding, Alexandre would be dealing with her ass in New York, on her own turf, but Whiskey cared for Venus and decided he wanted to give the lady a nice wedding gift, right before the vows.

"Well, let me start from the beginning, but I promise this won't take long…"

When he finished giving the rundown of the trifling trader's deeds, he could practically taste Venus' anger oozing through the phone.

"Where is she right now?"

"She's headed to this place called *Nuit Noire*. It's an underground district where you can get specialty bloods, charms, candles, Wiccan, Voodoo and Hoodoo love spell work, shit like that. Buncha witches and Vamps makin' and selling mostly girly love spell shit." He slid a cigarette out of his pocket and stepped outside to light it. "A lot of Haitian Vamps work the tents, too. For all I know, it's her last-ditch effort to get

Alexandre."

"I see… Well, I think I need to have a little chat with Fawn."

"Oh, really? Maybe you and she can have a girls' lunch or somethin', Bloody Marys and shit while you're over there." He smirked.

"Mmm hmm, yeah, sounds delicious. Thank you, Whiskey. You've made my fucking day."

"I figured it would, Beautiful. Besides, I don't just answer to Alexandre anymore. I answer to you too now."

"You don't answer to me. We're friends. No, actually we're family. I don't work that way, but I greatly appreciate this. Seems that my Bloodmate was going to handle her at a later date, but no, this type of betrayal needs a Queen's touch."

He chuckled at her words.

"I couldn't fuckin' agree more. Off with their heads!" And then he ended the call, laughing all the way to his motorcycle…

CHAPTER TWENTY-TWO

You Can't Hold a Candle to Me...

I N THE MASSIVE bedroom, the once crisp, white bedsheets were now splattered with blood, disheveled from several hours of incredible morning sex. Alexandre brought the fabric to his nose and inhaled, then smiled. They smelled like his mate. They'd been passing each other like ships in the night, only getting together to take care of necessary pre-wedding traditions and to fuck. Moments earlier, she'd stated she needed to run a quick errand before she was gone, swept away in the throes of wedding plans once again. He'd expected this, but not some other aspects of his life. Things had gotten complicated...

Flopping back onto the headboard, he ran his hand through his hair and closed his eyes. He hadn't spoken to or seen his mother since Victor's death. He imagined she'd stayed in that basement for quite some time afterward. He'd returned to his mansion to heal, but couldn't get the look in her eyes as she held his brother to her bosom out of his mind. Nevertheless, he'd moved forward with the planning of the memorial, though he refused to attend. The Council was taking care of it, following his orders to the letter. He picked up a glass tumbler full of fresh blood from the nightstand and took a small sip before setting it back down.

His cell phone rang.

"Hello," he stated as he stretched, feeling lazy.

"Greetings, King Marseille. This is King Ioham Santos."

"Ahhh, yes, my brother from Brazil." Alexandre had not spoken to Ioham in at least three years. "How are you?"

"I'm well. My Queen and I will attend your wedding this evening. In fact, we just landed in Paris."

"Splendid! That sounded rather English of me, didn't it?" he teased, causing the man to laugh.

"Yes, it did, but I imagine you're excited on your special day."

"I am..." Alexandre's smile slowly faded as he thumbed the sheets, twisting them between his fingers. He couldn't help but think of his Bloodmate... of the joy she'd brought into his life.

"I am calling also to offer my condolences for your departed brother, Victor, because I was told that is what we are supposed to do when a king loses his mother, father, brother or sister."

"Thank you. Unfortunately, it had to be done."

"It most certainly did. I heard about what happened during the Council session preceding this. With all due respect, I did not give a fuck about him and my entire family and, I'm sure, my subjects, are glad he is gone." The man's voice was full of venom. "He made a mockery of our trade agreements, interfered with negotiations while you were away in New York, and threatened our ally, the Monarch of Portugal."

Alexandre shook his head. "Yes, I remember."

"Good. As you may also recall, I had to have my secretary contact you several times during these ordeals. Thankfully, you were able to arbitrate but it was aggravating, to say the least."

"Yes, it appears Victor has left an indelible mark upon the world. However, since my mother is alive, I am treading lightly regarding what I say about the matter, though I understand your concerns and frustrations, please do not bring this up at the wedding or anywhere in her presence."

"Of course not. That is why I am discussing it now. In any case, I look forward to seeing you and meeting your bride. I hear she is a lovely Turned Vamp, and I am glad that you were brave enough to take the initiative to make this move, so that future generations may also be open to finding their mate amongst the T.V. community."

"Thank you for your words, Ioham. I am certain Venus will be honored for you to be in attendance and I look forward to seeing your wife, Izabel."

"Thank you. We will see you soon." And then, the call ended.

Alexandre sat for several minutes, his mind chasing thoughts he wished were buried, like his brother. He picked up his phone once more and dialed.

After the third ring, he heard her voice…

"Mother…"

"Yes?" He was quiet for a while, listening to her breathe. He used to enjoy that sound as a youth…

"Is there anything that you need from me?"

It was strange; no matter how much time had passed since she'd gone missing from his life, disappeared into nothingness, he still had reverence for her, deep respect that he could not shake. Mother was a force to be reckoned with. She'd been deemed one of the most unusually beautiful rulers of their kind. She had extraordinary, striking features… strangely lovely, a face you'd never forget. Over two hundred oil paintings existed of her. She was revered because of her strong warrior spirit, something hard to find in this day and age. Victor had always complained how much alike they were… Perhaps that had been the origin of all the tension between them.

"What I need from you, Alexandre, is for you to show by example how to rule. I need you to be what your father and I were, and more. You and Venus will create and hold our legacy in the palm of your hands. Everything I've done has been for France, our people and especially, my progenies. One day, when you become a father, you will not judge me any longer. You will understand the meaning of sacrifice and the need to put your offspring first. We have no true feelings, it's not in us, but we have an understanding when we create our undead. We know, as soon as that offspring is born from our womb, we will owe him or her *every*thing—most of all, protection. It changes you…"

"Please tell me, I have to know… how did you know to select Venus for my bride? I know that you heard her mother's prayer, and I of course know about the prediction, but you still had a choice. Ultimately, I could have chosen differently and so could you. We have free will. How did you know she'd be so perfect for me? I've never met anyone like her in my life…"

Mother took some time to answer.

"Everything was lined up perfectly… the stars, the moon, the planets and the sleeping sun that plagued our people for so long, erasing them from existence. The night Venus came into the world, you were angry. You were a young man, a new king, feeling things you were told you were never supposed to… things like loneliness." He hung his head. "You missed your family, and though you never told me, son, I always knew you craved that. The planets never lie; they choose who we are destined to love and be. Her mother named her after the Goddess of Love, Venus… right there under the stars. Your surname is the same as your father's, and his father's, and his father's… Marseille. Mars… Venus… Mars… Mars is the planet of war, leadership, rulers. It is masculine. Venus is love, creativity, intelligence and beauty. It is feminine. What a perfect blend…"

"That's incredible. You took it as another sign? The names?"

"It most certainly was. You are the last of us, Alexandre. Your father and I knew that our last two surviving sons were our last hope. We also knew that Victor did not have the temperament to rule properly. Those were private discussions that you were not privy to. So, we made a decision and sought out assistance... predictions. I declared that I needed to find you a proper mate, someone worthy to carry on our name. It was time for our people to embrace change. It was time that we accepted and allowed Turned Vamps as the mates of our offspring, because to me, this was proof that it was meant to be. I figured, if she was strong enough to get away from that plantation and find me, then she'd pass the final test if my suspicions were correct. It began with your *Sorcier Cadieux*, but yes, I had to investigate, to ensure it was her... make certain we had been right. So much was riding on this, child."

"So... you knew how I felt as a child. I was never to speak of it. The loneliness you mentioned was true. I wanted friends, but being Royal, I had few. My brothers and sisters were dying, and after a while, Victor and I were the only ones left. He never cared for me, and I never cared for him... but I helped protect him all the same. I gave him too much power, allowed him to pretend to be in control at times, anything to make him feel better... but nothing helped. He was determined to do what he did."

"Yes, because everyone has a true nature, Alexandre. You stayed angry for centuries. That is how you ruled so well... you were so callous and hard. It was beautiful. But you weren't happy. You stayed angry until the night Venus reached that cabin in the woods. Something within you seemed to realize that your loneliness would soon be coming to an end, because suddenly, I heard that you'd—"

"Thrown a party…" His eyes watered with blood as he recalled that very night. "I'd looked up at the sky and thought it was so nice out. I threw a big party in Paris. It was the first time I'd been happy in—"

"Since you were a little lad who'd met a new friend, that little human boy who smiled at you."

A trail of bloody tears fell from his eyes. The shame he'd felt from that incident never left him… his entire village practically destroyed. He rubbed his hands together, looking down, shaking, falling apart.

"Alexandre, I shamed you. Your father shamed you. We never spoke to you about it, but we shamed you because we'd warned you to steer clear of the humans and you disobeyed. But, as time went on, I realized I should not have done that, for were it not because of a Black slave woman, a human being in terrible pain, crying out to the Heavens for her newborn baby girl to have freedom, you may never have smiled again… ever. Venus proved herself, and so have you." They both drew quiet. "I must now attend my son's wake. I must go. I will see you when the time comes."

"Mother…"

"Yes?"

"Before you go, I have another question for you…"

"Yes, what is it?"

"Have you ever felt… love? I don't know how to describe this, but… that is the only thing that comes close to how I feel for Venus. I haven't told anyone but her, but… yes, this is strange to me. It's happened. Mother, I am in love. Of that, I am certain."

"Venus has a power over us all, Alexandre." He could hear the smile in his mother's words. "Her mere existence caused this. I believe it is because of her resolve and also because of how she changed after I claimed her. She never wished to fully let go of her life as a human, despite my trying to convince her otherwise. She wanted to blend in, to keep drinking coffee, teach art history and lick the sweetest of chocolate candies. The night I bit her, I felt different, too. No, my son, I've never felt love, but I have experienced deep levels of concern and caring since I've known her. I believe that, in her own way, while I travelled the world with her, teaching her, molding her and training her, she was teaching me, too. Perhaps, things were not as they seemed. Just maybe, we needed her as much as she and her mother needed *us*..."

Nuit Noire WAS filled with vendors selling juicy peaches infused with blood and expensive vases created by some of the most talented artists in Paris. These works of art were stuffed with herbs, talismans, and instructions on how to win love... as if it were a game. Venus walked around in black leather leggings, thigh high boots, and a fitted black turtleneck. Though she'd fed from her mate that morning, she was still hungry... in desperate need of some deer meat better known as Fawn...

She sniffed the air, her nostrils flared as her curly hair bounced from each hurried step. She paused upon turning a corner, picking up the distinct sounds of two vampires fucking on the side of the road, tearing at one another as if their lives depended upon it. One had long blonde hair, her legs in the air as a male vampire jammed his short, fat cock deep inside her, plunging away. Venus drew closer, inspecting the situation. She hoped the bitch getting plowed was Fawn, but no such luck. Turning away, she kept on, feeling the delicious chill in her bones as she drew closer to her prey.

Oh yes, there you are...

Fawn was standing nearby with her luggage at her side, talking to a vendor as she waved a blood candle about. Venus smirked and shook her head.

Bitch, what do you know about Hoodoo? Put that candle down. You should have spoken to the women in my family. They could have schooled you. She glanced down at her watch, then quickly approached. "Hello, Fawn." The Vamp jumped, then laughed nervously.

"Oh my! Hi Venus! Wow!" Fawn grabbed her scarf and closed her eyes, as if she needed a moment to catch her breath. "I didn't, uh, expect to run into you here! Aren't you supposed to be getting married? How could you have time to shop?"

Venus grinned at the woman and put her hand on her hip.

"Oh, today I got time, cuz..." Venus yanked the bitch by her arm and hauled her away from the vendor, candle still in hand.

"You have to pay for that!" the vendor screamed out in a thick French accent.

"I'm about to be Queen!" Venus replied. "I'll make sure you're squared away."

"Get your hands off me!" Fawn yelled out, her eyes big as saucers as she tried to break away. "What do you think you're doing? I am telling Alexandre about this."

"I don't think he'll be interested." Venus approached a red limousine and tossed Fawn inside like the trash that she was. The doors immediately locked. Sitting across from the bitch, she noted how her chest was heaving up and down.

"What is this about?! Where are you taking me?!"

"It's a shame for you to skip out on your boyfriend's funeral." Fawn blinked several times. "That's right, Fawn. I know all about what you and Victor had going on, how you threw my mate under the bus over and over again. Look, I'm sorry that you had feelings for Alexandre. I have nothing to do with that." Venus threw up her hands. "But what I *do* know is that he chose me, and instead of being a grown ass, mature woman about it, you went and sought revenge with one of his few last living relatives—his brother. You knew that mother-fucker was crazy, but you were so hellbent on being queen one way or another, you took the risk."

"I don't know what you're talking about. Whatever Victor may have told you are lies! He approached me about taking Alexandre down and I refused! Now sure, I tried to talk sense into Alexandre about you, but he didn't want to hear it." She shrugged. "I accepted that. I was even planning your wedding... it was going to be beautiful! Does that sound like someone who can't get over Alexandre?"

"Hmmm." Venus tapped her chin with her finger, pretending to mull over the matter. "In fact, it does. See, Fawn, you and I were both once human, unlike Alexandre and Victor. We have a menu, if you will, of those tricky little things called emotions that we can choose from at any given time throughout our lives. Alexandre and Victor don't know much about all of that. Consider it a weakness... and it can be, but in times like these, actions are quite revealing. I know you still recall what it felt like to be in love, to wish and dream, to be sad. Those emotions stay with us. They are not as strong as they used to be, but we *never* forget them."

Venus' eyes hooded as she tapped the side of her head, and then she leaned forward. She caught her reflection in the window—her eyes had turned the glowing amber color she'd seen for the first time during her blood bath. Fawn must've noticed too, for she trembled and recoiled to the farthest corner of the seat, as far as she could get from Venus.

"Where are we going? To Alexandre so he can kill me?"

"Ha! You wish." Venus made herself comfortable in her seat, tucking her thick hair behind one ear. "Nah, got a little surprise for you..." Venus reached into the center console and pulled out a chilled bottle of champagne. She poured herself a glass then downed it. Minutes later, they arrived at a place that looked as if it had been bombed. Fawn swallowed hard and looked out the window.

"Where are we? What is this place?"

Instead of answering, Venus leisurely got out of the limo. The driver stepped out and opened Fawn's door.

"You son of a bitch!" Fawn screamed as she looked up at Whiskey.

The bastard wore a hat that was far too small for his head. He grinned at her. Grabbing her by the waist, he hoisted the bitch over his shoulder then slammed the door closed behind him. The three walked a few feet then stopped when a strong stench filled the air.

"Oh my, smells like someone here is sick, got that dirty ass Bottom Feeder disease. Who could it be?! Eenie, meenie, miny, moe, catch a Bottom Feeder by its toe!" Venus chuckled.

"No... no!!!" Fawn's fangs descended as she wiggled about on Whiskey's shoulder, but it was simply no use. Several Bottom Feeders came out from their homes, looking around, feasting their eyes.

"Don't worry, they've been paid in advance to handle you. Now, isn't this fitting? This is called irony!" Whiskey chuckled at her words. "You tried to have me destroyed by B.F.s... Victor hadn't even come up with the idea—that was a Fawn original!" She cackled. "Like Netflix. Red is the new black, huh? I've had a blood bath, I feel abso-fucking-lutely rejuvenated! They put blood in there from Queens all over the world. It's magical. You see, I learned a little something from my fiancé. Our greatest fears and desires are what *truly* rule us. That's why he's so good at what he does, ya know? You were afraid of never having any true power in this life, and it's sad, because you had more control than you realized. If you had been decent to Alexandre, although he still would've never loved you, he would have looked out for you, made sure you didn't want for anything. You were the only woman he let get close to him before I came along, Fawn. Instead of seeing that as an honor, you tossed it in his face."

Whiskey set Fawn down, but held her close so she wouldn't run away.

"You stupid Black bitch! He doesn't love you! He doesn't love anyone but himself!" Fawn's voice quivered as she looked around, the fear stark in her eyes as the Bottom Feeders stared hungrily at her.

"First of all, you do know that he loves me. That is why you've gone to such lengths to do what you've done. Secondly, that whole racial thing is lame and played out, Fawn. I *am* Black. And proud of it, I might add. I can be a bitch at times, but stupid is something I could *never* be. Whiskey, let her go."

Whiskey released the woman and Fawn made a mad dash in the opposite direction. Venus and Whiskey got back inside the limo and waited… The prey was loose, and the games would soon begin.

The Bottom Feeders gave chase like a pack of hyenas. A few of them stopped and looked inside the limo, possibly trying to figure out if it was worth attacking her and Whiskey, too. She was prepared for that as well. She and Whiskey had more ammo, guns, and bombs on them to light up their entire township like the 4th of July. Venus rolled down the window a hair and peered at one who was loitering a bit too close, and for too long...

"Listen here, motherfucker... I was a Queen before my King even knew my name... now try me if you want to."

The Bottom Feeder stood up straight then went on his way. It was only a matter of minutes before they heard Fawn's earsplitting screams in the near distance. Whiskey started up the limo, and without another word, turned to drive away. As they left the area, Venus took notice of one of the Bottom Feeders holding a fistful of blonde hair... the ends stained in blood. Another held shreds of the Vamp's clothing, the expensive garments soaked in red essence. It was time that Fawn was returned to her people, for she was no better than them... at least they knew what they were and accepted it, feeding and feasting off peoples' pain and weaknesses.

"All right, Blood Queen... we've had our fun. Let's get you back to where you belong."

"And where's that, dear brother?" She smirked as she picked up the blood candle on the floor and gave it a sniff.

"In your rightful place... on the motherfuckin' throne..."

CHAPTER TWENTY-THREE

Here Comes the Blood Bride...

VENUS SAT ON the slate and stone floor in the cozy white cottage, the Queen Mother nestled behind her, enveloping her in a soothing cocoon, working a golden, wide-toothed comb through her thick tresses for her wedding night.

A fire was lit before her, the warmth so delicious, kissing her skin. The gentle tugging motion relaxed her after a hectic day, which she was certain was what her mistress had intended. Last minute preparations for her wedding were in full effect, but she didn't mind allowing Syà to take the wheel and drive it to the point of no return. The Vamp was into showy, beautiful, sparkly things, but Venus and Alexandre wanted a garden wedding, something traditional like the unions of previous French monarchs. The final touches to her gown were complete now, but she didn't look forward to being placed within the elaborate thing...

A frenzy of professional this and that had her in their

clutches. She'd had a pedicure, manicure, and now sported deep burgundy nails with a glossy topcoat. Her skin was buttery smooth after she and her appointed bridesmaids, all of whom turned out to be truly lovely upper echelon ladies, had a spa day. The finishing touches to her makeup had also been made, and the results were shocking to say the least. Syà insisted that the best makeup artist in Paris do the work. A man by the name of Louis Bernard, had turned her into a damn goddess. When she'd looked in the mirror moments prior, she barely recognized herself. She'd never seen such an impeccable makeup job, but she appreciated her own natural beauty as well.

How am I going to get into my dress without messing up my thousand-dollar face? Oh yeah… they pull it up from the bottom… Goodness gracious, this isn't my bag. I don't know if I'm coming or going…

Now here she sat in her bra and panties, while her soon-to-be mother-in-law styled her hair. It was apparently tradition—something else new for Venus to know. The fire crackled, and long moments of silence webbed between them. Gentle hands moved along her scalp as the Queen massaged it from time to time, soothing the sting after ridding the locks of occasional tangles.

"Geneviève, thank you."

"You don't need to thank me, dear."

Even though she couldn't see the woman, she could sense the smile through her words.

"I do. All of this time we've… I don't know." Venus smiled and lowered her gaze briefly, then looked back into the fire. "I missed you so much. You told me it was time for me to go, and I didn't know what that meant... but now of course I do."

"My acts were selfish, and I have no shame in that. You were a good match for my child, Venus. Had you not been, we would not have gone on this journey together."

"I understand that, but you still cultivated me. You cared for me. There were things that arose that I asked of you. You could have simply said 'no' and still had me... but you didn't. You can call it all selfish, but I disagree. You helped me solve problems, then taught me how to solve them myself." She took a long deep breath then gathered her knees beneath her chin and hugged her legs. "So that is why I am grateful to you. Not only that, you have a wonderful son... and you trusted me with him. At the very least, that deserves a thank you."

"You are as much his gift as he is yours."

Venus nodded; those words warmed her within. "What did you think of me the very first time you saw me, Geneviève?"

"When I first saw you, I thought to myself, 'What a beautiful young lady'," Geneviève began. "You'd already arrived at the cabin, letting me know you were built to last. Anyone who could escape from such a situation surely was made of pure grit."

She paused, dipped her finger in olive oil and rubbed it along her scalp, then continued to comb through her hair. "After I fed you, I ran you a bath and looked at your naked body. You were built to bring my son's offspring into the world, too. Alexandre comes from hearty genes. We're robust, strong from birth. You have nice rounded hips to carry the descendants, full breasts to nurse... a beautiful specimen you are." Venus cringed at the word 'specimen', but knew that was simply the way the woman spoke—she meant no disrespect. "When I took you with me to travel the world, you proved to be a quick study, quite intelligent and charming, too. Men—humans and vampires alike—fawned over you, but I knew you were spoken for."

"What about me annoyed you the most?" Venus asked with a smile.

"You had a big heart, and that irritated me to no end."

Venus chuckled at her words. The woman placed the comb down, then began to braid her tresses, tugging here and there.

"It wasn't funny to me, Venus. It meant that your survival could be challenged. You could be in danger." Venus threw her a glance from over her shoulder, seeing the concern in her eyes. "Your stubbornness to release what I was certain would be your demise angered me, but then, you surprised me." Venus turned away, her eyes fixated on the flames. How transfixing, how lovely they looked, jumping about in the hearth. "You wanted to kill the man who'd enslaved you and your family... you wanted revenge. Finally, you were coming into your own." Venus' eyes narrowed as she recalled that fateful night. "We'd been so many places, and when we were about to head off to Hungary, you stopped and said, '*Madame*, may I return to the plantation and give back the same pain that was brought to me?' I didn't hesitate... I knew you needed this. Your soul had dreamt of it from your birth."

"My mother's pain and death... my father's horrible life... my grandmother's never-ending sorrow... Someone needed to pay, and pay for everyone who was trapped in that nightmare."

"And pay they did. We headed back and arrived in the dead of night. With your new strength and vitality, you crept inside that big white house while they were asleep, beat the Master with his own whip, then stabbed him in the chest with his own hunting knife. You strung some of his neighbors from trees, hanging them just as they'd done to others... forbidden fruit. You did the same to his wife, but before you left, you chopped his dick off and shoved it up his ass for all to see..."

Venus grinned as the horrifically beautiful memories flooded back... yes, now Master wouldn't ever be able to rape again, not even in the afterlife. It had been a strange celebration, although to this day, she wasn't convinced it had been enough...

"You killed everyone, with exception of the newborn baby, though you confessed you wanted to, but your heart wouldn't allow you. I told you that child was just as guilty—alive due to pain inflicted, the sins of the father... That child would inherit the wealth made off your back but you insisted that a baby is pure, innocent. So you swaddled that baby in soft cotton cloths, placed her in a basket, and set her on the porch of a home a mile away. A part of me admired that you'd done that. You then headed off to the slave quarters, told them to run away, and set the entire plantation on fire. The rage in your eyes... I'll never forget it! The place was ablaze. It glowed so beautifully! The flames could be seen for miles!" Geneviève laughed. "And then, you cried..." Her giggles softened, then ceased.

Venus' smile faded.

"You looked at me and said, 'They have nowhere to go now, Geneviève... They'll just get caught, bought and sold again. The nightmare of slavery will continue.' I asked you why did you care? You were finally free. You replied, 'Because they told me about the cabin in the woods, and they're my people. No, we're not all related, but we're related.' I had to think about that for a moment, and then, I understood. So, I did what any mistress in my position would do. I went out with you into the night before the sun rose and rounded them up. I called in some help, and we got them on a boat, sent them to New York. You were happy again... It was *then* that I realized I had to stop trying to change you, my child. You had what you needed within you. You were a true survivor and your heart would not damage you.

"You'd managed to adjust, use it as a strength, not a weakness... you had balance. The world doesn't care about what's fair, but *you* did." Venus met eyes with her mistress once again, while batting away blood-filled tears. Geneviève leaned in to kiss her forehead, then turned her back towards the fire.

"The flames are so pretty tonight."

"They are you. You are the fire tonight. Your eyes are the color of those flames sometimes now, Venus."

"Yes, I noticed that. Why?"

"Sometimes the Bridal Blood Bath has that effect when you're fertile." Venus swallowed. "This is why your wedding was set for today. You're in heat, Venus."

"In heat?" Venus rolled her eyes. Now this she simply couldn't let go. Geneviève knew better. "I'm not an animal, mistress. And neither are you."

"We're *all* merely animals, my love. Beasts. Pretty paint on our faces and sitting down at a table with a fork and spoon doesn't change that fact. Don't get caught up in semantics. It's hard to resist the lure of mating when in this state while lying next to your lover. Your will may be strong, and my son's, too, but the heart and body want what it wants. Our true desires always eventually win. Glowing from within…"

"So now every time I'm ovulating my eyes will glow?"

"It's a signal, like a beacon to your mate, inviting him inside. It's not consistent… just enough to let your mate know your status, kind of like pheromones. All creatures, my dear, have the desire to procreate. While ovulating, you send a message to your mate that you can accept his seed, and if you feel threatened at any time during your ovulation period, your eyes may glow, too. Your eyes are beautiful whether they are dark brown or light amber… but perhaps, should you and Alexandre decide, tonight you will create a new generation. It's a beautiful evening for such a thing."

Venus sighed and realized she needed to speak to her mother-in-law candidly. The elephant in the room was overdue to be addressed.

"Mistress, I know that it is tradition to do such things on

the wedding night, but along with Alexandre marrying a Turned Vamp, we would like to do things in our own time, in our own way. I also may rule a bit differently than you had."

"How so?" Geneviève kept braiding her hair without missing a beat.

"Well, since Alexandre and I will be spending the majority of our time here in Paris, I would like to establish a museum of African, Native Indian and Asian art, for example. There would be discussions and classes on art history, a library, guided tours, things of that nature. I would own this museum and teach, too, and it would be my way of giving back to our community as well as fulfilling my passion. I'm aware that knowing how to fight is important, and I have no doubt I need to use those skills at times, but I want my legacy to be more than slaying enemies with a sword, Geneviève... How about we slay them with educating the future generations, too? I want to show our people more human artwork so that they may be better understood. You taught me, you fostered my love of such things. Let me explore. I wish for my children, and their children, to not have to live in fear—but should a situation arise, they will know how to handle it by any means necessary. Like their grandmothers, you and my mother, they will not be afraid."

Venus was prepared to argue with the woman, perhaps even get into a physical altercation, but instead she was met with silence. Geneviève placed the comb down and made Venus face her. She looked at her a long while before she spoke.

"As Queen, that is your right to do such a thing—to make provisions and live your life as you see fit. It is a bit unconventional for a Queen of your status to be teaching to our brethren, but of course, the world is ever changing, and we must follow our passions. However, please always remember that you are an example to others, Venus, and you must carry yourself in a proper Vamp way."

Venus nodded in understanding, pleased with how diplomatic her mother-in-law was being. And quite surprised about it, too.

"You and I may not always agree. I never believed that we would." She picked up the golden comb and went back to work on her hair. "You are headstrong, just like me, but I know you will do the right thing according to our laws and expectations."

"I will. I promise." Venus turned to smile at her and rested her hands on her knees.

"I will hold you to that. We do not play by the same rules as humans, Venus. We don't need to, we don't want to, and we *never* will. Humans are hypocrites. Pretending to be a way they are not in order to follow their religions, but they cannot follow those rules because they are unnatural. So in order to self-regulate, keep themselves in line, because they are animals, just like the rest of us, they try to control their impulses, but that only in the long run leads to perversions of what is simple and natural, meant to be. You can't reason with someone who lies to themselves all the time. They can't even accept their true nature how could they ever accept ours?"

"I don't completely agree with you, Geneviève, but I appreciate your perspective. What you are saying, your views, is part of the reason I want to open the museum. I know that you were hurt by human beings, but we've hurt human beings, too."

"I appreciate your viewpoint as well. My point is, do not try to force us to be anything that we are not, just as I have stopped trying to force you to forsake your birthright. We are rulers and we have a code of conduct that is to be upheld. You are now one of us, through and through. I trust you to be *true* to yourself, and to my son. Never forget the sacrifices made on your behalf. I know you must feel that I am old fashioned, but look where it has gotten me? I'm still here... Most everyone else in my bloodline has perished, but I am still alive, still thriving, still tasting the sweet essence of eternal life. That must mean something. My choices could not have been all bad, old fashioned or not."

"It does say something. It says a lot. I still have a lot to learn. I will be the first to admit that. I respect you more than you realize."

"I'm glad to hear that." Venus sighed as the woman jerked her head back and began working on a braid at her nape. "In our world, Venus, giving birth does not saddle you down. It doesn't mean your life is limited. In fact, you gain greater respect and control. You've brought fresh blood into the world... that is revered. You can do many things. Humans believe in women's limitations, but we know no boundaries, my Love... the sky is the limit."

Venus' entire body filled with joy. It appeared that Geneviève was open to change and learning, too.

"You do realize that this is all your fault." Venus smirked. "Because of you, I fell in love with art."

"Oh, trust me, I know. You were in love with museums from the moment I took you to your first one in Prague. I would buy you artbooks, and you'd sit there and doodle, paint beautiful portraits, write notes and study for hours on end. I was not surprised that when my son found you, that's what you were doing for a living. Daughter, you have my blessing. I… I care for you deeply. There. All done."

Venus stood to her feet and stretched, then made her way to the mirror. Her hair was done in elaborate, shiny black twists that flowed down her back. Two in the front had red ribbons wrapped in them.

Before she could express her delight, the Queen Mother approached her from behind. She gathered the twists and pinned them high, then placed a black and sapphire crown atop her head. "That's the final touch… You look beautiful, Venus."

"Thank you, mistress."

"Now, go to the seamstress and get assistance with wearing your gown. I will be joining the masses, sitting up front to watch my son marry his lovely bride. Tonight is made of sweet dreams." Geneviève ran her thumb across Venus' cheek and smiled. "And now, those dreams are your reality…"

ALEXANDRE GLIDED HIS hand over his hair, smoothing it into place before putting on his black and red top hat.

His black high-collared robe covered his suit beneath, and both had been tailored to fit his height and build to perfection. He looked at his reflection in a silver-free mirror, and smirked.

I look like some Hollywood type Dracula.

But it was tradition, and he had no problems following protocol in this situation.

He stood outside, surrounded by hundreds of guests, not including the thirty kings and queens that had showed up to support him during his unfortunate Council meeting then stayed to attend his nuptials. As they walked past, they extended their hands or bowed before taking their seats in the underground romantic quaint village of Louche Rouge.

This place was famous as a popular site for Royal weddings. His parents had been wed here, and their parents, too. There was a fountain in the center of town, believed to have been given magical powers in affairs of the heart—a superstition vampires of Pure Breed status scoffed at. Marriages were simply alliances and you were fortunate if you liked your partner at all. The cascade from the fountain was spell-casted from a half vampire/half witch from the 15th century, who *did* believe in love.

If couples drank from it, it was thought their love would never die. Alexandre didn't give that much thought, but it was an idealistic notion, he couldn't deny. He surmised his Coven only wished to take a sip to help fortify the lineage, forsaking the true intent behind the purified waters. Shaking the idea out of his mind, he checked the time. 10:00 P.M. A full white moon glowed in the sky, just like the one on the day he and his Love were born.

It looks nice here. Queen Syà really outdid herself.

Beautiful, plush red chairs were arranged in a huge circle to accommodate everyone on the expanse of green grass, and a black path had been set up down the middle. White lights had been strewn all around, and soft music played in the background—Daniel Caesar's, 'Get You' ft. Kali Uchis—creating a relaxed, lovely vibe. He took notice of the black, white, and red candles lit all around, perfuming the warm air. Bubbles moved about in the light breeze, emitted from a machine, as well as clear balloons.

I wonder what she's doing right now? I hope she's thinking beautiful thoughts...

He smiled, imagining his Bloodmate drinking a glass of wine, then feeling ill, but doing it anyway...

Whiskey tapped him on his shoulder, bringing him out of his deliberations. The two slapped hands and grinned at one another.

"Hey, Boss! Looks nice, right? Queen Syà did great, huh? She really came through!"

"She did... It's amazing that a queen would volunteer to

390

plan a wedding. She could have easily just appointed someone else, but she said she loves things like this. I'm impressed." They kept on making small talk, enjoying the music and their surroundings. "Hey, let me ask you something, Whiskey?"

"Sure."

"Fawn hasn't returned my calls." He readjusted his top hat, waved to a guest, then turned back towards his friend. "Do you have anything to do with that?"

Whiskey laughed nervously. "Yeah, maybe. A little bit..."

"No such thing as a little bit in this circumstance, ya bastard. That's like being a little bit vampire. Either you are one or you're not."

"I had a little to do with it, ya know." He shrugged. "But, uh, Venus had her day in court is all, all right? Someone had to straighten that bitch out. I was sick of 'er shit."

"How dare you, man?" Alexandre chuckled, surprised and amused all at once. He waved at the Queen of Turkey before she took her seat. Whiskey chuckled real easy like and shrugged.

"Come on, I know you wanted revenge but think about it, Alexandre—a cat fight is the ultimate vengeance, right? Think about it from Venus' point of view. Fawn was tryna take her man, interrupt what you two had goin' on. In fact, she was getting materials to try and work some silly ass love spell on you. This coming from the lady who said she didn't believe in that type of shit. You see how desperate she'd become?"

Alexandre crossed his arms, tucking his hands beneath his armpits.

"So, did my mate do what she sought out to do?"

"Yup. Came up with the plan all by herself."

Alexandre shook his head. "Hmmm, so Venus got down and dirty?" he asked with a raised brow.

"Nope. Didn't want to mess up all the work Syà had done, damn facials, the sacred blood bath, all that shit. No need for doing anything like that... so she got a little help... some pros at getting low 'nd grimy... the lowest on our totem pole."

That was enough for him. He understood, got the picture. It was uncanny, really. He'd never told anyone, not even Venus, but one of Fawn's greatest fears was being attacked by an angry, bloodthirsting mob, torn to shreds. He'd read it on her years ago. One of her greatest desires, was to marry him...

Venus is fighting smarter, not harder.

Her training had been put to good use. He'd always told her if she didn't have to get in the midst of it, then she shouldn't. This was a new world order. Using one's mind to get rid of a bastard was far more efficient, but being a lethal weapon was sometimes necessary, too.

Combat was crucial for his kind. They were warriors after all, but in this new land, the way the world had changed and evolved, there were more options now—like vampire armies focused on technology, mind over matter, and sometimes others who were more than willing to do one's bidding... He certainly appreciated that she'd attacked her enemy with the same weaponry the adversary in question had thrust upon her. It was fitting. In fact, it was beautifully logical...

A shabby looking fellow waddled up to him, his face reddened and a look of sheer terror in his syrupy light brown eyes.

"Sir, King! Excuse me, I'm sorry, but uh, I know I don't have the right to talk to you, to be here," the man uttered in French, "but the Queen said she'd pay for an expensive candle I made when some lady ran off with it. It took me four days to make that candle. I used the finest ingredients!"

Whiskey looked at the guy and burst out laughing. Alexandre shook his head and grinned.

"It's true. He's owed money," Whiskey explained.

"I'm sorry, young merchant. I didn't bring my wallet but yes, we'll take care of it."

"Wait, I've got mine." Whiskey pulled his out and removed several Euros from it. "Is this enough?"

The merchant greedily snatched the money. "Yes, that's plenty! Thank you."

The little guy turned around to leave but Alexandre tapped on his shoulder.

"Let me ask you something, vampire to vampire..." The little man seemed surprised to be spoken to that way, but his socio-economic status didn't make him any less of a man in Alexandre's eyes. "So, you believe those candles really work, huh?"

The merchant gave a toothy grin and nodded. "Only if the one using it believes it does. It comes down to a matter of faith." And then, the guy scurried off into the night.

Alexandre sucked his fanged teeth and looked around, nodding at people who were waving or raising their thumbs in his direction. The energy in the garden was magnificent, tangible, electric. He could smell the excitement; it raced within him, contagious as it was. Moments later, he and Whiskey stood surrounded by his groomsmen, all of them looking amazing in their black and red tuxedos. Bruce arrived with all the flowers, a greasy grin on his face as if he'd just finished plowing some primo pussy... Perhaps he had.

"Alexandre, please step into the circle," a Vampire Priestess directed as she pointed to the area directly in the center of the semi-circle of chairs. It was time for the wedding to officially begin...

ALEXANDRE STOOD ON the gold pedestal. All around him, his groomsmen, including Whiskey, were on bended knee, their gazes lowered to the ground. A red wine silk runner was placed before him, then spread towards the white house inside of which was his soon-to-be wife. Rahsaan Patterson serenaded 'Feels Good,' setting up the right atmosphere. The guests remained in their seats and turned to see the door of the cottage opening. Out stepped Venus, and the chatter began. The song melded into another, 'Butterflies' by Queen Naija, now playing at full volume. The snapping and flash of cameras commenced and the videographer moved his large equipment around, catching her from all angles. Alexandre swallowed as he stood erect, in more ways than one, his eyes keenly upon her while she glided on in a breathtaking black and red gown...

She reminded him of a dark fairytale princess. The petticoat layers had the skirt puffing out dramatically. The sweetheart shaped neckline flowed into a perfectly fitted bodice, her soft breasts partly spilling out, begging for a taste. Black layers of fabric adorned the skirt, followed by a row of red, then black once more. Her waist was cinched with a red and gold sash. As she drew closer, he could see the details of her makeup, her sparkling rare diamond jewelry, and his mother's ring on her right hand. A long, cathedral style black and red train trailed behind her, and atop her head sat the crown his own mother had worn during her wedding ceremony to his father.

"*Si belle!*" He placed his hand over his heart and couldn't help but smile proudly. She was his... they belonged to one another.

When Venus reached the halfway point, the guests stood up. Alexandre waved his hand towards her, forcing her body forward, making her float towards him.

"Come to me, my Love." Venus floated to him, so graceful. When they were finally face to face, he waved his fingers again and placed her down onto her feet, which were clad in delicate lace-up boots. The Vampire Priestess positioned one hand over Venus' and the other over Alexandre's. She spoke in French.

"Tonight, we join King Alexandre Marseille and Venus

Margaret Anderson in matrimony. King Marseille, please proceed." The Priestess reached for a golden chalice filled with blood and water from the fountain of lovers, then placed it to his lips. He sipped, then offered it to Venus. She tasted the rich libation, then handed it back to the Priestess. He then removed his top hat, and out fluttered red butterflies, causing applause to erupt from their guests. He tossed the hat onto the ground, and one of his groomsmen quickly picked it up.

"Venus Anderson, please proceed." The Priestess picked up an ornate dagger.

Venus took it and made a small cut across her wrist. She handed Alexandre the dagger, and he did the same. They pressed their wrists together and kissed one another. Her soft, juicy lips were the sweetest thing he'd ever known... Venus then took the lotus flower that he'd given her during her blood bath, the one she'd kept inside her for twenty-four hours, and handed it to him.

"The lotus flower is a sign of King Marseille's acceptance of his bride, and her mental, emotional, physical, spiritual and sexual devotion to him."

He placed it in his mouth and swallowed. One by one, the groomsmen stood to their feet and walked away, sprinkling white lotus petals along the way. Seventy-two bridesmaids came down the runner, two by two, arm-in-arm, donning long white gowns and black and gold chokers. They tossed red rose petals, each dipped in blood, in the air, then went to sit cross-legged around the couple. Alexandre wrapped his hand around Venus' neck and she did the same. Resting their lips against each other's throats, they closed their eyes and breathed, holding tight to one another as the Priestess spoke...

"'*Aimer ce n'est pas se regarder l'un l'autre, c'est regarder ensemble dans la même direction.*' This is a quote by Antoine de Saint-Exupéry. King Alexandre, please proceed."

Alexandre took a deep breath then fell to his knees.

"I did not know what love was for over four hundred years... and now, I do. I am not ashamed anymore. I tell you all that I feel things for this woman I have never felt for another and I say it proudly. I am the King of Blood, *le Roi Du Sang,* and I have met and fallen deeply in love with my Bloodmate, Venus Margaret Anderson, my *Reine Du Sang.* I am weak for no one but her. I am not in control of myself when we are together, and I love it. I have hoped for her since I was a youth and was told she would come my way.

"I have been to so many places in search of my Blood Queen, but only when the time was right did she appear. I found her in a strange place, a laundromat in Manhattan. She was trying to get blood stains out of her clothing while watching DIY birdhouse videos on her phone. She lived in the city, so I am not certain what for." Snickering ensued, and Venus chuckled. "But her being in that place meant so much more... She wanted to wash her sins away, and I wanted her to embrace them and not see them as sins at all. She was so different from me.

"How could we find common ground? Our beliefs were so dissimilar, we came from two different worlds. I come from a people that rule over others, she came from a people that were treated as lesser than, and controlled. But then, I remembered—she too came from kings and queens… long ago, in Africa."

His bride's chest rose and fell in a choppy fashion, her emotions rising, striking him, making him feel something deep and filling him with longing.

"She is the descendant of not only slaves, but of royalty, too. What type of man would I be to deny my heart of its true desire?" Blood flowed down his cheek as he poured out his heart. "I have fallen in love with a Turned Vamp, the first to be wed to a French Royal Pure Blood in the history of the country. I could not pick and choose the parts I wanted of her. I had to accept her in her totality. This week, I was on trial. This week, I was stripped of my status, my crown taken away. This week, my rank was reimbursed, my crown returned. This week, I had to kill my brother while my mother watched. This week, I had to pay for the burial of my brother, while my mother attended his memorial.

"This week, I marry my one true love." He stood to his feet, and the beautiful woman before him reached up and wiped the blood from his face. He took a moment, then turned to his mother, who sat, stoic, in her black lace gown, her head held high.

"Thank you, Mother, for finding my Queen and preparing her for me. There is no need for a wedding present, when you supplied the main attraction, the Blood Bride."

Mother nodded, and he returned his focus to Venus.

"Please exchange your gifts." The Priestess held out her

palm, on which sat two black and gold wedding bands. Venus reached for the bigger one and placed it on his finger. He did the same with hers. "I pronounce you, King Alexandre and Queen Venus, Vampire Monarchs of France. You may bite your bride."

He undid the tie from his cape and let the expanse of fabric fall at his feet. He then loosened his suit tie and collar. The priestess smiled as Alexandre took Venus into his arms. She shuddered in sweet anticipation. Slowly, he slicked his tongue along the side of her neck and he inhaled her delectable scent. His fangs descended and his heart began to race, beating within his chest like wild horses.

"Mmmm!" He pierced her flesh and drank from her rich, delicious blood. His cock strained against his pants as his desires for her leaped and clawed at his resolve.

"Venus, you may now bite your groom."

In her weakened state, her body wracking with orgasm after orgasm, she tried to hold tight to him. He helped her, bringing his neck a bit closer to her mouth after lightly flicking his tongue along her dripping wound. He groaned when her teeth sank into his flesh, drawing blood. He shook with emotion as they embraced, dancing in euphoria. Soft music played and black feathers started to fall all around them. The crowd cheered when she pulled away from his throat and he pressed his lips against hers. When the kiss ended, she looked into his eyes. Lust danced within them, then spilled out, making him weak at the knees.

"*Je te veux. Baise-moi.*"

"Ahhh!" He laughed. "Your French is superb now!" Then he whispered, "I want you, too … and yes, I'm going to fuck you senseless." She draped her arms around his neck and kissed him hard. He looked into her eyes as they shimmered a bright orange. "I can't resist you…" He slicked his tongue within her mouth, holding her close as the cheers grew louder and their friends and family playfully bounced around, singing and dancing.

Le Roi Du Sang had done the unthinkable.

He'd fallen madly in love.

CHAPTER TWENTY-FOUR

I Can See the Fire in Her Eyes...

THE PARISIANS KNEW how to party. These motherfuckers really did it big. Venus was spent; her voice had grown hoarse from laughing at the top of her lungs. She'd danced with ten different kings, spinning and carrying on and being passed around like a joint. A few even felt her up, the raunchy, horny bastards. She made sure not to let Alexandre know—his jealous rage was not something she was in the mood to experience that night. It would ruin the entire evening. She delighted in watching him dance with his mother.

Her mistress slipped him a small bottle while the two danced. She whispered in his ear, then he glided it into his suit pocket and Venus was curious as to what it contained. She'd never seen Alexandre fast dance before—it was absolutely hilarious! Her man was 6'6, and though he could fuck his ass off in the sack, he seemed a little bewildered about how to do the Wop dance the youth vampires were trying to teach him.

But, he was quite determined. After the third try, he finally got it and they cheered him on. There was a buffet of various blood treats and beverages, but the sparkling blood fountain was a big hit. It was mostly water, but it was lovely nevertheless.

King Zhang Wei and Syà were the life of the party, making everyone feel tipsy with mirth as they danced the night away, showing some of their cultural moves. The Queen had brought something magical to share with the crowd—a glass pipe filled with something rich and mind bending. Puffs of red smoke emanated from it, likely aiding in everyone's giddiness. At the end of the night, Venus pulled the zany Queen aside and kissed her cheek, loving her so. Syà hugged her close and pressed her head against hers.

"We'll be friends forever, Venus. Call me. I shall see you soon! I promise! Oh, and enjoy tonight!" The vixen winked and off she went as she and Alexandre retreated into a black carriage, fit for an upside-down fairytale. Initially, Alexandre seemed happy as could be, just as joyous as she was, but soon, his mood seemed to shift to a dark place.

"What's wrong?"

"Nothing, baby." He forced a smile. Alexandre balled up his fists, looking preoccupied and not speaking much on the ride to their private sanctuary, a retreat set up just for their special wedding night. He sniffed her, drawing closer, his expression intense ... perplexed, even. He adjusted himself on the seat as if his balls were hurting, and then sniffed her again. When they entered the premises for their honeymoon night, which looked rather unassuming from the outside, more like a small hotel, he walked up to an empty reception area. He rang the silver bell that reminded Venus of a little tit, and a tall, elegant man with silver hair approached.

The two shared no words, but a black paper bag was placed in her husband's grip before they went to their private chamber. Now, here she was, trying to understand what she was seeing... feeling... doing... Alexandre stated he'd be right back and before she could say anything, he disappeared. The balls of her feet throbbed as she slipped her boots off and dragged herself farther into the room.

"Shit." She looked around, unprepared for what she saw.

A small, shallow black marble hot tub stood in one corner, a waterfall of blood cascading from the rock walls into it. Sensual jazz music played, and she was all alone, looking to and fro... wanting him beside her.

"Alexandre?" she called out.

On both sides of the room, gorgeous portraits of the two of them hung on the wide red walls.

"I'll be there in a second, baby."

She heard him speak, but where was he? She couldn't figure it out. Perhaps it was the blinding red lights that bathed the room in deeper hues of burgundy, or maybe the strong incense and flickering candles that made her head a bit woozy. She went to pull back several layers of curtains that framed something rectangular in the middle of the room.

A massive steel and black bed.

Sitting high, the bed was equipped with thick chains and

restraints at the headboard and footrest. She smirked, her pussy throbbing at the sight. Tiptoeing up the stepstool, she sat on the black and white comforter. Soon, she realized she wasn't alone. She pulled the curtain back a little more to find Alexandre standing naked from head to toe, with the exception of his wedding band and the black chain around his neck. His muscles glistened as if he'd just stepped out of the shower, though he didn't appear wet. He picked up a remote and the music changed, the room turned a deeper shade of red, and one wall opened, exposing a huge fireplace already blazing. She smiled with delight.

As he approached her, she couldn't help but lick her lips as she sized up his thick, long, juicy dick that swayed with each step he took. He sat next to her and presented a white box with a white satin bow on it.

"This is for you, my Love." He leaned close and kissed her forehead.

Curiosity gripped her. She opened it and found a watch with a thick band inside, nestled on the satin lining, the face cracked. "That belonged to a friend of mine in New York. He was a Turned Vamp, like you. He was also an attorney. I had much respect for him. One day, he was murdered by another vampire. The reason doesn't even matter. Anyway, when he was knocked to the ground during the altercation, his watch had stopped right at the time of his death.

"I found out who killed him and avenged his death, but it was yet another time in my life, when I denied what I was feeling... I was alone again. Just like me and the little human boy who betrayed me… looking for you and wondering if I'd ever find you… I was all alone again."

He shook his head. She reached out to touch him, but he grabbed her hand and intertwined their fingers. "I hurt from that loss…" He hung his head for a brief spell. "I went out and killed and killed for seven days straight, Venus, and still wasn't satisfied. This watch reminds me of him. It's a testament to the fact that we must always be aware of our surroundings, not take this time here for granted, but it also reminds me of something he once said to me."

She wrapped her other hand around his and squeezed.

"What did he say?"

"He told me a last breath can never replace a first kiss." He pressed his lips to hers and the coolness of his flesh sent shivers down her spine. "What that meant was, he missed at times being human, feeling those emotions. His last breath as a human was transcending, but he'd died long before he was slain. His existence in my life, even though for only a brief time, made it easier for me to accept you, to stop running from our differences. He made me want to reach out a bit more, learn to trust. Not soon after that, I found Whiskey on the street. I began to look for people to gather around me, so I could *feel*… or at least, pretend to. I could pick up their energy… knew their fears and desires. All Whiskey wanted was to be cared about, to be trusted, to be wanted. There is nothing wrong with you, my beautiful Bloodmate, but maybe there is something wrong with *me*."

"Nothing is wrong with you, baby!" She released his hand

and drew him in for a kiss.

"Every time we make love, you make me feel so much better… I *need* to be inside you, baby." He took her in his arms and ran his hands roughly through her hair, laying her down onto the hard, massive bed.

Venus snarled and hissed as they clawed at one another. Her flesh stung from him dragging his teeth along her body, up and down, ravishing her as he ripped her dress apart with his bare hands.

"Fuck me… Shit!" Her body radiated with passion and desire. Perhaps this was what her mother-in-law had *truly* meant by being in heat. It was the worst yet most lovely feeling, like an addict needing a hit so badly. Alexandre gave a deep growl and snatched every stitch of clothing off her like some beast. He yanked her down the bed, jerked her thighs apart, and eyed the fresh tattoo between her thighs…

It was his full name, not just the initials, along with a white lotus flower. In a flash, he buried his face between her thighs, kissing and sucking on her clit as he ran trembling fingers against her tattoo. He devoured her like a final meal.

"*Tu est à moi!*" he roared between tense licks.

"Yes, baby… I'm yours, *all* yours."

Crawling up her body, he wrapped one strong arm around her waist then enveloped her hard nipple into his mouth. The heat from his tongue drove her crazy as he licked and sucked all over her tits. His hands roamed all over her ass and he cupped and squeezed her cheeks over and over.

Then, without preamble, he flipped her onto her stomach.

Biting into the pillow, she gripped the sheets when she felt his hot tongue return, darting in and out of her pussy as he held onto her ass with both hands. He wolfed her down, taking her whole, licking her entire soul. She cried out as she came, dripping like a leaky faucet into his awaiting mouth. His soft lips pressed hard against her nature, his tongue flicking faster than lightning against her bud. Venus' eyes rolled as she bucked and humped the sheets.

"I need you, please!" She clawed at the layers beneath them, tearing them to shreds like some wild cat. She was on the verge of tears... her rage, desire, and lust married, turning her into a monster. Flipping away from him, she shoved him hard onto his back with a swift kick to his chest. With a roar, he yanked her hair, making her curse and moan as she crawled up his thighs, dragging her nails, drawing blood before taking his huge cock into her mouth and sucking with all of her might. He moaned so loud, it echoed through her body. He pumped ruthlessly between her lips, fucking her oral cavity, balls deep. His back arched as he bucked, and she squealed and cussed when he grabbed her hard, pulling her away as if she meant nothing, and slammed her onto her back.

Forcing her thighs open once more, he ate her pussy roughly, then softly, licking and sucking as he drove his finger in her ass, fucking it, too. She pulled on his hair, wiggling and screaming... landing smack dab within a mind-bending orgasm. Her eyes rolled as he made her cum over and over, the bed under her ass drenched with her flowing juices.

He paused, his eyes hooded. He lunged at her and they

struggled. The brute wrapped his hand around her neck, forced her up from the pillow, and claimed her lips in a soul-crushing kiss. She grinded soft and easy against him as he worked his hand against her pussy lips... torturing her, making her hungry cunt cry. The music soothed her inner beast, the incense filled her nose with a strong, sweet aroma mixing with their sex. Like a sweet, gentle angel, he hooked his gaze on her, rubbed her hair away from her face, and lowered her down onto her back. Then, he reached for one of the hand restraints and locked her wrist inside it.

"You don't have to do that... I'll be good, baby," she cooed as her pussy continued to pour and her pelvis rocked, the aftershocks of her orgasm still working their torturous magic.

"I know you'll *want* to be good, baby... you'll want to be so good to your *Roi Du Rang*, but you'll fail, my Love. I have to keep you under control tonight... Your scent was so strong on the ride over; it was divine, so fucking inebriating. I'm going to make you mine. I'm *taking* you. Don't deny me."

He grabbed the other wrist restraint, cuffed her, and then administered the same treatment. She arched and sighed when he ran his tongue gently along her inner thighs, then traced her pussy with his finger and the tip of his tongue. He kissed her tattoo and massaged it, then kissed it once again, as if for good measure, though she was certain it boosted his ego, made him feel rather proud. Bilal crooned through the speakers—'White Turns to Grey.' The deep bass of the music vibrated through her damn body, but his touch was so much more devastating.

He made her fall apart from his hands, his kiss… the way he looked at her with those cool, crystal blue eyes…

Beneath her, his pelvis flush against her ass, he kissed her neck from behind and grinded against her hungry flesh, real slow and nasty. Wrapping his arms around her stomach, he claimed her, holding her steady. Her heart hurt with its harsh beating. He sank his teeth into her neck, and she was done for. She trembled with blood pouring down her shoulder, onto him and the sheets below. She writhed in delight, her body exploding like a million shattered rainbows dipped in golden bombs. She screamed out so loud, she heard something shatter, perhaps a window as he entered her with brute force.

"FUCK!" he screamed, thrusting deep and slow. She looked down at her stomach and saw his fucking dick imprint going in and out of her pelvis, lifting the skin with each plunge.

"Baby! Please!" she begged, helplessly pressing her groin into him. It hurt *so* good, she thought she may pass out. The music went on and on, and he moved to the beat, rocking his hips back and forth as he went impossibly deeper, forcing her ass against his stomach. He sped up the pace, tore her apart with his love. When he yanked her arms and legs, the chains and restraints rattled hard, one of them almost tearing from the steel post as she screamed and hollered, cumming hard on his cock. He reached down and stroked her clit while he possessed her … pounded her … faster… faster… faster…

He's not fucking me… he's mating! Shit! It feels so good! SO DAMN GOOD! HURTS… SO… GOOD! He's killing me!

409

As if reading her mind, he kissed her cheek so softly, so sweetly.

"I'm giving you my baby right now, my beautiful *Rein Du Sang*… I know you want this as much as I do. Don't fight it. I couldn't resist you. Your body and soul told me what it wanted!" Her pussy ached as he had his way with her, thrusting his thick muscle in and out of her like a piston, and she fell apart against him. Cupping one of her breasts, he flicked her nipple, making it hard, then sucked her neck and layered gentle kisses all over her shoulder.

"*Merde!*" he yelled, riding her from behind. She hollered out, hissing, fangs exposed, eyes glowing and rocking against him. She snatched one arm free, the chains dragging and smacking the bed as her mind went white…

"Show me your greatest fears and desires, my Love… GIVE. THEM. TO. ME."

Rice fields flashed in her mind… Grandmama humming, Mama holding her tight, her mistress braiding her hair with pale, slender, heavily jeweled fingers…

Tears flowed from her eyes, the blood of four hundred fucking years of oppression! The chains around the ankles, the collars around the necks!

I AM HUMAN! I AM NOT THREE-FIFTHS OF A MAN! MAMA! DADDY! I LOVE YOU! SAVE ME!

…I AM NOT YOUR SLAVE!

She sobbed angry, happy, furious tears!

Venus broke free from the other restraint as her lover continued to rock inside her, holding her tighter against him now that her mind had taken her asunder. He cooed and kissed her, protected her, loved her... his own tears now blending with hers.

"I love you so much, my Blood Queen!" His voice cracked as he spoke those words. The bed rocked violently against the floor as he pumped ruthlessly inside her. Her eyes fluttered once again, then rolled back...

She could feel the water of the creek sloshing against her feet... see herself running for dear life in the forest... staring at the full moon above her head, blood all around... hear pounding African drums beating from the ancestors... the pages of a Bible flipping about in fast motion—a book she was told would save her, but one she had not been able to read...

Someone with worn, dark, beautiful hands shook a doll in her face...

Grandmama!

The old woman's smile lit up her mind like a thousand lights! Her pitch black, smooth skin became the galaxy, the cradle of civilization... free from bondage. Venus arched her back and fell back against her king as waves of violence and lust hit her all at once. She gnashed her teeth, screamed for mercy. His kisses were urgent, his body cold against her warmth...

Little black children running, smiling, laughing... nooses hanging from trees, one with a body still swaying from it...

Alexandre hugged her tighter, kissing away her pain. Her tears flowed nonstop—the hurt, the hatred, the love...

He moaned loud, deep and guttural, waking her from her thoughts. And he kept on fucking her but then, he paused, jerked, then went still…

She felt the rush of his liquid love flowing within her as he breathed hard in her ear, his heart beating so loud, it rivaled the African drums in the recesses of her mind. His entire body shook against her, settled, then started to tremble once again…

When she looked around, regained her bearings, she had both hands loose and one leg. She smiled and wiped the bloody tears from her eyes with the back of her hand. She looked over her shoulder at him, and he was spooning her, smiling down at her…

She turned her head to look up at him. "You're so fucking beautiful," she whispered to him.

He kissed her and caressed her cheek.

"Not as beautiful as you." His chest heaved, his face registering raw emotions. After a few moments, he slid out from behind her and undid the restraint on her right ankle, setting her free. He slowly got up from the bed, leaving her lying there, listening to that song over and over, staring up at the ceiling, feeling peace like she'd never known.

She'd not been bred… she'd made love and created life…by *choice*.

Moments later, he returned with the black bag he'd been given when they first came into the private hotel. He set it next to her, reached inside, then removed a bottle of diamond shaped bottle of perfume, a little glass bottle of blood, and a beautiful diamond anklet. She removed the cap on the perfume and sniffed it.

"Oh, this is nice! Beautiful!"

"I had it made for you. It's called Venus. It reminds me of you."

She thrust her arms around him and hugged him tight.

"That's so sweet, Alexandre. Wow." He picked up the diamond anklet, reached down, kissed the top of her foot, and hooked it around her ankle. He then tried to hand her the bottle of blood.

"I've had enough blood tonight. Goodness, I'm full."

"This is no ordinary blood…"

Her brow arched. "Oh really?" She gathered the sheets against her.

"Really. Go on, take a sip." She removed the cork and tasted it. "It's good… wow. Whose is it?"

"Mine, as a baby. My mother had held onto it for my wedding night, hoping it would one day be used. It's to help you." He ran his hand along her stomach, smiled, then stood up. He reached for her. She placed her hand in his and he led her to the blood-filled hot tub in the corner of the room. He helped her inside it, then joined her, sloshing about as his long legs moved to and fro until he got settled. Lying back, his body slick with the red fluid, he looked so fucking sexy.

Unable to resist him, she straddled him, and he simply lay there with his arms outstretched. His eyes hooded as he smirked, looking up at her, waiting to be crowned. She lowered herself onto his stiff cock and rocked against him, working her way down until he was fully inside of her. She rode him as Eric Bennet crooned 'Femininity.'

She had no idea where the bastard had got it from, but he suddenly pulled out a black and white striped cigar, lit it, and watched her through half-sleepy eyes that glowed bright. His fangs were partially exposed as she bounced on him, forcing him to rock back and forth. He kept casually smoking his cigar, pumping ever so slightly inside her, following her rhythm. In no time at all, she came hard against him, her self-control completely lost.

He blew out smoke from the corner of his mouth, then cupped her around the back of her neck and slid his long tongue inside her mouth. When he pulled away, he looked into her eyes.

"Let me tell you one thing we've got on humans, baby…"

"What?"

"When I tell you I want to love you until the end of time, I know that's a real possibility… not just words." He grabbed her hair, jerked her head to the side, and bit her, showing no mercy…

8 months later…

HE COULD BARELY hold his damn breath…

Whiskey winked at him, trying to offer comfort. It didn't

work. Alexandre had just made it to New York the previous day. He still had a thriving law practice there that he needed to check on from time to time. He'd hired a few top-notch lawyers to make things smoother. Venus had attended this trip with him, despite being eight months pregnant. He'd been staunchly against it, but she'd insisted, saying she needed to check out a few things in person for her art museum in Paris, which was successful. And she missed being in the city, too.

"Shit!" He slammed his fist into the wall and the damn thing fractured, leaving a big ass hole where his hand had landed. "I should have insisted she stay in Paris! I should have told her no! She doesn't listen!"

"Boss, it's okay… She's in good hands."

"She's in early labor… this is no good!" He started to pace back and forth in the lobby of the private infirmary, a place catering specifically to vampires up in Harlem. Venus had had a rough pregnancy, but she'd worked through it. She'd had great doctors, supportive friends, and of course, him. It was tradition for them to not find out the sex of the baby until birth, but due to her increasing weight at a drastic pace, they did discover that she was in fact having twins. He heard her faint screams from the room she was in down the hall, and his heart stopped. He marched back towards the door, prepared to demand answers and lend comfort, but Whiskey pulled on his shirt and made him stop.

"Boss, no, no, no! They said you can't go back in. You're too worked up."

He hissed and turned back around, murmuring and stomping. Just two hours prior, things had appeared fine... but then she began to bleed. Badly.

"Ahhh! Oh, God!" He sat down on a couch and covered his ears, rocking back and forth as he heard his bride screaming for dear life.

I did this to her... I should have waited! Why couldn't I control myself on our wedding night?! She wasn't ready... What have I done?!

Venus had a strong pain threshold. He could only imagine what she was feeling. What would cause her to yell that way? And then... just like that, it stopped... everything went quiet. He looked up at Whiskey, and their gazes locked. And then, he heard a baby crying... and another.

He jumped to his feet, laughing, his heart beating a mile a minute. The door opened and there stood the doctor, a big smile on her face.

"Come on in, King Alexandre... it's time for you to meet your son and daughter."

He nearly lost his mind as he rushed down the hall and into the room. Venus lay in the bed, looking tired but happy, holding a baby in each arm. Both were wrapped in white blankets, their bodies pale as snow, their hair black as a starless night.

"Is she okay? Are you okay?" He went to her and kissed the top of her head.

"Yes, honey, I'm fine." Venus chuckled. "We got one of each!" A happy red tear rolled down her cheek. "Here, hold your daughter." He reached for the baby, then jerked back. "Come on, Alexandre!" she scolded. "You couldn't possibly be afraid to hold your own offspring!"

He chuckled, trying to play off the fact that he was terrified. Babies were so fragile. What if he crushed her? He swallowed, puffed out his chest, then took the baby into his arms. As he looked down at her, he rocked her slowly and in that moment, he fell in love for the *second* time. Her sky blue eyes glowed like balls of light as she looked up at him, as if searching for answers.

"Hi! I'm your father... your daddy," he said softly before kissing the baby's forehead. "You're lovely... truly you are." His heart beating fast, he held their beautiful creation in his arms.

"What are their names?" one of the nurses asked as she cleaned up around Venus, tossing bloodied tissues and towels into a can.

"Well, we didn't know exactly what we were having so we came up with two boy names, and two girl names. Since we had one of each, we said the girl, in that case, would be named, Océane Geneviève-Chloe Marseille—Chloe was my mother's name—and our son would be—"

"Julien Alexandre Marseille. My father's first name was Julien," Alexandre explained.

"Those are very nice names, King Marseille. Your queen did very well. She should be fine." Venus nodded in agreement as if she were an expert on the matter. "She is a quick healer so she should be back on her feet soon. The babies appear quite healthy, despite being premature. We want to watch them overnight if you don't mind, especially your son. He is a bit yellow under the eyes. I doubt it's anything serious… just want to make sure he doesn't have an infection."

"Of course, totally understandable…" He sat down in a chair near his wife, cradling his child.

"We'll leave you two alone."

The room cleared, leaving only the two of them behind.

"You want to switch?" Venus asked softly after a few moments of silence.

"Uh, yeah…" He adjusted himself in the chair. "I'm just a bit overwhelmed… in a good way." She nodded in understanding as he got to his feet, gave her Océane then held his son for the first time. She slipped down her gown and put her breast to his daughter's mouth. The little girl began to nurse right away.

He stared at his son.

Si parfait…

The newborn's eyes were light brown with flecks of gold and amber, and his hair a bit curlier than his sister's. "He's beautiful…" He laid a gentle kiss on his son's small, pouty lips. "Hey, baby… You think it was this morning's four-hour fuckfest that caused this?" He shot her a look, then shook his head in disbelief. "You know, because they shouldn't have been here right now. You should have been pregnant for a couple more months since it was twins… They take longer."

Venus burst out laughing and shrugged.

"Well, your mother and my doctor said everyone is different. With me being a Turned Vamp, my gestation was longer than, say, your mother's, since she was a Pure Blood. They said generally no one should be giving birth to twins before eight months, Turned or not, so really, I have no idea... We haven't slowed up in that regard. I wasn't told to not have sex; in fact, it was encouraged. All I know is that they are here and healthy. All is well. Looks like she's finished."

She stretched her arm and yawned. Venus placed the baby on her shoulder and burped her. He couldn't help but smile. His mate was a natural.

"Let me hold her again." He reached for his daughter.

"Are you sure?"

"I have to get the hang of this sooner or later." He smiled. She handed the baby back and he stood to his feet, both of the babies now nestled in his arms. "Whiiiskey! Open this door. I could bust it down with my foot, but I doubt the staff here would appreciate that." He laughed then kissed each of them on the top of their head. Soon, the door opened and he stepped out.

"Awww, man! They're beautiful!"

"One boy, one girl! They're perfect." Whiskey smiled then leaned in, looking at them more closely. "They look like both of ya!"

"Yeah, they do."

"Boss, hold his neck! Geesh! Haven't you ever held a baby before?!"

"Oh, shit! I thought I was! And no, I haven't! It didn't look too hard on the video on YouTube." Whiskey rolled his eyes. "I figured, how hard could it be?!" Alexandre's mind was racing, his thoughts going everywhere, with no rhyme or reason. Adrenaline rushed through him, elation fueled him, the whole nine. There was no way to explain the joy he felt at that moment... Love at first sight *did* exist, after all. Whiskey chuckled, grabbed his phone out of his pocket, and began to call people on his behalf, sharing the good news.

"Hey! Yeah, they're here! Twins! Boy 'nd girl!"

Alexandre stood there eavesdropping then skipped to the side when he was hit in the arm with a swinging door.

"What the hell!" Venus had come bursting out the room, her IV still attached in her hand. "Get back in the bed," he ordered, tired of her ignoring doctor's orders, and his, too.

"I gave birth, I didn't die!" She rolled her eyes. "Relax! I was tired of lying there anyway." She leaned forward and kissed his cheek. He immediately calmed down, grinned and kissed her back. She walked up to Whiskey and took the phone to tell King Zhang Wei and Syà the babies' names. Whiskey took the boy from his arms and cradled him like a pro...

I hope one day he has children of his own, too. I think Whiskey would make an excellent father.

He cradled his daughter once again, kissing her, rocking her, falling impossibly further in love.

Everything felt so surreal...

He stroked her hair, then glided his finger against her soft, pale cheek. She cracked a slight smile... He ran the pad of his thumb along her gums and laughed... he could feel the sharp ends of her incisors that hadn't yet burst through her gum-line...

"In due time, my Love… you'll be drinking blood straight from the vein before you know it."

He couldn't wait to get back to Paris and have a grand party to celebrate the arrival of his offspring, and introduce the latest members of his family, with his beautiful Queen. He held up Océane in his arms.

"You are a Marseille… you are the future, the fruit of a forbidden love shared between a Pure Blood and a Turned Vamp. You and your brother are the pathway to change, a new day, a new beginning for France, and the world. One day, you will be *La Reine Du Sang*, and your brother will be, as my first-born son, the next *Roi Du Sang*… Happy Blood birthday, my Love. *Je t'aime…*"

The End

Did you enjoy this story?

Then please leave a review! This book took a lot of time and dedication for the author to write, so leaving a review is one of the coolest and most helpful things you can do! It only takes a minute or two.

Thank you so much!

Please join Tiana Laveen's newsletter to get the latest and greatest updates, contest details, and giveaways!

You can join her newsletter at:

www.tianalaveen.com/contact.html#newsletter

www.tianalaveen.com

About the Author

Tiana Laveen is a USA Today Best Selling author. She was born in Cincinnati, Ohio though her soul resides in New York.

Tiana Laveen is a uniquely creative and innovative author whose fiction novels are geared towards those who not only want to temporarily escape from the daily routines of life, but also become pleasantly caught up in the well-developed journeys of her unique characters. As the author of over 45 novels, Tiana creates a painting with words as she guides her reader into the lives of each and every main character. Her dedication to detail and staying true to her characters is evident in each novel that she writes.

Tiana Laveen lives inside her mind, but her heart is occupied with her family and twisted imagination. She enjoys a fulfilling and enriching life that includes writing books, public speaking, drawing, painting, listening to music, cooking, and spending time with loved ones.

If you wish to communicate with Tiana Laveen, please follow her on Instagram, Facebook and Pinterest.

www.tianalaveen.com

Le Roi Du Sang Music Directory

In many of my previous books, I have included a Musical Directory. The songs mentioned during the scenes in this novel truly do help set the mood and give the reader an additional layer of understanding and depth to any particular scene. The songs in this book are included below, but please note, they may not be in the exact order that they appear in the text.

If you discover new music via the mentioning of these songs in this novel that you enjoy, as many of my readers have professed to having done so in previous works, please purchase a legal copy of the song by the artist/band. This can be done on iTunes, Amazon, and many other credible music vendors. That is how you show your appreciation to the creators of this wonderful music and of course, you are then able to play it as much as you like, wherever you are in the world at any given time.

Thank you and enjoy.

1. Gary Clark Jr. – 'Bright Lights'
2. Jungle – 'Casio'
3. PVRIS – 'White Noise'
4. Juice Newton – 'Angel of The Morning'
5. Moonchild – 'Cure'
6. H.E.R. – 'Focus'
7. Donny Hathaway – 'Love, Love, Love'
8. Otis Redding – 'Pain in My Heart'
9. Daniel Powter – 'Bad Day'
10. Alabama Shakes – 'Sound & Color'
11. Phony Ppl – 'Why iii Love the Moon'
12. Jorja Smith's – 'Beautiful Little Fools'
13. $UICIDEBOY$' – 'Paris'
14. BEETHOVEN (is mentioned – no specific song)
15. GHOSTEMANE – 'Mercury'
16. Elton John – 'Candle in the Wind'
17. Otis Redding – 'I've Been Loving You Too Long'
18. Knoc-Turn'al's – 'Muzik'
19. The Animals – 'House of the Rising Sun'
20. Alan Walker – 'Faded'
21. Jacques Brel – *'Ne me quitte pas'*
22. Daniel Caesar – 'Get You' ft. Kali Uchis
23. Rahsaan Patterson – 'Feels Good'
24. Queen Naija – 'Butterflies'
25. XXXTENTACION – 'Guardian Angel'
26. Iggy Azalea – 'Bounce'
27. Eric Bennet – 'Femininity'
28. Kelly Rowland – 'Ice'
29. Eddie Money – 'Take Me Home Tonight'

30. Red Man – "I'll Be That"
31. Beyoncé – 'Naughty Girl'
32. Valley of Wolves – 'Chosen One'
33. Queens of the Stone Age – 'Make It Wit Chu'
34. Jane Birkin and Serge Gainsbourg – *'Je T'Aime, Moi Non Plus.'*
35. Tank – 'Dirty'
36. Christina Perri – 'Human'
37. Isabella – 'More Than Words'
38. The Bonfyre – 'Automatic'
39. Iggy Azalea – 'Bounce'
40. Gabriel Garzón-Montano – 'Sour Mango'

Made in the USA
Las Vegas, NV
09 April 2022

47123853R10267